"MY, WHAT A PITIFUL, PENNILESS PAIR WE ARE, MY LORD."

Magnus moved beside her. "Pitiful indeed—ye with her matchmaking aunts and I in want of a wealthy bride." He exhales into the night. " 'Tis a shame we are not able to help each other solve our problems."

"*Help each other*?" Eliza snapped her head around to fully look at him. "Yes…help each other," she repeated.

As though lost in thought, Eliza played her gloved fingertips across her pink lips, making Magnus want to taste them all the more. He felt a stir below.

Damn it all. Where was a stiff chill breeze when he needed one? "We shoud rejoin the others," he said, opening the door.

She raised a digit in the air. "A moment, if you will." She looked at Magnus once again, studying him. "I believe I might know a way we can help each other." Her eyes glinted with excitement.

"Really? How so?"

A sly smile spread across Eliza's face as she drew him away from the doors. And her prying aunts. "I want to discuss an *arrangement* with you."

ALSO BY KATHRYN CASKIE

Lady in Waiting
A Lady's Guide to Rakes
Love Is in the Heir

Rules of Engagement

Kathryn Caskie

FOREVER

NEW YORK   BOSTON

Cover design by Diane Luger
Cover illustration by Franco Accornero
Hand lettering by David Gatti
Book design by Giorgetta Bell McRee

Forever
Hachette Book Group
237 Park Avenue
New York, NY 10017
Visit our website at www.HachetteBookGroup.com.

Forever ia an imprint of Grand Central Publishing.
The Forever name and logo is a trademark of Hachette Book Group, Inc.

Printed in the United States of America

First Paperback Printing: May 2004

10 9 8 7 6 5 4 3 2

For my family,
with all my love and gratitude.

Acknowledgments

Though writing a novel is thought to be a solitary endeavor, such was not the case as I wrote *Rules of Engagement*. Many friends, fellow authors, and experts in their fields lent me a hand when I needed it most.

My sincerest gratitude to:

My parents, Edward and Sylvia Smock, who fostered my dreams and encouraged me every step of the way.

My dear friends, Deborah Barnhart, Denise McInerney, and Pamela Palmer Poulsen, who poured their hearts and souls into this book, and willingly suffered through more drafts than the Geneva Convention would deem humane.

Friend and fellow author, Sophia Nash Ours, who not only told me what color copyediting pencils to buy, but graciously took my hand and guided me through the entire publishing maze.

Acknowledgments

Cindy Haak and Cheryl Lewallen, who even from miles away served on my front lines by offering sage critique and lending support during my journey.

Celeste Bradley, Anita Gordon, Eloisa James (my very patient mentor), Cathy Maxwell, and Mary Jo Putney, exquisite authors all, who generously took time from their own busy schedules to read my work and offer pearls of wisdom that elevated my craft to a new level.

USAF Colonel Don Higgins at the Pentagon for his help in identifying sources for early nineteenth-century military stratagem, and to Nancy Mayer for her assistance with Regency-era research and fact-checking. Any possible errors are completely my own.

Melanie Murray and Beth de Guzman, who took a chance on an unknown author and made my dream come true.

And finally to my wonderful agent, Jenny Bent, whose guidance has been invaluable. Thanks for believing in me.

Rules of
Engagement

Rule One

*Those whose ranks are united in purpose
will be victorious.*

London, April 1814

Eliza Merriweather watched her sister pace the floor of their great aunts' Hanover Square town house with such unforgiving force that she was compelled to examine the Turkish carpet for damage.

"If your aim is to wear a hole through to the wood, Grace, you've not succeeded. Best pick up your gait." Eliza grinned through the tendrils of steam rising from her teacup and relaxed back against the blissfully plump settee.

With an exasperated sigh, Grace halted. "I shall wait as long as it takes, Eliza. I *will* have your promise."

Eliza set the blue and cream teacup on the table and crossed her arms over her chest. "I told you I would behave. What more would you ask of me?"

"To refrain from making a spectacle of yourself at every turn, else I shall never find a husband and this entire season will be for naught!"

Eliza laughed. "Oh, how you go on. Do relax, Grace, else

before you know it, strawberries will be erupting all over your pretty face."

With a little gasp of horror, Grace's gaze sought out the ancient looking glass on the wall and she frantically patted her cheeks, as if probing for any indication of blemish.

"Darling, you know I desire your happiness beyond my own, but I do not know how much pomp I can endure."

As Grace turned her head back to Eliza, a frustrated groan slipped out through her clenched teeth. "If you will not step into formation for my sake, then consider our aunts. Can you not do as they ask, at least for the season? You owe them that much—and more."

"No one is more grateful than I for their generosity. Heavens, they took us in. I have not forgotten."

"They did much more than that, Eliza." Grace sat down beside her. "They saw our sister into Mrs. Bellbury's School for Young Ladies. Even if our parents still lived, we never could have afforded Meredith's fees and tuition."

"I realize that, but—"

"*And* our aunts have agreed to sponsor a season for us both. The least you could do is smile through a few balls."

Eliza blew a dark wisp of hair from her face. "Yes, I could manage to survive a few. But why? I have no intention of marrying. *None*."

"But Eliza—"

"*No,* my mind is set. Once this infernal season is through, I am off to Italy. I will not be dissuaded from studying painting. I won't. So I ask you, why should Aunt Letitia and Aunt Viola waste their money on gowns and adornments for me?"

Grace exhaled through her nostrils, drawing Eliza's attention back to her. "I do not understand what you hold against marriage. I, myself, cannot think of a more honorable state for a woman."

"I hold nothing against wedded bliss." *If such a thing*

exists. In all her life, Eliza had never seen evidence of it. And most certainly not at home.

Rising, Eliza moved toward the window where a half-finished painting perched on a wooden easel, awaiting her return. With great care, she lifted it in her hands.

Breathing in the welcoming scent of the oils, she tilted the canvas slightly toward the window, allowing the afternoon light to illuminate the sun-dappled landscape she'd rendered.

"I am an artist, Grace." Still clutching the canvas, Eliza turned. "But unlike Mother, I will not allow the gift God has given me to wither and die simply because a husband demands my full attention. My art means too much to me."

Grace shook her hands in the air. "La, Eliza. Not all men are like Father. Many husbands encourage leisure pursuits."

"Encourage, yes. But with marriage comes children." She raised a sardonic brow. "There go your leisure hours. Then there will always be parties and balls to attend. And of course the staff and household must also be managed—"

"Stop." Grace clapped her hands over her ears momentarily. "Yes, a married woman has many responsibilities. But that is no reason to detest marriage so."

"I do not detest marriage," Eliza said, setting the painting against the easel back once more. "I just do not choose it for myself. After all, I see nothing wrong with following my heart instead of Society's dictates."

Eliza crossed the room and plopped down next to Grace. "Besides, not everyone excels at domestic and social pursuits so well as you, my dear." She hugged her sister close, smiling as Grace's soft golden curls tickled her cheek.

Grace nudged her away, trying very hard not to grin.

Coming to her feet, Eliza moved before the waning fire. "My, but there is a chill in the air. What do you say we ask Mrs. Penny to brew a bit more tea?"

"I will not give in so easily," Grace replied. "I will have your promise. You know what this season means to me. I cannot have you spoiling it. Swear it."

"All right." Eliza placed her hand over her heart. "I swear I will do as our aunts say. But once the season has concluded, I have *other* plans." Eliza widened her eyes. "Sufficient?"

"It will have to do, I suppose."

Eliza laughed as she extended a hand and drew Grace to her feet. Arms linked, they passed the bell pull and instead headed into the passageway for the cozy warmth of the kitchen.

In the late General's well-stocked library, Viola Featherton returned a marble-papered book to its low shelf and straightened her aching back, feeling every one of her seventy-four years.

"The gels' season must begin on proper footing," she said, turning to face her plump twin. "What will we do if we cannot find the book, Sister?"

"Stop fretting. We'll find it. Just keep looking," Letitia chided. "I tell you, it's here somewhere."

Viola was doubtful. Already scores of books had been removed from the shelves and stacked on the desk and in piles on the floor.

Resting her slight weight against her ebony cane, Viola fought back a grimace as she watched Letitia scour the eye-level library shelves. The division of labor hardly seemed fair, for if she was not mistaken, Letitia had not bent for a book even once, while she, herself, had spent the last hour upon her knees. Still, Viola knew she shouldn't begrudge Letitia. After all, her sister was the eldest, by three minutes anyway, and therefore less able to stoop than Viola. At least, so Letitia had claimed.

Mr. Edgar, their frosty-haired manservant, was perched near the top rung of a wheeled library ladder. He glanced down nervously, then squeezed his eyes closed.

Letitia set her hands on her ample hips and looked up at him. "Do open your eyes, Edgar. We shall never locate the book if you insist on such nonsense."

Edgar opened one eye, then the other, and hurriedly scanned the books on the top shelf. "I am sorry, my lady. I do not see the volume up here. May I come down now?"

"Might I suggest trying the shelves behind the glass doors next?" Viola asked, smiling sweetly at Edgar as she gestured with her cane to a bookcase several feet away.

The manservant bit his lip and eased his foot down a rung. Before he could fully descend, Letitia impatiently grasped the ladder and tried to push it toward the next set of shelves.

Edgar grappled for the shelf to steady himself, but instead, three oversized volumes came away in his hands. Eyes wide, he fell to the carpet with a thud. Two wavering towers of books teetered and then toppled over him.

"Edgar!" Viola caned her way across the carpet to him. "Are you injured?"

The manservant winced, but shook his head.

"You should be more careful, Letitia," Viola scolded, as she pulled a thick crimson tome off Edgar's chest and handed it to her sister. "You might have injured him."

But it seemed Letitia paid Viola no mind. Something about the book seemed to snare her interest. She slid her thick spectacles onto her nose, then turned the volume over in her hands. Her rheumy eyes brightened. "Viola, I believe Edgar has done it."

Pushing a pile of books from the library table, Letitia placed the volume on its polished surface. Her pudgy finger raced across the first two pages. She looked up at Viola. "Yes! He's located Papa's book of rules."

As Edgar climbed out from beneath the hillock of books and began the arduous task of replacing the volumes on the shelves, Viola steadied herself against her cane and joined her sister.

Her hand trembled with anticipation as she drew her lorgnette from the drawer, then held the glasses to her eyes. Squinting, she tilted her head until her poor eyes could make out the title page's bold heading.

"Why, you're right, Sister. This is it!" She gazed up at Letitia, feeling a pleased smile warm her lips. "We should begin tonight, don't you think?"

"Absolutely. Right away, in fact." Letitia whirled around. "Edgar, have our grandnieces meet us in the parlor— *immediately*."

Eliza and Grace were seated in the parlor when the click of walking sticks in the passageway heralded their aunts' arrival.

With great solemnity, Aunt Letitia and Aunt Viola took their places before the Pembroke table and stood as though an announcement of great import was to be made.

Aunt Viola cleared her long throat and began. "Years ago, Letitia and I were about to enter our first season when our mother died. Even for some years after the mourning period, in deference to our father's deep despair, we did not partake in the season's festivities. We were not courted. We received no offers despite the General's esteemed standing in society." A forlorn sigh escaped her. Then, quite suddenly, Aunt Viola's eyelids fluttered and she gasped a quick warning. "*Spell . . .*"

Viola's chin hit her chest and she wavered to and fro as her eyelids fell shut.

With nary a trace of worry on her round face, Aunt Letitia guided Viola back into a seat a second before her sister's knees buckled beneath her.

Then, seeming confident Viola was not about to tumble from her chair, Aunt Letitia turned once more to face Eliza and Grace.

"Now, where did she leave off?" she asked.

"Y-you received no offers," Eliza offered helpfully as she glanced at Viola, who showed no sign yet of waking from her spell. Her aunt's sudden sleeping spells were a regular occurrence in the household, and though the suddenness of them always startled Eliza, she knew she needn't be concerned. Aunt Viola would awaken soon enough, fit as a filly on a spring day.

"Right you are," Aunt Letitia replied. "When Papa died some years later, we reentered Society. But we were past the marrying age and were put on a shelf as *spinsters*." She reached for her sleeping sister's hand and squeezed it. "You cannot imagine the half life of a spinster. Never quite belonging. Never truly loved or appreciated—"

"But Auntie," Eliza cut in, "you are free to make your own choices. You are independent. No one tells you what you can and cannot do with your life—"

"And no one shares my bed at night. No children come to visit me. I have no grandchildren to spoil. Do you not understand, Eliza? A spinster's course is a lonely one." Tears glittered like starlight in Aunt Letitia's lashes.

The heartbreak in her aunt's voice prickled the backs of Eliza's eyes. It would be different for her, she told herself. She had her art, after all.

Aunt Viola's hand jerked, bringing a smile to Aunt Letitia's lips. "Good, good. Sister is returning to us now," she said, settling Viola's hand back atop her own knobby knee.

She looked at Eliza, then at Grace. "The point of all this

is that we do not intend to allow the same fate to befall either of you." With a precise nod, she signaled to Edgar, who crossed the room and placed a thick red book before the elderly aunts.

Eliza stared at the dusty tome and puzzled over its significance. Rising, she moved to the Pembroke table and ran her finger across the book's faded gilt title. "*Rules of Engagement*," Eliza read aloud. She looked up at her aunts for further explanation, but they only smiled back with delighted expectation.

Opening the heavy book to its middle, Eliza quickly scanned its pages and saw it was filled with military ruses and stratagem. This was even more perplexing.

What were her aunts planning to do with a book on strategies for war? Eliza snapped her head upright. "I do not understand."

Aunt Viola raised her head slowly, then snorted and grinned. She took Letitia's proffered arm, and, finding her balance, moved to the table and closed the book. She tapped a nail on the fading cover. "Read the title, dear. *Rules of Engagement*. It's a primer, you see, on how to get engaged."

Aunt Letitia clapped her hands. "With this book, we have all the strategies necessary to see both you and Grace engaged by season's end. 'Twill be like the season we never had."

Eliza wavered, trying to make sense of what she'd heard. But there was no sense in this. None whatsoever.

Her aunts had mistaken a military strategy text for an instruction manual for getting engaged!

"Auntie, this book is—"

Grace clasped Eliza's hand and pulled her back to the settee. "Remember your promise, Eliza."

"But Grace, you do not understand, this book—"

"I do not *need* to understand. Can you not see what this means to them?" her sister whispered.

Eliza looked at Aunt Viola, who was now cradling the precious rule book in her hands. She turned to Aunt Letitia, whose eyes were alight with hope.

Eliza squeezed her lids closed. Oh, for mercy's sake. She couldn't do it. Couldn't tell them the truth. Not without breaking their hearts.

Opening her eyes, Eliza forced a smile. "This book is *exactly* what we need. How lucky for us that you remembered it."

Grace released her pent breath.

Skirting the table, Aunt Letitia pressed a kiss to Eliza's cheek. "We knew you both would be pleased. We shall begin at once. Edgar, bring the sherry. This is a celebration!"

Eliza and Grace joined their aunts around the table as Edgar served the libation.

A giggle of excitement escaped from Aunt Viola's lips as she set the book down again and opened it. She positioned her lorgnette and focused on the large dark heading at the top of the page—no doubt all her aging eyes could make out. "Rule One," Aunt Viola read. "Those whose ranks are united in purpose will be victorious."

"We have achieved our first objective," Aunt Letitia announced. "From this moment onward, we are one in our purpose—to see you both engaged by the end of the season."

"Hear! Hear!" Grace cheered, looking toward Eliza.

"Hear, hear," Eliza murmured, staring with shock at the crimson book between them.

What sort of madness had she just agreed to?

Rule Two

Take action before he can discern your strategy.

With a muffled cry, Eliza burst from the Presence Chamber at the Court of St. James's and yanked from her hair the wretched white plumes that had caused her disgrace. Even now, standing in the gilded drawing room amid the shocked stares of London's ton, she could not believe what she had done.

"Really, Eliza. This tops it all." Grace pushed through the crowd at the door and trailed not two steps behind. "You sneezed on her. You spewed saliva in Queen Charlotte's face. *Three times,* no less!"

"Grace, please. Is not my own humiliation enough?"

Pressing her way through the undulating surge of courtiers, Eliza spied the grand staircase and made for it at once. In just a few moments, she'd be safely inside her aunts' carriage, putting as much distance as possible between herself and the damnable palace.

Just as Eliza's slipper touched the first step, Grace snatched her wrist and jerked her aside.

"You disgraced us all," her sister rebuked. "We will never live this down. Never."

"I hardly think all the blame can be placed on my shoulders," Eliza replied. Looking past Grace, she noticed a circlet of London's first set watching them intently.

Eliza lifted her chin. She didn't care in the least what the ton thought of her. Though the season had only just begun, they'd already written her off as . . . what was it now? Oh, yes. A hopeless hoyden. After today's sneezing incident, no doubt this snide assessment would make its way through the whole of fashionable London before nightfall. Yes, the entire incident was mortifying, but Eliza had to own that even this nightmare suited her purposes perfectly well.

When Grace, too, realized the onlookers' scrutiny, she drew closer to Eliza. A look of warning flashed plainly in her eyes.

Eliza sighed. "Surely you do not think I sneezed on purpose."

Grace merely stared back at her, clearly waiting for an explanation.

"It is not as though I *asked* to wear these vile plumes." Pinching the frothy feathers between her thumb and index finger, she held them at arm's length, as if they were crawling with vermin. "You know how feathers affect me. My eyes are watering so badly I can scarcely see."

Ignoring Eliza's statement entirely, Grace snapped open her pierce-work fan and flapped it before her delicate face. "What must the queen think of us, or the ton for that matter? Word will travel, you know. We will be blocked from every respectable drawing room in London, I am quite sure of it."

"Oh, calm yourself, Grace. I'm certain the queen has all but forgotten the episode by now." Eliza raised the offending plumes eye-level, turning them thoughtfully through her fingers. "Besides, since all debutantes wear these absurd white feathers during presentation, I truly doubt I am the first to *spew,* as you so daintily put it, on the queen."

"I fear, Lizzy, you are mistaken," a plaintive voice said.

Eliza turned to see the plump Lady Letitia and willowy Lady Viola, bearing down on them in identical gowns of lavender satin and blond lace.

Aunt Letitia fretfully wrung her handkerchief as she wedged her turnip-shaped form between the two young women. "I have it on good authority that you *are* the very first."

"Really? The very first?" Eliza looked from one aunt to the other. As humiliating as her presentation had been, she was not about to take a simple sneeze, or three, so gravely. And neither, she decided, should they. "Then I must make it my solemn mission to ensure this tragedy never befalls another debutante. I shall petition the queen, at once, to ban all ostrich feathers from court."

"Oh, dear," Aunt Viola gasped, frantically looking to Aunt Letitia for help. "We cannot allow her to do it, Sister."

"Now, now, Eliza will do nothing of the sort," Aunt Letitia answered. "Will you, gel? You've caused quite enough stir for one day, don't you agree?" She punctuated her statement by jabbing the point of her index finger into Eliza's back and starting her down the staircase. "The queen has finally retired, so to the carriage, my loves. Quickly now."

While they waited in the noisy, bustling entry hall for their conveyance to draw up through the crowded line, Aunt Viola grasped Eliza's hand and squeezed it reassuringly. "Do not fret, Eliza. It's all over now," she said softly. "You have been presented. And, as you know, dear, presentation is the first step in making a good match."

Eliza cringed. "If that sort of thing matters to you," she muttered.

Aunt Letitia clucked her disapproval. "Did I hear you right? *If* that sort of thing matters?"

Eliza withdrew her hand from Aunt Viola's gentle grasp

and faced Letitia's formidable countenance. "Please do not misunderstand me, Auntie. I do appreciate your efforts, for Grace, that is. But I am not inclined to find a husband. You know that."

Aunt Letitia swatted down Eliza's comment as though it were a winged insect headed for her nose. "Nonsense, child. Now that the season is under way, you will have the time of your life."

"Assuming she survives *this* disgrace," Grace added.

Eliza ignored her sister's comment. Instead, she gave her aunt a noncommittal nod. "I am sure you are right. But since I possess few of the traits desirable in a wife, I seriously doubt any offers shall be made for my hand."

"Pish posh," Aunt Letitia said. "You are fair and clever. The gentlemen will be queuing up to call upon you. You will see, Lizzy." She gave a sidelong glance toward Viola. "For we have a plan, do we not?"

Aunt Viola's ancient eyes sparkled with excitement. "We do indeed, Sister."

A *plan*? *Oh, no, they mean to use the rule book, don't they?* Eliza shuddered at the thought. To her dismay, that slight movement made her nose itch. She was about to . . . *Oh God, not again. Not here.* "A-achew—"

At the wet blast, Aunt Letitia looked Eliza full in the face, her eyes suddenly narrowed. "Oh, for heaven's sake. Give me the feathers." Snatching the white plumes away, Aunt Letitia shoved them at Viola, then pressed her own handkerchief into Eliza's empty hand. "Do see to your nose, Lizzy. It's as wet as a pup's."

A moment later, their footman, liveried in pale Featherton lavender, stepped into the hall to signal the arrival of their carriage.

With great exuberance, Aunt Letitia waved her arms to

shoo the young women through the burgeoning crowd as though they were a pair of particularly dim-witted sheep.

Eager to leave the scene of her blunder, Eliza started for the door, when she noticed Aunt Letitia's handkerchief was missing. Whirling around, she spotted the crumpled bit of lace on the floor and dashed back, stooping to retrieve it.

"Eliza, do hurry," Grace called out from the doorway.

"Coming." Eliza straightened, then turned on her heel for the door, only to slam into a blue wall of some sort. Pain shot through her face.

Oh, what now? Opening her watering eyes, Eliza found her nose flattened against what appeared to be a brass button. She tried to see whom she'd run into, but was too close. Teetering on her heels, she pitched backward.

Firm hands seized her shoulders, steadying her on her feet.

Eliza inched her head upward. The button was attached to a silk gold-shot waistcoat, and the waistcoat to a very large man. Her gaze climbed higher still, until at last, she found herself looking straight into the gentleman's face. She gulped.

Pale eyes, glinting like quicksilver, stared down at Eliza. As she marveled at their sterling color, she saw in them the faint reflection of her own heart-shaped face and wide sherry-hued eyes. *Criminy*. It was like looking into two small mirrors.

Thick waves of ebony hair, drawn back in an unfashionable queue, set off the man's strong chiseled features.

Her gaze slid down along his jawbone, over the blue beginnings of beard just beneath the surface of his faintly bronzed skin.

His body, too, was well defined, suggesting years of physical activity.

And he was tall, standing fully a head above any other

gentleman in the hall. Eliza wondered how she'd missed seeing him earlier.

She took a half step backward. Like her, this man did not belong at the palace. Oh, he was polished enough. His tailor had done well by him, supplying formal garb of the first quality. But somehow, his well-muscled form seemed ill-at-ease within its perfect seams.

Nay, this was no refined gentleman who stood before her. There was a ruggedness about this man, a maleness she could very nearly taste.

"I beg yer pardon, miss. Are ye all right?"

The low burr of his voice, hinting of highland heather and distant moonlit moors, hummed through the whole of Eliza's being, thrilling her so fully that she was rendered mute.

He eased his palms from her shoulders, trailing them down the length of her arms to her gloved hands, where his fingers entwined her own for a scant moment before releasing them.

A pleasurable tingling swept up her fingertips, heightening her senses to the very roots of her hair.

"Eliza?" A light hand touched her elbow, causing her to start.

She turned her head and found Grace at her side. The thick scent of lavender assailed her senses, and Eliza realized her aunts had also returned and now stood at her right.

"We lost you in the crowd at the door. Are you well, gel?" Aunt Letitia asked.

Aunt Viola's bony elbow nudged her sister's plump side, drawing Letitia's attention to the handsome gentleman.

"Oh, my," chuckled Aunt Letitia. "I'd say so."

Heat rushed into Eliza's cheeks, but somehow, through her embarrassment, she found her voice. "I am fine."

The gentleman smiled. "Glad to hear it."

Eliza's heart throbbed in her ears. "I . . ." Dash it all. *Compose yourself, Eliza.* Suddenly, her hand seemed to lift of its own accord and, with her aunt's handkerchief, she polished the gentleman's waistcoat button. *Say something.* "I do apologize. I hope I haven't tarnished your button."

Oh, that was witty.

He reached out and stilled her hand, sending a wild jolt racing up her arm.

"'Tis just a wee scrap of metal, miss."

An uncharacteristic flutter of nervousness took hold of Eliza. She lowered the handkerchief and looked up at him through her lashes, offering a shy smile.

"Please excuse my niece, kind sir." Aunt Letitia leaned close to the gentleman, dropping her voice to a confidential tone. "You see, she has only just been presented and I fear she is still somewhat shaken by the experience."

The gentleman arched a brow. "Aye, I seem to recall her rather *memorable* entrée. Miss Elizabeth Merriweather, I believe."

Eliza's cheeks flamed hotter still. Without knowing what else to do, she dipped into a deep curtsey. *Egads,* she was acting like . . . well, like one of those plumed jingle-brains milling around the palace! What was wrong with her?

"Please forgive my impertinence," the gentleman said. "Allow me to introduce myself. I am Magnus MacKinnon." Then he winced and struggled to correct himself in the next breath. "Or rather . . . Lord Somerton." He bowed low before them.

"Of course you are. The *fifth* Earl of Somerton, to be exact," Aunt Viola chimed in.

Aunt Letitia sidled closer. "What Sister meant to say, Lord Somerton, is that we were briefly introduced at Harper musicale last week."

The earl smiled. "I am honored ye remembered me."

Aunt Letitia snapped open her fan and swished it through the air. "How could we ever fail to remember *you,* my lord." She glanced around him with a hawkish eye and, likely seeing no female relation nearby, promptly introduced Eliza and Grace.

Eliza winced inwardly. A titled nobleman. He might as well have dangled a sparkling betrothal ring before her matchmaking aunts. Her only hope now was that he was already attached to another, else there would be no restraining Letitia and Viola.

The thought had just broached Eliza's mind when Grace shoved a flaxen curl behind her ear and charged forward. "My lord, is your wife also at court this day?"

The earl lifted his brows at Grace's none too subtle inquiry. "I am *not* married."

"Then you are here with your betrothed?" Eliza blurted before she could stop herself.

One corner of Lord Somerton's mouth lifted in amusement. "I am quite unattached, if that is what ye are seeking to ascertain, Miss Merriweather."

Humiliated at her gaff, Eliza averted her gaze.

Wasting not a moment, Grace lifted her hem from the floor and inserted herself between them. "Unfortunately, your marital status matters not a bit to my sister. For you see, Eliza has no interest in marriage," her sister confided. "I, on the other hand . . ."

At her sister's brazen remark, Eliza choked. Her gaze sought out the palace doors, and if Aunt Letitia had not snared her arm at the very instant, she would have bolted for the carriage.

Eliza unobtrusively wrenched her arm from Aunt Letitia's grip, but she was hardly free. Her aunts' fervent whispers told her they were already hard at work plotting to ring her finger.

"A debutante uninterested in marriage?" Lord Somerton's light eyes fixed on Eliza's.

"My sister has grander plans for life, you see," Grace said, not bothering to veil her sarcasm. "She plans to become a great artist."

"Pay no attention, Lord Somerton. Eliza's painting is merely a silly diversion," Aunt Letitia said hastily.

"Much more than a diversion." Aunt Viola's thin brows shirred at her sister's statement. "Our Eliza is quite a skilled portraiturist."

"An artist not interested in marriage." The earl shook his head slowly. "I am greatly saddened by this news, Miss Merriweather."

"Saddened?" Eliza asked.

"Most certainly. For ye see, 'tis my firm hope to find a wife this season." An all-too-apparent twinkle appeared in his eyes.

"Indeed?" *Having a bit of fun are we?*

"And, I must confess, from the moment I first saw ye, my heart was sworn to yer service." His grin broadened as he lifted Eliza's hand and pressed it to his broad chest.

One corner of Eliza's lips pulled upward. "Is that so?"

"Och, aye." The earl turned to her aunts as if to await their reaction to his game.

Aunt Viola and Aunt Letitia's gazes locked and their eyebrows waggled mischievously as their over-rouged cheeks rounded with perceptive smiles. *Prime quarry.*

Oh, dear, Eliza thought. He's gone too far with his folly. And now the matchmakers were at the ready. She had to say something, do something, find some way to shift the conversation.

"Lord Somerton." Like a sugar sweet, Eliza savored his name on her tongue. "We have not met before, I am sure of it, though your title is not altogether unfamiliar to me."

At her words, the earl dropped her hand. For a scant second, his eyes darkened. It was unlikely anyone else had noticed, but she'd seen the subtle change.

"My brother bore the title before me," he said. All warmth had retreated from his voice, despite his attempt to even his tone. "He oft visited London. Perhaps ye made *his* acquaintance."

Unnerved by his curt reply, Eliza fabricated a soothing smile hoping to mollify him. "I am sorry, my lord. I . . . cannot say. But then, I have met so many people during my short time in London."

"I see," Lord Somerton replied, his voice softening in the span of a breath.

A sudden commotion outside, followed by howls of complaint about the position of the Featherton town carriage, cut the uneasy conversation short.

"Lord Somerton," Aunt Letitia twittered. "We are ever so pleased to have met once more." She extended her hand to the earl, and he politely took it.

"The pleasure has been all mine," he said, bending low.

Aunt Letitia colored profusely, and a petite giggle fluttered from between her vibrant, painted-on red lips.

Urged forward by her sister, Aunt Viola slipped her fragile hand before the earl as well. "Mayhap we shall see you again," she giggled.

"I would say 'tis almost a certainty," Lord Somerton replied. He nodded to Grace, then, turning away from the others, took Eliza's hand in his.

The earl bowed low over her glove, then, as he rose up, shot her a wink. A wink! And at court, no less.

Eliza arched a chastising brow, but he only grinned, then turned back to her elderly aunts.

"Good day, ladies," he said, ever so politely, as if nothing had happened. But, of course, as far as her sister or aunts knew, nothing had.

"Good day, Lord Somerton," her aunts chirped merrily, a sentiment echoed by Grace as they departed for their carriage.

After boarding their conveyance, Eliza leaned toward the cab window and idly watched as Lord Somerton climbed into his own town carriage and disappeared from sight.

But as she settled back in her seat, Eliza realized her mistake. Her aunts had been watching her, and now sat, pleased as can be, with amused, knowing grins curving their lips.

"I am *not* interested in Lord Somerton," she told them.

"Whatever you say, Eliza," Aunt Letitia replied. Then both her aunts cupped gloved hands over their mouths and giggled.

Eliza rolled her eyes. *Oh, dash it all.* It was all too clear. Her aunts' matchmaking campaign had begun, and Lord Somerton, heaven help him, had been marked their primary target.

Rule Three

Use local guides to gain the advantage of ground.

Dozens of beeswax candles flickered before gleaming gilt-framed mirrors, imbuing the Greymont ballroom with a magical golden glow.

Though several routs and musicales had christened the new season, tonight's event was special. It was the first society ball, a crowning affair, attended by every member of the ton, including the new Earl of Somerton, whose name, much to his chagrin, seemed to linger on every debutante's lips.

"I do say, Somerton," his uncle, William Pender, nodded his bald head toward the glittering crowd, "you're making quite an impression on the ladies this eve."

With a sigh of disinterest, Magnus eyed the giggling misses prowling ever closer. "Dash it all, I am about to be pounced upon. That's all I require."

His uncle cleared his throat. "Actually, 'tis *exactly* what you require—and the very reason I urged you come to London. You must snare a rich bride before the season ends, and the city is dripping with candidates." Pender tipped his mottled red nose toward a gathering of ladies nearby. "Look there, for instance."

Reluctantly, Magnus turned his gaze. Eight young women, bracketed by a clutch of eagle-eyed matrons, stared eagerly back.

Pender leaned close. "They're all but salivating. I'd wager two thirds of them would wrestle on this very dance floor for the chance to marry an earl. You need do nothing but choose one and your financial problems are solved."

Magnus's lips went taut, but somehow he managed an uncomfortable smile. "As much as the sight of wrestling debutantes would amuse me, sir, my need to marry may no longer be so . . . pressing, shall we say?"

Pender had no more than moistened his lips with his cordial, when he abruptly lowered the glass. "What say you? I thought the fate of Somerton lay poised beneath an auctioneer's gavel."

"Ye are correct, sir. But I am not without resources. Some months ago, I used what funds were left at my disposal to purchase the majority share in a shipping venture. Lambeth orchestrated the whole thing. Shipping's in his blood. His father owned a fine ship in his day, did ye know?"

Disappointment hardened his uncle's features and his voice quavered. "I should have known," he managed. "Gambling away what little you have, just like your brother."

Magnus drew his brows close and ground out his reply. "I am not speaking of gambling. I have made an *investment*."

"'Tis gambling just the same," the old man said. "And here I thought you better than that. But no, it seems you are cut from the same plaid as your father and your brother before you."

When Magnus looked away to quell his rising ire, Pender

caught his shoulder and brought them face to face once more.

"And yes, I did know that Lambeth's father owned a few ships. Hell, a few years ago, all of London knew—that he sunk his own ship to claim the insurance money. You've done it now, lad. You're in league with a cheat."

"Lambeth is a good man, Uncle. I've entrusted my very life to him and he's never failed me," Magnus replied evenly, tamping down the flaring embers of his anger.

Pender disgustedly shook his head. "Do you not understand that I rely upon you for my very existence? And I'm not the only one. Hear me, boy, you cannot lose the Somerton fortune. You have a responsibility to the family. 'Tis time you realize it and do what's necessary to preserve our livelihood—*marry*."

"Dinna *ye* understand, Uncle? 'Tisna about the money, or that pile of stone the MacKinnons call home. 'Tis the land. The land that three hundred souls depend upon for their livelihood," Magnus said. "*They* are the reason I am here. The reason Somerton must not be lost."

Pender exhaled a long, slow breath. "Damned fool thing your father and brother did, breaking the entail just so they could sell bits and pieces of Somerton whenever it suited their empty pockets."

"I agree, 'twas foolish and self-serving. But 'tis done, and I am the poor soul charged with trying to save what my kin worked so hard to tear apart."

"Don't envy you, Somerton. Not one bit." Pender's jaw muscles rippled and tensed, but he remained silent for several moments. At last, he turned his sharp nose to Magnus. "But if you are intent on playing this ill-advised hand at least be smart about it." Positioning his elbow against his side, he waved a gaunt hand across the debutante-filled ballroom. "Cover your bet."

Magnus's face felt hot. This was his life, damn it. His predicament. He would handle it in his own way. "Be assured, Uncle, I am not above marrying a dowry to save Somerton," Magnus finally said. "But, I will do so only as a *last* resort."

Pender's brows met and fluttered upward. "I have given you my advice, boy. I expect you to take it."

Or not. Magnus gave his head an evasive nod. It was sage advice, marrying for money. Certainly less risky. But he'd wagered nearly everything he had on *The Promise* and would see his shipping investment through.

Marking an end to their conversation, Magnus turned to watch the dancers circle and weave, then fall into two perfect lines as the orchestra's last note played out.

Every last one of them was pressed, polished, and starched, in garb as well as a demeanor. How foreign these people seemed.

Why, he wouldn't even know how to begin to look for a wife amongst the Quality—let alone a rich wife. He was a Scot after all, not a prim Londoner. Aye, he was schooled in England, could feign Society's manners when it suited, but the wilds of the Highlands drove his heart and ran thick through his veins.

The set had just concluded, when he noticed in the distance a young woman, her visage obscured by a lace fan, leaving the floor with an extremely well-appointed gentleman.

He watched as she slipped a crimson-edged card from the placket in her gown and covertly slipped it to her dance partner. The gentleman read the card, then stared at the woman, mouth agape, as she turned and left the dance floor.

The odd exchange would not normally have interested Magnus, but the fact that the young woman now stared directly at *him,* did. Magnus watched her join an animated crescent of matrons, whose backs faced him as they conversed with their esteemed hostess.

He was about to look away when the bold miss turned, peered over her fan, and brazenly eyed his form from head to toe.

What the devil? Now she had his full attention.

Bemused, he watched as her curious gaze crept leisurely up his body, titillating him. *Ye wicked lass.* A wry grin lifted the edges of Magnus's lips.

Within the span of a breath, their gazes met, giving Magnus pause. In that instant, he almost convinced himself that he knew those eyes. Bah, quite unlikely. He'd only been in London a few short weeks. Still, there was something oddly familiar about them. Magnus bowed his head in address.

But as the woman took heed of his notice, her large dark eyes rounded and she lurched as though splashed with a dipper of ice water.

Magnus pursed his lips in satisfaction. *Serves ye right, my bold little chit. Now lower yer fan and let me see who ye are.*

As if to defy him, the young lady raised her blasted fan higher still, concealing her face completely. Then, grasping her gossamer white and blue gown in her hand, she turned, giving her back to him.

Why, had that brash miss just issued a challenge? Intrigued, Magnus turned to his uncle. "What do ye know about *that* lass?" he asked, nodding toward his once ardent admirer.

Pender's face brightened. "Glad to hear you have taken my advice." He raised his quizzing glass and peered across the dance floor. "Now, which gel has caught your eye?"

"'Tis impossible to see her face from here, but she is standing just to the right of our hostess, Lady Greymont."

"Ah, yes," his uncle said, spying her.

Magnus's spirits lifted. "So ye know her?"

"Actually, no. But I am sure our hostess can arrange an introduction, should you desire it."

"I believe I would," Magnus replied, if for no other reason than to alleviate his growing boredom.

Brows lifted high, his uncle's quizzing glass promptly dislodged from the fleshy fold beneath his eye. The eyepiece dropped to his lapel, where it swung on its golden chain, ticking away the moments until he could catch their hostess's attention.

It was then that Magnus noticed that three gentlemen standing nearby held the same crimson-edged cards he'd seen the woman give to her dance partner. He edged closer, hoping their conversation might shed some light on the mystery woman's identity.

"Just who does she think she is?" Magnus heard one of the men ask, prompting the other two to cast their disbelieving eyes at their own cards again.

"She's an odd one, that's for certain. Headstrong too," the shorter of the three replied. "She's got the curves of a goddess but the stones of a man."

"Say what you will," the last of the three said. "I admit, she mightn't be the sort to marry, but I suspect she'd make a lively bed partner for some lucky gent. Just look at her luscious mouth."

All three chuckled wickedly in agreement, until they noticed Magnus standing close by. Then, as if cued, the men tucked their cards into their pockets.

"Ah, good," Pender finally said. "Lady Greymont is headed our way."

Magnus straightened his back and awaited their hostess. He had to know just who the woman was who could inspire such conversation.

A few short moments later, Lady Greymont reached the

far corner of the dance floor and greeted Magnus and his uncle. But before Magnus could request an introduction to the spirited lass across the room, Lady Greymont made a request of her own.

"Lord Somerton," she said, "I simply must introduce you to one of the most enlightened women I have ever met. Will you allow me?"

"Most certainly," Magnus replied, hesitantly offering her his arm.

Lady Greymont laughed at his delay. "No need to worry yourself. Miss Merriweather is tolerably handsome, I assure you."

Magnus's heart slammed into his ribs. "Ye dinna mean Miss *Eliza* Merriweather?"

"You are not already acquainted with her, are you?"

"Only informally." *So far*. Magnus couldn't believe his good fortune and wondered at the serendipitous cascade of events that must have occurred to bring them together once more.

Lady Greymont pulled a frown. "Oh, dear. I did so hope to be the one to introduce you to your future wife."

"Future wife?" Magnus glanced at Pender then, donning an amused smile. "Uncle, ye did not tell me that matchmaking was such a competitive sport in town."

Lady Greymont laughed, playfully nudging Magnus. "My, you haven't been in London long, have you? Matchmaking, my lord, is *the* game of the season."

Eliza's middle clenched when she saw Lady Greymont leading Lord Somerton and an elderly gentleman directly toward them. "Oh, Auntie, you didn't."

"Well of course I did, Lizzy," Aunt Letitia admitted, tapping her cane on the floor with excitement.

Eliza watched nervously as he moved steadily forward,

his gaze hot upon her. Tiny beads of moisture sprang up along Eliza's hairline and between her breasts. She swished her fan before her face hoping to regain her composure. "I told you, I have no interest in Lord Somerton."

Aunt Letitia chuckled. "We know what you *said,* my dear, but Sister and I saw the way the two of you looked at each other at court. 'Tis a love match in the making if we ever saw one."

"A glorious match, to be sure," Aunt Viola added. "The trick, of course, is making Lord Somerton realize it. Hence the need to employ Rule Three."

Eliza turned to her aunts. "Rule Three?" she asked, warily. From the corner of her eye she could see Lord Somerton was nearly upon them.

Aunt Letitia nodded. "Rule Three clearly states that local guides should be used to gain advantage."

"And Lady Greymont is our hostess," her aunt Viola added. "She is our—"

"Local guide," Eliza said, completing her aunt's thought.

"Quite right." Aunt Letitia leaned close to Eliza. "By using this strategy, you will be able to beat the other young ladies to the prize."

"The prize being?" Eliza asked. *Twenty feet away. Fifteen.*

"Why, Lord Somerton, of course," her aunt whispered.

"Of course." Eliza's gaze drifted heavenward as she pleaded for divine intervention.

Magnus's lips curved with delight as Lady Greymont drew him toward the very debutante whose less than delicate gaze had intrigued him only moments before—Eliza Merriweather.

Miss Merriweather, ye are full of surprises.

Wide, golden-brown eyes broached the upper rim of

her fluttering fan and she stared, unblinking at him as he approached.

Magnus broadened his stride, forcing Lady Greymont to double her step merely to keep up with him.

"My, you are an eager chap," his hostess quipped as they quickly closed in on Miss Merriweather and her family.

"How can I be anything less than eager, my dear lady? Ye said it yerself, my future wife awaits."

Lady Greymont chuckled between gasped pants for air and graciously guided Magnus and his uncle into the Featherton ladies' intimate circle of conversation. There, she introduced him, once more, to the elderly sisters.

She gestured to Eliza next. "May I present—" She stopped then. Still winded from the trot across the ballroom, Lady Greymont laid her hand upon her chest and inhaled deeply.

Magnus stepped into the momentary gap and turned to the young woman now skulking behind her fan. "The legendary Miss Merriweather, I presume?"

Eliza Merriweather slowly lowered her fan and politely dropped him a curtsey. "My lord."

An unplanned smile formed on his lips, which, to his great surprise, was returned by Miss Merriweather. She blushed, then muttered something to herself and quickly looked away.

"I daresay," Lady Greymont managed, "they do look quite handsome together. Do they not?"

"Oh, indeed they do," the reed-thin aunt, Viola, replied, with an elbow nudge to her sister. "Most handsome."

Magnus lifted Eliza's hand and bowed low. Beneath the pads of her gloved fingertips, his palm heated with exhilaration. How small and fragile her hand looked in his. As his gaze took in her lithe form, Magnus straightened his six-foot-and-a-hand frame, suddenly feeling larger and stronger than ever before.

Behind her, he could see that the orchestra readied to play. Dancers were beginning to assemble on the floor. Now was his chance to separate Miss Merriweather from her aunts.

"If ye're not already engaged, Miss Merriweather," he persisted, "may I have this dance?"

Eliza looked at him then, and narrowed her gaze. "I fear I must decline, Lord Somerton. I . . . find myself rather fatigued."

"Nonsense," her aunt Letitia countered, giving her grandniece a furtive shove forward. "My niece would be honored to dance with you, Lord Somerton."

Her other aunt, Viola, took his arm and drew him still closer to Miss Merriweather. "Eliza is new to elevated Society, you see, and still shy as a spring blossom."

Magnus lifted a brow as he eyed the glaring young lady. *Shy* was not a word he would ever use to describe the woman standing before him. He offered Eliza his arm. "Shall we?"

She paused another moment then reluctantly laid her gloved hand on his proffered arm.

At her touch, Magnus's chest swelled. He puzzled over his odd sense of exhilaration. Maybe marrying a dowry wouldn't be so distasteful after all—not if it came wrapped in a package so delectable as Miss Merriweather.

While they moved about the dance floor to the music, Magnus became aware of the marked change in Eliza's appearance from their first meeting. Her face, no longer flushed from sneezing, was a delicate ivory oval, framed by sable locks swept into a mass of glossy ringlets atop her head.

When she looked up at him, he remembered how red and

swollen her eyes had been at court. Now, he could scarce take his gaze from the intriguing swirl of brown and gold blinking up at him. His pulse quickened.

"All eyes are upon ye this evening, Miss Merriweather," he told her as she danced a tight circle around him, wreathing him in her faintly lavender scent. "It seems ye've captivated the ton."

"That, my lord, I sincerely doubt." Eliza gazed deeply into his eyes as he took her hand and moved alongside of her. He felt her hand tremble and watched as her gaze darted nervously around the crowd rimming the dance floor. But then she seemed to relax.

"No one is looking at *me,* my lord. Rather, as the new Earl of Somerton all eyes are upon *you* this eve."

Magnus laughed softly. "While I have my doubts that all eyes are upon me, I do know of one pair that were indeed."

Eliza lifted her chin in challenge. "Are you referring to me, my lord?"

"I saw ye ogling me from behind yer fan."

"Are you implying that my study was inappropriate?" She arched a questioning brow.

Magnus raised her hand in the air and turned her around. "Dinna fash, Miss Merriweather, I didna mind in the least."

Eliza glowered at him, her brief delay causing her to fall behind in the dance. A wash of pink rose into her cheeks. She scurried to catch up with the other dancers.

On the eight-count, she drew alongside Magnus once more and laid her hand atop his. "You are *quite* mistaken in your presumption, my lord. I am an artist. A painter. Artists often study life to inspire their art."

"That's right. Yer sister mentioned ye were an artist." Magnus bit his lip to prevent a grin from taking hold. "I understand now. So . . . ye were just wondering how I might look without my clothes—for a classical painting, perhaps?"

His jest, however, did not hit its mark. She did not appear the least bit shocked.

"No, I was simply noting your military stance," she replied. "Which is odd, I thought, as I was certain you had introduced yourself as an earl."

"My, ye've a fine eye, Miss Merriweather. I've only recently journeyed from the Peninsula."

"Really?" She peered at the skin around his eyes, and as if something finally made sense to her, she added, "I see."

Magnus nodded. "I had just returned to Scotland when I received word of my brother's death."

She lowered her thickly lashed eyes. "My apologies, my lord. I am very sorry for your loss."

He bowed his head in concordance.

As if sensing his shift in mood at the mention of his brother, Eliza took events into hand. "No more talk of sad matters though," she added quickly, "this is a ball, after all." She placed her slender hand in his and twirled twice, when once was all the particular dance required.

Her laugh that followed tinkled like bells and she had him again. A pleasurable shiver iced his skin and Magnus's spirits lifted. Just what was it about this lass that charmed him so?

As Miss Merriweather came round to face him, Magnus caught her hand and stilled her step.

She inclined her head and stared up into his eyes. Their gazes locked for just a moment overlong.

"My thanks, Miss Merriweather," he said.

"Thanks?" she asked, her chest rising and falling as she worked to catch her breath.

"Why, for the dance. The music has ended." Magnus released her and gestured to the silent orchestra. All at once, he found himself strangely regretting the loss of feeling her hand in his.

Eliza gave an embarrassed laugh. "So it has."

Her eyes sparkled with vitality and Magnus realized how different she was from any woman he'd ever met. Though she'd been in his company only a handful of minutes, she already affected him like no other.

Perhaps finding a suitable wife, of *his own* choosing, wasn't going to be so difficult after all. He looked down at her and smiled. Aye, not so difficult at all.

"Would ye care to take a respectable turn about the ballroom? I am certain yer aunts would agree to it."

"No doubt," Eliza replied, shifting her gaze to the two old women, who stood chatting with two young bucks. Then, if he wasn't mistaken, he heard her sigh.

"I would be most pleased to join you," she said, fashioning a smile for him. "After all, the moment I return they will simply start their matchmaking games again."

Magnus nodded to her aunts, who waved their fans enthusiastically as he and Eliza circled past, making him feel like a child on a merry-go-round. "Matchmaking, you say?"

"Sadly, yes. They are bent on seeing me engaged before the season's end."

"Forgive me, Miss Merriweather, but I seem to recall yer sister mentioning that ye have no intention of marrying."

"You are correct, my lord. Unfortunately, my aunts see my painting as a frivolous amusement that occupies my time until they can secure a husband for me. I, however, hold my art above all else, and have no intention of giving up my painting aspirations to marry. Hence the need for these." She reached into the hidden placket in her gown and withdrew several cards, edged in red. She handed one to Magnus.

Thank you for not calling on Miss Merriweather.

Magnus looked up from the card and met her proud smile. "I dinna understand."

"Really? 'Tis quite simple." She snatched the card from his hand and shoved it back into her pocket. "I need these to help repel potential suitors."

"Your aunts do not know of yer . . . cards, I assume."

"Of course not. I have been quite careful with my distribution. I am not so naïve as to believe they will never learn of the cards, though by the time they do, I shall likely have passed out enough to reduce potentials by half or more."

Magnus stared at her, considering the odd young miss. "Why are ye so armed against marriage, lass? 'Tis hardly the usual stance for a woman of yer position."

"Well, sir, mine is hardly the *usual* position." Sparks of light seemed to flicker in Eliza's eyes. "You see, if I can remain unattached through just one mandatory season, I can claim my inheritance and use it to finance my studies abroad."

"Is that so?" Magnus lifted an amused brow.

"'Tis." Eliza shined a bright smile at him. "I needn't marry to claim the money, as I'd first feared. I found a loophole in my father's will. It's all quite legal, I assure you," she proudly added.

Magnus curled his lips upward as he slowly guided her around the perimeter of the room. "Ye're most . . . *unconventional,* Miss Merriweather."

Eliza smiled back at him. "Why, thank you, Lord Somerton."

As they neared the crowd mingling before the orchestra, the closeness of the room amplified.

"Such a crush tonight." Eliza snapped open her fan and swooshed before her face. "I do wish our hostess would have limited her guest list so those attending might be able to draw more than a single breath."

Magnus laughed in agreement then gestured to the glass-paned doors leading to the garden terrace. "Shall we step outside, perhaps?"

Eliza glanced uncertainly across the ballroom at her aunts.

Magnus stopped. "Oh, fergive me. Ye require a chaper-one."

"A chaperone? Heavens no." Eliza swept him with a ver-tical glance. "Though you are the burly sort, aren't you? Nonetheless, I think I can trust you."

"Can ye now?" He tipped her a sardonic grin as they stepped into the refreshing night air.

Eliza narrowed her eyes teasingly at him. "You are not planning to ambush me with an offer are you, Lord Somerton?"

"Why, no. Not *tonight* anyway."

She smiled at that. "Good. Because an offer from an earl would complicate matters—my aunts, you see."

Eliza flashed a quick smile then walked to a flickering Chinese paper lantern, dangling from the far end of the balustrade. She touched it with her fingertips and slowly spun it around. "No, I do not need *any* offers this season."

Magnus pondered her statement. "What will ye do if a genuine offer is made?"

Eliza's hand halted abruptly over the bobbing lantern. She spun on her heel and approached Magnus cautiously. Stopping only a breath away, she looked him in the eye with all seriousness. "That simply will not happen."

"Why not? I noticed several of London's finest watching you as we danced," he countered.

"No one will make an offer. Once they learn of the piti-ful state of my portion they will be off to hunt doves in grander fields."

Pitiful state of her portion? Magnus felt the bite of

disappointment keenly. She had no money. Despite sterling appearances, she was not the chance solution to his financial problem. He should have known. It had all been too perfect. *She* had been too perfect. Too easy to become attached to.

"Ye believe that, do ye?" he asked.

"Oh, most certainly. You see, my sisters and I were not born into wealth as you were," she told him. "Though our mother was wellborn, our father was a commoner, as are we. But, after we mourned the passing of our parents, our great aunts kindly took us in and introduced us into Society."

Magnus regarded her closely as she spoke. She really was an uncut gem. Just how old was she, he wondered. Two and twenty, perhaps? She appeared quite young, but displayed a confidence the other debutantes he'd met sorely lacked.

"Oh, yes, we may don the finest gowns and wear brilliants in our hair, but we are still fresh from the countryside." She looked up at him and laughed, then dropped a low curtsey. "So here I am, mingling with the ton with dirt under my nails and barely a penny to my name. Well, save a few quid I've managed to save for my passage to Italy."

Magnus applauded her performance. "'Tis a great pity ye're penniless, Miss Merriweather, but there are those who might make an offer despite yer financial state."

"True," she sighed, but as she leaned her back against the balustrade her eyes brightened mischievously. "But with just a bit of effort, I believe I can ensure that not one suitor my aunts deem worthy will make an offer."

"Not one suitor?" Magnus said. "Were I in a position to do so, Miss Merriweather, I would challenge that brash remark. But alas, my fortune is also somewhat wanting at the present." He turned and looked up from the topiary garden into the night sky.

"Truly?" Eliza moved beside him. "You are no threat at all? But, why not, may I ask?"

Magnus looked down into her curious eyes. "Verra well. 'Tisna as though polite society is not already acquainted with my situation." He swallowed hard and began. "When my brother died, I inherited not only the earldom, but his debts as well."

"Oh, dear." Eliza innocently patted his coat sleeve and looked up at him with sincere compassion.

Magnus glanced quickly at her hand on his arm, then inexplicably at her moist lips. He turned away and drew in a cleansing breath. "If I canna cover his notes by the end of the season, all that I own, including my home, Somerton Hall, will be lost."

She peered up at him with her huge doe eyes. "So you must marry well or lose everything."

"Not entirely, but it may come to that," he replied.

Eliza gave a frustrated groan.

At her odd response, Magnus looked up and noticed that her attention was no longer focused on him, but inside the ballroom. Turning around, he saw that her aunts watched them from behind a potted palm just inside the door.

"Just ignore them. It's what I've decided to do. Attention will only encourage their antics." She turned away to rest her hands on the marble rail. "My, what a pitiful, penniless pair we are, my lord."

Magnus moved beside her. "Pitiful indeed—ye with yer matchmaking aunts and I in want of a wealthy bride." He exhaled into the night. "'Tis a shame we are not able to help each other solve our problems."

"*Help each other?*" Eliza snapped her head around to fully look at him. "Yes . . . help each other," she repeated.

As though lost in thought, Eliza played her gloved

fingertips across her pink lips, making Magnus want to taste them all the more. He felt a stir below.

Damn it all. Where was a stiff chill breeze when he needed one? "We should rejoin the others," he said, opening the door.

She raised a digit in the air. "A moment, if you will." She looked at Magnus once again, studying him. "I believe I might know a way we *can* help each other." Her eyes glinted with excitement.

"Really? How so?"

A sly smile spread across her face as she drew him away from the doors. And her prying aunts. "I want to discuss an *arrangement* with you."

Rule Four

*Employ diversion to distract opposing forces
from the true objective.*

Lord Somerton eyed Eliza speculatively. "What sort of *arrangement*?"

Before she could reply, there was a sudden squeal of moving hinges. Eliza swung around. The French window doors to the terrace, which had been left only ajar before, were now wide open.

Narrowing her eyes, she focused beyond the threshold at the wavering potted palm and the two pairs of faded blue eyes blinking through its waxy leaves. Eliza exhaled.

"Not here," she whispered, taking the earl's arm. "Let us return to the ballroom. Between the music and conversation, it's less likely we'll be overheard."

With a wary nod, Lord Somerton escorted Eliza through the open door and past her aunts, who still watched them secretly through the leaves of the potted greenery. At last they stepped onto the expansive dance floor, where they joined a dozen other couples waiting for the music to begin.

Standing so near, it was difficult for Eliza to keep her

eyes from her partner's glossy ebony hair, from searching out the lean cords of muscle disappearing beneath his coat.

But the artist in her yearned to see more. She swallowed deeply.

Oh perdition. She should just paint his portrait and be done with it. Get him out of her head! Then perhaps her mind would be her own again.

"Ye spoke of an arrangement," he said, almost impatiently.

Eliza glanced up. "Oh, err—yes." Gathering her composure around her like a shawl, she set her eyes casually on the orchestra and leaned close to Lord Somerton so she wouldn't be overheard.

"As circumstances would have it, I am in need of a diversion," she told him. "A feint, if you will, to draw my aunts' attention and divert them from their matchmaking activities."

The earl's brows nearly slammed into his hairline. "And ye would like *me* to be that distraction?"

"Yes, I would."

"And why would I consider taking on such a role?" he asked softly.

"Because I am in a unique position to help *you*."

"Help *me*? With what exactly?"

"With finding a wealthy wife, of course."

Lord Somerton's eyes widened just as the music began. He missed his step, faltered, and crushed Eliza's left slipper with his heavy foot.

Eliza winced, but continued with her offer as they danced. "Being a debutante myself, I shall be able to investigate possible marriage candidates for you."

At that, Lord Somerton's firm hand caught hold of her arm and he led her promptly from the dance floor where he deposited her upon the damp floorboards before the punch bowl.

"What exactly do ye mean?" he demanded. While his eyes conveyed seriousness, his mouth smiled agreeably for the obvious benefit of the other guests.

"It's quite simple, really," she replied, taking the lemonade he offered her. "I will learn which young lady is most amiable and whose countenance, *and purse,* are most suited for a man of your position."

Lord Somerton considered her words. "Interesting notion."

"If you desire, I will go so far as to befriend her to discover the exact amount of her dowry."

He lifted a brow.

"You doubt me?" Eliza raised her chin. "Young ladies often share information that men deem too private to discuss. I assure you, Lord Somerton, you will never learn as much about a potential bride's family as you would through me." Eliza smiled brightly. "Join me in this arrangement and together we can save Somerton."

"A most intriguing proposition, Miss Merriweather."

Eliza held her breath in anticipation of his answer. The seconds passed slowly. Too slowly. Why wasn't he answering?

All he had to do was pretend interest and her aunts would have no need to bombard her with potential suitors. Hadn't she positioned it well enough? Was this not the perfect solution for them both? Evidently not.

She had to think of something else. Had to sweeten his prize. Then, Eliza came upon the perfect solution . . . for them both.

"I will paint your portrait," she added.

"My portrait?" He rubbed the hazy beginnings of stubble on his chin.

Was that a hint of intrigue in his voice?

"I am quite a skilled painter," she proudly told him.

Eliza studied his reaction. From the look on his ridiculously handsome face, he was mulling over her offer. "I am certain your heirs would want a portrait of the fifth earl—the man who saved Somerton for future generations."

He chuckled dryly. "Ye've figured me out already, have ye? Aren't ye the clever one?"

"Yes, my lord." Eliza turned her face up to his and smiled. "Come now, you must realize that spending time with me would benefit you in other ways as well. Look around you. I count at least six marriage-hungry mammas ready to thrust their daughters at you the moment I leave your side."

The earl looked around the ballroom.

Close, so close. Eliza scattered a few more crumbs before him. "But, make your attentions to me known, and they will be quick on the trail of some other titled bachelor—until you are ready to select a bride, of course."

Lord Somerton drew a deep breath through his nostrils then exhaled as he glanced around the ballroom once more. He turned to look at her.

"While I am certain I will live to regret this, Miss Merriweather, I will agree to this *arrangement* of yers."

"*Marvelous!*" Eliza said, a bit louder than she meant to.

"I'll pose as yer dutiful suitor for the season and ye—"

So eager to begin, Eliza cut him off before he could finish. "I will investigate potential brides for you and paint your portrait then, shall I?"

"Aye," he agreed.

Eliza bounced gleefully on her toes. Both painting and snooping would keep her mind occupied—until this egregious season was at its end.

With his acceptance of this arrangement, her future *and* her thoughts would be her own once more.

Late the next morning, Eliza sat at the table swirling a silver spoon through the steaming tea Mrs. Penny had poured.

She glanced at the case clock in the corner. It was already eleven in the morn. Eliza slumped in her chair. They had returned from the Greymont's ball only five hours earlier.

She would never survive the season.

Aside from Mrs. Penny and the rest of the Featherton's meager house staff, Eliza appeared to be the first to rise. This she had done primarily out of habit, for had she thought about it, she certainly would have remained in bed well past the stroke of noon to catch up on her sleep like a good debutante.

But tired as she was, the day already held great promise. Thanks to her "arrangement" with Lord Somerton, it was the first day of this absurd season that she would not have to worry about her aunts' militaristic matchmaking ploys.

Yes, after seeing an attentive Lord Somerton at her side last eve, her aunts would believe an offer from the earl forthcoming in due time. Why, she could even drop a few veiled hints of her own interest and bolster this belief.

Eliza leaned back in her chair and smiled. No unwanted suitors. No strategies from that deplorable rule book. Why, her inheritance and ticket to Italy were as good as hers.

Now her aunts could move on to finding a young man for her *dear* sister Grace. Eliza chuckled with wicked delight at the prospect.

Mrs. Penny eased up behind Eliza and stood over her with teapot at the ready. "Drink that one down and I'll pour you another. Your aunts told me to perk you up by whatever means necessary this morn."

Eliza raised a quizzical brow. "Perk me up? Whatever for? The rest of the house is still asleep."

"Not the ladies. They've been up for two hours or more," Mrs. Penny said. "They're working on a project in the library."

"Really?" Eliza had no doubt what that *project* might be. She was quite sure a certain red leather book was being studied in preparation for yet another clever maneuver.

She should take care to hide that odious book from her aunts—and Grace. It would not do for her sister to learn the true purpose of the rule book and set her aunts' mistaken strategies to rights.

After finishing her cold meat and fruit, Eliza made her way to the library where she found her aunts Letitia and Viola. As she expected, they were bent over *Rules of Engagement,* lorgnettes in hand.

"Good morning," she said, smiling.

"Eliza! I am glad you've finally risen," Aunt Viola responded, looking up from the book. "Please sit down. We've not much time."

"Not much time?" Eliza asked, hesitantly lowering herself into a cushioned chair.

"To discuss Rule Four, of course," Aunt Letitia answered.

Eliza dropped her chin to her chest and closed her eyes. "Rule Four?" she murmured.

"Why, yes," Aunt Letitia said. "Do not toy with us, Lizzy. We know you are already acquainted with Rule Four."

"Am I?" Eliza hadn't the faintest idea what they were talking about.

"You shifty tod," Aunt Letitia said with a knowing grin on her lips. "You must have stolen a glance at the next chapter."

Eliza rose from her chair. "I am afraid I do not—"

Raising her palm, Aunt Letitia silenced her. She held her lorgnette to her eyes and read the dark heading aloud. "*Rule Four. Employ diversion to distract opposing forces from the true objective.*"

"D-diversion?" Eliza sank nervously back into the chair.

Aunt Viola shuffled over and placed her hand on Eliza's shoulder. "Your offer last night to paint Lord Somerton's portrait was simply inspired."

"What?" Eliza tried to leap up, but her aunt's firm hand held her in place. "You know of m-my offer?"

Aunt Letitia chuckled. "Why, you do not think Lord Somerton would call on you without seeking our permission, do you?"

Eliza stared at Aunt Letitia. He'd *already* sought out permission? Why, they'd only struck their deal last night.

"I must say, Eliza, how utterly brilliant of you to come up with such a plan," Aunt Viola said, undisguised glee plain in her eyes.

"Plan?" Eliza asked. Surely he would not have told them about their *arrangement*.

"Why, to paint his portrait of course." Aunt Letitia lifted the strategy book and hugged it to her ample bosom. "You really are an innovative miss. Now Lord Somerton will *have* to call on you frequently—for his sittings."

With her bony finger, Aunt Viola poked each word into Eliza's arm. "What better way to prevent his lordship from calling on other young ladies."

Eliza rubbed the throbbing divot in her arm, and stared up at Aunt Viola. Why, she had not really considered that their little arrangement would force Lord Somerton to spend a goodly amount of time with her *outside* the season's events; would require him to call on her even between sittings for his portrait. Her heartbeat quickened.

Not that this would be all bad. For his dutiful company

would preclude her from being hauled around family-to-family, house-to-house like a dusty cart of coal.

In fact, the more she considered it, the more she liked the idea of spending time with Lord Somerton. He was witty and intelligent. He challenged her and made her laugh, which was more than she could say for any of the other dreary bachelors she'd met in London.

And, though she'd never admit it to anyone, were she looking for a husband, which she absolutely *was not,* the ruggedly handsome earl might be exactly the sort of man she'd set her cap for.

Aunt Letitia squinted at the clock across the passageway. "Heavens! I've completely lost notice of the time. Lord Somerton will be here soon."

The downy hair on the back of Eliza's neck prickled. "Lord Somerton is coming here? *Today?*"

"Yes, dear," Aunt Viola said.

At the clop of hooves in the street, her aunt glanced out the window. She then hurried back and fretfully fingered Eliza's heavy, loose locks. "I fear you will not have time to pin your hair."

Eliza rose and started for the door. "I shall have Jenny help me. She is quite nimble of finger."

"Even she is not fast enough," Aunt Viola said. "Lord Somerton has just arrived."

Eliza's world seemed to momentarily slow around her. The repetitive thud of the doorknocker blasted like cannon fire through the cavernous entryway.

"What? Here—now?" Eliza paced the carpet, drumming her fingertips on her lips. "Please tell Edgar I will receive Lord Somerton in the courtyard."

Eliza flattened a bird's-foot crease in her morning gown with her palms and finger-combed a few stray curls into place, then turned to leave the library. As she reached the open door, she whirled around.

"I shall require my drawing tablet, pencils . . . No, wait. *Charcoal*. Oh, bother! I cannot seem to think." Eliza squeezed her fists tight, struggling to compose herself. "Please ask Edgar to bring *all* my sketching supplies. Thank you."

Was that a scowl he detected?

Magnus looked at the young woman standing in the center of the rose-framed courtyard, her eyes narrowed, fists clenched.

"A thousand pardons, is this not Seventeen Hanover Square?" he asked. "I had hoped to call upon Miss Merriweather, the *delightful* young woman with whom I had the pleasure of dancing last eve."

"Oh, stop it, Somerton," Eliza huffed. "You know all too well why I am cross."

"On my honor, I do not."

"I do *not* like surprises." She walked over to a rose bush and ripped several blood red petals from the early bloom. She crushed them in her hands and let them flutter to the brick paving. "When my aunts informed me, only moments ago mind you, that Lord Somerton was coming to sit for his portrait, I was quite taken aback."

"Why is that? Ye agreed to paint my portrait."

"I did, yes. But when I realized that my aunts knew about the portrait I promised, I feared what else they might know." She strode across the courtyard and then spun around to face him. "Did you tell them anything more?"

"Are ye referring to our arrangement?"

She thrust her hands into the air. "Of course, our *arrangement*."

Magnus caught a flicker of movement in the windows

above and moved toward Eliza. Cupping her hand in his, he bowed over her slender fingers and pressed a quick kiss atop them. He felt her tremble beneath his mouth. "Yer aunts are watching us from an upper window," he whispered.

"Oh, I see. Which window?" Eliza asked quietly. She plastered on a demure smile and fluttered her lashes.

"Very nice touch," he remarked, then glanced upward at the two lavender-frocked old ladies who unabashedly peered down at them. "They're standing at the second floor window, behind ye."

Eliza laughed as though she were having a grand time. Taking his arm, she led Magnus to a small bench under the shade and privacy of an oak situated in the center of the courtyard.

"I do not believe we can be observed here," she told him, flattening her palms to her lap. "Now, will you tell me how much they know?"

"Do ye think me daft, Eliza? Our bargain would be meaningless if yer aunts knew of it."

It was then he noticed that she was staring at him, blinking like an automaton.

Magnus waved his hand before her face. "Are ye well?"

She swatted his hand away. "Of course. I was merely taken aback by your familiar use of my given name."

"My, ye are an odd sort, aren't ye? Ye think nothing of studying a man's form as though it were a piece of fruit, yet ye're stunned by my innocent use of yer name."

Eliza swallowed deeply. "Well, I have not yet given you permission to address me in such a familiar manner."

Magnus grinned. "I beg yer forgiveness, Miss Merriweather. Might I use yer given name?"

She glanced warily at him. "I suppose it would be all right. But only in private, mind you. I have my family's reputation to think of."

Magnus raised his brow. "Of course ye do." He glanced up through the verdant leaves to the window where Eliza's aunts stood and chuckled at what he saw. "I daresay, yer aunts are most resourceful."

Eliza looked quizzically up at him.

Magnus gestured through the new leaves to the upper window. Two sets of mother-of-pearl opera glasses were trained on them.

Eliza groaned and rested her forehead in her hand. "I do apologize." She slowly raised her head.

Magnus laughed and waved at Aunt Letitia and Viola. Instead of fluttering to an interior room, as one might expect those caught in the act of spying to do, the two old ladies happily waved back at him.

"No need to apologize," he told her. "They are most . . . entertaining."

The sole door to the courtyard opened and the manservant entered with a large tablet of paper and a wooden case. When he departed, Eliza silently tacked paper to a board from the case, then laid out an array of pencils and charcoals on the small table beside her. She sat down on the chair and looked up at Magnus.

"You may sit over there." She gestured to the iron garden chair opposite the small table beside her. "Come now. Don't dawdle."

"I had no idea ye would wish to begin so soon."

Eliza stilled and looked him in the eye. "Didn't you? I thought that was why you were here," she said. "Turn your head to the right just a bit. That's it. Now lift your chin slightly."

Bristling at her order, Magnus shifted uncomfortably.

Eliza set her hands on the gentle slope of her hips. "What is this now? Unaccustomed to taking direction from a woman?"

"Nay. I am unaccustomed to taking orders from most anyone."

"Oh, I see, *General,*" she teased.

"That would be Lieutenant Colonel," he corrected.

Eliza sucked in the seam of her lips to conceal a grin. "No matter. Although I am not a commissioned officer, as long as you sit in that chair, *I* am in charge." With a passive face, she snatched up a wedge of charcoal and carefully laid it to the paper.

Magnus chuckled at her game. She never failed to amuse.

With her left hand, Eliza crossed two long brushes and held them at arm's length in front of him. She squinted one eye, then held the makeshift cross before her page and began to draw with quick sweeping strokes.

"Did ye just wink at me?" Magnus asked.

"No." Eliza did not seem at all appreciative of his sad attempt at levity. She shot him an overwrought glare, though the smallest hint of a smile curved her lips.

"Might I ask what ye're doing?"

She positioned the brushes before him once more. "I am blocking your features. I need to sketch a few studies of you before I paint. Do not speak."

"How long will this take?"

Eliza exhaled and lowered the brushes. "Blocking? Or painting your portrait?"

"The portrait."

"Well, Lord Somerton, that all depends on you."

"Me?"

"Yes, and how many times you interrupt my work."

The corners of Magnus's lips lifted. He didn't give a damn about the portrait. She could be drawing stick figures for all he cared. Nay, he simply enjoyed Eliza's refreshing company and her ability to make him forget his money troubles . . . if even for a short while.

With naught else to occupy his time, as Eliza studied every nuance of his face and body for the portrait, Magnus afforded himself a gratifying study of his own.

Softly-curled sable locks fell loose about Eliza's shoulders, seductively cascading down her back in thick, silky waves. Magnus imagined those glossy tresses sliding over his bare skin and bit back a pleasurable sigh. By God, she was a beauty, in face as well as form—from her long pale throat, high breasts and slim graspable waist, down to the delicate turn of her ankles.

He could well understand how any man could be distracted by Eliza, despite her less than perfect reputation. "They call her the hellion of Hanover Square," one well-meaning patroness had whispered to him at the Greymont's ball. But that only made Eliza more interesting to Magnus.

He, himself, had never managed to adhere to Society's rigid rules and mannerisms. Not when his father carted him off to Eton, where his instructors thought it their sacred duty to the Realm to beat his wild Scottish nature and brogue from him. Nor in the military, where his impulsiveness regularly rippled his regiment's crisp lines.

Pity Eliza did not suit his pocket. Otherwise, she fit him so well. Magnus's gaze rose warily to Eliza's eyes. It would not do for his guilty indulgence to be detected.

At the moment, however, Eliza was thoroughly engrossed with her work.

Magnus watched her face, entranced, as her pink tongue moistened her lips and her skin took on a slight sheen as she concentrated her attention on the page at hand.

As her focus grew, she drew faster, blended and smudged with the tips of her fingers and the side of her thumb. Three pieces of charcoal, of varying sizes, now poked out between the fingers of her left fist as her right hand moved ceaselessly over the paper.

At length, Eliza lifted her eyes from the page. "Lord Somerton, if you did not expect me to begin this morn, might I ask why you are here?"

"Merely to discover if ye were serious about our arrangement. I see now that ye are."

"I am quite serious, I assure you," Eliza confessed. She lowered her wedge of charcoal and frowned. "Now you've moved." Setting her board aside, she walked toward Magnus. Framing his face with her hands, she leaned close and tilted his head upward. "Oh, I've smudged you."

Magnus breathed in her fragrance as he plucked a linen from his waistcoat and handed it to her. "Lavender."

"Yes. Fine nose you have, Lord Somerton." Eliza looked at him and gave a little smile. "Our lady's maid, Jenny, bottles its essence in the stillroom for my aunts. Do you like it?"

"I do," he said, breathing deeply of her.

Eliza leaned in to the remove the mark from his cheek, and suddenly Magnus felt the tip of her breast lightly rub against his chest. He looked up, and their gazes locked.

Magnus's breath seized in his throat and for the briefest of moments, he had the oddest notion that he should kiss her. He straightened his back and blinked, surprised at the power and suddenness of the urge.

He knew he mustn't. She was a lady, an innocent. Not some camp follower vying to share the warmth of his cot. He should remain the gentleman. He definitely should.

Eliza likely read his base intentions for she backed away, retreating behind the relative safety of her drawing board. When she looked at him again, he noticed her cheeks were flushed.

He wasn't the only one who'd felt the intimacy of the moment.

Nervously, she shifted her gaze to the upper window. She

gave a relieved sigh. "Thankfully, my aunts are no longer watching, Lord Somerton."

"Magnus," he said, glancing up at the window. "Call me Magnus. After all, we are going to be spending quite a lot of time together during the next weeks."

Eliza nodded as she looked back down at her page. Finally after several moments, she started drawing again, but there was a tenseness to her stance now. A string of silent words seemed to form on her moving lips as though she were auditioning them, phrase by phrase, on her tongue until she found the right combination.

"We might as well make the most of this time, do you not agree, Lord—Magnus?" she said at last.

He grinned. "What have ye in mind?"

"If I am to carry out my half of our arrangement, I believe we should discuss the qualities you find desirable in a woman."

"Verra well."

"Wealth is a given," she said matter-of-factly, not lifting her eyes from her work.

"Sadly, aye."

Eliza swallowed hard. "So, let us begin with her . . . *body*."

Magnus suddenly coughed, surprised by her frankness.

Eliza bit her pink lips every so slightly, then slowly lifted her eyes to him. "You needn't worry. I shall not judge your choices. You may speak plainly with me, as if I were a gentleman friend."

Not bloody likely, Magnus mused.

Eliza held him firm in her sight, stubbornly awaiting an answer.

"Her body . . ." Magnus's gaze centered on Eliza's own lithe shape as he thought about what to say.

She squirmed under his gaze and shrank farther behind the drawing board.

Magnus straightened in his chair. "I—I do apologize," he said. "I didna mean to make ye uncomfortable. I only sought to frame my reply using yer form as reference."

"Oh, I see." Eliza lifted a suspicious brow, but set the board on the table and rose. With a wry smile, she raised her arms from her sides, allowing Magnus a delightfully unhindered view of her.

A rush of heat swept Eliza as she felt him study every curve and crease of her body.

Beneath her shift, her skin tingled, dampened. She pressed her thighs together, willing away the unexpected, yet all too potent, new feelings building deep within her.

Then he spoke. "I have no preferences." His gaze continued to devour her as he rose and came to her.

Eliza's heart pounded in her ears as he closed the gap between them. Slowly, she turned her eyes upward to meet his.

"Were my bride to resemble ye, Eliza, I would be most content." He slipped his fingers beneath her chin and ran his thumb over her bottom lip, tilting her mouth upward to his.

Eliza gasped a broken breath, scarcely able to believe what was happening, but she rode her instincts onward. Without thinking, she opened her mouth to him.

But then, Magnus abruptly drew back his head. Confusion knit his brows as he stared at her mouth, then at his own hand cradling her chin.

"Damn it all," he muttered. He lowered his hand and abruptly stepped back. "I shouldna do this."

Eliza didn't know what to say. Didn't know what to do.

"I should leave now." Magnus's gaze focused on the pavers beneath his feet.

She nodded her head dumbly.

Without looking at her again, he turned and walked away, leaving Eliza standing in the courtyard. Confused. Embarrassed.

Alone.

She dropped into a chair and stared at the courtyard door.

After only one day, her brilliant "arrangement" was fast becoming a huge mistake.

Rule Five

Pretend inferiority and encourage his arrogance.

The night mist, thick and ghostly white, swirled about the coach as it skidded across the slick cobbles. While her aunts excitedly exchanged Society gossip with Grace, Eliza gazed out the small window, her shoulder thumping rhythmically against the door as the coach clattered through the wet streets.

The town carriage drew to a rough halt just as a bell in a distant clock tower struck ten, heralding their arrival at Lord and Lady Hogart's fashionable home.

Despite Grace's claim that their invitation to tonight's supper was much coveted by elevated society, Eliza was not at all eager to attend yet another tiresome Society event—especially at the home of the famously ill-tempered Lord Hogart.

Already this week, she'd suffered through three horrid routs and to her dismay *and* her aunts' keen notice, Lord Somerton had not attended any of them. Nor had he returned to sit for his portrait! Eliza feared her aunts' belief in his romantic interest in her was growing woefully thin.

Thankfully, her matchmaking aunts had not pitchforked

her any new suitors, but Eliza had no doubt they would soon if Lord Somerton could not be counted upon as her match.

Eliza drew her mantle close to ward off the dampness of the evening and peered through the open door as the footman let down the stairs and helped her aunts and sister alight from the carriage.

Through the tall candlelit windows of the manse, she saw a sizeable crowd of elegantly dressed ladies and gentlemen. She focused on a tall dark-haired man standing with his back to the window. Her heart began to pound.

Was it Lord Somerton?

He had to be here this eve. Just *had* to be. Didn't he realize what a predicament his inattention had put her in? He was her partner, after all. Despite what happened in the courtyard, he was to be her . . . well, her salvation.

Eliza took the footman's hand and reluctantly stepped out into the night. "We're dreadfully late," she said, her gaze drifting through the window once more.

Aunt Letitia snickered. "Why yes, I do believe we are." She glanced at her sister.

"Pity that," Aunt Viola added. "Now all eyes will be upon us when we enter." She raised her gloved hand to her lips and tried, without success, to conceal her delight.

With mouth agape in awe, Grace stared up at the massive brick house, then made for the door.

Aunt Letitia lunged forward and managed to catch Grace's arm. "Calm yourself, Grace," her aunt scolded. "It would not do to appear overeager."

Grace nodded her head. "You are right, of course. But how can I douse my excitement when my future husband may be standing just inside?"

Eliza groaned at her sister's ridiculous enthusiasm, catching Aunt Letitia's notice.

"We shall not have any of *that* this evening, Eliza," her aunt warned.

"Yes, Auntie," she murmured.

Aunt Letitia waved off their footman before he could lift the doorknocker, then drew Eliza and Grace aside. "Now remember, Grace, tonight we are employing Rule Five. *Pretend inferiority and encourage his arrogance*."

Eliza wrinkled her nose. "What good will that do? I should think a man would prefer an intelligent woman as his match."

"It is my impression that Rule Five means that men enjoy talking about themselves," Aunt Viola said softly. "They will think you most amiable if you simply listen or ask questions that allow them to expound upon their own virtues and strengths."

"Oh, of course," Grace replied, bobbing her head like a pigeon.

The grand door opened before them at last and Eliza affixed a smile to her lips. What a simply glorious evening lay ahead.

After their party was announced, they were greeted by their hosts and led into an expansive drawing room. But for a few murmurs from the farthest reaches of the room, conversation stopped as the other guests turned to observe the band of latecomers.

Eliza barely cared. She was taken immediately with the elaborate decorations. Shimmering swathes of crimson and gold radiated from every wall to a central sparkling chandelier. It was as though she had stepped inside a sultan's tent. She marveled at Lady Hogart's creativity.

In place of chairs, large jewel-toned silk pillows were tossed in mountainous piles on the floor. Several men and women lounged upon them, chatting casually.

Grace was awestruck. "You see, Eliza, this is what life has in store for us. We have only to find suitable husbands."

Eliza stared pointedly at her sister. "Grace, you are so naïve." She was about to explain herself when, through the crowd, she caught sight of Lord Somerton and his uncle, William Pender, standing before the hearth. An unexpected thrill cut through her middle.

"*Somerton.*"

Grace followed Eliza's gaze. "So it is," she said in a rather bored tone. "And his uncle, Pender, too."

Eliza's cheeks drew up with her smile. Thank God, she was saved. At once, she started through the swarm of exquisitely dressed bodies on her way to Magnus.

But Grace's arm slid around her waist and held her in place. "Eliza, you cannot race across the drawing room to a bachelor. It simply isn't done."

Eliza blinked back at her sister. "Then how, pray, am I to speak with him? Shall I shout from here?"

Her sister glowered at her. "Of course not. We'll walk *together,* mingling as we go. No one can fault you then."

Eliza fired a breath through her nostrils. "Are you sure? I wouldn't want to jeopardize your chances for a good match."

Grace, who was already scanning the field for her own prospects, paid Eliza's comment no mind, and the two set off through the vibrant room together.

As they strolled casually between the pillow mounds, Eliza held Magnus firm in her gaze, wishing she could see with whom he and Pender were conversing. But it was just too crowded. Still, she could make out Magnus's dark blue cutaway coat, crisp white waistcoat and fawn breeches. By Jupiter, he looked dashing.

A gentle warmth crept into her cheeks as her gaze drank him in, greedily swallowing every detail.

While they continued their walk through Society's finest, Eliza began to notice more than one lady frown at her as she passed. Criminy, they were looking at her as if she had stepped in . . . wait a minute. Had she? Pausing, Eliza surreptitiously peered down at the sole of one slipper, then the other. They were clean. She glanced down at her gown next, but there was not so much as a wrinkle to mar her appearance. Why were they looking at her that way?

Then, she heard a snippet of conversation that made everything clear as Austrian crystal.

"No, 'tis true, I tell you. They were together at the Greymont's ball," a stout woman said to her escort. "I own, as unseemly as we may all think it, Misfit Merriweather *is* the apple of the earl's eye."

How Eliza wanted to laugh. If they only knew the truth.

Then as a clutch of ladies moved aside, Eliza saw something that stilled her step.

"Is something wrong?" Grace huddled against her as a horde of party guests surged by them.

"No, of course not." But there was something wrong. Something most unexpected. Magnus was speaking with another woman.

Though the woman's back was turned to her, Eliza could see that she was every bit as lovely as Magnus was handsome, with a graceful, swanlike stance and deep emerald gown. Twinkling blue brilliants adorned her copper hair, which tumbled down the back of her pale neck in soft curls.

But the presence of this woman was not what troubled Eliza so. It was Magnus's reaction to her. Why, his eyes appeared lit from within as he spoke with the lady.

Heavens! What would her aunts think if they saw Lord Somerton fawning over another? Oh, this was bad. Very, very bad. Their ruse was already on weak footing.

Catching her image in the hazy mirror beyond, Eliza

raised her hand to her own unadorned, ordinary brown hair. She glanced down and grimaced at her simple pale blue gown.

With an audible breath, Grace interrupted Eliza's assessment of her own lacking appearance. "I cannot believe it. Lord Somerton is flirting with that—that *woman*."

"No, he isn't," Eliza replied, trying with all her heart to appear unaffected. "He is . . . simply being polite. This is a party after all."

How she wished her words were true.

It bothered her to see him with another. Not because she was jealous. Certainly not.

She was just . . . disappointed. He should be taking their *arrangement* more seriously. Did he not realize he was jeopardizing everything?

Grace narrowed her eyes at the earl. "He obviously does not realize you are in attendance. I shall tell him you are here," she said, pumping her arms as she charged forward.

Eliza reached out to stop her sister, but her fingers only caught the air.

"Wait!" The word was barely out of Eliza's mouth, when the toe of Grace's left slipper caught the edge of the carpet and she tumbled, belly first, onto a mound of golden pillows.

Her sister's eyes rounded in mortification, but within a blink, Grace had jerked herself into a sitting position. There, she came nose to nose with a concerned young man kneeling beside her. Grace raised her eyes to peer up at him. A slow smile spread across her lips.

Eliza rushed forward to help, but her sister's coy expression told her nothing was amiss, despite the fact that she was now rubbing her ankle. *The wrong ankle.*

"Are you all right?" Eliza knelt to her side.

Her sister smiled blandly. "I think so, though I seemed to

have turned my ankle." She batted her thick lashes at the young gentleman, who offered her a supportive arm as she leaned back against the pillows.

"I shall inform our aunts." Eliza stood and smoothed the front of her gown.

"No need." Grace was simply glowing in the light of the young man's attention. "I believe I just need to sit *here* and rest for a bit. Go on, Eliza. Find Lord Somerton. I am sure that—" She gestured to the gentleman hoping, obviously, to coax an introduction.

"Uh . . . forgive me. Dabney, Mister George Dabney, at your service." He was a barrel-chested gentleman, the sort more suited to hunting pheasant in the country than attending an elegant party in London.

His hair was a pale blond, nearly the exact shade as Grace's, which contrasted greatly with his huge chocolate-colored eyes. Or, perhaps his eyes only seemed overlarge, for they were dark with excitement and firmly affixed on Grace. "I will see to your needs, Madam—"

"*Miss,*" Grace corrected. Then, as if upon hearing the boom of her own voice, she colored and lowered her tone. "That is . . . Miss Grace Merriweather."

"In that case, it would be my distinct pleasure." Dabney remained at Grace's side on one knee, but for the briefest of moments, turned his head as though he was looking for someone. Then his searching stilled.

Eliza rode his gaze across the room to where Lord Somerton and his lady friend stood. Was it possible he was acquainted with Magnus . . . or perhaps the young lady?

"You are too kind, Mr. Dabney." Grace looked up. "You see, Eliza, I shall be fine. Mr. Dabney will watch over me. Won't you, kind sir?"

Dabney whipped his head around to face Grace. "Of

course." He fashioned a broad smile, but once again, his gaze flitted across the room.

Eliza studied her sister, fighting the upward drag of her own lips.

Feigning injury. *Pretending inferiority.* Mayhap she underestimated the logic behind her aunts' Rule. For in her sister's case, its application elicited the desired effect. Grace had snared a potential suitor's attention.

Aunt Letitia, who'd obviously observed the whole commotion, bustled forward. She greeted Mr. Dabney most enthusiastically and made sure Grace had survived her fall before turning her consideration on Eliza.

"Come with me, Lizzy," her aunt whispered, her command hissing like lard in a hot skillet. "There is naught you can do here and if I am not mistaken, I believe I see Lord Somerton standing near the hearth—and he is *not* alone."

"Oh, I know," Eliza began, gesturing emphatically in Magnus's direction. "His uncle, Mr. Pender is . . ." But as she jerked her head around and saw Pender conversing with Lord Hogart several paces from the hearth, her words faded on her lips.

Magnus was alone with the copper-haired young lady. Eliza winced. "What I meant to say, Auntie—"

"*Now.*" Her aunt's firm hand pressed against the small of her back and suddenly Eliza found herself propelled before Magnus.

The earl's eyes widened the moment their gazes met. Clearly he had not expected to see her this eve. Or, mayhap he was still shaken from their moment together in the courtyard. Yes, far more likely, Eliza decided.

But Magnus quickly recovered and greeted both Eliza and Letitia warmly.

Eliza smiled and held his gaze as long as she could without bursting with burning color.

When she glanced away, Eliza noticed a stern-looking older woman standing beside the fiery-haired young lady at Magnus's right.

Aunt Letitia seemed to recognize the pair of women and her countenance quickly lightened. "How lovely to see you again, Mrs. Peacock, Miss Peacock," she exclaimed, then began her own introductions.

Mrs. Peacock was a bone-thin woman with a nose like a beak and three signature peacock feathers stuffed into her gleaming jet hair.

Aunt Letitia placed her hand on Eliza's shoulder. "Eliza, surely you remember Miss Peacock? She accompanied her father to the Smitherton rout early last month."

The young woman with the flaming hair turned her head then and looked straight at Eliza.

Yes, she remembered Caroline, all right. Caroline Peacock had to be the most selfish chit in all of London—nay, surely all of England.

"Of course. Wonderful to see you again." Eliza affixed a stony smile to her lips to mask her blatant lie.

When last they met, Eliza's party had just arrived at the Smitherton rout, when Grace, looking utterly beautiful in white satin, drew the notice of several suitors, robbing Caroline of their attention. In a fit of jealousy, Miss Peacock plowed into Grace, *accidentally* spilling a glass of red claret down the front of her white gown, ruining forevermore the embroidered bodice of worked fleurs-de-lis.

When Grace collapsed into tears, Eliza snatched up the claret decanter and, had Letitia not prevented it, would have emptied it over Caroline's perfectly-coiffed head.

But Magnus, Eliza realized with some disgust, seemed oblivious of Caroline's foul character. For he gazed admiringly at her as she prattled on about the rising cost of tortoiseshell hair combs.

Then, something caught Eliza's eye, and she suddenly realized how Caroline had earned Magnus's undivided devotion.

Miss Peacock's breasts were elevated, by some hidden contrivance no doubt, and now sat perched atop her bodice like two plump oranges on a tray—offering themselves up to be devoured.

Now feeling pathetically inadequate, Eliza forced her gaze to return to the woman's face. To her great fortune, Caroline Peacock was not possessed of her mother's sharp appearance. In fact, much to Eliza's utter vexation, her features were as graceful as her form.

Just then, Caroline's critical gaze swept Eliza from head to toe, concluding with an amused flick of her copper brow.

"Such an elegantly simple gown, Eliza," she said, without an ounce of sincerity. "But then I told you as much at the Smitherton rout? It is the same gown, is it not?" She smiled politely, then shot her mother a wry glance.

Mrs. Peacock's thin lips drew inward, stifling what Eliza was sure would have been a smirk.

Caroline glanced across the room and, spotting Grace chatting with Mr. Dabney, sneered. "How *fortunate* that your younger sister is also out this season. But I suppose, since you are still unmarried and she is well of age, your aunts had no other choice."

Eliza bit back the heated retort simmering on her tongue when she noticed Aunt Letitia's left eye begin to twitch. The poor dear was trying to temper her anger, but none too successfully. Surely even Miss Peacock could see that the old woman was about to ignite.

Hoping for a distraction, Eliza nudged her aunt toward Lord Somerton, earning Letitia a neat bow.

Then, the earl looked warmly at Eliza, a second or two

overlong, for his gaze felt more like a touch. Eliza curt-
seyed. "Lord Somerton."

A whisper of a smile touched Magnus's lips as he grasped
Eliza's hand and raised it toward his warm mouth. "Miss
Merriweather. As always, a great pleasure."

He did not kiss her hand this time as he had done in her
aunts' courtyard, evidently choosing this eve to play the
mannered gentleman. Or so Eliza had convinced herself
until his thumb gently stroked her inner wrist, causing her
pulse to quicken and throb beneath his touch.

A hot blush raced through the thin skin of her cheeks and
neck. His touch both embarrassed and flattered her, but
more than anything, it pleased her immensely.

Hurriedly, she glanced at the two Peacocks. Thankfully,
Eliza being a social oddity of the first order, what had actually transpired between she and Magnus passed completely
beneath the notice of either woman. But their familiarity
with each other did not.

Mrs. Peacock assessed the pair of them for one overlong
moment before speaking. "You know each other then?"

"Yes, they do," Aunt Letitia cut in. "*Quite well,* too, if
you take my meaning."

The edge of Mrs. Peacock's lip trembled almost imper-
ceptibly. "So you know of my daughter and Lord Somerton's betrothal."

What? Magnus . . . betrothed to Miss Peacock?

Letitia's hand tightened painfully around her forearm.
Eliza's blood seemed to drain downward and puddle in her
toes, making her feel confused and oddly light in the head.
It can't be. She stared up at Magnus and saw the muscles of
his jaw tense.

Why had he claimed to need a rich bride when he had one
all along? Eliza stifled a small laugh then. The reason was
blinking back at her. Caroline herself. How unlucky the poor

man was to have formed a connection with such an utter shrew. She could not blame him for wishing to cry off.

He did not love Miss Peacock. That was clear. Else why would he have thought to kiss *her* while in her aunts' courtyard? At least, she thought he had been about to kiss her. After all, she had no real experience with these matters. But the way he looked at her. How he made her feel all warm and tingling inside.

"Miss Merriweather," Mrs. Peacock cut in. She took Eliza's hand and deliberately drew her away from Lord Somerton. "Though I was unable to attend the Smitherton rout, I know you somehow, do I not?"

Eliza thought a moment, but was sure she'd never seen the woman before. "I don't believe—"

"Of course!" Mrs. Peacock's eyes narrowed as she finally made the connection. "At court. I recall your presentation to Queen Charlotte. You *sneezed* on her, I believe." She leaned back on her heels and slid a sidelong glance at Magnus as if waiting for his reaction.

But before Eliza could say a word, her aunt surreptitiously hoisted her silver-headed cane behind Mrs. Peacock and lightly flicked the tallest feather. Several fuzzy blue shreds detached.

Oh, no, Auntie. Eliza watched in horror as the feathers fluttered through the air as if drawn by invisible threads to her own face.

Wisps of blue fluff rained down on Eliza causing her nose to itch. It twitched, and before she could cover her mouth, a tremendous sneeze shot right into Mrs. Peacock's face.

"Oh! I beg your forgiveness," Eliza exclaimed. "The sneeze came upon me so suddenly . . . I—"

Mrs. Peacock opened her mouth wide. "W-well, I never!"

Aunt Letitia smiled triumphantly. "You are quite correct,

Mrs. Peacock. Eliza did sneeze. As you can see, she is quite ill-affected by feathers. Pity, isn't it?"

Caroline glared at Eliza. "If you are unwell, Miss Merriweather, perhaps you should stay at home."

"Oh, Eliza is quite well," Aunt Letitia said. "As long as there are no *peacocks* flitting about."

Caroline and her mother gasped.

Auntie, please stop.

Tears flooded Eliza's itching eyes. There was no holding them back now. *Blast.* She dug inside her reticule for a handkerchief, but everything was fast becoming a complete blur.

"Excuse us, *please*," Caroline sniped.

With an icy backward glance, the Peacock pair made for the withdrawing room.

Magnus brought his fist to his mouth to conceal a grin.

Tilting her head back, Eliza blinked several times to clear her watering eyes. "Oh, Auntie. How could you?"

"Love and war, dear. All's fair," Aunt Letitia replied, dropping her own handkerchief into Eliza's hand.

As embarrassing as her sneeze had been, Eliza had to applaud Aunt Letitia. The Peacocks had gotten no more than they deserved. She only wished her nose had not been her aunt's weapon of choice.

"Well then. My work is done," her aunt declared, clasping her hands together. "I shall leave you two lovebirds to sort out this Peacock engagement nonsense." With that, she turned and tottered off in Aunt Viola's direction.

Magnus exhaled a long breath. After several days and nights immersed in sorting out his late brother's muddled affairs, he was at last alone with Eliza, a moment he'd longed for since he first accepted Lady Hogart's invitation.

As gazed down at Eliza, and couldn't help but notice, with some amusement, that her eyes and nose were almost as red as the crimson panels billowing overhead. He had to own, he was a bit relieved by her newly blotched appearance. Perhaps now he could focus on what he must do, instead of being distracted by her beauty.

But he doubted it. Eliza's allure went far beyond her lovely face. Beyond her all too clever mind. Beyond the gentle curves he so longed to feel pressed beneath him.

Could it be that he simply yearned to taste the forbidden fruit? That he wanted her because he could not have her? She had no dowry to recommend her; no standing in Society, as his uncle oft reminded him. No riches to save Somerton. Why did he want her so badly?

Eliza was fast becoming a weakness for him, and if he wasn't careful, she could become his addiction. For even now he craved her, as surely as his brother had craved drink and cards.

But he would not allow his desires to overtake his life as his brother had. He was stronger than that. Had to be.

He would steel his impulses and do what he must to save Somerton. But then, Eliza looked up and his heart thudded in his chest.

This wasn't going to be easy. Taking a deep breath, Magnus readied himself for the battle about to wage within.

"Would ye like to sit down?" he asked her.

"Thank you, but no," Eliza replied, appearing remarkably unscathed by the whole feather ordeal. "I shall be fine as long as there are no more peacock feathers—or *aunts* about." Wide-eyed, she glanced around the room, as if on the lookout for the elderly marauders.

"And thank ye, Miss Merriweather," Magnus said, "for rescuing me."

"Rescuing you? From the Peacocks?" Eliza exhaled a skeptical laugh. "You did not appear to be in want of a rescue—except from Mrs. Peacock, perhaps."

"Well, yer aunt handled that problem quite efficiently, in her own inimitable style."

"That she did." Eliza raised her hand to cover a mischievous grin. But Eliza said not another word. She simply tilted her head upward and stared at him as if waiting.

Magnus laid his arm across the mantel and set his boot atop the fireplace fender. "Ye would like an explanation."

"An explanation, my lord?" She blinked her eyes innocently. "Just because I have learned that you are, in fact, *betrothed,* while you had previously contracted with me to help find you a rich bride—is hardly reason enough to think I might require an explanation. Is it?"

Magnus knew she deserved the truth—that in the end, he'd likely have no choice other than to marry Miss Peacock. But in his heart, admitting this was akin to resigning himself to that inevitability. And he could not do that, not when a mist of a chance to solve his financial woes still rode the waves. Nay, he had to believe his world would right itself given enough time.

He opened his mouth to give Eliza her reply, hoping, in some burst of genius, he would come upon the right words. But just then, a butler entered the drawing room and announced that supper was served.

Relief flooded his mind. "Miss Merriweather, ye shall have your explanation. Of that ye can be sure. Soon."

Twisting her lips a bit, Eliza smirked at his delay.

"Shall we?" Magnus offered his arm to Eliza.

Hesitantly, Eliza slid her arm around his.

Magnus drew her body close as he guided her into the dining room. Through the wool sleeve of his coat he could feel the warmth and softness of her breast, pressing against his upper arm. He swallowed deeply, aware of his snug-fitting breeches, thankful that he would soon be sitting down.

*   *   *

Eliza found supper a less than enjoyable experience. While she had the good fortune to be seated at Lord Somerton's right, Caroline Peacock was placed to his left. Chatting incessantly, Miss Peacock did her utmost to monopolize Magnus's attention, much to Aunt Letitia's chagrin, judging by the pinched expression on her round face.

This left Eliza at the conversational mercy of their host who sat to her right.

After two hours of dreary conversation while supping *á la Française,* Lord Hogart returned, most inadvisably, to his cups and the news that had dominated the front page of every newspaper for two weeks—the raging storms at sea.

"F-four hundred men have drowned," he slurred in an overloud tone, drawing the attention of everyone at the long, narrow dining table. After several glasses of wine, his bulbous nose had gone red, and beads of sweat greased his thinning hairline. "And the cargo," he added. "Well, I dare not even imagine the losses."

This turn of conversation put a number of the guests ill at ease. One gentleman quietly excused himself from the table, while others shifted uncomfortably in their chairs. To Eliza's surprise, Magnus was included in their number.

She saw him exchange a meaningful glance with his uncle, before stabbing a bit of fish flesh with his knife, only to stare down at it for several empty moments. As Hogart droned on, Magnus squeezed the blade's mother-of-pearl handle until the beds of his nails went as white as the linen beneath his plate.

"Thankfully, none of the western shipping lanes have been affected by the tempest," their host added.

This bit of news, though meaningless to Eliza, seemed to assuage Magnus, who relaxed his grip on his knife.

Eliza studied the Scotsman from the corner of her eye.

Why had he appeared so concerned about the storms? He could not be an investor. He had no money. He'd admitted as much to her.

Or was this, too, another of his fabrications? Eliza pondered this as she glanced up at their hostess.

Lady Hogart was not blind to her guests' discomfort, as her husband seemed to be. She clapped her hands together, breaking the tension in the room. "My husband acquired a stunning chestnut at Tattersall's only last week," she began.

Bleary-eyed, Lord Hogart glared at his wife and with a loose wave of his hand, dismissed her. "Do not try to quiet me, Madam. Besides, you know nothing of horseflesh. Best keep your mouth closed rather than embarrass yourself before our guests."

Lady Hogart raised her napkin to her lips as tears began to catch in her lashes. Rather than risk another rebuke, she uttered not another word.

Eliza's heart went out to her. Amid the lavish meal and elegant home, Lady Hogart was an unhappy woman, trapped in a marriage to an ogre of the first order. She diverted her gaze from Lady Hogart, as she hoped others would do, to afford their hostess some dignity. As she did so, Grace's astonished gaze caught her own.

Eliza lifted a knowing brow. *This is what marriage does to a woman,* she wanted to say.

Lord Hogart lifted his crystal goblet and gulped the wine from it. "What right have the Americans to British merchant ships? They are running amok, I tell you," he growled. "We should deal with them swiftly and firmly. 'Tis our duty and our right, just as 'tis a husband's duty to control his wife."

The tears welling inside Lady Hogart's lashes spilled over and trickled down her cheeks.

Eliza seized her fork, her knuckles paling with her grip. She drew in a breath, preparing to speak her mind, when

Lord Somerton brushed her hand lightly, causing her to pause and glance up at him.

"I would agree with ye, Hogart," he said. "Our relationship with America should be like a marriage."

Eliza caught her breath. She turned and stared at Magnus. Surely he did not agree with their beast of a host!

Out of the corner of her eye, she noticed Aunt Viola shaking her head and wiggling five fingers just above the lip of the table. *Rule Five. Pretend inferiority.*

Hogart lifted his quizzing glass to his eye and peered at Magnus. "Glad to hear you agree, Somerton."

Magnus raised his palm. "Allow me to finish, if ye will."

This, Eliza decided, she should like to hear. Folding her hands in her lap, Eliza leaned back in her chair and allowed Magnus an unhindered view of Lord Hogart.

"Our relationship with America should be like a marriage—" he turned his eyes and caught Eliza's gaze, stunning her with his attention. "A partnership, in which both grow as a result of merging their strengths and resources."

Eliza looked down at her napkin. A relieved, and admittedly surprised, smile tugged at her lips.

She glanced up at Magnus again and studied his profile. Perhaps there was more to this Lord Somerton than she gave him credit for. Perhaps much more.

When supper concluded, the ladies took their leave, allowing the gentlemen their brandy and imported cheroots in the privacy of the dining room.

Eliza, who had no desire to be chastised for allowing Miss Peacock to wholly monopolize Magnus's attentions at the table, occupied herself by chatting with another young lady who was also *enjoying* her first season. Eventually though, she succumbed to the inevitable and joined her aunts and sister near the hearth and awaited her rebuke.

"I cannot do it, Auntie," Grace was quietly telling Aunt Letitia. "The man is marginally attractive, but he has the intelligence of . . . *a slimy garden slug*. I cannot pretend inferiority any longer."

"A garden slug, say you? Hmm," Aunt Letitia replied distractedly. She flipped her fan open and waved it before her face, casting a disappointed eye on Eliza all the while. "Then, perhaps he is not the match for you, Gracie."

"I daresay he is not," Grace whispered, "but I fear he may feel otherwise."

Aunt Viola's eyes grew bright. "Do you anticipate an offer?"

"I do not know." Grace's face grew pale. "Perhaps."

Eliza looked at her sister. "Surely not after one evening."

Grace wrung her hands. "I believe Rule Five might have worked too well. Since we are new to London, I had not been warned of his dull character. My efforts likely afforded him more female attention than he has received in years."

Eliza bit her lips, preventing a guffaw.

The rumble of sliding pocket doors drew Eliza's attention. At last, the men had finished their libations and tobacco and were now rejoining the women.

"There's Somerton, gel. Go get him!" Aunt Letitia's hand slammed into Eliza's back and shoved her toward the center of the room. "Hurry now."

Eliza took a step forward, more determined now than ever to have her explanation of Magnus's supposed engagement.

But the two Peacocks, unnaturally fleet of foot, surged forward and met Lord Somerton and Mr. Pender as they emerged and together the four of them walked to the other side of the room. *Blast!* Caroline had usurped her again.

Mr. Dabney, a son of a baronet and therefore a commoner by the high ton's standards, was the last guest through the doorway. His eyes scanned the room, brightening when he noticed Grace.

Grace's eyes grew round. "Lud! Here comes Mr. Dabney now. Please excuse me." With her words still loose in the air, Grace made a hasty retreat for the ladies' withdrawing room.

Eliza turned away and reluctantly rejoined her aunts, but it was no use. She could not stop her gaze from drifting back to Magnus. He was supposed to be posing as her suitor, not cavorting with that heifer, Miss Peacock. She had to speak with him *now*. Had to know if he was truly engaged to her.

Then, as if summoned by her wishes, Magnus lifted his eyes and found hers. One corner of his mouth pulled into a slight smile and he playfully fluttered his eyebrows at her.

A wash of heat suffused her cheeks, and she turned quickly away, trying again to follow her aunts' conversation. How she abhorred Society's ridiculous rules. Were she a man, she could just stride across the drawing and demand an interview. But a lady could not. A lady must be patient.

A moment later, Eliza found the courage to glance in Lord Somerton's direction to monitor his conversation. But as she turned her head, she nearly jumped from her slippers. Magnus had left the Peacocks with his uncle and was now standing directly at her side.

"Miss Merriweather," he said, with a polite nod.

With gleeful grins, Aunt Letitia and Aunt Viola silently receded into the next circle of conversation tactfully leaving Eliza alone with the earl.

"I do beg yer pardon. I know ye wish to continue our conversation, but it took a little longer than I'd hoped to extract myself from Miss Peacock's company."

"Y-you should have signaled me," Eliza said, vaguely alarmed at the shrillness of her own voice. "I would have come to your rescue."

Magnus lifted a speculative brow. "Ye do not find Miss Peacock agreeable?"

"How could I make such a judgment? I barely know her."

Eliza glanced across the room to where Caroline Peacock was now happily conversing with Mr. Dabney. Surprisingly, she did not appear at all bored, as Grace claimed to have been. In fact, Caroline actually seemed to be enjoying their chat. But then, Eliza chuckled to herself, cows were not known for their intelligence, were they?

Turning back to Magnus, Eliza tilted her head and studied him for a moment. "But *you* find her agreeable, my lord."

"She seems amiable enough. Her manners are superb. Very handsome too, I must admit," he said thoughtfully. "But Miss Peacock was my father's choice of bride for *my brother,* the late Lord Somerton."

Eliza lifted her brows. "For your *brother*? So you were never . . . and you let me think . . . well, fancy that." An odd feeling of relief washed over her. "Though, I daresay, the Peacocks seem to be under the impression that Caroline is to marry *you*."

"I am well aware of their wishes. Caroline was to be a countess when she married James. Now that he is gone and the title has passed to me—"

"She has set her cap for you."

"Aye. Or rather, her parents have." Magnus gestured toward Pender, who stood across the room staring back at them with a critical eye. "And, my uncle is doing all he can to convince me of her suitability, given my situation, ye know."

Eliza's mood lightened. Their *arrangement* could remain in place. After tonight, they'd only need to bolster appearances a bit, that's all. She smiled inwardly, for she could do little more to release the pent tension. Her corset was too tight to take the deep cleansing breath she longed for.

"I have inherited much from my brother. Somerton Hall, a mountain of debts . . . of which I am working to rectify. But I never wished to inherit his betrothed. After all, I know so little of her." He hesitated a moment before continuing. "Though, it would do no harm to learn more . . . I mean, in the event my current course of action doesn't pay out."

"Current course doesn't pay? What does that—" she muttered. Then, his former words registered. Eliza's jaw dropped before she could gather the wits to react calmly. "Wait a moment, please. Are you asking me to investigate *Miss Peacock*?"

Magnus lifted two cordials from a passing footman's tray and handed one to Eliza. "It would be imprudent to count her out simply because she had an attachment with my brother, would it not?"

"Y-yes, I expect so."

"I know ye've been introduced to both Miss Peacock and her mother. I do not believe I am requesting too difficult a task of ye. We do have an *arrangement*."

Eliza steadied herself. "*We* do," she emphasized, hoping he would take her meaning and realize the trouble his inattentiveness had caused her with her aunts. "And I've been meaning to discuss it with you."

Magnus chuckled. "Have I neglected ye this eve, Miss Merriweather? If so, I do apologize," he said, his mesmerizing silvery-blue eyes piercing the distance between them.

She looked down at her slippers. Suddenly, Eliza felt very foolish. She was acting like a jealous ninny. After all, in a few short weeks she'd be in Italy, and Lord Somerton would be naught but a distant memory.

Eliza sipped her cordial twice, then swallowed the remaining ruby-hued liquid and replaced her glass on the silver tray as the footman circled by. "Of course, I will investigate Miss Peacock for you,"—she spotted an iridescent feather shred on the carpet and squashed it with her foot—"in accordance with our arrangement."

"I am glad you agree."

When Eliza looked up at Magnus again, his gaze was once more focused on the Peacocks—nay, likely *Caroline* Peacock and her breasts! *Typical man.*

"Lord Somerton." Eliza exhaled. "I say, Somerton."

Eliza looked down at her own small breasts and sighed. Magnus was all but ignoring her. She looked across the expansive drawing room at her aunts, whose concerned expressions told her that they, too, were witness to Magnus's preoccupation with Caroline Peacock.

Well, this would not do. Would not do at all.

Bah! She had to think of some way to regain his attention and keep it. But how? Caroline had the clear advantage.

At that moment, it came to her in all clarity. Reaching into her reticule, she withdrew her aunt's handkerchief and balled it in her fist.

Keeping a watchful eye on Magnus, whose attention had strayed across the room to Caroline once more, she turned her body toward the wall and wedged the handkerchief inside her corset, beneath her breasts. Then she whirled around and faced Magnus once more.

"Lord Somerton?" she said.

Magnus redirected his gaze to her. "Hmm? Ye were saying something, Miss Merriweather?" Suddenly his gaze dropped and his eyes seemed almost to bulge in their sockets.

"Yes, yes, I was," she said, as calmly as she could manage with her breasts poised to pop out of her gown. "I will investigate Caroline Peacock and anyone else you choose, but I shall require your help on the morrow."

Magnus seemed to struggle to drag his gaze up to Eliza's face. "My help?"

"Whether you realize it or not, as of tonight our *arrangement* is in tatters. My aunts are likely already plotting an offensive to revive your interest in me."

"Is that so?" A roguish grin eased across Magnus's lips. "Then just leave everything to me. Oh," he added, as if he had forgotten something. Magnus reached into his coat pocket and withdrew a handkerchief. "Here ye are."

Eliza looked the square of linen and then blankly back at Magnus. "I am quite recovered, I assure you. Why should I need a handkerchief now?"

Grinning, Magnus balled the linen in his hand then pressed it into her palm, with a quick glance at her chest.

His gaze lingered so long that Eliza was compelled to follow his gaze to her handiwork. She gasped at the sight. One breast sat high, like Caroline's own, threatening to spill from her low neckline. One. Just one.

The other lay hidden demurely inside her gown.

"Oh!" Eliza was positively mortified.

Magnus winked. "So ye'll have a matched pair, *lassie*."

Rule Six

*Advance troops ensure the tactical plan
is carried out.*

The wide sterling tray, expertly laid with tiny cakes and dried fruits, glinted in the waning late afternoon sunlight as Edgar settled it upon the tea table before the four ladies.

Eliza gazed across the lip of her teacup at Grace and her two aunts. They sat together in the parlor, as had become their daily habit, gathered around the tea tray . . . again. *This* was the life they wanted for her. This dreary, boring, pastry-popping, savory-supping existence.

"Of course, I wrote all about the Hogart's party to dear Meredith," Grace was prattling on as she absently fingered each blush satin rose ringing the base of her right sleeve. "Poor thing, tucked away at school, missing out on all of the excitement."

Eliza laughed. "Oh, yes. Isn't London *all* the crack?" She hurried the teacup to her mouth, hiding the wiseacre grin itching her lips. "Still, I suspect Meredith is better off at Mrs. Bellbury's school, protected from city excitement."

Aunt Viola nodded in agreement. "Our Meredith is quite

spirited. And at her impressionable age, I daresay London is not the place for her."

Tipping her cup, Grace washed back a half-hearted sigh. "Still, Meredith seems quite disappointed to be missing out on the fun. And she won't even come out for another two years."

"Before she knows it, her season will come," added Aunt Letitia, pecking with her plump finger at the crumbs on her plate, in a most unladylike fashion.

Eliza rolled her eyes. Meredith didn't know how lucky she was to be spared from this horrid season. Besides, according to Mrs. Bellbury's letters, their sister was keeping herself—and the staff—quite entertained.

The dinging bell in the tall case clock sounded the six o'clock hour and soon after Eliza heard Lord Somerton's resonant voice in the entryway. She looked up from her teacup, nearly spilling its steaming contents on her azure silk walking dress.

At last. Eliza settled her porcelain cup down on the table, and as she did so, noticed Aunt Letitia covertly nudge Aunt Viola, who returned a decidedly conspiratorial wink.

Eliza shook her head. There was only one way to keep her aunts at bay and their abominable rule book locked away in the library. And Lord Somerton held the key.

Grace hurried her teacup to the table. "Eliza, you neglected to mention Lord Somerton was to call."

"Did I?" Eliza glanced anxiously toward the doorway.

Wasting not a moment, Grace pinched her cheeks and bit her lips until they blossomed rosy red, then pasted on a gleaming smile to await their guest's entrance.

Aunt Viola shook her head. "You needn't bother primping, Grace. Lord Somerton has come for our *Eliza*."

"I am aware of that, Auntie, but it is possible he has

brought along a gentleman friend," Grace replied. "It never hurts to look one's best."

Eliza fought the urge to comment and instead looked through the doorway to the entry hall. There, her gaze fell upon a golden wedge of light that retreated across the marble floor and vanished with a click of the front door's heavy lock.

A moment later, Edgar appeared with Lord Somerton and led him into the parlor.

Eliza donned a wan smile and rose to nod a quick greeting to Magnus. His calling was not a surprise, but his presence made Eliza uneasy nonetheless.

For yet another night, Eliza had not slept well, her mind troubled by the persistent image of Magnus gazing upon Miss Peacock at the Hogarts' supper.

It had taken some time to accurately label what she'd been feeling, nearly all night in fact, but now she knew the beast for what it was—*jealousy*.

This was something she could not abide. Because for jealousy to exist, Eliza knew there must also be a certain level of caring. And goodness knows she could not allow that. No, affection for the man would only serve as an obstacle to accomplishing her ultimate goal of leaving for Italy at the end of the season.

It would be best for all if theirs remained purely a business relationship, and nothing more.

As Magnus came to stand before her, and she smelled his fresh-washed scent, a little quiver in her middle built into a slow burn. Boldly, he lifted her fingers and pressed a soft kiss atop her bare hand. She glanced up, sure her family had witnessed his transgression, but they had not. Their view had been blocked by his broad shoulders as he bent down.

Surely he knew it highly improper to kiss an unmarried woman's hand—and yet he persisted, whenever he thought he might do so unobserved. And Eliza could not seem to pull herself away. The roughness of his shaved chin against her knuckles made her skin tingle—and made her wonder how it might feel if he kissed her . . . elsewhere.

No, no, *no*. She mustn't allow this.

Damn your handsome face. Eliza drew in a breath and reminded herself, once more, that Magnus could be her business partner and nothing more. *Nothing more*.

"Good evening, ladies," Magnus said, turning to nod to each of them. "I trust I haven't come at a poor time."

Aunt Viola offered her hand to Lord Somerton. "Not at all. You are a welcome guest in our home any time you care to call."

Next, Aunt Letitia extended her hand to Magnus. When he neared to take it, she snatched up his wrist and hauled him before her. "What brings you to our home this late afternoon, Lord Somerton? Come to join us for tea—or perhaps something a bit sweeter?" She tilted her head toward Eliza, hooted merrily, then released his wrist.

Eliza cupped her eyes with her hand and cringed. "Auntie, *please*."

Both aunts burst into laughter.

Magnus smiled too. "I came to sit for another study. Though, I also had hoped yer niece might consent to join me for supper at Vauxhall Gardens. The evening should be quite mellow, and the entertainment is reported to be superb this eve."

"Oh, Vauxhall Gardens!" Aunt Viola tugged on Eliza's arm. "Doesn't that sound delightful, dear?"

"Indeed." A tenseness seized Eliza. An evening at the Pleasure Gardens. *This* was how he planned to set things to rights with her aunts?

Only yesterday, she might have commended him for his ingenuity. But today, the thought of being alone with

Magnus terrified her. In fact, now that he had played his hand and reestablished his supposed interest in her, she wished only that he'd leave. *Now.*

"A jaunt to Vauxhall Gardens sounds incredibly romantic to me." Grace sighed and blinked her eyes dreamily. "You could leave right away, in fact. You see, there's no need for more blocking. Eliza has already begun to paint, and there isn't daylight enough for a proper sitting. La, you should see the canvas. I've never seen such a grand likeness. You will be most pleased."

"Oh. Ye've already begun?" Magnus looked up at Eliza, quite surprised. "Then perhaps ye would be so good as to allow me to see the portrait . . . to view yer progress."

"Of course. The canvas is in the library. I shall fetch it for you," she replied, eager to leave the room and put as much distance as possible between them.

"No need. I shall accompany ye and save ye the exertion of moving the painting," Magnus offered, his long legs carrying him to the doorway before Eliza had even skirted the tea table.

"Please do not trouble yourself, Lord Somerton." Eliza waved him away.

"I assure ye, 'tis no trouble at all." His lips parted and he leveled her with a dashing smile.

She glanced down at her bodice, half expecting the pounding of her heart to be visible through the fine silk of her walking gown. When she looked up again, she saw Magnus's silvery eyes had followed her gaze.

Mortified as her chest flushed a deep crimson red, she rushed past him and headed for the corridor. Glancing back over her shoulder, she saw him grin, tip his head to her aunts, and follow her.

Lifting her skirts, Eliza flew to her easel and turned it so that the painting might catch the last rays of golden light.

But before she could step back, she felt the heat of Magnus behind her. She turned her head slowly and saw him studying the canvas over her shoulder.

"You are quite talented, Eliza. I can see why painting holds such significance in your life."

"I . . . I am far from being finished," she said, turning around in the breath of space between him and the painting.

It was then that she realized her mistake.

Magnus peered down at her, his mouth partly open.

She watched, unable to move, as his tongue slid over his full lower lip, making her feel like a tasty morsel he was about to sample.

Though she inhaled faster, Eliza could not take in enough air. Nor could he, it seemed, for his chest heaved as if he'd just returned from a hard ride.

His eyes, always so pale and cool, now glowed with the blue heat of a candle flame, threatening to ignite her. And, indeed, warmth was building within her, intensifying the dull ache that burned in the pit of her belly.

Magnus reached out and brushed her cheek with his knuckles.

Without a thought, her head turned of its own accord, and her lips swept over the base of his fingers.

"Eliza," he whispered, and her insides turned to liquid. He touched her face and turned it upward, slowly touching her mouth to his. He groaned as he tasted her, as his tongue gently explored the curve of her wanting lips, the smooth slickness of the inside of her mouth.

Blood pounded in her temples as he fed on her, as she consumed him. Oh, God. She never thought it could be like this. And she wanted more. She wanted to hold him, to feel him against her.

And he answered her silent call. His hands fell away from her cheeks and he pulled her tightly into his embrace.

He clutched her to him and her hips slammed against his as a sense of urgency overtook her body.

At once, she felt his rigid hardness against her pelvis and she pressed herself intimately against it. *This is wrong. Wrong.* But she could not stop herself. This new, forbidden sensation excited her as never before and she became aware of a growing dampness between her legs.

Somewhere in the recesses of Eliza's mind, she registered a knock at the library door, but she was powerless to acknowledge it. She was listing in a sea of pure sensation.

Then she heard the door open.

"Eliza, my dear," came Aunt Viola's soft voice.

Magnus pulled away from her and swung aside, clearing Eliza's view of her aunt. Eliza ran four fingers through her hair, securing her loosened curls beneath a hair pin.

"Oh my! I had no idea . . . you'd been gone for some minutes and I, well, thought perhaps you might need some hel—." Aunt Viola swooned. "Oh heavens. *Spell*—"

Magnus lurched forward and caught Viola as her body plummeted toward the gleaming floor. He looked up at Eliza, concern flashing in his eyes as he carried her aunt to a plump chair beside the hearth. "Call for a doctor," he ordered. "Hurry now!"

Eliza crossed to her aunt, and, seeing she was in no danger of falling from the chair, settled the old woman's shriveled hands in her lap. "No need. She'll be fine. Just having one of her spells, that's all."

Magnus came to his feet. "What sort of spell?"

Eliza took Magnus's hand and drew him away. "Sleeping spells. She succumbs to them two or three times a week. High emotion or surprise usually brings them on."

"Ye mean, like the shock of seeing ye in my arms," he whispered.

Eliza looked away from him then, and suddenly became

extraordinarily interested in her fingernails. "Err . . . yes, that might do it." She glanced at her aunt then. "No need to whisper though. We shan't rouse her. She will wake in a minute or a few hours. Nothing we do will change that."

A slight smile brushed Magnus's lips, making Eliza wish she hadn't as good as told him they were alone.

She turned to finish the task of returning the easel to its earlier position. Magnus moved to help her, jumbling her senses all over again.

Reaching out to steady the painting, his hand accidentally brushed her own. Worried eyes greeted her. "Eliza, I—"

"I do not wish to talk about what happened, if you don't mind," she said, averting her gaze and focusing on the task at hand.

"I just wanted to say I am sorry. I should not have—"

Eliza steadied herself and quietly implored him. "*Please*." The worst thing that could have possibly happened, *had happened*. She had wanted him to kiss her and he had. And it was tender, passionate and wonderful . . . but over. And it would not happen again. The moment had served its purpose.

She'd gotten him out of her system. That was a good thing. Perhaps now she could stop thinking about him and start making plans for Italy.

"Verra well, then." He glanced up at her, twice, but respected her wishes and did not press the matter again. Silently, Magnus turned to leave the library, but caught notice of her canvases leaning against the far wall.

He crossed to them and thumbed through the paintings one at a time, resting those he'd already viewed on his upper thigh. Eliza peered at the shadowed space beneath his waistcoat where the paintings now rested. Every curve of his musculature was visible through the tight doeskin breeches men favored these days.

One curve in particular. One overlarge curve. *Jupiter!* She stifled a gasp and looked quickly away.

"These are stellar, Eliza," he said, unaware of her embarrassment. "I had no idea. No idea at all."

"Y-you act surprised." *Do not look down. Focus on what he is saying.*

"Surprised, to say the least. I thought that yer painting was simply a female fancy—that yer talent was, perhaps, above average, which is why ye sought to study in Italy."

Eliza rounded the library table, temporarily forgetting her discomfort, and stood before him. She folded her arms and dared him to overstep his bounds.

He eased the paintings back against the wall and moved before her. "But Eliza, yer work . . . I've never seen anything like this."

She looked away to avoid the strength of his gaze and saw *Rules of Engagement* lying on the table. What was it doing out and in plain sight no less? Only a day had passed since she'd climbed the library ladder and replaced the book on the highest shelf, hidden away from Grace and the two matchmaking strategists.

But here it lay again. A quizzing glass lay poised on the open pages magnifying the chapter heading.

Rule Six
*Advance troops ensure
the tactical plan is carried out.*

She squeezed her eyes tight for a moment. She daren't even consider how her aunts were planning to enact that strategy. But she had no doubt Rule Six would unfold that very eve.

Stretching out her fingers, she quickly brushed the

magnifier to the table and slapped the heavy manual shut before Magnus could see it.

"I am so glad you hold my talent in such high opinion," Eliza said as she opened the table drawer and quickly hid the book inside. She nudged the drawer shut with her hip and looked up again just as Magnus came to stand before her.

He lifted her chin with the pad of his index finger. "Yer talent is not a matter of opinion. Yer paintings are brilliant—that, my dear, is a fact. Anyone who would say otherwise would have to be blind."

That voice of his. Its deep timbre hummed through the most inappropriate place. Just then, from the corner of her eye, Eliza saw her Aunt Viola's head move. She turned, expecting to catch her aunt watching them, but by the time she did so, her auntie's head was resting on her chest, and her eyes were clearly shut. Had she imagined it? No, Eliza knew better. Her aunt was spying on them.

Blood coursed into her cheeks and she pulled away from Magnus.

"Thank you, my lord," she muttered, so distracted by the proximity of his body that she busied herself by straightening the handle of the quizzing glass so it lined up with the angles of the table. Lud, she was acting quite the goose!

"W-we should rejoin my aunt and sister. I'll call Jenny to sit with Viola," she stammered as she breathed in the almost woody scent of him.

Heaven help her. She wasn't over him! She should raise her hands in the air and surrender to her aunts this very moment. Her *arrangement* with Lord Somerton was putting her heart in much more jeopardy than her aunts' maneuvers ever could.

"Lead the way, lass," Magnus said in a burr that made her breath catch.

Flustered though she was, Eliza folded her arms across

her chest and hoisted a pleasant smile. It was important that she appear calm when they rejoined her aunt and sister, as if nothing of consequence had occurred.

And from the feel of her gently upturned lips, Eliza was sure she had achieved the essential serene countenance she sought. That is, until she caught her reflection in the passageway mirror and the term *constipated* flashed in her mind.

"Now, what say ye to a trip to Vauxhall?" Magnus asked Eliza the moment they entered the parlor. He was quite sure Eliza's aunt Letitia would accept his invitation for her, if she did not.

Why he was so intent on escorting Eliza to the Gardens, he did not know. All he knew, since he saw her at the Hogarts' party, was that he wanted to be alone with her—Eliza Merriweather, the Society misfit who had not a penny to her name.

"Vauxhall?" Eliza's eyes widened almost fearfully.

He wanted to tell her she needn't worry. That he'd made a mistake by kissing her, but that he was in full control of his faculties now. That he would not allow his passions to rule his mind and body again.

Still, one small taste of her plump lips was not enough to satiate his need. And, if there was even a small chance of stealing her kiss again, he knew in his wicked heart, he would take it.

Suddenly, Eliza's eyes sparkled with excitement. "Why don't we make a party of it?" She turned to her aunt Letitia. "You will join us, of course. It *is* a lovely evening."

Magnus teetered, unprepared for Eliza's clever turn of the situation. A group outing was *not* what he had planned.

But thankfully, her aunt Letitia waved her linen napkin in the air, dismissing the thought. "Bless you, Lizzy, but I am much too old to stroll anywhere but through my own parlor."

Lady Viola suddenly appeared in the doorway, apparently no worse for her supposed spell. She released a regretful sigh and nodded in agreement. "And I am much too weary. But *you* may join them, dear." She gestured to Grace. "Though pray, do not be too awfully rigid in your chaperoning."

Magnus could see the tension in Eliza's shoulders disperse as she quickly took to the idea.

"Yes, *do* join us, Sister."

Grace grimaced. "Chaperone? But I am unmarried."

Lady Letitia pulled a playful scowl. "Pish posh, child. Do you wish to go to Vauxhall or don't you?"

Magnus felt his plan to be alone with Eliza slipping from his grasp.

Grace smiled up at Eliza and then flashed her teeth at Magnus as well. "I should be most pleased to join you."

"Wonderful," Magnus droned.

With a little giggle rolling from her lips, Grace leapt to her feet and charged into the hallway. Then, she paused and gave first her gown, then Eliza's, appraising glances before concluding with a relieved smile. "Our gowns are perfectly appropriate for the Gardens, do you not agree, Aunt Letitia?"

"Quite," Aunt Letitia replied. "Might as well leave now."

"May we, Lord Somerton?" Grace asked.

Magnus exhaled slowly. "Of course. My carriage awaits."

Taking her proffered bonnet from Edgar, Grace whirled around, her face positively alight. "Who knows whom we might meet along the way?"

"That's our Grace," Eliza whispered to Magnus. "Never missing an opportunity to hunt for a husband."

As the three turned to leave the house, Lady Letitia called

out. "We do hope you will join us for a refreshment when you return, Lord Somerton."

"Yes, you must return this evening," Lady Viola added.

Magnus smiled brilliantly at the two aunts. "I would consider it an honor, ladies."

The two aunts giggled like milkmaids as he, Eliza, and Grace walked out the door and headed for his waiting carriage.

"Now, will ye tell me why yer aunts were giggling so?"

"Lord Somerton, with my aunts, one can never be too sure," Eliza said. "Suffice it to say, they are up to something *grand*."

Rule Seven

When birds startle and flee,
you are about to be taken unaware.

From the moment they passed through the Kennington entrance of the pleasure garden, Eliza was dazzled by the spectacle of Vauxhall. Thousands of dappled glass lanterns glittered through the profusion of trees, flickering like huge colorful fireflies in the coming night. Honeyed music hummed through the throngs of London's elegantly garbed elite as they strolled down the well-lit Grand Walk, seeing and being seen.

Still, Eliza wished with all her heart that she could be anywhere else. *With* anyone else but Magnus.

Absorbed in the sights, Eliza and Grace blindly followed Lord Somerton through the tree runs, past the domed rotunda and dazzling piazza of five arches, to one of many supper boxes near the center of the pleasure garden. There, they dined on sweetmeats, paper-thin ham, dark cherries, wine of prime vintage, and delicate cakes while enjoying the lively music of a full orchestra.

Grace sighed. "Have you ever seen a place so grand?"

"Indeed, I have not," Eliza admitted.

"I own, I could stay here forever, Sister."

Forever? Eliza had already been here an hour too long. After the way Magnus had boldly pressed his lips to hers, making her smolder inside—even now, how could she possibly endure an evening with his body so close to her own? She flipped open her fan and waved it madly before her hot cheeks.

Suddenly, from the far side of the shrubbery, there came a burst of familiar voices.

"Oh, my foot! You've stabbed it with your cane, Viola!"

"My apologies, Sister. Shan't happen again. But you mustn't shout, else we'll be discovered."

Magnus blinked outward into the night and slowly rose from the table. "I daresay, are those yer aunts on the other side of the hedgerow?"

Eliza turned in time to see two elderly women, disguised in black dominos, ducking behind a hedge of boxwood. She lowered her head and sighed, for the masks did not conceal the identities of the two snowy-haired women.

"I should have guessed they would appear," Eliza said.

Grace nodded her head. "Yes, they were protesting joining us much too strongly."

"Shall we ask them to join us?" Magnus asked.

Eliza rose and glanced over at the wavering bushes. "I . . . think not."

Magnus stared back at her, perplexed. "Are ye sure?"

"Oh, quite." Eliza sat down again and lifted a bit of ham with her fork. "After all, they seem quite content to creep through the hedgerows just now, and I should hate to spoil their fun."

Eliza breathed in the refreshing night air as they strolled along the Grand Walk a short while after their meal. She hadn't seen her aunts in well over twenty minutes, and had almost convinced herself they had gone home, when she realized Grace was no longer nearby either.

She glanced around and saw that her sister had fallen behind to watch a band of jugglers. "We should wait for Grace," Eliza told Magnus, as she reached out her gloved fingers to catch a white moth flittering past her nose.

She did not want to be left alone with him, even in such a public place as the Garden.

As several couples of the Quality passed them, curious glances riding astride their greetings, Magnus caught up Eliza's hand and placed it atop his arm. He smiled, as if expecting to be congratulated for good behavior.

"You know, you really do not need to play the ever-attentive suitor, my lord," Eliza said. "It is not as though you are truly courting me."

"I do nothing by half," he replied evenly.

At his touch, Eliza's body trembled. She looked up at him, at his mouth, and remembered the depth of his kiss. Her knees begin to wobble with the potent memory. "No, I don't suppose you do," she managed.

Noticing that Grace was now moving slowly toward them, Magnus coaxed Eliza into an easy stroll once more. "Ye've already assessed my character, have ye, Miss Merriweather?"

"Miss Merriweather is it? My, my. Until this moment, I do believe I was Eliza."

"Yes, and I was Magnus. Is there something troubling ye?"

Eliza lifted her chin and looked into his eyes. She could never admit what was truly wrong—that her body quaked and logic seemed to fly out her ears whenever he was near. Or, that she feared she was developing feelings for him— feelings that would ruin everything.

She took a deep breath and feigned a smile. "Naught is wrong. Truly."

She longed for a more believable answer to his question. Finally, something, inane as it was, came to mind. "I just feel that while you have maintained your end of our bargain, playing my suitor, I have not taken my promise to you seriously."

Magnus studied her. "Ye're painting my portrait."

"Yes, but, I have barely begun to investigate possible brides for you. I've not even quizzed Miss Peacock—though I have my doubts she is the one for you." Eliza focused her gaze on Grace, who strolled leisurely a short distance behind them.

Magnus turned and began walking again. "I see."

"Then you will not mind if I ask you a few questions."

"What sort of questions?"

"The sort which will help me determine your preferences in a bride." Eliza quickened her step, and then turned to block his path, halting him. "For instance, is intelligence important to you?"

"Intelligence. Aye."

Eliza exhaled. "Do not be so forthcoming, my lord. I am having difficulty taking in so much detail."

Even silhouetted against the bright lanterns lining the Walk, she could see his grin.

"All right. Intelligence is verra important to me. More so than other attributes. I should like my bride to be well read, and current on events and politics. Quick-witted. Clever. She should be fair of face, with a pleasing form."

"Much better."

"And rich." Magnus stared blankly at her with eyes that could only be described as startled.

"What is it? Do I have something in my teeth—a leaf of

parsley, perhaps?" she said, trying to make light of whatever was bothering Magnus.

"Other than the last qualification," he admitted in a rather surprised tone, "I could be describing ye."

At his words, a warm tingle raced through Eliza's body, making her highly aware of his proximity and the fact that they were, for all intent and purposes, alone.

Needing to do something other than stand and stare, Eliza began to walk. Magnus remained at her side, but no words came to either of them for an uneasy handful of minutes. The tension between them deepened until Eliza felt compelled to break it.

"Where do you suppose Grace has wandered off to?"

As if in answer, she saw Grace hurrying toward them, a lanky, silver-haired man and a roving band of musicians in pursuit. Eliza opened her eyes wide. "What is Edgar doing here?"

Magnus pivoted and stared down the Grand Walk. "Yer aunts' manservant?"

"The very same."

Scanning the trees along the Grand Walk, Eliza quickly spotted her aunts hiding in a leafy stand of elms.

Grace ran to Eliza and clutched her arm, steadying herself while she caught her breath. "It appears . . . our aunts mean to provide us with . . . some entertainment," she said between shallow gasps for air.

"Yes, I see." Eliza glanced about looking for an escape route. "But I intend to enjoy this evening. And, being serenaded by tin-eared street musicians is not what I deem entertainment." Eliza turned to Grace. "If you care to join me, I plan to leave this very instant. If not, I will see you soon enough at the house."

"I am not racing off anywhere," Grace whined. "My new

boots are squeezing my feet. I will ride home with our aunts. Lord Somerton will escort you back."

Magnus seemed quite pleased with the prospect, which made Eliza more than a little nervous. "Logical solution, really." A grin slid across his lips.

"Very well, then." With a quick glance toward her aunts, Eliza snatched up her walking skirt in her hand, readying herself to leave. "Shall we?"

At that very moment, Aunt Letitia burst from the trees, waving her cane in the air and pointing a pudgy finger in their direction. Immediately, Edgar whistled for the hired musicians, who picked up their instruments and scurried down the Grand Walk toward them.

"Aye, let's go." With that, Magnus grabbed Eliza's arm and yanked her down a narrow pathway like a Viking with his prize.

Gravel popped from beneath their boots as they raced far from the reach of light from Vauxhall's busy center. They turned down a narrow walk closely lined with trees and ran down its length.

Eliza was fast becoming disoriented. Lud, how would they ever find their way back? Her eyes searched for landmarks, but in the growing darkness there were none. Then, almost too late, she saw a ragged painted sign. Throwing a glance back over her shoulder to read it, she immediately wished she hadn't. Lord above! They were headed down the scandalous Dark Walk.

Magnus caught her waist and pulled her into a tangle of bushes along the trail. He cupped his hand over her mouth to quiet her heavy breathing from the run.

She should not allow this to happen. She knew this, but her blood surged with the excitement of the chase and the way he held her just now.

He lifted his hand from her mouth and she turned her eyes upward to look at him. In the blue light of the three-quarter moon, she saw a mischievous grin slip over Magnus's lips as he peered through the profusion of beech leaves bracketing the walk. On the other side of the branches, the band of confused musicians paused, then set off in another direction, passing them by.

Eliza laughed softly, surprised they had managed to lose the band so quickly. "Once they reach the Walk's end, they will realize where we've gone."

"Well, we canna have that. Come with me, lassie. This way."

Without batting a lash, Eliza looped her arm through Magnus's and allowed him to lead her farther down the pathway to decadence.

The Dark Walk certainly stood up to its lewd reputation this night, Magnus mused. He'd thought it was supposed to be closed off to the public, but they passed one impassioned couple after another, all in various states of undress. He could certainly understand why it should be closed. Still, Eliza appeared both shocked and fascinated and could not seem to look away from the couples. Nor did she release his arm.

At last, they came upon an unoccupied marble bench and sank down upon it. "I doubt very much that they will find us now," Eliza said.

"I should think not." Magnus's grin faded from his lips as he became uncomfortably aware of the woman sitting so close to him, her bosom still heaving from their escape. Damn, she was beautiful. He felt his gentleman's control slip, then fall, and there he let it lay.

Without further thought to what could and could not exist between them, he gently cupped Eliza's chin in his hand and turned her face until it was lit by a single wand of moonlight breaking through the trees.

She looked up at him, blinking rapidly. His touch had surprised her, but she didn't pull away.

"We appear to be quite alone." He stroked the side of her cheek with his forefinger.

"Yes." Eliza closed her eyes and drew a small breath through her moist lips.

Magnus leaned toward her, intent on pressing his mouth to hers. Business arrangement be damned. His arms encircled her and with one hand pressed into the small of her back, he drew her deeper into his embrace. His lips touched hers softly.

With an angel's sigh, she eased her arms around him and pulled him closer. The soft contours of her breasts pressed against the muscles of his chest. He could feel her heart pounding through her gown. It was nearly his undoing.

He knew he should restrain himself. She was a lady after all. But oh God, he wanted her so much.

Crushing her against him, he claimed her mouth, hungrily parting her lips with his thrusting tongue. He heard her gasp, but he was past all thought. All he knew was his need for her.

Shivers swept across Eliza's skin.

Maybe it was the wine she'd sipped at dinner, or the run down the Dark Walk, but the touch of his lips seemed to drug her senses, making her want more. Making her quiver from within.

She was shocked at her all-too-eager response to Magnus, but she could not pull herself away.

His warm mouth trailed down the column of cool skin at her throat with unbearable tenderness. She threw her head back as he planted a searing kiss in the hollow of her throat and held him against her, weaving her fingers through his thick hair.

He moved his kisses lower still, until she felt the wetness of his mouth in the valley between her breasts. The air was cool on the sweet trail of his making. She sucked in her breath as he brought his hands round her shoulders and down her arms.

With a tug, her bodice was pulled aside, and in an instant, Magnus dragged the peak of one breast into his mouth.

Her eyelids flew open. Like a burst of icy wind, this revived her senses.

"No, no . . . we cannot—" she gasped. "No!"

Eliza freed her fingers from his thick dark hair and lurched back. Leaping from the bench, Eliza readjusted her bodice then stood back staring at him. She panted to reclaim her breath as the blood pounded in her temples and her face grew hot.

His breath still heavy, Magnus stared back at her before resting his elbow on his knee and lowering his head into his open palm. "I . . . apologize. I overstepped."

"Yes, you did." Eliza paced before the bench, fanning herself with her mesh reticule that dangled at her wrist. "But you did not venture there alone."

It was as if her composure was under attack. She drew in a deep gulp of cool air and exhaled it, before looking at him again. "You understand, this must never happen again."

"I know." Magnus looked up at her. "But lass, ye drove me near out of my mind with yer touch, yer kisses. And I'd be lying if I didna tell ye I enjoyed it verra much. And I believe ye did as well."

"Precisely." Eliza glanced into the dark trees around them to ensure they were completely alone before uttering her next words. "The experience was . . . quite pleasurable, but it is a fruitless endeavor. You know as well as I—we can never have more than a . . . business relationship. Never!"

Magnus came to his feet. "Tell me why."

"*Why*?" Eliza staggered back a pace. "I should think the answer quite evident. For one reason, you must marry an endowed woman to save Somerton. I am not that woman."

His dark brows arced mischievously. "Forgive me, Miss Merriweather, but I find ye most graciously endowed." He glanced at her breasts and smiled wickedly.

Eliza folded her arms over her chest and cast a hot glare at him. "You know very well what I mean."

"Indeed, I do. But I have every faith that my financial crisis may be resolved soon—without the need to marry for money. So ye see, a relationship between us may be possible after all."

Eliza lowered her arms then set her hands on her hips. "Do you think my reluctance is all about you and your needs? Mightn't I have reason to avoid a relationship as well?"

He shrugged.

She felt a shriek of frustration well up inside her. "I have every intention of leaving for Italy at the conclusion of the season. I—I cannot allow some romantic notions to muck up my plans."

Coming to his feet, Magnus closed the space between them and slid his warm hands over her shoulders. "If yer so-called plan was the least bit logical, I would agree with ye."

Eliza shoved her hands against his chest and pushed him away. "You—you think me illogical?"

"Nay, I think yer plan illogical. What sort of life do ye envision for yerself in the future?"

She was incensed. "I am not without some skill, my lord."

"I do not doubt your talent, but ye are a woman."

Indignation almost choked her. "And what exactly do you mean by that?"

"Ye know, as well as I, that Society is not kind to women who choose to live outside its bounds." Magnus returned to the bench, sat down, and eyed her. "If ye leave for Italy to become an artist, ye can never return to yer life as it is now."

"And what sort of existence have I now? All I want is a life of my own. A life where I make the choices for my future."

"Ye have that now."

"Do I? What choices can I make for myself? Which gown to wear? Which party to attend?"

"Is that so terrible?"

Eliza stood before Magnus wanting to shake him. Why did it matter so much that he understand?

"Don't you see? I've lived for someone else my entire life. I was nursemaid to my mother and grandmother until they died, then I cared for my father. I lived completely for others. *That* was my life."

"And now?"

"Now I have no true responsibility. My sisters are older now. I have a chance. A chance to fulfill my dreams, my goals."

"But at what cost, Eliza? Will ye sacrifice yer sisters to pursue yer dream?"

She blinked at that. "I would never harm my sisters."

"Nay, not purposely. But the moment ye leave for Italy, yer sisters' chances of marrying into good families will be ruined. No gentleman of Society will wish his family name to be connected with a scandal. And that is precisely what yer jaunt to Italy will become—a scandal."

Eliza couldn't believe what she was hearing. But his words were true. All of them.

"I hope for Grace's sake that she marries before the season concludes. Then there is yer youngest sister, Meredith, is it? Will ye write her future as well?"

Eliza pressed her hand over her face convulsively and sank down on the bench beside him. "I had not thought of it in quite those terms."

"I was certain ye had not."

Eliza raised her chin and looked at him. "Before you spout anymore of your sanctimonious drivel and warn me about scandal, please recall just who led an unmarried woman down the Dark Walk only moments ago."

Magnus nodded his head thoughtfully. "Touché, my dear."

"And besides, Meredith is safely tucked away at school where my behavior is unlikely to abrade her. And Grace, well, once an offer is made for her hand, which I have every confidence will be soon given her verve to become engaged, she will also be safe from the sting of my influence. So, my lord, I simply need to come up with an acceptable way of leaving for Italy. It cannot be too difficult. Mayhap . . . we shall say I have gone to visit a long lost relative. One way or another, I will go to Italy. I will become a great artist."

Magnus stared at her in disbelief. "Ye are most determined, Miss Merriweather."

Eliza smiled. "Why thank you, Lord Somerton. I am glad you are finally beginning to understand."

A loud snap of a branch diverted their attention to the footpath. Instinctively, Eliza retreated into the safety of Magnus's arms. She could not see anyone, though she could hear shuffling about in the grove beyond.

"There they are," came Viola's whisper. "You may begin."

The smooth tones of a violin broke from the darkness and enveloped Eliza and Magnus in song.

Magnus smiled down at Eliza. "Might I add, Miss Merriweather, that yer aunts are equally determined."

Eliza broke their embrace. "That they are, indeed."

Rule Eight

Know him as yourself, and the engagement
will never be endangered.

It was nearly eleven at night when the barouche carrying Eliza and Lord Somerton returned to Hanover Square.

Still wary after her aunts' clandestine escapades at Vauxhall Gardens, Eliza gave a cursory glance out the window before disembarking. She scanned the exterior of the house, mentally preparing herself for yet another assault drawn from her aunts' detestable strategy book.

The curtains in the front parlor swayed mysteriously, then suddenly, two noses appeared between the center break in the velvet drapes. Eliza exhaled with exasperation.

"You need not see me inside, my lord," she said, hoping Magnus would see her to the door, then do the considerate thing and take his leave.

Why, even now she pulsed with his nearness. She could not look at him without recalling the sweet thrill of being crushed in his embrace, his tender lips pressed against her bare skin.

Wanton thoughts swarmed like bees, humming wickedly

through her body, heightening her womanly senses. She ran her tongue over her lower lip, her mouth anticipating, craving, what her mind did not want to allow.

Why, at that moment, just one honeyed word from Magnus could spur her to do something she'd regret. Eliza shifted uncomfortably in her seat. She snapped open her fan hoping to cool her face, which, like another part of her anatomy, had grown exceedingly warm and damp.

Appalled at her body's reaction, she turned away to gather up her wrap and reticule from the leather seat cushion. Was it too much to hope that he would simply go home?

"It seems my aunts have already arrived," she told him. "And, if I am not mistaken, we are about to be ambushed."

When the stairs were let down, Magnus climbed out of the cab and raised up his hand to Eliza. Amusement, heightened by something sharper, flickered brightly in his eyes.

"Bring them on, I say. I'm up for the challenge," he said.

With that, Eliza's hopes for a quick farewell dissolved. As she rose from her seat and emerged from the carriage, she reached out for Magnus's hand, but suddenly thought better of it, and stepped down from the conveyance unassisted.

She saw him wince at this small slight, but she could not hold his hand, even for a moment. Even the most innocent of his touches meant danger for her.

If this evening had proved one thing, it was that she was simply incapable of being near Magnus without her body resonating like a bell, her mind turning to the most depraved of thoughts. Heavens, a kiss was all it had taken to persuade her to bare her breasts to him—in a public place no less.

Eliza's body simmered with the memory. Oh, she was doomed. Doomed. Where had her self-control gone? One thing was for certain, she could not remain in his presence until she bettered her grip on her resolve.

She looked up at Magnus. "Bring them on? You are courageous, my lord, or perhaps simply very foolish. My aunts are not to be underestimated."

"Of that, dear lady, I am sure," Magnus replied.

"Very well then," she said with a small sigh. Straightening her gown, Eliza raised her chin and charged ahead to the front door. "I did warn you," she called out as her silk skirts swished past him.

Before her foot mounted the second step, the front door swung wide. Her aunts, Letitia and Viola, pushed against each other as they vied for prime position, shoving poor Edgar back against the door's raised panels.

"Welcome back," Aunt Viola said sweetly.

"And I trust you had a marvelous evening at the Gardens," Aunt Letitia said, as she and Viola followed Eliza and Magnus into the parlor.

"We did, indeed." Magnus flashed a roguish glance at Eliza, sending a flutter through her middle.

"I trust your evening was relaxing, aunties."

The two old women exchanged nervous looks.

"Our evening was not the least notable," Aunt Letitia replied, "so we shall hear all about yours."

Catching up Eliza's right arm and Magnus's left, Aunt Letitia marched them across the passageway to the music room.

Aunt Viola entered behind them, stopping before the pianoforte to slide her hand almost affectionately along its top. "How was the music this eve?" she asked, her eyes wide with false innocence.

"Delightful," Eliza said, and fought back the amused smile spreading across her lips.

"Most delightful," Magnus agreed, as he leaned on the pianoforte and flashed a grin at Viola. Then he turned his gaze on Eliza, even as he replied to her aunt. "In fact, we were most fortunate during our *walk* to be serenaded by a strolling violinist."

Walk, indeed. Eliza squirmed at the thought of what really had gone on at Vauxhall.

"Really, a violinist? How romantic!" Aunt Letitia sucked her lips into her mouth and turned away. A silvery titter emanated from her direction.

Eliza looked around the room and realized her sister was nowhere to be seen. "Where is Grace?"

"She is in the library with a gentleman friend." Aunt Viola happily clasped her hands together.

"A gentleman?" Eliza was more than a little intrigued.

"Yes, dear. From what Gracie has told us, she became separated and was about to go in search of you when she quite literally bumped into a young man she'd known for years."

Aunt Letitia bustled forward. "Well, after she left word of her plans with Somerton's coachman, she allowed the young man to deliver her home in his new curricle. Fancy one too, I own, with a family crest emblazoned on the door. Though, with my poor eyesight, it might have just as easily been a fanciful split of mud."

"Family crest?" Eliza was utterly flabbergasted. "Do you know this gentleman?"

"Sister and I hadn't the pleasure of knowing him until this very eve." Aunt Letitia put her arm around Eliza's shoulder to calm her. "But I believe you know him, Lizzy."

"I do?" Eliza said with astonishment.

At that moment, the click of boot heels in the passageway echoed off the music room's walls. Eliza glanced up to see Grace proudly cross the threshold on the arm of a young gentleman.

"Eliza, Lord Somerton," Grace began, seeming hardly able to contain herself. "I present Lord Hawksmoor."

"Hawksmoor? H-how do you do?" Eliza blinked as she rose from her curtsey. She gazed at the fair-haired gent, who happily twirled a sterling-capped walking stick through his fingers. Her aunts were right. Somehow, she did know this gentleman. He seemed familiar. Quite familiar.

"Forgive my surprise, my lord," Eliza began. "Hawksmoor Hall was but few miles from our home . . . near Dunley Parish. Are you attached to it?"

Lord Hawksmoor bowed at the waist. "Indeed. Hawksmoor Hall is my home. Inherited it from my uncle." He looked at her then, as if waiting for something. "Do you not recall our last meeting, Miss Merriweather?"

"I certainly feel I should." Eliza studied the young man intently, then shook her head in defeat. "Oh, I am sorry, my lord. Have we met?"

From the corner of her eye, Eliza saw Magnus straighten his back and take a step from the pianoforte toward her.

"How can you have forgotten?" Grace laughed. Then, she raised her finger in the air. "Perhaps I might prompt your memory." Closing her eyes, Grace puckered her lips and leaned toward the young man.

Momentary shock at her sister's unseemly pose faded when realization dawned. "*No*. It cannot be!" Eliza exclaimed.

Grace and Lord Hawksmoor nodded then burst into laughter.

Eliza stared at the two. "I do not believe it." Then she felt the heat of Magnus as he moved alongside of her and every drop of blood in her veins rushed to her middle.

"Perhaps someone will share the reason for such amusement with the rest of us," Magnus said, edging near enough that his boot brushed her slipper.

Both aunts lifted their brows expectantly.

Magnus focused his gaze on Eliza. "Miss Merriweather,

are ye acquainted with this gentleman?" he asked, distinctly piqued.

Eliza glanced at him. That could not be jealousy in his eyes. Certainly not. Couldn't be.

"Miss Merriweather?" Magnus urged, almost sternly.

"I—I." At that moment, Eliza wasn't at all sure what Magnus had asked her until Grace stepped into her breach.

"I daresay she is acquainted with Hawksmoor," Grace replied, as she gasped for breath between girlish giggles.

Eliza focused her eyes upon Hawksmoor, who was propping his cane near the door. Then, all at once, she began to laugh quite unexpectedly and clapped a hand over her mouth. "I *do* remember him. It must have been ten years ago, at least."

"That's right," Grace confirmed.

Eliza laid one hand to her breastbone and gestured to Grace and Lord Hawksmoor with the other. "One afternoon, I went to collect Grace from the orchard. It was early autumn, and she had been picking apples. But when I arrived, I saw a boy was about to kiss her. I shouted for him to stop, but he kissed her anyway, then took off willy-nilly through the trees."

Grace cut in. "Eliza gave chase, of course, and being ever so light of foot, caught him at the river."

Hawksmoor stepped forward. "Where I kissed her as well. Of course, then she pushed my face into the mud until I swore I would not try to kiss her *or* her sister again."

The two aunts hooted merrily, chuckling until they clutched their middles and gasped for breath.

Magnus's brows migrated toward his nose. It was clear he did not seem to see the humor in the situation. "And ye, sir, were that ill-mannered lad."

"Yes, I was at Hawksmoor that month visiting my uncle, you see," Lord Hawksmoor replied, flashing a broad grin.

But as he noticed Magnus's dour expression, his smile evaporated and his gaze shifted to the polished tip of his Hessian boot.

"And have ye?" Magnus asked coolly.

Hawksmoor glanced up, confused. "My lord?"

"Have ye kissed Miss Grace since?"

Aunt Letitia's laughter ceased abruptly and she leaned forward so as not to miss his reply.

The young man was taken aback. "Why, of course not. I gave Miss Merriweather my word, did I not?" His gaze drifted from Magnus and fell lightly on Eliza.

Aunt Letitia passed behind Grace and the young man, then using her hands as makeshift bookends, pressed the couple together until their shoulders met.

She looked to Eliza. "Dear, perhaps this young man should be released from the promise you coerced so many years ago."

Eliza laughed as she studied the young man, though she knew her aunt was quite serious. "You are Reginald Dunthorp."

"Yes, well . . . Lord Hawksmoor now. I have held the title for three years."

Aunt Viola sidled up to Grace and patted her grand-niece's hand before depositing it atop the young man's forearm. "Lord Hawksmoor, you have come to London for the season? Mayhap to find a wife, hmm?"

"Auntie, *please*." Though Grace protested the remark, she did not seem truly discomfited by her aunt's comment. Instead she drew close, wide-eyed, and breathlessly awaited his answer.

Lord Hawksmoor puffed his broad chest out, not seeming to mind being the center of such focused attention. "I have come simply to enjoy the season's events," his tone hinting that this was hardly the truth.

"I do find London's sights most diverting," he added. At that, Hawksmoor's gaze firmly affixed itself to Eliza, giving her the uncomfortable impression that she was being assessed.

Magnus must have noticed Hawksmoor's gaze too, for much to Eliza's surprise, he protectively folded her hand over his arm as though claiming her for his own. Her heart fell into patters at his presumptive gesture.

But then, as if detecting deficiency in Eliza's own charms, Hawksmoor's attention shifted abruptly back to Grace.

"Of course, I do hope to marry someday," Hawksmoor said.

Scarlet bloomed on the round apples of Grace's cheeks. The smile she returned him was alive with unbridled delight.

Just then, Edgar shuffled into the music room with a decanter of cordial on his tray along with several glistening crystal glasses.

Aunt Letitia smiled broadly. "Perhaps some music might be in order?"

"And some libation," Aunt Viola chirped as she caned her way back to the pianoforte. "As they say, time flies when you're having rum!"

At Aunt Viola's mangled adage, Eliza saw a bud of a smile unfold on Magnus's lips, which put her more at ease.

"Do ye play, ma'am?" he asked, stepping blindly into her aunt's well-laid trap.

Sheer happiness lit Aunt Viola's eyes. "Why, yes, I do. And Letitia sings like a bird, doesn't she, Eliza?"

"She does indeed," Eliza said. *A bit . . . like a crow.*

Aunt Letitia did not wait for an invitation to perform, but bowled through Grace and Hawksmoor to reach the mahogany cabinet where she began earnestly flipping through music.

Heaven help them all. With a sigh, Eliza glanced through the glass doors and checked the time on the clock in the passageway. It was going to be a very long night.

When Aunt Letitia began to rifle through the sheet music for the fifth time, Lord Hawksmoor seized with gusto the opportunity to plead an early appointment and was quickly escorted by Grace to the door.

Eliza looked expectantly at Magnus, sure he would follow Hawksmoor's lead, but she had no such fortune. To her vexation, Magnus seemed perfectly content to remain in the music room. How much more could she endure? Already she'd caught him watching her *three times* as her aunts obliviously played on. Why, he'd made her a nest of frayed nerves.

A moment later, Grace pranced into the room, her hands clasped over her heart. "Have you ever seen such a handsome creature as Lord Hawksmoor?"

Eliza found her lips forming a knowing grin. Grace was smitten with Lord Hawksmoor, just as she had been in the orchard on that day so many years ago.

Aunt Letitia drained her glass completely, then tottered over to Grace and took her hand. "I think we may have found your match, Miss Grace." She looked to Viola. "Do you agree, Sister?"

"Oh, indeed, I do!" Aunt Viola rose from the bench. "We should discuss our next move at once—in the library." Her white brows excitedly lifted and fell like goose wings in flight.

Aunt Letitia agreed and rang a diminutive silver bell. When Edgar arrived, she whispered something into his ear causing the the manservant's wild gray brows to lift higher and higher with each of her hushed words.

"Y-yes, my lady," Edgar shook his head the second he turned away from her to leave the room.

Aunt Letitia took Grace's arm and followed Viola to the door, then turned back to Eliza and Magnus. "The three of us will be in the library for a short time before we retire."

Oh no! Eliza'd forgotten to hide the rule book again. It was still sitting inside the table drawer, wasn't it? *Blast.* They were sure to find it. And what if Grace was to discover the text's true purpose and explain it to their aunts?

Magnus came to his feet, a little too tentatively for Eliza's taste. "I should take my leave as well."

Softly, Eliza exhaled. *At last.*

"Leave? No, no, no. I shan't hear of it." Aunt Letitia shook her head and gestured for him to sit. "Please stay and finish your refreshment, Lord Somerton."

Eliza snapped her head around and stared in astonishment at her aunt. *"No,* Auntie, the earl is right. It is quite late."

"No, not another word, Eliza. Please stay Lord Somerton and keep my dear niece company. It is so *seldom* that she has a gentleman caller."

Magnus grinned at Letitia's well-aimed jab, but tipped his head and accepted her assignation.

The edges of Aunt Letitia's painted lips curved upward. "After all, the night is still young for those of fewer years. Good night, Lord Somerton. Lizzy."

Aunt Viola and Grace bid them good eve as well, and the three left for the library across the passage.

Her aunt's exit sent Eliza's pulse pounding. This could not be happening. She could not be left alone . . . with *him.*

Not one minute later, Edgar entered the room carrying a tray weighted with sweet wine, fruit, and sugar biscuits. He dutifully laid out the fruit knives and plates on a crisp bed of linen then set about refilling their glasses. As he turned to leave, he hesitantly handed Eliza a folded slip of stiff paper.

Eliza, who'd been fidgeting with her aunts' music to avoid Magnus's watchful eyes, looked up. "What is this?"

"A message from your aunts, Miss." Edgar bowed slightly then hurriedly crossed to leave the room. When he reached the door, he turned. "I am sorry, Miss Merriweather. Pray, do forgive me."

Eliza's momentary confusion shifted to astonishment as Edgar closed the glassed-paned door behind him and turned the key in the lock. "No!" she cried out. "Edgar, you can't do this."

The elderly manservant winced and mouthed a short apology once more, then disappeared into the darkness of the corridor.

"What the devil?" Magnus leapt to his feet and rushed to the door. He tried to turn the handle. "He's locked us in."

Eliza dropped the note on the silver tray and hurried to the door to tug on its brass handle herself. "I can't believe they did this!"

"*They*?" Magnus peered through the glass, looking to see if someone were near enough to help them.

"My aunts," she hissed. "You do not believe Edgar would do such a thing of his own accord? The ladies bade him to do this, of that I am certain."

"That note may give us an explanation," Magnus suggested.

"No doubt." Furious at her aunts latest maneuver, Eliza stomped back to the table and snatched the note from Edgar's silver tray and began to read. "Oh, *no*."

"What does it say?" Magnus reached for the note.

Eliza swiped the bit of paper behind her back. "Nothing."

"'Tis something, else we would not be locked in this room."

"Oh, very well, *here*." Eliza thrust the paper before him. She bit nervously into her lower lip as he unfolded it. "It is an excerpt from my aunts' strategy book." She sank to the bench as Magnus began to read.

Rule Eight
*Know him as yourself, and the engagement
will never be endangered.*

Appearing bewildered, Magnus looked back at her. "What does that mean?"

Eliza fought to swallow the lump that had uncomfortably risen in her throat. "I believe the message means that we are being given time to get know each other more . . . intimately."

"Intimately?" Magnus lifted a single brow. "Ye do have two very open-minded aunts, Miss Merriweather."

Eliza shot a glare at him. Already she could feel hot, itchy blotches erupting across her chest.

One corner of Magnus's lips lifted. "No need to fret. I gather what ye mean. But I do not understand where this edict from yer aunts is derived."

Eliza drained her glass, refilled it, and finished a second glass. She nearly dropped the crystal as fire erupted in her throat.

"Bad as all that?" Magnus asked.

Eliza coughed, but nodded furiously. "Worse," she squeaked.

Magnus crossed the room and sat in the wooden chair opposite her. His warm hands reached out and caught her nervously bouncing knees, stilling them. Steadying her. "It canna be that bad. Come now, explain."

The sympathetic smile on his face gave her just enough courage to admit all she had neglected to tell him when he agreed to her arrangement. The moment she regained her voice she began. "As I briefly mentioned, my aunts have a strategy book entitled *Rules of Engagement*."

"I am acquainted with it. 'Tis a well-known military strategy text for war."

Eliza nodded. "That would be the one." She widened her eyes and looked at him, then shifted her gaze to the note.

Magnus silently read the message once more. He snapped his head upright. "Well, I'll be damned if this isna drawn directly from the text."

"Yes," Eliza managed.

A surprised laugh erupted from Magnus's lips. "I have to ask, Eliza, why are yer aunts quoting military strategy text?"

"Well . . . err . . . Oh, bother. I do not know where to begin."

"Eliza, please." He shook the note before her. "How is this excerpt connected with our being locked in here?"

She slapped her hands atop her thighs. "You must understand something first." Eliza sucked in a deep breath then expelled the truth of it. "My aunts do not know that *Rules of Engagement* is a strategy text . . . for war."

Magnus cinched his brows, but gestured for her to continue.

"They are quite old, a tad addled, and their eyesight is very poor, you see. I believe they can only make out the larger chapter headings and are under the mistaken impression that *Rules of Engagement* is a strategy manual for becoming engaged to be married."

Magnus cocked his head. "I beg yer pardon."

Eliza lowered her head and sheepishly looked up at him through her lashes. "They are using the book's strategies to secure offers for Grace and me before the season ends."

"Ye are joking with me."

"Sadly, no." Her voice was small and meek. "It is all quite true, I'm afraid."

Magnus remained silent for a long moment, then, to her complete surprise, threw back his head and laughed as she'd never heard him before.

Eliza's nervousness dissolved and a small giggle tickled her own lips. "I suppose it is rather amusing at that."

"Quite rich, indeed," he said, fighting to compose himself.

Eliza listened to his deep, masculine laughter, wondering why she'd not admitted the depth of her aunts' matchmaking schemes before. He did not seem concerned by it in the least.

When his amusement waned, a gradual mask of confusion slipped over his face. "Eliza, if ye have been aware of their mistake all along, why have ye not explained it to them? Ye could put a stop to their schemes immediately."

"Because it would break their hearts." Eliza rose and began to slowly walk a circle around the room. "You see, when they discovered the book in the library, I think they believed their father had purchased it when their mother was ill, to help guide the two of them through their first season. But when their mother later died, their father fell into despair, and the two girls were never afforded a season of their own."

"So in their naïveté, they're using the book now to guide ye and Miss Grace."

"Exactly." She returned to the bench and sat down. "Through us, I believe they are enjoying the season they never had."

Magnus exhaled slowly. "So ye and yer sister are going along with their schemes to make them happy."

"Yes, well—" Eliza twisted uncomfortably. "Grace does not know the true nature of *Rules of Engagement*. She has not opened the book, as I have. And she will not if I can help it. What strife that would cause."

"Good lord, Eliza! Yer sister is unwittingly using military stratagem to snare a husband?"

"Err . . . yes." She lifted her chin. "But I have promised myself, if ever the Rules endanger her reputation . . . or her chances for an offer, I will inform her immediately."

"How magnanimous of you." Magnus leaned back in his chair and began to laugh anew.

Eliza narrowed her eyes at him. "Will you please tell me what you find so amusing?"

"Just the way yer mind works."

Eliza looked down her nose at Magnus, hardly amused. "Well, my mind cannot seem to configure a way out of this room. Perhaps you will assist me." Eliza rose and moved to the door. She peered out into the corridor through one of the glass panes and pleaded in full voice. "Do let us out! *Please!*"

Silence was her answer.

"Grace and Aunt Letitia must have gone through the far door and retired to their chambers," she reported to Magnus, who remained comfortably seated. "There's no sign of them."

Eliza pounded her fist on the glass and shouted for a few more minutes before accepting defeat and slumping down onto the piano bench. "Viola's still in the library. I can just see the top of her head, but she must be asleep. And, there's no waking my aunt once her eyes are closed, believe me."

"I am not surprised she's abed." Magnus flipped open his gold watch and glanced at the dial. "Lady Viola took a fair draft of her . . . *ehem* . . . refreshment and it is quite late— or early, I should say."

"The fault is your own, you must concede," Eliza said, launching a glare at him. "Why didn't you depart? You might have taken your leave with Lord Hawksmoor and saved us both this odious fate."

Magnus cocked a brow. "What, and take the chance Hawksmoor might return? Not bluidy likely."

Eliza crossed her arms. "Why would Hawksmoor return this eve? You are making little sense."

With a nod of his head, Magnus gestured to a silver-topped walking stick leaning against the door frame. "That is his stick, is it not? Now he has a reason to return, when-ever he chooses. Oldest ploy in a bachelor's book of games. I saw the dark way he looked at ye. He fancies ye. Mark my words."

"My lord, you are certainly mistaken. He favored Grace."

"Only after I took yer hand. Dinna fool yerself, Eliza."

"Well then, I must thank you for playing my suitor and for alerting me to a potential problem." Eliza moved to the door and rapped upon it once again. "Though I daresay, Hawksmoor is the least of my worries," she muttered.

"Now, ye canna be speaking of me . . ." Magnus grinned at her.

Why couldn't she manage to keep her lips sealed and her thoughts inside her brain? She had to get out of this room!

"Of course not. I was referring to my aunts." Hoping to see Magnus had swallowed her lie, Eliza turned her head and glanced over her shoulder. "Your turn now."

Magnus was leaning back in his chair with his arms propped comfortably behind his head. "Yer pounding and screaming has brought us no closer to release. 'Tis clear yer aunts will release us when they are ready and not before, no matter how much noise is made."

Eliza growled, then plopped down before the pianoforte and began to peck out a tune. "I fear, then, we must resign ourselves to the fact that we are locked here together for the night."

"Aye, it seems we must," Magnus agreed. "So why don't ye sit down and talk to me about what happened in the Gardens."

"Talk? Oh no. I am quite through with that discussion. Care for a game of cards instead?" She nervously glanced up at Magnus's striking face, and when their eyes met, she felt her belly flip-flop.

Heaven help her make it through this night . . . a virgin.

After three laps of the clock's minute hand, and a dozen tedious games of piquet, during which she repeatedly ignored Magnus's attempt to discuss the evening at Vauxhall Gardens, Eliza's weighted eyelids began to droop from the dreadful combination of the early hour and her aunts' blasted cordial. She leaned against the door, forced her lids abnormally wide, and tightened her grip on the pearl-handled fruit knife she held protectively before her.

Eliza stared bleary-eyed at the drained bottle of cordial before her wishing she hadn't passed the time with a glass in her hand. Magnus, by comparison, seemed perfectly unaffected.

"I fail to understand how you can sit there so agreeably when we are trapped in this glass cage," she snapped, her defenses failing miserably.

Magnus rose from his chair and moved deliberately toward her. "Must be the scenery. For it certainly isna the conversation. But of course, that is about to change."

"There is nothing more to discuss," Eliza protested for the tenth time, but her voice was quavering as she helplessly watched him near.

"Oh, lass, but there is." Magnus loomed above her now. "What happened in the Gardens was no accident and we *will* speak of it." Sparks of excitement seemed to flash in his eyes as he stared down at her. "Admit it, lass. I know ye feel something for me, Eliza. Feel it down to yer verra toes."

"You're wrong," she managed to say. "Ours is naught but an arrangement of convenience."

Then suddenly he was standing before her, reaching out to her. Too tired to twist away, she closed her eyes as his fingers trailed along her jawbone, welcoming the pleasurable tickle as he brushed the skin beneath her ear. She sighed as he slipped his hand back to cup the nape of her neck and drew her closer.

Slowly, she lifted her lids, gazed into his eyes, and was startled by the purposeful glint she saw in them.

What am I doing? With feeble intent, Eliza raised the dull blade threateningly, but Magnus only chuckled at her well-meant defense.

"Enough games. Enough words, lass."

Her eyes tracked Magnus's left hand as it reached between them, twisted the small knife from her grip and cast it skidding to the floor.

Now empty of her weapon, Eliza's fingers curled toward her wrist, but Magnus gently pressed them open and touched his lips to her palm. The moist heat from his mouth made her tremble, even as he leaned back and threaded his fingers with hers.

Her breath came in pants when he pulled her from the bench and drew her to her feet. He yanked her into his arms, fanning his fingers to press against her back until their bodies were so close that she could feel his heart thudding against her.

She knew he was about to kiss her, and lord help her, she wanted him to. Needed him to. Slowly, she tilted her chin up, closed her eyes, and stood motionless, breathless. Waiting.

Then she felt him, felt his tongue brush her lower lip,

tasting her. Teasing her. Coaxing her mouth open to him. At long last, he kissed her fully, his tongue masterfully exploring every recess of her mouth. There was no escape. She was helpless to resist him. Helpless to refuse him anything.

The longer he kissed her, held her, the weaker her knees felt. Then, his hand was suddenly on her breast.

Good lord! Eliza's eyes snapped open. Had she been a proper lady, she would have certainly fainted dead away! Then it occurred to her. Mayhap there was a way to stop him. Stop herself.

In the next moment, Eliza's eyelids fluttered closed and her body fell limp in Magnus's arms.

"Eliza? Eliza?" Magnus held Eliza's wilted body in his arms, stunned. He shook her. "Damn it, Eliza! Answer me."

She was breathing, he could see that. Had the silly chit fainted? Nay, not his Eliza. She wasn't the sort.

But still, despite his calls, his pats to her cheeks, she made no response. Magnus laid her out on the wooden floor, turning her on her side so he could release the row of small buttons at her back then loosen her stays. Then, he settled the candelabra on the floor beside her and waited, but his ministrations made no difference.

Eliza had worked so hard to avoid him for the past few hours. To put space between them. And he'd given her that, even given in to her marathon card games for a time. She was just so damned adorable, so transparent as she struggled against the physical urges inside herself.

But then he pushed her. Tried to make her admit the feelings she denied. And she had admitted them. Not with words. Nay, he felt it . . . in the way her body softened against him. In her passionate response to his kiss. Her feelings for him, her need for him, were as certain as daybreak.

But look where his manipulation had gotten him. *Bluidy*

hell. He had to get her out of here. Had to get help. Snatching the fruit knife from the floor, Magnus hurried to the door. He knelt down and examined the door's brass hardware, then slipped the knife's point into the keyhole and turned it little by little until he felt the lock release.

Movement in a reflection in the glass caught his notice and he was astonished at what he saw. Eliza was watching him, mouth fully agape at his success in unlocking the door.

But within the seconds it took for him to come to his feet and turn around, Eliza's head was back on the floor. Her eyes closed. Magnus stifled a chuckle. So this is how it was to be?

Ach, 'twas time he left anyway. He had an early morning meeting with *The Promise*'s other investor in two hours time. "First light at the docks" the card had read. And Magnus intended to be there, despite his long evening, for *The Promise* was scheduled to make port by morn. And, it was just possible that his financial shortfall would come to an end and a life with Eliza could begin.

Magnus exhaled a sigh, then slid his hands beneath Eliza's warm body and raised her gently into his arms. "Come with me, sweeting," he whispered softly against her ear as he carried her above stairs. Magnus felt his way along the dark passageway until his hand connected with a cool door handle. He pressed it and pushed the door open with his boot.

In the glow from the flickering golden flames in the hearth, he could make out the lines of a bed near the window.

"Who is there?" came a shriek.

He recognized the voice as Grace's. "Hush now." He carried Eliza toward Grace's bed.

"Lord Somerton? What are you doing in my bedchamber?" Her tone was frantic. "If you touch me, I shall scream."

"I have Eliza in my arms. May I lay her down with you?"

"Y-yes," she stammered. "I suppose. But why—"

He settled Eliza on the bed, then bent close and whispered in her ear. "Ye win this time, lass. This time." But as he felt her slow breath on his cheek, he realized she didn't hear him. The cordial had already ushered her to sleep.

Turning, Magnus passed through the doorway, then paused with his hand on the door handle. In a finger of moonlight, he could see that Grace's startled eyes were as wide as her open mouth. "Good night, Miss Grace."

"G-good night, Lord . . . S-Somerton."

Magnus descended the stairs, stopping only to gather up his coat and hat before heading out into the night.

As his waiting hackney drew up before the house, a sudden movement from across the street snared Magnus's attention. His muscles tensed, every nerve fired, as he peered around his vehicle. A dark carriage, nearly invisible in the cushion of fog, had stopped two houses up the street. The cab window was open, this he could see, but little more. Suddenly, for a scant second, a flame illuminated the hack's ebony interior.

Magnus squinted his eyes, but the dull glow from the lit tip of the cheroot was all he could see.

He had the distinct impression he was being watched.

Rule Nine

*During the early morning spirits are keen,
during the day they flag, and in the evening
thoughts turn toward home.*

"West India Import Dock, guv'nor," the hackney driver bellowed as he pulled the horses to a jerking stop.

Magnus rubbed his weary eyes and peered out the window at a row of brick warehouses before him. Packed cheek-by-jowl, the five-story buildings buffeted an endless dock lined with bobbing, thick-masted ships.

He stepped from the hack into the cool morning air, flipping a heavy coin to its driver, who circled the horses around, and headed down the damp paving stones in the direction he had come.

Magnus breathed deeply of the air blowing off the Thames, drawing into his lungs the vaguely salty scent of the wooden ships beyond.

He glanced warily behind him, scanning the shadowy slants of gray between the buildings. But he saw nothing. The carriage that had paced his hack through the wet streets of London was no longer anywhere to be seen. That was something to be thankful for at any rate, but unnerving just the same.

He had no clue as to who had been following him. *Ach,* if he had indeed been followed at all. London was a busy city and movement in the early morning, by tradesmen, barrow girls and shopkeepers, was not uncommon. He'd do well to dampen his military acuity. Forget his training. London's streets were not trenches in a battlefield after all.

Putting his suspicions aside for the time being, Magnus reached into his coat pocket and withdrew the card he'd received the afternoon before.

Twenty-two, West India Import Dock. First light.

It was not quite six in the morn, though twenty ships already filled to capacity the thirty-acre Import Dock basin.

Though tired beyond words, Magnus's mood remained light and he whistled as he walked. He was almost sure that at any moment he would spot the ship he'd bet his future on—*The Promise,* sitting low in the water, heavy with precious cargo.

He recalled *The Promise*'s distinctive rigging and scanned the forest of masts for a glimpse of her. For with the ship's arrival, the financial challenge his brother bequeathed could be put to rest—and he could begin the season anew by offering for the woman who'd come to mean everything to him—Eliza.

A smile came to his lips as he remembered the warmth and softness of her against him in the music room. The seductive curve of her body. The fullness of her lips. The faint scent of lavender in her hair. He drew a half breath, remembering.

"Heads up, sir!" came a warning shout.

Magnus looked up. A coach-sized crate dangling from a crane whooshed toward him.

Mirthful thoughts of Eliza instantly evaporated as he dove from the crate's path just in time to avoid being flattened beneath its bulk.

"Damn it all." Magnus's heart pounded as he crawled to his feet. He blinked at the hulking crate and adjusted his coat, shaking off the shock of near catastrophe.

The slap of clapping hands drew his attention to a small doorway all but cloaked in morning shadow.

"Well done, Somerton." Charles Lambeth stood just outside the next factory with a toothy grin on his narrow, freckled face. "But just where was your head, man? Hitched to a bit of muslin, I'd reckon."

Though they were from different worlds—Magnus a peer, and Charles Lambeth, the son of a merchant—they had served together at the Peninsula, where war-born hardship sealed many an unlikely alliance. There, amidst the death and suffering, they had become fast friends.

Magnus crossed the wharf and gave Charles's shoulder a good-natured cuff. "There ye are, my good man. Why the summons? *The Promise* arrived on schedule, has she?"

Lambeth's smile dissolved. "You'd best come inside."

Despite the coolness of the morn, buds of perspiration moistened Magnus's brow as he followed Lambeth into a small room off the main warehouse. It was clear the news he'd hoped for was not to be had. "Come now, what's wrong?"

Lambeth looked out the casement window toward the basin. "We should wait for the other investor." There was an unnerving edge to his voice this morn.

"If there is something amiss, I demand to hear it now," Magnus replied, his own tone hardening. "Ye know of my situation. My life is crated inside that ship—my future."

Exhaling his breath, Lambeth gazed at the floor as if collecting his thoughts. Slowly, he turned his eyes upward to Magnus. "I think it best if you take a chair."

Magnus pulled a ladderback forward and sank into it. "This news disna sound promising."

Clouds of dark worry gathered in Lambeth's eyes as the door swung open and the second investor, Porter Hanover, Lord Dunsford, entered and took a chair.

"What's going on to rouse a man so early from his bed? *The Promise* has arrived, hasn't she?"

Lambeth dispensed with the greetings and instead set himself to the business at hand.

"Last night, I received several reports of an immense storm crossing the western shipping lane. Yesterday, The East India Company confirmed the loss of two ships."

Magnus came to his feet. "And *The Promise*?"

Lambeth shook his head. "I cannot say. She has not been included in the reports thus far. I hope for the best."

"Hope for the best?" Dunsford leapt up. "Is that all you can offer us, *hope*?"

"Sadly, yes," Lambeth replied, his gaze scraping the floor once more. "Gentlemen, we must have faith."

"Faith?" Dunsford repeated. "You sound like a bloody vicar!"

Lambeth moved toward Dunsford and laid his hand on his arm to calm him.

Dunsford smacked it away. His brows bunched as he narrowed his eyes. "You know, I should have listened to the players at White's—even *they* cautioned me against this gamble." Dunsford pointed his finger at Lambeth. " 'The apple doesn't fall far from the tree,' they said."

"What's that supposed to mean?"

"That you're just like your father—a swindler."

"You bloody whoreson—" Lambeth charged at Dunsford.

Magnus launched himself between the two men as Dunsford lunged toward Lambeth, who snatched up a ladderback in his hands and hoisted it over his head, prepared to strike.

Thrusting his shoulder before Lambeth, Magnus then caught Dunsford's lapels and threw him bodily into a chair.

"Calm yerself, man. There have been no loss reports on *The Promise*. Until we know more, we must assume all is well."

Once certain Dunsford's temper was diffused, Lambeth slowly lowered the chair to the worn wooden floor. He set his hands upon the top rung and leaned against its worn back, dropping his chin to his chest.

Dunsford rested his head in his hands. "I'll be ruined, you know." His voice was thin and shaking. "If this ship is lost, I'll be ruined."

"We'll *all* be ruined, Dunsford." Magnus gazed out the window at the rocking ships in the basin. "Each of us knew the risks when we laid our guineas on the table. And with that risk came the possibility of tremendous profit—which might still be ours. If we dinna lose our heads, that is. Even if the cargo is gone there's always the insurance."

Dunsford shrugged. "At least we have that."

Lambeth turned away from them then, and without a word, simply gazed out of the small casement window.

Muted shouts from the wharf workers outside joined the creak and groan of docked ships, as each man silently dealt with the gravity of the situation in his own way.

Finally, Dunsford dragged himself to his feet and extended his hand to Lambeth. "Accept my apologies, my good man. It's just—"

Lambeth nodded and reached for Dunsford's out-stretched hand. "I know. I am worried as well." He clasped Dunsford's hand between both of his own and shook it.

This simple gesture seemed to ease Dunsford's mind, but Magnus was not so oblivious to the barely controlled anger still seething behind Lambeth's eyes.

Dunsford contritely offered a watery smile, then turned to Magnus. "Share a hack, Somerton? Might as well conserve what coin we have left, eh?"

Magnus exhaled a small laugh. "Indeed." They moved toward the door and he looked back at Lambeth. "Ye'll let us know if there is any news?"

"You know I will." Lambeth pressed a compassionate smile on his face and followed the two men to the door.

Magnus walked along with Dunsford toward his awaiting carriage, worry weighing like ballast in his heart. If *The Promise* did not make port soon, he could see only one other way to save Somerton. Lord, he didn't even want to consider it.

How could he even think of wedding another? A sudden shiver swept up his neck and over his scalp as he finished his thought—when he was falling in love with Eliza.

As they readied to board the hack, a pale-haired man tipped his polished beaver hat as he passed.

Magnus responded likewise. Though the man's face was partly concealed by the hat's brim, he seemed familiar somehow.

Once the two men had settled inside the carriage, Magnus leaned forward and peered through the small cabin window. A gleaming black carriage emerged from a shadowed alleyway. He watched as the blond man boarded it.

A carriage had paced his hackney during the night. And now a gentleman, clearly out of his element, appears at the basin. This was all too smoky by half. Or, just a coincidence.

Still, Magnus was sure he knew the man from somewhere. But from where?

Later that morning, William Pender set his teacup on its saucer and pushed his breakfast plate aside with such force that bits of bread sailed from the plate and broadcast across the table. "So the ship is missing."

Magnus said nothing, knowing exactly where the conversation was leading.

The disappointment in his uncle's eyes was raw and barely tempered. "It's missing and still you have not found a bride."

"The ship is not missing." Magnus, who had not yet put head to pillow, was in too dark a mood to have this discussion. "She simply has not yet *arrived*. The storm has crossed the western shipping lanes, and she's delayed by the foul weather. Simple as that."

His uncle leaned his bony elbow on the dining table and twirled the wild hairs of his shaggy gray eyebrow between thumb and index finger. "I vow you'll be the death of me yet. Why will you not heed my advice and marry Miss Peacock?"

Magnus nodded to the hovering footman, who filled his cup with the steaming, rum-splashed fruit tea his uncle was so fond of drinking.

"I dinna intend to rush into an ill-advised marriage just to hedge my bet. If I am going to bind myself to another for life, it will be to a woman of my choosing. Anything less is naught but a receipt for years of misery. I've seen it more times than I care to recall."

"What about that Merriweather gel?" his uncle asked. "You seem to be quite taken with her. Though, I must warn you, Somerton, her social position is not quite the thing. Rather an odd one, she."

Magnus glared at that. "Watch where ye tread, Uncle."

Pender groaned quietly and shifted in his chair. "I only meant . . . err . . . does she at least have money? Her aunts certainly have guinea aplenty."

"I greatly enjoy Miss Merriweather's company. But our relationship has nothing to do with money."

His uncle shook his head. "My dear boy, all relationships between men and women of Society have to do with money."

Magnus shifted in his chair. "Not this one."

The old man reached across and plucked a heel of bread from his plate. He popped it into his mouth then washed it down with a loud sip from his teacup. "You know, it has been whispered that her father did not adequately provide the gels. True?"

Magnus sighed. "True enough, I suppose."

His uncle exhaled, making clear his annoyance. "Then why do you continue to romance her? She can offer you nothing. Might even knock you down a rung with the ton, you know. Don't want that. Don't want that at all."

Magnus opened his mouth to speak but Pender lifted his hand. "Now, now. Do not hush me. I know you don't want to hear this, but it's the truth."

Magnus shrugged off the comment as best he could. His relationship with Eliza was no one's concern but his own. He brought the teacup to his lips and drank from it, cringing at the tea's sugary fruit taste. "Really, Uncle, I dinna know how ye manage to drink this swill."

"I drink it because I enjoy its sweetness. It takes the edge off the morning." Pender turned and looked pointedly at Magnus. "There is no use trying to evade my question, Somerton."

"Which is what?"

William Pender grunted with frustration. "Why do you

continue to connect yourself to Miss Merriweather when you know you must marry money or lose everything?"

Magnus lifted a brow at his uncle. "Because I enjoy her company." Magnus's lips curved upward. "Her sweetness takes the edge off this whole damned mess."

His uncle chuckled at that. "Ah, a tasty little diversion, is she?"

Magnus did not care to dignify that comment with an answer. Instead he turned a hard eye on the old man.

Pender sneered down his nose at Magnus. "Diversions have a time and place, but now is not one of them. Your family estate is at risk. It is time to find yourself a suitable bride with a very large dowry. Marry Miss Peacock and your financial troubles are over."

Magnus narrowed his eyes. "*I* will decide when it is time. Not ye, or anyone else." Slamming his cup to the table, he shoved back his chair and stalked from the room, knowing all the while that his uncle was right.

"Wake up!" Grace shook Eliza roughly.

Folding her fingers around the woven counterpane, Eliza pulled it over her head.

"*Finally,* you're awake. Just how much cordial did you have? I couldn't rouse you at all last night."

"Go away."

"You are in *my* bed, Eliza."

"Really?" At the moment, Eliza couldn't quite recall how she came to be in her sister's bed. All she knew was that her head pounded like a mason's hammer and her sister's shrieking was not helping matters in the least.

Grace folded her arms at her chest. "Are you going to tell me what happened?"

"What do you mean?"

"Do not toy with me! Lord Somerton put you in my bed

last night. I spoke with him, Eliza. I did not dream our conversation. He carried you into my room and laid you in my bed. He asked if you could share it, and I told him you could. What else could I say? A man was holding my sleeping sister in his arms in the middle of the night!"

Eliza tried to shake the drink-induced cobwebs from her mind. Sitting up fully, she noticed she was still dressed in the walking gown she wore to Vauxhall Gardens. Then it dawned on her. "Oh yes, he used the fruit knife to pick the lock and free us from the music room last night."

Grace blinked stupidly at her. "You were locked in the music room?"

"Our aunts had us locked in, then forgot about us. They had a bit too much cordial, I suspect."

"Do you mean to tell me you were locked in the music room nearly all night with—*a bachelor*?" She slapped her hands to her cheeks. "Lord help us, Sister, if anyone should learn of this."

"No one will—as long as *you* keep quiet." Eliza played the evening through in her mind. It took but a moment before she recalled Magnus's mind-tumbling moonlight kiss at Vauxhall, then again in the music room. Her cheeks burned hot as a taper.

"What are you grinning about?" Grace moved closer and studied Eliza's face. "Why, you're blushing!" She gasped. "What happened in the music room, Eliza? He did not try to kiss you, did he?"

Eliza turned away from her sister's scrutiny.

"You need not even say it. He *did!*" Grace tore the covers from Eliza. Leaping from the bed, her sister raced around to the other side and grabbed Eliza's shoulders hard. "Answer me!

"Yes! Yes, he kissed me. Are you satisfied? He kissed me on the Dark Walk at Vauxhall, then in the music room."

Grace straightened her back slowly. With her hand cupped over her mouth, she staggered to the tub-chair and sank into it. "The *Dark Walk*? Scandalous. Why, it is one thing after another with you, Eliza. Our family is surely ruined."

"We are *not* ruined. Lord Somerton and I were not observed," she said, adding softly, "so far as I know."

Grace's lashes flew up. "But you do not know for sure? *Oh dear*. What shall we do now?"

Her sister thrummed her fingers on her lips until her mind seized upon a logical solution—at least logical to Grace's way of thinking. "I have it," she exclaimed. "No one could truly fault you too harshly for kissing your *betrothed*."

"What are you saying, Grace?"

"That you must marry Lord Somerton."

"What? Have you gone mad?"

" 'Tis the only way. If you were seen *kissing* Lord Somerton, and you do not announce your betrothal, I will have no chance to make a good marriage. Nor will our sister, Meredith. You will have damned us all with your impetuous behavior."

Eliza looked down at the counterpane, absently tracing its weft with her forefinger. "I do apologize." She looked up into her sister's eyes. "But I cannot marry Lord Somerton."

Grace leapt to her feet. "Why not? You obviously feel something for the man, or you would not have let him *kiss* you."

Eliza scrunched her fingers in her hair. "Yes, I admit it. I hold a certain . . . fondness for him."

"Then why will you not consider marrying him? Is it because of your dreams of becoming an artist? Well, you should have considered that before his lips were hot upon your mouth."

Eliza flinched at the sting of her sister's words. She bowed her head. "It is not that at all, Grace."

"What is it then?"

"*He* cannot marry *me*."

Grace folded her arms over her chest. "He cannot or he *will not*? Because if he refuses, even after he has all but ruined you, then we shall have to ask Aunt Letitia and Aunt Viola to pay a call to his uncle, William Pender. *He* is a gentleman and will see that his nephew does the proper thing by you."

Meeting her sister's gaze, Eliza sighed. "Lord Somerton did nothing that I did not wish."

Grace blinked, thrice.

Crawling out of bed, Eliza moved before the hearth. "I wanted his kiss." *His touch. I wanted . . . him.*

Her sister opened her mouth, quite obviously shocked, but she said not a word.

"Grace, you have to understand. What happened between us was as much my fault as his." Eliza turned from the bank of graying embers to face her sister. "And I do not regret it."

Grace began to cough on the words she'd ingested. She pounded her chest until she was able to form sentences again. "But still, you will not marry him?"

"Grace, you know I have no intention of marrying anyone. I will be leaving for Italy soon enough. Besides, even if I changed my mind, and I most certainly have not, *he* cannot marry *me*. His brother left him naught but a penniless earldom walled thick with debt. He must marry a woman of means before the conclusion of the season or he will lose his lands and home to his brother's creditors."

"His estate was not entailed?"

"No." Eliza looked down at her hands. "His father and brother broke the entail years ago." She looked up at her sister. "So you see, he must marry well in the coming month, or Somerton is forfeit."

"Oh dear, oh dear . . ." Grace went to the washstand and filled the basin. She splashed her face with cool water then rubbed it briskly with her hands as if to sharpen her senses.

Fumbling for a linen, she dried her hands then turned to Eliza. "I do not understand. If he cannot marry you, then why does he continue to court you? It makes no sense."

Eliza drew a deep breath. It was time to confess.

"Because I *asked* him to do it—to keep our aunts from parading me before an endless queue of suitors."

Grace's eyes grew wide until Eliza feared they would burst from her head. She was clearly as shocked as she was confused.

"But if he must marry by the end of the season—"

"Well, that's my end of the bargain. I am to investigate potential brides for him."

"*No*." Grace's eyes went round as her wash basin. "I don't believe it. This whole time . . . the two of you . . . your relationship . . . it has all been a *charade*?"

"Well, yes. That's how it started out anyway. Our arrangement seemed so logical then."

"Logical? Eliza, if the ton ever learned of your game, our family would be disgraced forever." Grace held her hands to either side of her head. An odd cry welled up from deep inside her sister's throat and bore out into the room.

Eliza took Grace's shoulders in her hands. "I am sorry. I should have seen this eventuality coming." She slid her palms down Grace's arms then sat down on the edge of the bed. "Indeed, I daresay I would have, had I not been so determined to leave for Italy at the end of the season."

Grace looked up at her, blankly. "There is no other answer,

Eliza. You must sever your connection with Lord Somerton. You must put an end to all of this. *Now*."

Eliza sighed. "I am quite aware of that. But it isn't that easy."

Grace cocked her head. "You can do it."

"I cannot."

"Why not?" Grace folded her arms, demanding to know.

Eliza swallowed hard. "Because, I think I love him."

Rule Ten

*There can be no engagement
unless both sides are willing.*

From the corner of her eye, Eliza noticed Grace glancing at her with sullen annoyance. "How long do you intend to remain angry with me?" Eliza finally asked as she passed the pot of chocolate they shared at breakfast.

Grace leisurely sipped from her cup. "Until you admit the peril you've placed us all in with your reckless behavior."

Eliza released her breath and peered into the swirling depths of her cup. "I meant no harm."

"You never do." Grace narrowed her eyes at Eliza. "Still, you must avoid Lord Somerton at all costs—for the good of the family."

Eliza sighed. "London Society is not so very large. We are certain to cross paths. Even if I wanted to avoid him, I could not. We travel the same circles."

Her sister stared back at her with impassive eyes. "You are just making excuses to continue seeing him."

"I am merely stating facts." Eliza spread a thick pat of butter over her toasted bread. "There is no way to avoid him, especially since I have formally agreed to paint Lord Somerton's portrait. I must fulfill my half of our arrangement and complete it."

Grace refilled her own cup, then looked pointedly at Eliza. "If you must paint *his* portrait, then do so. But do it when and where our aunts' watchful eyes will prevent any improprieties on his part."

He is not the one I am worried about, Eliza thought, with some trepidation.

"Good morn, my gels," Aunt Letitia called out as she entered the dining room. She bent and pecked her nieces' cheeks with her thin lips, then eased herself into the dining chair opposite Eliza. No sooner had Aunt Letitia raised a finger and asked Mrs. Penny for a willow powder for the dreadful pain in her head than Aunt Viola staggered blindly into the room with her left hand cupped over her eyes.

She felt her way around the table, overturning a pot of gooseberry jam onto the crisp white table linen, much to Mrs. Penny's vexation.

Once she located the empty chair beside Grace, Aunt Viola lowered her shielding hand, only to jerk and squint in the morning light. "Would you do me the kindness of drawing the drapes, Mrs. Penny? The sunlight seems particularly harsh today."

Eliza allowed herself a slight grin. It seemed both her aunts suffered the ill effects of too many glasses of cordial the night before.

After the drapes were closed, and Aunt Viola's eyes were able to open normally, it did not take long for both aunts to begin their morning assessment of Eliza's tired appearance.

"Heavens, look at your eyes. Did you not sleep well last eve?" Aunt Letitia squinted as she slowly lifted her teacup to her lips.

"I doubt I would have slept a wink if I had the attentions

of a gentleman as fine as Lord Somerton," Aunt Viola added, winking at Letitia. She, alone, laughed at her pale joke until her head began to bob, causing her to wince. She slapped fingers to her temples and began to massage them vigorously.

"I've had very little sleep," Eliza replied matter-of-factly.

"Really? The cordial did not ease you into slumber? I slept quite soundly," Aunt Letitia admitted.

"Yes, I am quite aware of that." Eliza took a deep breath and tried to rein in her anger. "Which is why *I* spent the night securely locked in the music room with Lord Somerton."

Aunt Letitia's gaze met with Viola's. "Oh, heavens," she gasped, raising her fingers to her lips.

Aunt Viola lifted her brows. "I thought you said you were going to unlock the door, Letitia."

"No, Edgar gave you the key."

"Which I gave to you, Sister."

"Stop!" Grace finally shrieked, leaping up from her chair. "It does not matter now. The point is Eliza spent much of the night alone"—her voice fell to a whisper—"with a *bachelor*."

Before Grace's charge was barely out of her mouth, Aunt Viola's lids began to twitch. "*S-spell* . . ." With a thump, her head came forward and her face immediately dropped to her plate, the blow thankfully cushioned by a short stack of toasted bread with jam.

"Auntie!" Eliza cried.

"Oh calm yourself, Eliza." Aunt Letitia came to her feet and righted her sister in the chair. "You see, Sister is fine." Dabbing a napkin to her tongue in motherly fashion, she wiped the remnants of gooseberries from Viola's chin.

The instant Aunt Letitia sat down again, Grace slapped her hands down on the table and leaned toward her. "What do you suppose the ton will think of this, Eliza? Auntie? What say you? Can you not see this is dreadful, simply dreadful?" Grace collapsed back into her chair as if her heavy words had exhausted her.

Aunt Letitia pondered Grace's words for a moment then giggled. "Well, I suppose if Society learned of it, they would expect Lord Somerton to marry Eliza."

"M-marry Eliza?" Aunt Viola's eyes fluttered open. Slowly she turned her head and looked at Eliza. "Did he make an offer, dear?"

"An offer? No, he did not," Eliza replied, looking sharply from one aunt to the other. "I am sure he was much too frustrated to think of anything other than escaping the music room."

"Pity," the aunts' voices sounded in unison.

Grace ground her teeth. "Am I the only one who recognizes the problem? This is a *disaster*. Why, this might seriously impact Hawksmoor's or any eligible bachelor's interest in me. I want to know what we are going to do about it and I want to know *now*."

Eliza took Grace's hand in her own and patted it. "There, there, Grace. Calm yourself or you'll be having strawberries for breakfast."

Grace snatched her hand away and began feeling for eruptions on her face.

"That's right, gel," Aunt Letitia agreed. "What happened in the music room was an accident, a minor transgression. Nothing to get all hubbity, tubbity about."

"It is not only what happened in the music room that I am worried about," Grace exclaimed. "Eliza—"

Eliza's heel met Grace's shin with a hearty kick, effectively stifling her sister's next words while earning herself a nasty glare.

"You need not worry, Grace." Eliza smiled sweetly. "I

sincerely doubt anyone observed Lord Somerton leaving the house. Still, I will right the situation."

"Viola and I will assist you, of course. After all, we are at least *partly* to blame," Letitia said, while Aunt Viola nodded in vigorous assent.

Partly to blame? Eliza choked on her chocolate, spewing chocolate spots over the table linen.

Mrs. Penny sighed loudly.

Aunt Letitia rapped on her niece's back. "Are you well, Eliza?"

With her napkin, Eliza dabbed the chocolate droplets from her lips, then nodded. "Yes. But please, Auntie, allow me to handle this on my *own*."

Aunt Letitia gave her sister's bony forearm a covert nudge. "As you wish, Lizzy."

Eliza cringed and gazed down at her lap. For the briefest of moments, she considered confessing everything to her aunts. Considered ending this complicated charade now.

But as she listened to her scheming aunts chattering away at the table, she knew a confession would be the wrong course.

The season was fast drawing to a close, and if she was no longer connected to Lord Somerton, her aunts would work doubly hard to see her engaged to another.

"Now that that is settled," Grace began, "you both should know that Eliza has decided she will no longer receive Lord Somerton."

Eliza glowered at her sister. "That is not what I said."

Aunt Letitia lifted the ribbon of her quizzing glass and leveled her eyepiece at Eliza. "Then what did you say, Lizzy?"

Eliza inserted a wedge of toasted bread into her mouth. She raised a finger, indicating she needed to finish her bite, hoping to buy a few precious moments in which to craft her reply.

A haughty grin curved Grace's lips. "Yes, Eliza. Tell us what you said."

Her sister knew full well Eliza was not about to confess to her aunts her feelings, her love, for Lord Somerton. Where would she be then? Halfway down the aisle, that's where!

Lifting the cup of chocolate to her lips, Eliza washed the bread down her throat. "I simply said that while I intend to fulfill my obligation to paint Lord Somerton's portrait, I do not believe the earl and I are suited."

Aunt Viola chortled, her mirthful snorts sending Aunt Letitia into fits of laughter.

Eliza rose from the table. "I do not understand what you two find so amusing."

Her chuckles withering on her lips, Aunt Letitia wiped her eyes with her napkin. "My dear, Viola and I have never seen two people more suited than you and Lord Somerton. The attraction is obvious."

"You are clearly a match in intelligence and temperament. Why do you deny your feelings?" Aunt Viola tried rather unsuccessfully to conceal her amusement.

"I deny nothing." *Or rather everything.*

"Are you so set on studying painting in Italy that you cannot see a love match right before your eyes?" Aunt Letitia's tone sounded suddenly quite serious. "Think about it, Lizzy."

Emotion welled up in Eliza's throat and spilled from her lips before she could stop it. "Why should I, Auntie? Nothing I can say or do will change the fact that there will be no match. No offer. *Ever.*" Her eyes began to sting and Eliza turned for the open door. She wasn't about to let anyone see what a ridiculous goose she was.

Grace rose and followed Eliza from the dining room.

Letitia exchanged concerned glances with her sister. "What do we do now, Sister?"

Viola's eyes widened excitedly. "The rule book?"

"Right you are."

Later that day, a refreshing breeze swept into the courtyard, sending the pale green leaves veiling the paving stones into wild, undulating spirals.

Eliza sought refuge there. Refuge from her sister and her aunts. Refuge from her own thoughts, her own feelings. As she had done so many times in her childhood, she sought to lose herself in her painting.

Loading her brush with pigment, Eliza touched it to the canvas, to her portrait of Magnus. With a deft hand, she swept it from the strong line of his jaw to the cleft in his chin.

She had thought it would be difficult to complete his portrait without him sitting before her. Even with the three charcoal studies she'd completed—all but one drawn completely from memory.

How wrong she had been. Unlike any of her past models, she had no need to see Magnus to capture his likeness. Every line and curve was carved deep in her mind: the garnet highlights in his ebony hair, the inquisitive arch of his brows, the high plane of his cheekbones. Eliza knew the hue of his lips . . . and their taste.

All she needed to do was close her lids and he would be there once more, silvery-blue eyes glinting in the moonlight as his mouth descended to kiss her.

She caught her breath, remembering the shivers of pure excitement that had pricked her senses unbearably. Until, at last, his firm lips had moved against her own, igniting an explosion of pleasure within her.

The faint thud of the doorknocker jarred Eliza back from her musings. She opened her eyes and, through the French window, saw Edgar scurrying to answer the door.

Eliza's stomach clenched. Was it Magnus? She fought the urge to rush inside to know for sure and instead wiped her hands on a paint-spattered cloth. To pass the moments, she cleaned her brushes, organized her oils, all the while keeping a watchful eye on the door for any sign of movement.

Finally, Edgar turned into the interior hall once more. Eliza's heart pounded with anticipation.

It had to be Magnus.

What would she do now? Refuse his call?

Grace was right. For the sake of the family she must. She should not risk Grace and Meredith's futures on a flight of fancy.

Momentary infatuation. That's all her feelings were. Artists were prone to such obsessions of the heart. She'd read all about it in one of the questionable French magazines Aunt Viola kept hidden under the settee cushion.

But another part of her wanted to see him. Wanted to be with him. Wanted to feel the heated pressure of his lips upon hers. Just one more time.

Hesitantly, Eliza laid her brushes on the table and started for the door. But Grace reached Edgar first. Eliza watched as Grace glanced out into the courtyard, smiled and waved her back. Then her sister made a quick adjustment of her skirts and followed Edgar to the front rooms.

Eliza stopped midstride. *Hawksmoor. Of course*. Grace had made no secret of the fact that she was thoroughly infatuated with the man, and he, obviously aware of her feelings, must have returned for an interview.

The breath she hadn't even realized she'd been holding exploded from her lips. She didn't know whether she felt relief or disappointment.

Returning to her painting, she gazed wistfully at Magnus's image on her canvas. Everything had been so simple until *he* came into her life.

After Edgar left him to wait in the Featherton's lavender-bedecked parlor, Magnus peered out the window at the grand homes framing Hanover Square. His thoughts wound tightly about Lambeth's news of *The Promise*'s disappearance.

What now? If his ship was truly lost, if his one chance to earn the money he needed to save Somerton was gone, what could he do?

Pender's words rang out in his mind, "Marry Miss Peacock and all your troubles will be over." But Magnus knew that was far from the truth. His troubles would be just beginning. For how could he marry Caroline, when his heart called out for Eliza?

God, how he needed the ease of Eliza's company. Somehow, he knew that only when he was with her again her, smelled the lavender in her hair, felt her soothing touch, would he feel balanced once more.

"Lord Somerton?"

Magnus's spirits lifted immediately and he turned from the parlor window expecting to see Eliza standing before him.

Instead, he saw her sister. Grace's lace-skirted arms were folded securely over the bodice of her scarlet gown and a tight frown thinned her lips to threadlike slashes of watery pink.

"Miss Grace." He bent quickly into an awkward-feeling bow. "I trust ye are well."

"I am." There was a coldness to her reply. A bite.

"I have come to call on yer sister."

Grace lifted her chin ever so slightly. Her bearing was

stiff; her smile forced. Something was definitely wrong. "Eliza is not taking callers today."

Magnus cocked his head. "I believe she may see me if she knew I was here."

"I fear you are wrong, Lord Somerton."

He was unnerved by her icy reply. "I . . . I dinna understand."

"Don't you?" Her voice was firm. "My sister has tired of your *arrangement*."

Magnus lifted his brows, surprised to hear that term, of all she could have selected, from her mouth. "Our *arrangement,* did ye say?"

"Yes. Oh, do not be coy with me," Grace snapped. "I know all about it. And I do not approve!"

Magnus stepped toward Grace. "I see."

"At last, you understand. Oh, I know this season is all a game to you and my sister, but actions have consequences, Lord Somerton." Grace narrowed her eyes. "Consequences that could be disastrous for this family!"

"I assure you, I would never do anything to harm this family," Magnus said with all sincerity.

Grace's eyes grew wide. "How can you say that?" she all but roared. Then, gathering herself again, she lowered her voice. "You have already compromised my sister, sir. If anyone knew of this *arrangement* of yours, Eliza—nay, *all of us,* would be ruined!"

"I swear to ye, if ever my relationship with yer sister caused her harm, I would hope to do the honorable thing by her."

"You can *hope* to do the honorable thing, hope all you like, but we both know you cannot marry her."

Grace's words slapped Magnus's face as harshly as if she had used an open palm. He swallowed deeply, then looked up at Grace, saw her shake a little from the blow she'd dealt him. "I must speak with Eliza."

"I . . . I will not allow you to harm her anymore."

Magnus raised his hands in supplication. "I only want to speak with her."

At that, she lifted her palm to him and turned her head away. "Good day, Lord Somerton." Grace crossed the parlor to open the door and stepped into the passage. A stiff finger poked in the front door's direction.

Magnus stood in the center of the parlor, wholly stunned by his dismissal, when Lady Letitia appeared at the threshold. He rushed forward in her direction, hopeful that Letitia would do that which Grace would not, and tell Eliza he was there.

"Lord Somerton, Edgar told us you had arrived. How lovely to see you," she chirped. Viola drew up behind her and together the two old ladies beamed at him, then at each other.

Grace stepped in between Magnus and her aunts, then folded her arms at her chest again. "Lord Somerton was just leaving."

Edging her way around Grace, Lady Viola pressed forward. "I am so sad to hear it." A childish pout pursed her face.

Letitia stepped forward, too, and poked her head through the parlor doorway and looked about. "Where is Eliza?" she asked, glancing up at him.

Grace beat him to the reply. "She is not taking callers."

"Really? How odd." A worried look flitted across Letitia's face. She clasped her sister's hand and gave it a quick squeeze.

"Well then," Viola said, doffing worry for a polite smile. "We do hope we will see you at *the theater* this evening. I understand Kean's performance tonight at *Drury Lane* is to be superb. *Eliza* is quite looking forward to it."

"Drury Lane," Magnus echoed with a smile. "Yes. Perhaps I will see ye ladies there this eve."

"Wonderful," the aunts chimed together.

Grace narrowed her eyes at Magnus as he retrieved his hat from Edgar and started through the open door.

He turned and smiled. "Until this eve then, ladies."

As Edgar closed the heavy door behind him, Magnus turned and looked back, fighting the urge to reenter and demand to speak with Eliza.

Why had she refused to see him, to talk with him? Well, she would explain herself soon enough. Tonight, in fact.

He would see to it.

Rule Eleven

The element of surprise can restore a situation.

Sweeping the train of her crimson gown aside, Eliza nervously took her seat in her aunts' private box at the Drury Lane Theatre.

The smell of the freshly lit candles filled the still air, their glow gilding the scattered dust motes drifting past Eliza's eyes as her vision adjusted to the low light.

Voices welling up from the patrons seated below, and from those comfortably ensconced within the crescent of boxes wrapping the auditorium, drifted skyward to the domed ceiling in a cacophony of sound.

With a forced air of nonconcern, Eliza rested her hand on the wide rail and scanned the patrons filing into the theater from the outer vestibule.

Of course Magnus would be in attendance this eve. His presence was assured after her aunts' well-meant attempt to reverse Grace's handiwork. The very thought made her quiver with an uneasy blend of anticipation and dread.

"Sit back, Eliza," Grace whispered. "I know you are looking for *him*. I should never have told you he'd come by this afternoon."

"Him?" Eliza allowed her gaze to float from the musicians in the orchestra pit to her sister. "I'm sure I don't know what you mean, Grace."

Aunt Letitia leaned close. "I believe she is referring to Lord Somerton, dear."

"He is sure to be in attendance tonight," her aunt Viola added. "We practically invited him, you know."

"Yes," Eliza said, "so Grace has informed me." Her aunts' indirect summons could not have been worse timed for her, of course, but also for Magnus, should he arrive. For if he wasn't yet stricken with worry over the eventual loss of his home due to his brother's debts, tonight's play, Massinger's *New Way to Pay Old Debts,* would likely whisk him to the breaking point.

The orchestra began to play and the massive curtains lifted to reveal the great actor, Edmund Kean, portraying the beleaguered Sir Giles Overeach.

Eliza heard Grace giggle in nervous anticipation. Her sister had discussed little else all week. Kean was dark and mysterious, and his talent was rumored to be so stirring, so powerful, that his words had sent a score of patrons into convulsions only the night before.

Eliza sighed all the same. She had no desire to be here. In the back of her mind she could hear Kean's emotional oratory, the gasp of the audience, the trill of the musicians' instruments, but, like voices over a rushing river, all nuances were lost.

Her mind was on Magnus and how she would respond when he arrived. Just where was he?

Straining her eyes against the dimness, Eliza searched for Magnus, row by row, in endless tedium. But it seemed useless. There were too many gentlemen, all dressed far too similarly. When she had all but given up, a tall ebony-haired man entered the box nearly opposite the theater from their own.

Her stomach knotted. Eliza leaned forward for a better look, then whispered to Aunt Viola. "May I please borrow your opera glasses?"

"Of course, dear."

Eliza took the glasses in her trembling hand and raised them slowly to her eyes. The gentleman came into clear focus.

A familiar tingling sensation swept through her. *Magnus*.

Eliza sat frozen for a moment, hoping that if she did not move, he mightn't notice her. But he did see her. More than that, he outright stared with an expression so fierce, that Eliza flinched. The opera glasses slipped out of her gloved hand, then slid from her lap and thudded at her feet.

Grace shot Eliza an annoyed glance as she bent and scrabbled beneath the bench until her fingers felt the smooth mother-of-pearl case. Snatching them up, Eliza hurried the opera glasses to her eyes.

Magnus came to his feet and gestured to her, then pointed at himself and the exit to his box.

Eliza gasped. He could not expect her to leave her aunts and meet with him now, could he? If so, he was quite addled. She shook her head vehemently.

He nodded and thrust his finger at her.

No, she mouthed.

Suddenly, Magnus turned abruptly and disappeared through the opening at the rear of his box.

Eliza's heart drummed against her ribcage. He was coming for her. Part of her thrilled at the notion. The rest of her quaked. Despite thinking about him all day, she wasn't the least bit prepared to face him.

But minutes passed and there was no sign of him. Eliza fidgeted. She pivoted, angling her body ridiculously, so she could see the doorway in the rear of the box. More than an hour dragged by, fraying her nerves like basket reeds.

At the end of the second act, the audience roared with applause, startling Eliza so that she bounced right off the bench and plopped, bottom first, on the floor.

"Oh, Eliza. Is not Kean *amazing*? Such a talent." Grace asked, casually reaching out an arm to help Eliza to her feet. Grace was adrift in the rafters, so taken with the performance that she did not seem to register that Eliza was not in her seat.

But her two aunts noticed. They grinned behind furled fans, though they said not word as Eliza settled herself on the bench once more.

Below, patrons accepted drinks from runners or rose to mingle with one another. The loud buzz of conversation rode upward on a sudden swell of heated air to the box where Eliza and her family sat.

Aunt Letitia waved her fan to acknowledge another theater patron then turned to Eliza. "I had hoped we would see your young man, Eliza. I have not seen him. Have you, Sister?"

"I own, my eyes are not what they used to be. In fact, I fear our Lord Somerton could have been sitting at the box opposite ours and I would not recognize him in the dim light."

Eliza's eyes went wide. So Aunt Viola *had* seen Magnus. She was sure of it.

Aunt Letitia rapped her cane on the floor. "Where are our refreshments? Eliza, do be a dear and see what is keeping our box attendant."

"What?" Eliza gulped audibly. She couldn't go. Not alone. Not when Magnus could be waiting for her just outside the box.

"Please, dear. I am quite parched," Aunt Viola prodded.

Eliza glanced, wild-eyed at Grace. "Will you join me, Sister?"

"Oh . . . of course," Grace said, finally realizing something was amiss. "I could do with a short stroll to the grand saloon before the performance resumes."

Placing her hand on the rail, Eliza rose from her seat and gave Lord Somerton's empty box one last glance. *Still empty.* With arms linked, she and Grace moved into the outer passage and headed for the grand saloon.

Grace patted Eliza's hand. "You may rest easy, Sister. I do not believe Lord Somerton is here."

"He *is.* I saw him."

Grace's brows lifted. "Where?"

"He was sitting opposite our box. Aunt Viola saw him. Likely Aunt Letitia as well. Which is why I have been sent to see about the refreshments. Those clever old women are not nearly as thirsty as they would have us believe."

Grace's eyes grew large and she shielded Eliza's body with her own. "Stay behind me. If he spies us, I will distract him whilst you make your escape."

Eliza sighed in exasperation as she resumed her place beside her sister. "Don't be daft, Grace. We are all civilized adults. If he wishes to speak with me, I have no objections to spending a moment simply conversing." *What a lie that was.*

"You did not see him in the parlor, Eliza. He seemed quite agitated when I told him you had tired of your arrangement and that you wouldn't see him."

"You should never have spoken to him."

"So you've said, twice now." Grace shrugged her shoulder as they walked together down the sweep of stairs. "I fail to understand why you are so upset with me. I simply said what needed to be stated—for all our sakes. You would not have done it."

"I would have, but in my own time." She stopped her sister at midway down the stairs. "Please, Grace. Do not interfere again."

"Very well. I am sure he understands the situation now, anyway for I was quite clear." Grace glanced at the gathering of polite society at the foot of the stairs. Her eyes suddenly lit like a torchlight and she clutched Eliza's arm. "Look there. Is that Lord Hawksmoor?" She leaned against the rail. "But . . . it can't be. Reggie told me he needed to return to Dunley Parish for a fortnight, and he was to leave today."

Eliza followed Grace's gaze. *Oh dear.* It *was* Reginald. And he was not alone. Instead he was in the company of a stylish slightly older woman, whose face Eliza couldn't see.

Grace withered dramatically against the stair rail. "He is with another," she said, all confidence leached from her voice. "I don't understand this. I thought he . . . fancied me."

"I am sure she's nothing more than a family friend whom he'd invited to the theater long before the two of you renewed your acquaintance last eve."

"Do you really think so?"

"I do." Eliza took Grace's arm and led her back up the staircase. "Now go back to the box and wait with our aunts. I shall wish him well for you."

Eliza knew she oughtn't wander about alone, especially with Magnus lurking somewhere nearby, but she had little choice. She couldn't allow Grace to approach Lord Hawksmoor and his lady friend in her current state of distress. Knowing her sister's inclination to overreact, even if Hawksmoor was innocent of Grace's suspicions, her sister might act brashly, jeopardizing any possible offer in their mutual future.

Grace gave one last fretful glance at her beloved, then,

with her chin nearly resting on her chest, she entered the shadowed passage leading to the Featherton box.

Turning, Eliza started back down the staircase. When she neared the bottom, she steadied herself against the rail and looked up to search for Lord Hawksmoor. Instead, she saw Magnus, standing only ten feet away no less, his brow drawn deep in a scowl.

Lud! Whirling around, she put aside all notion of speaking with Lord Hawksmoor and scampered back up the treads as fast as propriety would allow.

When Eliza reached the top, she threw a frantic glance over her shoulder. Magnus trailed her and was not a dozen steps behind. *Perdition!*

Her slippers barely touched the floor as she rushed down the dark passage toward the Featherton box. She would be safe there. Surely he wouldn't dare intrude—not after the way Grace had berated him earlier.

She hurried around the curve, taking a quick glance over her shoulder again.

She'd barely turned her head forward again when she plowed right into a heavyset gentleman standing before the entrance to her aunts' box. "Oof!"

She bounced backward off his belly. Her feet tangled in her short train and she hit the floor hard—again. How she wanted to scream!

"Oh, sakes alive!" The startled gentleman grasped Eliza's arm and assisted her to her feet. "I do beg your pardon, miss."

"Thank you. Oh no. Please," she muttered as the man continued to fuss over her, waving his handkerchief ridiculously while trying to brush carpet fibers from her gown. "Do not concern yourself, sir—*really*." Eliza batted at his hands. "Please stop, sir. I am *fine* for goodness sake!"

She swung her head around. Magnus was closing fast.

There was no chance of escaping inside her aunts' box now. Snatching up her skirt, she rounded the man's substantial girth and dashed madly down the passageway.

"Eliza, wait," Magnus called in a raised whisper.

She didn't bother to turn around. Peering down the dimly lit corridor, she edged past the gaggle of patrons and rushed down the passage.

The corridor ended at a narrow door. Unlike the other doors leading to the boxes, this one was devoid of all ornamentation.

Taking a deep breath, Eliza tugged at the pull. The hidden hinges squealed, the door opened and she slipped into a midnight black passageway.

Her breath seemed amplified as she ran down the narrow hall, as did the sound of the performance. Her path must somehow have taken her backstage.

There was a whine of metal behind her. Eliza spun around, her eyes wide yet blind against the darkness. *The door.*

"*Eliza,*" came Magnus's low voice.

Frantically, Eliza searched for a place to hide. She stretched out her arms and ran her fingers along the walls on either side until she felt the outline of a door. When at last her hand brushed the cool metal of a door pull, she eased the handle down and stepped into a room as black and soft as thickest velvet.

"Eliza?" she heard Magnus call. "I only want to talk. Dinna run from me."

She stood silently in the dark until her eyes began to burn. She was acting like a child avoiding punishment. At the very least, she owed Magnus an explanation for her behavior.

Cautiously, Eliza groped her way toward the door, but when she reached for the latch, she felt only stacks of cloth.

The door had to be near. Her grasp on direction could not be so askew.

She plunged her hand through piles of fabric, hoping to find the door or even a bare wall, but there was nothing but swathes of wovens in every direction.

This was unbelievable. She was lost in a nest of cloth. A whimper of frustration burst from her mouth.

"Eliza?"

Thank God, he'd found her. "Yes. I am here, Magnus. I cannot find the door."

"Dinna worry, I'm coming."

Step by small step, Eliza moved toward the sound of his voice, but tripped over a heavy bundle on the floor. An avalanche of cool silk cascaded down around her.

She tried to stand, but could barely move. "Blast!" she was as tangled in fabric as a fine chain in a cluttered jewelry box.

"Eliza? Are ye all right?" His voice sounded concerned this time.

"Yes, but I'm caught. I need your help." She had yet to even see Magnus and already embarrassment scorched her cheeks.

The mechanical turn of the door handle drew her gaze blindly to the left. "Magnus?"

"Aye. Where are ye?"

"Here," she squeaked. "Down here."

"Stay still. I'll get a candle from the outer passage. I canna see a bluidy thing in there."

"Please hurry." She felt utterly ridiculous as she sat in the dark listening to the muted thuds of Magnus heading down the passage. For another minute she fumbled to free herself from the tumble of silks, satin, lace, and cording. Then, at last, she saw the flame of a single candle.

"Magnus?"

"Aye, lass. Stay where ye are. I'm coming for ye."

Then, Eliza saw the flame move as Magnus's dark silhouette lodged the taper in what had to be a sconce on the wall. She saw him turn and move toward her, then felt his fingers graze her breast. She gasped as his firm hands ran boldly down her sides to her waist.

Effortlessly he drew her from the tangle of fabric and lifted her to his chest, waiting for the twisted cloth to fall away before allowing her to slide slowly down his body to the floor. "Milady," he whispered with a muffled chuckle.

"Oh, stop it, Somerton. I am sufficiently humiliated already." And she had no one to blame but herself.

As her eyes adjusted to the candlelight, she realized she'd stumbled, quite literally, into the theatrical company's storage room. Aside from the cottons, satins, and velvets piled to ceiling against every wall, there were several ornate costumes, in various states of creation, strewn upon a narrow trestle table in the center of the room.

"Thank you for rescuing me," she whispered, but in the dimness, her words seemed loud and harsh. Eliza brushed her hair from her eyes, realizing she must look a tumbled mess. "Now if you will excuse me—"

Magnus's expression darkened. "Dinna be so hasty," came his resonate reply. His fingers suddenly wrapped around her arm and pulled her against him. "I believe ye owe me an explanation."

"An explanation?" she repeated.

His grip on her tightened. "Why wouldna ye receive me today? Why did ye go so far as to dive into a mountain of cloth to escape me?"

Oh, how she wanted to tell him—*everything*. But how could she explain? If he could only feel the turmoil inside of her every time she looked into his eyes, every time she felt his touch.

"What's wrong, Eliza?" His breath brushed her cheeks.

She sucked in a breath and tried to clear her mind.

"I waited for ye in the parlor." His hands ringed her arms, holding her firmly. I waited but ye sent Grace in your stead."

Eliza sighed. "I did not *send* Grace. She took it upon herself to speak with you." Twisting, she struggled to free herself from him.

Magnus tucked her arms behind her and pulled her firmly against him, knocking a whoosh of breath from her lungs.

"Eliza, we have an *arrangement,* do we not? I only sought to uphold my half of the bargain." His tone was smoldering.

She looked up at him in confusion. Their so-called "arrangement" had nothing to do with this. Nothing to do with what she heard in his voice, saw in his eyes. Humiliation, anger, hurt, all flaring into something greater. Into *desire*.

Breath rushed hot and violent from his nostrils, searing her cheeks. Her own breathing quickened involuntarily and her heart thudded within her breast. She fought to rein in her response to his nearness, to his overpowering maleness. But it was useless.

"You know why I didn't receive you—why I cannot be alone with you," she managed.

"Do I?" Magnus released her arm, catching her waist instead. Eliza wriggled, but he took her chin firmly in one hand and turned her face upward.

She had to get out of here. The looming darkness was making it too easy to forget what was right—making her *feel* everything and think nothing of propriety. She had to leave before something happened she'd later regret. She struggled again, but his arm held her against him as surely as a steel band.

"Why, Eliza?"

She pushed against the stone wall of his chest. "*Please*."

His hands fell away then, allowing her to depart if she so desired. But she couldn't leave—not when he still held her by the heartstrings.

She backed away, until she slammed against a wall of fabric bolts. "Because this is no longer a game."

"What do ye mean?" he asked in a low, resonant tone as he prowled ever closer.

"We pretended attraction, but we really weren't pretending, were we?"

"Nay," he said, closer still. His breathing was heavy.

"We wore ridiculous masks of love for all to see, but—" She stopped.

Magnus closed the space between them in a single stride. He slammed his hands on either side of her, pinioning her with his body. "What were ye going to say, Eliza?"

"*N-nothing.*"

"Then do not speak. But ye will tell me." He grabbed her and pulled her roughly into his arms. He took her chin in his hand and turned her mouth up to his. Then, with a look of determination, he pressed his moist lips against her mouth.

And she melted helplessly against him. His muscles pressed down on her, his tongue urged her mouth open, tasting and caressing her, making her hunger for more. She shuddered and clutched him to her. Outside the room, the sounds of the play and applause of the audience dissolved into nothingness. She was lost in the darkness, bound by the intensity of her senses.

All she wanted was to touch Magnus. To be touched.

Magnus shrugged and she heard his coat hit the floor. At once she felt his burning palms on her own shoulders, pushing her gown's lace sleeves down and away.

"Magnus," she breathed.

Cupping her buttocks in his rough hands, he pulled her

against him, forcing her to acknowledge the dark walk she was treading once more.

Lord, help her. What was she, an unmarried woman, doing? This was positively shameful. But the point of logical thought had passed. Her body and conscience had warred, and her body had won.

Magnus trailed his left hand down her outer thigh with exquisite tenderness, making her body flinch with expectation. Sliding his fingers behind her knee, he drew her leg up to his hip, then pressed the bulge of his erection between her thighs.

Eliza gasped with shock, but her body thrilled. Through the thin sarcenet of her skirt she could feel his heat, his hardness, against her. Against the one place where she seemed to need him most. Her body arched wantonly.

Magnus rammed against her. Eliza opened her mouth, but the sound was muted as Magnus crushed her lips with his own.

She wanted to surrender.

Consequences be damned.

She clung to him as he slid his right hand between them and rode it along the inside of her quivering, raised thigh. She felt his fingers push away her thin chemise and then softly brush the downy curls he found there.

His touch teased her, his wicked fingers seeking out and stroking the nub inside her gently swollen inner folds. His longest finger slipped up inside of her. Flinching with surprise, Eliza gasped against his mouth.

Magnus thrust his tongue inside her mouth where it swam with her own, as his fingers stroked her slippery curves, probed her far too intimately. Eliza drew her head back, turned it away, and squeezed her eyes tight as she pressed her hips toward him, forcing the pressure.

A tense heat built within her, winding her so tightly that

she ached where he touched her. His fingers moved faster, plunged deeper inside of her as his thumb stroked her most sensitive place.

In a mounting frenzy, she instinctively ground herself against him. She sucked in a breath and held it, biting her lower lip lest she cry out. Suddenly, his other hand was at her breast, pulling the lace-edged sarcenet low. He slid his hot palm over her nipple and squeezed gently making her moan.

Stop! her mind suddenly screamed.

Stop now before it is too late. She brought her fist to her mouth as his hand played out its final notes. All at once, fire seemed to blaze through her and she cried out. Her hands flung out, fingers splayed against his chest, as a gentle warmth surged through her body. "Oh God . . ."

Eliza rode the drugging sensation downward, lowering her foot to the floor and slipping her hands behind Magnus's back. She hugged him to her. "You've spoiled everything," she whispered huskily. "I never meant to give you my heart. Never wanted to. But I have. Damn you, I have."

Magnus leaned back as if stunned by her words. "What did ye say?"

A crash of applause broke the intimacy of the room.

Startled by the sound and knowing that soon the outside corridors would be flooded with people, Eliza stiffened. "The performance—it's ended!" Her voice shook.

Magnus's voice remained calm and even. "Yer aunts will be looking for ye."

Her mind was still awhirl, her gown askew, and no doubt, in the light her face would be as scarlet as the ruby pendant at her throat.

She felt the sweet heat of his hands upon her as he pulled her chemise into place and repositioned her dress. She slid her gown's capped sleeves higher on her shoulders.

"What will I tell them?" She twisted and shook to straighten her beaded overdress.

He bent and kissed her lips once more, softly, slowly, and her breathing slowed.

"Tell them ye met me in the grand saloon and we spoke. Nothing more. Just remain at ease and they will think nothing amiss."

"You're right." Eliza nervously finger-combed her hair and felt for the door handle. When she found it and had just pressed the door handle, Magnus caught her arm.

"But this is far from over, Eliza." His eyes blazed in the candlelight. "Far from over."

And she knew he meant it.

Rule Twelve

When ignorant of your quarry and of yourself,
you are in certain peril.

Gray slashes of rain pelted the hired coach, drumming the cab's slick black roof and fogged windows with an almost savage tempo. Magnus exhaled, frustrated that he'd been reduced to lurking in the darkness outside the Featherton home. He slammed his fist against the glass and rubbed a porthole in the condensation. *Dammit, Eliza, where are ye?*

After the previous evening, he knew she would be suspicious and would not receive him, willingly anyway. Everything had gone wrong at the theater. He'd only meant to talk with her, calmly, to find out why she would not see him. But instead, he'd lost control, had given in to his baser instincts. And yet, he didn't regret one moment of the passion that raged between them in the darkness of the storage room. The touch of her lips, the feel of her soft curves against him. Their night together would remain in his heart forever—for he knew they would likely never share another.

In the sobering light of morn, the truth of his dire situation laid plain his future. And he had to face it like a man:

Unless *The Promise* survived the stormy seas and made port, which seemed less and less likely with each passing day, he and Eliza could never be together.

Tonight, he needed to explain everything to her. Apologize and beg her forgiveness.

And so, he waited for Eliza to leave the house—he'd wait all night if he had to—for his moment to catch her alone. He knew he must remain in gentlemanly control this time. Resist every urge to sweep her into his arms. He only hoped he could do it.

Eliza glanced out the window. A fine mist supplanted the rain, which had fallen so heavily minutes before. Her aunts and Grace would be leaving soon—without her—if her ploy was successful.

Lifting the back of her hand to her forehead, and with as much dramatic flare as she could muster, Eliza collapsed into the chair beside the hearth. "My apologies, Aunt Letitia, but I fear I am unable to attend the *Spectacular* at the Serpentine. I am far too fatigued."

"Cannot attend?" Aunt Letitia stammered. "But everyone will be there, Lizzy—*everyone.*"

Aunt Viola patted Eliza's shoulder. "Come now, surely you do not wish to miss the fireworks or the parade of fanciful gondolas. This event is quite the to-do, you know."

Peering into the mirror over the mantel, Grace pulled enough golden curls from beneath her bonnet to frame her face. She bit her lips and puckered them, then smiled prettily at her own image.

As Eliza slumped miserably in her chair, she noticed that her sister watched her in the mirror's reflection, her blue eyes soft with concern.

"Even Lord Somerton is bound to attend," Aunt Viola added.

"Auntie!" Grace whispered harshly. Whirling around, she surreptitiously shook her head, warning her aunt to avoid the subject.

Eliza gave a long, drawn out sigh. Yes, Magnus likely would attend, which is exactly why she wasn't setting a slipper outside the house.

After last night at the Drury Lane, she could not risk seeing him again—not until she was in control of her pounding heart and ridiculous wilting knees.

"Not that I do not trust you alone, mind you . . ." Grace lifted a suspicious golden brow at Eliza. "But I may need your help. It is possible we might encounter Lord Hawksmoor at the *Spectacular* and I thought you might speak with him about . . . well . . . about the woman he escorted to the theater."

"Grace, I told you, Lord Hawksmoor's attention is in your basket. If you see him, do not make a cake of yourself by bringing up what you *think* you saw at the theater."

"I suppose you're right. Though I do wish you would come," Grace replied. "The *Spectacular* is the *place* to be this eve. Only a mutton-head would stay at home."

"A very *tired* mutton-head," Eliza replied, adding a long sigh for effect.

Concern cinched Aunt Viola's brows. "You are not ill, are you, dove?" She raised her hand to Eliza's cheek. "You do not feel overwarm."

Eliza shook her head. "There's no need to fret, Auntie. I am well. Just too weary to spend the evening strolling around the Serpentine."

Aunt Viola glanced at her sister, who chewed her lower lip in indecision.

"Is something wrong?" Eliza asked. "Why is it so important that I attend this eve?"

"Well," Aunt Viola began, "since we were all going to the

Spectacular, I had given the staff the evening to themselves, but I shall call them back if you will be at home."

"No, no, no," Eliza said, waving the idea away. "Do not ask them to remain on my account. I shan't be in need of their services."

Grace slipped her arms into her spencer and fastened it. "Now that the rain has let up, we'll miss the firework display if we do not leave at once."

"Grace is right." Eliza rose and shooed them all toward the door. "Go now and enjoy yourselves. You can tell me all about it in the morning. I will just finish my tea and be off to bed."

"Very well, Eliza. Good night," her aunts chimed as one.

"Good night," Grace echoed, as she and her aunts stepped through the door into the cool, misty night.

Eliza pressed the door closed and exhaled her breath through her nose. "Good *night.*"

At last, the house was quiet, so still that the only sound Eliza could detect was the almost imperceptible creak of her stays as her lungs filled with air. For several moments, she held still, not wanting to so much as ripple the settling calm.

But then a secret smile burst onto her lips and she laughed aloud. Dropping her head back, she gleefully flung her hands outward and spun round in a wild circle. By stars, it was good to be alone, even if she had to feign fatigue to achieve it. But her charade was justified. She just could not take the chance of facing Magnus again.

She thought of what had passed between them in the theater storage room and flushed with the memory. Had the play not ended when it did, who knows what she might have done? It had been as if she'd taken complete leave of her senses.

Oh, that she could whisk Magnus and this blasted season

from her life. Everything would be so much simpler with only her art to fill her days . . . and nights. At the thought, she started for the parlor where her easel now stood, but caught sight of Grace's kid gloves lying on the entry table.

Just then, the doorknocker slammed twice to its rest. Shaking her head at her sister's forgetfulness, Eliza snatched up the gloves and carried them to the door.

"I've got them, Grace. You'd forget your head if it wasn't tied down by your bonnet," Eliza called out as she made her way to the door. As she passed the mirror, she paused and plucked the pins from her hair. She shook her curls loose, hoping to make it appear she was already preparing for bed, and happened to notice one of her crimson-edged "Thank you for not calling" cards on the floor. Lud, what was that doing down there? She'd been so careful to keep those hidden!

Scooping it up, she hid it behind her back and swung the door wide. But it was not her sister wanting her gloves, nor their footman. Her breath caught in her throat.

Magnus removed his hat and politely bowed his head. "Good evening, Eliza."

"W-what are you doing here?"

"I told ye last night, we must talk." Without waiting for an invitation, Magnus walked through the doorway and passage, then entered the parlor.

Eliza glanced frantically about. Lord above! How did she get herself into this mess? She closed the door slowly, took a deep breath, and followed him. "You cannot stay."

"Why not?" he asked, moving toward her.

"Because we are alone. Receiving you now would be improper."

"I saw yer house staff leave, then yer aunts and sister. I wondered why ye were not with them."

"Y-you were watching the house?" Eliza drew her brows angrily, but her body tingled peculiarly inside.

Magnus dropped his hat on the corner table then settled back comfortably on the settee. "I could not chance missing ye this eve. How fortunate for me that ye chose to remain at home."

"I am . . . fatigued."

Magnus lifted a brow and one corner of his mouth lifted slightly. "Are ye truly, Eliza?"

Eliza folded her arms over her thudding heart. "*No*. I am not, as a matter of fact." She lifted her chin. "I did not venture out this evening because I did not wish to encounter *you* again. Not after we . . . you—well, you were there." A prickly blush swept her cheeks.

"Aye, I was." The easy smile that had played at the corners of his mouth faded from his lips. "Which is why I am here this evening. We have matters to discuss."

"Really?" Eliza turned away from Magnus. She went to the fire, which to her dismay had already been banked for the night, and pushed her crimson-edged card deep into the embers. "I do not think we need to discuss what happened *ever* again."

She heard Magnus rise from the chair and suddenly felt his hands on her shoulders, turning her. Eliza stiffened the moment their eyes met, but she could not make herself look away.

"*Eliza* . . . stop this," he breathed, angling his mouth toward her own.

She turned her head away. "Please do not say my name that way."

He slipped his fingers under her chin and brought her back to him. "Why not?"

She bowed her head and closed her eyes so as not to look

at him. "Because your tone promises things that can never be."

"Lass, I'm sorry . . . I—"

Magnus gently touched her cheeks and drew her face upward to his. She felt his lips brush hers, softly, tenderly. Her eyelids suddenly felt weighted, wanting to close and welcome his kiss.

No, no! She flicked her eyelids open. She wouldn't do this. Not again. Eliza stepped to the side, thrusting her finger accusingly at him. "You see? You see? *This* is why we cannot be alone. Not even for a moment."

Magnus's eyes widened, as if surprised by his own actions.

Rising up on the balls of her feet, Eliza raced behind her easel, hoping to shield herself from his clever seduction.

"Is that my portrait?" he asked, starting toward her again.

She glanced down at her painting. "Err . . . yes, of course it is. Or . . . will be." When she looked up again he stood only a breath away. "Stay where you are."

"Would it make ye feel more at ease if ye painted while we spoke?"

Eliza assessed him narrowly.

"I shall not leave until we discuss last night." Magnus lifted his brows. "But I will remain on *this* side of the canvas."

Eliza squinted her eyes at him, then, wanting to speed his departure by whatever means she could, nodded cautiously. She lifted a brush and pointed its fine tip toward him. "I will agree. *If* you keep your promise and remain on your side of the canvas."

"When will yer staff and yer aunts return?" His question sounded ever so casual. "I want to be sure that we have plenty of uninterrupted time—to talk."

"We shall have plenty of time. But once we've finished, you will leave at once. Agreed?" Eliza clarified.

"Of course."

Eliza dabbed small mounds of pigment onto her palette, glancing warily at Magnus all the while. Agreeing to this was insane. But what other choice did she have? He was right. They needed to settle what had happened between them once and for all.

When her preparations for painting were complete, she stepped from behind the easel to position him, her subject, in the chair.

"Would you please turn your head to the right a bit. No, lift your chin a little higher. No, not that high."

Magnus stared blankly at her, causing Eliza to fire a frustrated breath.

"Oh botheration. Let me . . ." Tentatively, she reached out her hands and nervously laid the pads of her fingers against his beard-roughened chin, drawing it slightly upward and to the left. From her vantage, she looked down at his moist lips, unwittingly reminding herself of the wickedness of which they were capable.

Her breath hitched, and she knew he heard it, for like a sprung trap, his arms shot upward and cinched her waist.

Startled, Eliza looked down into the luminous, and oh so dangerous, silver eyes peering up at her.

"Y-you promised to behave," she feebly reminded.

"I only promised to remain on my side of the canvas."

In an instant she felt his moist breath tease her breast through the thin muslin of her gown. She closed her eyes and gasped at the feel of it. "Magnus, *please*." Though her mind objected, her tone was smooth and sultry, transforming her meaning from "please stop" to "please do it *again*."

He looked up at her then, appearing torn, almost as though he was struggling and didn't know which direction to turn. "I wish ye knew how hard this was for me. Christ, ye must know how I feel. And I know ye feel something for me too."

"Do you?"

"Aye, ye love me. I know ye do." As he spoke, his fingers moved behind her and deliberately loosed the bow at her back, allowing the satin ribbon to fall at her sides. "Why do ye deny it?"

"L-love?" She cleared her throat, trying to appear unaffected. But as his hands worked free the four tiny buttons at her back, her breath came faster, her heart beat wildly. "Where do you come up with these notions, my lord?"

Magnus held her snugly, imprisoning her against him, but heaven help her, she had no desire to escape.

"Tell me. Tell me, lass." His deep voice hummed against her throat as he spoke, as he kissed her, and she shivered with pleasure. "Tell me that ye feel what I feel. I just need to hear it once. Only once."

"I cannot," she managed, but inside a strange excitement grew.

"Nay?" he whispered, drawing her back so he could read her eyes.

The separation of their bodies was all Eliza needed to think more clearly and logically. "Because a relationship is impossible. We both know it. Why complicate matters with words that cannot change that fact?"

"Because it matters to me, Eliza." At once his eyes flashed an imperious warning. Before she knew what had happened, Magnus tumbled them both to the plush Turkish carpet and had rolled atop of her.

Shock at his actions quickly erupted into excitement. Breathing in his musky scent, she savored the all too carnal feeling of his hard body pressed so intimately against hers.

With a determined look in his eyes, Magnus claimed

her mouth. His warm lips urged hers to part, to open for him. Eliza did not resist. Could not. She did as his mouth commanded.

Closing her eyes, she slid her arms around his neck and clung to him, as their bodies rocked with the gentle rhythm of their breathing.

Then, she felt his mouth lift away. She opened her eyes to see him peering down at her, and she sighed softly.

"Tell me ye dinna want this, Eliza. Tell me ye dinna want to be with me and I will go now," he said, his voice low and husky with passion.

She shook her head, then looked away.

"Why, Eliza? Say it!" He thrust against her pelvis as if to force her to speak.

She said nothing. Could not deny it.

"Ye canna because ye want me as much as I want ye. We belong together, lass. I know ye feel it too."

Eliza turned her head to peer into his eyes once more. "Listen to me. What we feel is of no consequence. You must marry another or lose everything."

"Nay," he whispered. "I will have *ye*. I must. And if . . . *when* my ship arrives in the basin—"

"Your ship?" Eliza blinked. So she had not imagined his reaction at the Hogarts' supper. "You invested in one of the ships in the storm?"

Magnus looked away, then rolled beside her and slowly exhaled.

"Why didn't you tell me?" Her voice sounded oddly strangled. "Why would you have me looking for a rich bride, when you never needed my help at all?"

Humiliation infused Eliza. *Devil take you*. She had to get up, get away from him. She tried to slide upright, but her skirts were caught beneath his body. She pushed against him, pounded at his chest, trying not to whimper foolishly.

"Stop it, Eliza. I was going to tell ye. *Tonight,* in fact," he said, trying to catch her flailing hands. "Stop."

But she wouldn't. If she did, she would start to cry. Eliza clawed at her dress, then shoved at him again. But he was too heavy.

Magnus caught her wrists then and pressed them down into the carpet on either side of her head.

"Ye are going to listen to what I have to say." His eyes were dark and roiling as a storm ravaged sky, but she looked straight into them as he spoke.

"I dinna mean to deceive ye. I only wanted to be with ye. That's why I agreed to your ridiculous *arrangement.* I dinna give a damn about yer investigations or even the portrait. I only wanted to be with *ye.*"

The moment she heard him speak those few simple words, her eyes began to sting. *He only wanted to be with her.* The same way she wanted to be with him.

He released her wrists then and she rubbed her eyes with the backs of her hands. "But your ship—" she sputtered.

"If she arrives in the basin, my financial problems will be solved." A thin smile, borne of hope, shone down at her. "And we could be *together.*"

She lowered her hands and stared at him, stunned. He actually believed his ship would make port. Or he wanted very badly to believe it. She could see it in his eyes. He hoped for a future—together. But she could not.

"When we—" he began, but Eliza laid a finger over Magnus's lips, silencing him.

"The whole of London knows of the storm—of the ships lost." Not wanting to see the disappointment in his eyes, she rolled closer to him and rested her forehead against his thudding heart. "I know you must adhere your hopes to your ship, but I cannot. My future lies in Italy."

"Eliza, there's been no report yet—"

"Shhh. It doesn't matter. You know as well as I that we cannot see each other again. Not the way we have been. The temptation to be together is too strong for either of us to bear." She ran a finger down the muscled slope of his chest, savoring the feel of him one last time. "You must forget me. You have a responsibility to your family, to the people of Somerton."

"Eliza," Magnus whispered. "Don't you think I've tried? I tried all the way to yer doorstep this very eve. But I canna do it. I can no more forget ye than I can forget to breathe."

He lifted a long dark curl from her shoulder and drew it to his lips as he leaned closer to kiss her. "I will never leave ye. Ye're mine. *Mine*." He raised his mouth from hers and gazed deeply into her eyes. "And I am yers. *Forever*."

And she knew it was true. It would not take a ring of gold to bind her to him. Eliza knew in her heart, from this moment, she was his, and would always be. A sob began working its way up her throat.

If only they could be together, the way he envisioned. But it was impossible. How she wanted to believe in his world. A world where money and position didn't dictate who you must marry. Where Society's fickle rules didn't determine a woman's destiny.

For one night, just one, she wanted to believe in the possibility of a life together.

This time, when Magnus's mouth came ravenously down upon hers, she did not pull away. Instead, she opened her mouth to him.

Magnus slipped his right hand along the carpet then upward into the small of her back. He pulled her solidly against him. His lips left her mouth and swept across her cheek to the hollow behind her ear. He kissed her, again, lower still.

When he lifted his lips from her, Eliza plunged her fingers

into the dark tumbles of his hair, not wanting his kisses to stop, trying to urge his mouth back to hers.

His breath came faster as he rose up from her, leaving her laying before him on the carpet as he loosened his cravat and unwound it with unbearable slowness. He dropped it to the floor, then leaned close and nipped her mouth teasingly with a quick kiss.

She chased his lips with her own, but he sat back on his heels, out of her reach, as he eased off his coat, then his waistcoat, and dropped them both to the floor.

Eliza reached out and grasped his shirt to pull him close, but instead his shirttails slipped from his breeches.

A dark smile lifted Magnus's lips. Taking her boldness as an invitation, he peeled his shirt over his head and cast it to the carpet as well.

In the glow of the candlelight, his body appeared hard and angular, his skin golden and smooth. *My God.* She'd never seen anyone formed so perfectly.

Hesitantly, she reached out her hands to touch him, needing to feel the suppleness of his warm skin beneath her eager fingertips.

He sighed with approval as her bare hands met his rippled stomach and rode its cut plane upward to the muscled curves of his chest.

"Magnus," she whispered as her fingertips brushed over his nipples. She watched them harden and tighten under her touch, and felt a pleasurable twinge between her legs.

Magnus leaned over her and once more he kissed her, harder this time. More urgently.

She moaned against him, knowing at that moment that tonight she would give everything. Take everything. Feel no regrets.

Magnus seemed to read her thoughts and his seduction became ever bolder.

Eliza watched his appreciative eyes twinkle as he boldly slipped her dress off her shoulders and pressed it down until it bunched about her middle; its sleeves wringing her wrists like bracelets. He looked into her eyes as he bit the tie that cinched her shift and tugged it loose. Slowly, his fingers drew back the linen until her half bare breasts rested atop her corset.

Eliza swallowed hard. This time there was no darkness to quell her modesty, and she struggled to cross her arms over her breasts to conceal her nakedness.

"Nay." He ran his fingers lightly over her skin, drawing goose bumps to the surface. "Ye're beautiful."

Eliza said nothing, only stared up at him, her breath coming in short pants as her excitement mounted.

One after the other, he took her hands in his and pulled them from the rumpled sleeves of her dress. Slowly, he pressed a kiss into each of her palms, then drew her arms up and laid her hands near her shoulders, pinning them there in silent command.

He leaned down over her, and suddenly his lips were upon her throat, sending her heart pulsing madly as he kissed her. His hand slid up over her corset, over her ribs and higher still.

He pulled down the thin chemise covering her breasts and cupped one in his hand, making her groan with pleasure as he trailed a path of kisses across her chest. He stopped at last, allowing her only one scant breath before he closed his lips slowly, tantalizingly, over her nipple.

The sensation sent her mind spinning, and she reached out to grasp him in order to remind herself this was not a dream—this was really happening. She sucked in a breath and clasped her hands to his head, running her fingers through his hair as he devoured her, driving her ever closer to delirium.

Just when she thought she could take no more, his hand moved slowly down her body to her ankle. Without a word, he trailed his fingers slowly up her silk stocking, nudging upward her chemise and gown, leaving it bunched at her waist. His hand stopped only when it touched her lightly between her thighs, making her body quiver with anticipation.

Eliza clung to Magnus as he kissed her, touched her. She pulled her mouth from him. "Magnus," she panted. "Now."

Magnus looked deep into her eyes, questioning, yet wanting.

"Yes." Her courage soaring, she wedged her hand between their bodies and fumbled unsurely at the buttons of his breeches until the flap opened and she felt him. His erection stirred and pulsed against her palm, exciting her wildly as she led him to her center. She didn't know for sure what she was doing. All she knew is that she wanted him there, needed him *there*.

Magnus stared at her, his eyes dark and primal.

She nodded slowly. "Forever," she said, knowing this was what he wanted to hear. "*Forever,*" she repeated, her breath uneven, but her words sure.

Magnus kissed her deeply, then moved his body between her legs, parting them with his knees. He leaned over her and put his hand between her legs, touching her, stroking her. She arched beneath him.

Her fingers splayed, she clung to the broad plane of his back, urging him onward as he moved between her thighs.

Magnus closed his eyes and groaned as he skimmed her wetness, filling Eliza with exhilaration, with a female power she'd never before known.

This was it. After this moment, there would be no turning back. Ever. Her life would be forever changed. She would be ruined in the eyes of the world, but she would not stop now. For her heart was already his.

"*Forever,*" he whispered as he positioned himself over her then pressed his hardness slowly into her.

Eliza whimpered softly and tensed as he filled her. Deeper, he moved and soon the initial burn and sting of his claiming of her subsided.

He rocked against her, slowly at first, then faster.

She felt her body stretching, tightening around him, drawing him deeper. Surprising rivulets of tingling warmth urged her to move her hips, to meet him thrust for thrust. The drugging sensation grew, intensified, and she closed her eyes, allowed herself to be consumed by the core of heat emanating from the place where their bodies met.

Magnus drew up on his arms and watched her as he moved within her. He drove into her again and again.

Eliza bit her lower lips and thrashed her head against the carpet. She locked her legs around Magnus's waist and held him tightly to her, controlling the pressure as he drove onward. Bucking against him, she cried out as something inside her ignited, then flared, sending liquid flames shooting from her center to every part of her body.

Magnus arched up suddenly and she felt him strain.

"Eliza—" With a groan, he rested atop of her.

She clutched him to her. Not wanting to move. Not wanting to let the moment end.

Magnus kissed her. "We are right for each other, lass."

A smile of contentment lifted her lips. For several minutes more, she stroked her fingers through his hair, down his back, and lower still, until, to her surprise, she felt his arousal—*again*.

Wholly confused, she looked up and saw that he watched her intently. Suddenly the front door's latch clicked loudly. Eliza's eyes snapped wide. She gasped.

Magnus cupped his hand over her mouth to quiet her. *Her family had come home!*

Rule Thirteen

Use bait to draw him into secure ground.
Here, his strengths can be compromised.

"Someone is here!" Eliza's breath seized with panic in her lungs.

For several seconds she remained completely still beneath Magnus, listening to the creak and groan of yielding floorboards as several people entered the hall. Gradually, the pounding faded as the group ascended the stairs.

Magnus rolled upright, snatched up his linen shirt and pulled it over his head. With a speed that astonished Eliza, he buttoned his now overtight breeches and hurried into his waistcoat.

Shooting her arms into her sleeves, Eliza hoisted her chemise and bodice into position, then scrambled to her feet. She whirled around, turning her back to Magnus. "My buttons," she pleaded as she tugged down the hem of her gown.

With the speed of a lady's maid, Magnus's nimble fingers fastened Eliza's gown, then he slipped on his waistcoat.

"*Hurry,*" Eliza said, tossing his coat to him.

As she moved toward the door, Eliza wrung her hands

and glanced frantically about the room for a means of escape. Her gaze focused on the large windows facing the street. "You will have to climb through the window. There is no other way."

"The window?" Magnus lifted his brow and flashed a sardonic grin as he haphazardly tied his cravat around his throat. "Ye must be joking."

"I assure you, I am not." Eliza stared at Magnus with amazement. Though she shook with fear of being discovered, he seemed quite calm.

"I should think being caught together by yer aunts greatly preferable to explaining to all of London why an earl was seen climbing from yer parlor window."

A voice drifted into the room from the passageway. "Eliza? Eliza, dear. Are you here?" It was Aunt Viola.

She heard the click of walking sticks on the floor just outside the door. Saw the brass door handle depress. *Lord, help us.*

"Answer her," Magnus whispered, "as though nothing is wrong."

Eliza nodded her head. "Yes, Auntie," she replied feebly. "I am here."

She looked frantically to Magnus. *Do something. Please.*

Magnus suddenly snatched up one of Eliza's paintings from the stack of three propped against the wall. He held it before him, covering the telltale bulge in his breeches, just as the door opened.

"Lord Somerton!" Aunt Viola gasped and gaped at them in utter astonishment. She looked behind her at Aunt Letitia and Grace, who stared back at him with equally startled expressions.

Magnus bowed slightly, keeping the painting centered over his body. "Ladies."

Eliza stepped in front of Magnus. "You have returned quite early. Did you forget something, perhaps?"

Aunt Letitia poked her cane into the Turkish carpet and moved toward Eliza. "How could we enjoy ourselves at the *Spectacular,* knowing our dear niece sat all alone at home?"

"Oh Letitia, how you go on," Aunt Viola broke in. "It started raining again. The event has been postponed, so we came home." She cast a frown in Magnus's direction. "Of course, we could not have guessed you would be entertaining Lord Somerton whilst we were gone."

Eliza's felt her ears reddening. "I just—."

Magnus cut in. "Miss Merriweather had offered me one of her paintings. I only thought to take her up on her kind offer, while I visited with her and her family."

Eliza spoke up. "I explained that we never received his card, else my family might have remained at home to receive him." She could feel Grace studying her and saw her glance surreptitiously at her skirts for any rumpled sign of a dalliance with Magnus.

"I am sorry we were not at home to receive you, my lord," Aunt Letitia replied, somewhat unsteadily. "It is only by the grace of coincidence, *it seems,* that our Eliza was here."

"Will you not sit down, Lord Somerton?" Aunt Viola gestured to the chair beside the fire.

Eliza saw Magnus glance casually at the straining fabric beneath the painting.

"Uh . . . no thank ye. I was just leaving," he said most convincingly.

Aunt Letitia took one exasperated look at the wide canvas in Magnus's hands and shook her head. "Lord Somerton, you need not carry the painting through the damp streets. I shall have our footman come by with it on the morrow. Let me take it from you now and give it to him." She reached out and caught hold of one corner of the frame.

Magnus held fast to the painting—his shield from certain embarrassment, even as Aunt Letitia tried valiantly to tug it from his hands.

"My, such *large* . . . hands you have, my lord," Aunt Letitia quipped, casting a wry glance at Viola. "Do help me with the painting, Sister."

When Aunt Viola enthusiastically joined in the tug-of-war, Magnus turned to Eliza, his eyes pleading for assistance.

"Aunties, *please,*" Eliza pleaded as she gently pried her aunts' hands loose from the gilt frame. "Lord Somerton came here with the sole purpose of retrieving this painting."

The minute the women's fingers left the painting, Magnus lurched away from the two determined old ladies. "I am afraid I have already overstayed my welcome. I shall take my leave."

He turned to Eliza and manufactured a perfectly genteel smile. "I must thank ye again, Miss Merriweather, for gifting me with such an extraordinary painting. If ye do not object, I will take it home with me *now.*"

"Of course, Lord Somerton. Thank you so much for coming."

With the canvas pressed securely against his hips, Magnus bid farewell to the ladies, backed his way to the door, and made a swift departure.

"My, he left in quite a hurry, did he not?" Grace commented.

Eliza furrowed her brow. "He only came for the painting but obviously noted my fatigue and departed quickly so that I might rest." She turned and moved to the banked fire.

"Of course, dear. I am sure you are right," Aunt Viola replied, raising a gloved hand to conceal an all too discerning grin as she followed Letitia to the settee.

Grace moved shoulder-to-shoulder beside Eliza. "Thanks

to the rain and our early return, you have been saved from the stain of impropriety once more."

She leaned forward and took Eliza's shoulders and turned her to face her. "What will it take to make you see what damage your actions can wreak on this family?"

"I do apologize." Eliza removed Grace's hands and stepped away. "But I did not invite Lord Somerton here. He came of his own accord."

Aunt Letitia exhaled loudly. "There, you see, Grace? This was not some grand scheme hatched between his lordship and Eliza. She knew nothing of his plans to visit."

Grace eyed her doubtfully and Eliza prayed she would not reveal her "arrangement" to their aunts.

"Still you should know better than to ask a *bachelor* into the house when you are home alone." Angry red blotches erupted across Grace's cheeks.

"Calm yourself, Grace. You have worked yourself into strawberries again," Aunt Viola tittered.

"What?" Grace released Eliza and peered into the gilt-rimmed convex glass above the mantel.

In the reflection, Eliza watched her sister pat her finger pads across her splotched cheeks. A horrified expression contorted Grace's face a moment before she whirled around.

"My face! Do you see?" Grace whined to her aunts. "Do you see what she's done to my face?"

Aunt Letitia tapped her stick twice on the floor. "Grace, I assure you, no one is to blame for the blotches on your face. Go to your chamber, clothe yourself in something dry, and relax your nerves."

Grace shrieked with frustration then started for the door.

Eliza turned in behind her, attaching herself like a shadow. Aunt Letitia's cane suddenly shot between them, blocking Eliza's escape.

"Eliza, *you* will remain here. Sister and I will have a word with you."

Nodding her head, Eliza turned and sat down on the fireside chair. Inwardly, she cringed, quite aware that she deserved any punishment her aunts might levy upon her. As far as Society was concerned, her transgression was grievous to say the least.

But it was oh so wonderful too. Her body never felt so alive, even if a little sore. She felt heat begin to suffuse her face at the memory.

Her aunts took their places upon the sofa. Aunt Letitia began quietly. "I am greatly pleased that you have decided to put aside your plan to study art in Italy to pursue Lord Somerton. But, Eliza, what you did tonight was very, very risky."

Aunt Viola waved her hand. "Do not misunderstand, we do applaud your determination and ingenuity, dear."

Confusion knit Eliza's brows. "I am sorry, I do not know what you mean."

"Do not play coy with us, Lizzy," Aunt Letitia continued. "It is quite clear you consulted the rule book *again* and set out to use its strategies on your own."

Eliza cocked her head and a small laugh pushed through her teeth. "What ever gave you that idea, Auntie?"

"Why Rule Thirteen, of course," Aunt Viola replied softly.

"Rule Thirteen?" Eliza gulped.

Aunt Letitia rose and left the parlor, returning moments later with the scarlet rule book, much to Eliza's shocked dismay. Her aunt turned the brittle pages carefully, then lifted her lorgnette to her eyes and began to read the heavy black text at the top of the page. "*Use bait to draw him into secure ground. Here, his strengths can be compromised.*"

"You baited Lord Somerton with your offer of a painting, dove, did you not?" Aunt Viola's voice was soft and gentle.

"Oh, of course she did," Aunt Letitia broke in. "We

understand what you were trying to accomplish, gel, but you mustn't attempt these strategies alone. We must discuss the Rules before venturing into the field."

Aunt Letitia snapped the book closed and set it on the tea table, as Aunt Viola crossed the room to Eliza and placed her hand on her shoulder.

"In the future, please allow *us* to guide you." Aunt Letitia joined Viola and Eliza at the hearth. "Our experience with London Society is far greater than your own and you may benefit from our knowledge."

"Yes, Aunties." Eliza released the air pent in her lungs.

"Well, shall we also change our clothing?" Aunt Viola asked her sister. "Don't want to catch our death, you know."

"Quite right." Aunt Letitia lifted Eliza's chin with her index finger. "Chin up, Lizzy. Tonight was no loss. Why, if I read Lord Somerton's countenance correctly, you have him by the . . . *collar*." With that, the two aunts giggled and left the room, closing the door behind them.

Exhaling her relief, Eliza turned and moved to the mantel. She rested her elbows on its surface, then, laying her head on her arms, closed her eyes. She had somehow escaped the harsh reprimand she had feared was coming her way.

But what had she done? Why was she so powerless against his touch? One kiss was all it took. Once kiss and all thoughts of Italy were gone. All consideration for her family, banished. Her mind held only one thought. *Magnus*.

At the click of the door lock turning, Eliza lifted her head and gazed into the mirror. In the reflection, she saw Grace move behind her. Felt her sister's hands on her shoulders.

"Are you all right?"

Eliza turned to face her. "You are not angry anymore?"

"How could I be? Once I collected myself, I realized that you were in no state to react logically. That's why I intend to help you."

Eliza opened her mouth, fully intent on arguing that she needed no help at all, when she realized, to her great dismay, Grace was right. Utterly, right. When it came to Magnus, logic seemed to leap out the window . . . even if *he* wouldn't. "I don't know that anyone can help me now."

"That is where you are wrong, Sister." Grace wrapped her arm around Eliza's waist and led her to the sofa. Once seated, she took Eliza's hand. "The way I see it, you have but two *real* choices that will not end in this family's ruin."

Eliza cocked her head. "As many as that—two?"

"Yes," Grace said in a matter-of-fact manner. "Your first choice is to marry Lord Somerton of course."

Eliza came to her feet. "Does it not matter to you that he has not asked me to marry him?"

"Eliza, do not be daft. At least twice now, he has compromised you. It would not take much to convince the earl to do the honorable thing and marry you."

"We've had this discussion before. Despite his fanciful beliefs, marriage is an impossibility. I am virtually penniless. So, unless the worlds align in the heavens, he must marry a woman with a fine dowry. A woman who can help him save Somerton from the creditors."

"Then you have no other choice but to choose my second option. Stay away from him, for all of our sakes." Grace looked down and slowly drew a paper from the placket opening in her skirt. "Take this."

"What is it?" Eliza took the sheet and turned it over in her hand. It was a document of passage. She looked up at her sister for explanation.

"I used what money I had to secure passage for you to Italy."

Eliza was dumbfounded. "I—I cannot accept this."

"You can, and you will. The ship sails on the thirtieth day of July, evening tide."

"But Grace, the cost . . . you cannot afford to do this for me."

"I didn't do it for you alone. I did it for myself and our sister as well. Your leaving is the best course of action for you—and more importantly, for the family. Otherwise, at your current trot, it is only a matter of days before Society turns its back on us all forever."

"I see." It all made sense.

The only problem that remained, in Eliza's mind anyway, was avoiding Magnus until the thirtieth of July—and that was still a few weeks away. But she had to keep her distance. They had proven, on nearly every occasion, they could not be trusted alone. Not with dratted lustful impulses spurring them on.

"Mayhap, Eliza, with the billet of passage in your hand, and knowing you have an ally within the family, you will find it easier to avoid Lord Somerton until you set sail—or until he marries someone else, of course."

At those words, Eliza stared mutely at Grace.

"Eliza?"

"Marries someone *else,*" she repeated thoughtfully. "Yes, that's it." Abruptly, she yanked Grace into a tight hug, then released her and started for the door.

"Wait!" Grace reached out a hand. "Where are you going?"

Eliza glanced back over her shoulder and smiled brightly. "To the library—to find Lord Somerton a bride. *Tonight.*"

The spent candlewick dipped into the melted beeswax and began to sputter, forcing Eliza to accept her conclusion, as much as she was loathe to do it. She took once last look at the list of names she'd scratched off her foolscap sheet. Only one debutante's name remained. She cringed.

Sitting before her aunts' rosewood writing desk, Eliza matched her own observations of the season's most eligible debutantes with Magnus's list of desirable wifely attributes. And now, after two long hours, she had come to the unsettling conclusion that only one woman was perfectly suited: *Caroline Peacock.*

She was everything Magnus was hoping for: beautiful, charming, poised, intelligent, accomplished and cultured. But perhaps most important, she was rich. If Society gossip was to be believed, Miss Peacock's dowry alone was enough to wipe out Magnus's debts entirely.

Caroline Peacock had only two faults Eliza could ascertain: her social-climbing family and her personality. Neither of which seemed to concern Magnus. He would just have to resign himself to the fact that his late brother's betrothed, Miss Peacock, was the most logical solution to his dilemma. Besides, the chit's family *wanted* her to marry him for his position in Society. No other suited Magnus's situation so well.

Sliding back her chair, Eliza rose from the desk with a strangled whimper. Her course was clear.

On the morrow, at the Hamilton musicale, she would release Magnus from their arrangement after supplying him with the name of the debutante most suited to his financial, intellectual, and *physical* needs. Eliza swallowed the bitter taste of jealousy seething within her.

Her hands trembled as she folded the sheet and glanced down at the small square of foolscap in her hand. She was doing the right thing. What had to be done, for the good of her family . . . and Magnus.

If only it didn't hurt so much.

The next morning, though the sun had taken its mount in the sky only an hour earlier, Lloyd's Coffee House was abuzz with activity, the large wooden box-seats were already filled with merchants, bankers, and underwriters conducting the risky business of insuring ships and their cargoes.

Magnus had just entered the coffeehouse, determined to learn the status of *The Promise* when, all at once, the din of voices quieted. All eyes seemed to focus on a young man who'd entered the expansive chamber from the private Subscribers' room. Both gentlemen of wealth and of lesser means parted to let the man through.

"It's the Secretary to the Committee," Magnus heard one man whisper to another. "Heard this morn that Bennett was to post the new reports about the ships in the western lanes."

The Secretary tacked several long sheets to the wall, then turned and disappeared into the Subscribers' sanctum once more.

Immediately the crowd cinched around the postings. Shaky fingers ran down the lists of lost ships and scattered cries of anguish erupted from the crowd.

Magnus hesitantly made his way through the group of investors. Leaning over the squat gentleman in front of him, he ran two fingers down one list, then another. And another. Nothing.

He pored over the intelligence posting from agents in the West Indies. Again, nothing. Not one mention of *The Promise*. With a growl, he tore the last list from the wall and swept the carefully penned column with his gaze.

A senior waiter, who'd obviously observed his frustration, stepped forward and carefully wrested the posting from him. "Might I be of some assistance, sir?"

Magnus glanced up at the young man, but found his mouth dry and wordless.

"You can check the Arrival and Losses Book for more information," the waiter told him, gesturing to a large green vellum volume perched on a wide podium. "If the ship's insured against any sort of loss, it will be listed there. And what ship isn't these days, eh?"

Dropping a few shillings into the waiter's ready hand, Magnus silently moved to the podium. There he stood for more than an hour, devouring its pages for any sign of his ship. Still, there was nothing. Not a single mention of *The Promise*.

He beckoned the young waiter. "Is there any other place a ship might be listed?"

"No, sir. Everything is recorded in *The Book*." The waiter tapped a finger on the thick volume. "The ship, my lord, she *was* insured?"

"Of course—" he started, but then the young man's question slapped Magnus coldly, halting any further utterance.

Was it possible Lambeth had lied about the voyage being underwritten? Forged the documents? Magnus felt the blood drain from his face. He gripped the podium, steadying himself. *Nay, it canna be.*

"Are you well, sir? Can I find you a chair or some brandy, perhaps?"

A mingling of anger and a sense of betrayal welled up inside Magnus. With a trembling hand, he dug inside his pocket and withdrew a guinea for the waiter. Then, he tugged at his coat sleeves and dragged himself to the staircase.

He would go straight to the Import Docks. He had to find Lambeth. Had to know for sure.

But in his heart he already knew the terrible truth of it.

The Promise, awash in the largest storm of the year, had not been insured.

Seething with anger and the pain of his friend's betrayal, Magnus slammed open Lambeth's dockside office door.

Lambeth's head whipped round and he leapt to his feet. "Good God, Somerton!"

As their eyes met and the full brunt of Magnus's fury registered with Lambeth, the ruddy color of his face faded to lime white.

"What brings you here so early?" Lambeth stammered. He leaned casually against his desk, though his fingers twitched.

"I think ye know the answer to that," Magnus growled, shoving a ladderback chair aside. "I've spent the morning at Lloyd's going through *The Book,* reading the intelligence reports."

"Have you now?"

"Dinna dally with me. *The Promise,* was she insured?"

Lambeth lowered his head.

"Answer me!"

"She was. When I sold you the shares *she was*."

Magnus moved toward the desk. "What do ye mean? Either the ship and her cargo are insured, or not."

Lambeth closed his lids for a moment, then lifted them and looked into Magnus's eyes. "Four underwriters insured her for the voyage. Four. But when later they learned who my father was, they cancelled the insurance."

"You told me your father was innocent."

"What did you expect me to say? That my da was guilty as the day is long?" He paused then and let his gaze trail across his desk. "He did it. He sank his own ship, and her worthless cargo, to collect from Lloyd's. He made a fraudulent claim. Though they could never prove it, they knew. *They knew.*"

Dumb with shock, Magnus stared at Lambeth for some moments before finding words. "Why didna ye admit it to Dunsford and me? We might have used our influence to change the underwriters' minds," he managed at last.

Lambeth looked into Magnus's eyes. His voice grew thin. "I had hoped that a group of underwriters in Edinburgh could insure her. But Lloyd's intelligence web is too tight. All the underwriters knew about my father." He collapsed into his chair.

Magnus exhaled until his lungs burned from lack of air. He returned to the door and closed it behind him, using the time the small task afforded to calm himself. He leaned back against the door, casting his gaze through the small window to a ship settled in the basin beyond. "And *The Promise*?"

"There's been no word from any of the ports. No sightings of her by any of the captains. She's missing, Somerton." Lambeth drew a bottle of brandy from his desk, along with two glasses, which he filled with luminous amber liquid. He held a glass out to Magnus.

Magnus drained the glass, then took the other glass and drank that too. Lambeth filled the glasses again and stared back at him, as if waiting for a response.

Magnus shoved his hands through his hair. "We're ruined."

"Nothing is for certain, Somerton."

Magnus sighed. "And the sun mightn't rise in the morn either."

"Listen, I haven't told Dunsford yet. Please, don't inform him about the insurance. Not yet. I know I can salvage our situation. I just need some time . . . a few days at most," Lambeth pleaded. "After all, there is no evidence that she is lost yet. I can come up with something. I know I can."

Magnus looked up at Lambeth and shook his head. He came to his feet, snatched the bottle of brandy from him, and opened the door.

"Please, just a little more time," Lambeth begged, as Magnus turned and walked through the warehouse to the docks.

Magnus wandered down the wharf and slowly climbed into his waiting hackney cab. *He was ruined.*

"Where can I take ye, guv'nor?" the driver called out.

Without thinking, he responded. "Seventeen Hanover Square."

He had to see Eliza.

Rule Fourteen

Do not dwell in desolate ground.

Eliza pressed her palm against the cool rippled glass and gazed at the sky above. Low ashen clouds blanketed the city, heavy with droplets primed to fall at the slightest provocation. In all her life, she never could abide a morn so dreary, but today it befitted her mood.

Her hand slid from the glass and wearily she settled herself in the chair beside the smoldering coal fire, lifting the delicate china teacup to her lips.

Her eyelids were throbbing and sore, no doubt swollen, after a night spent agonizing over what she must do this eve—say good-bye to Magnus forever. How would she bear it? Not only must she see him and Caroline together, but be the instrument of their engagement. Mrs. Peacock would be most pleased. At last the selfish hag would have everything she wanted: a title for her merchant-class family.

But Magnus would have to endure both Caroline *and* her horrid mother. *Dreadful.* Eliza was beginning to feel sorrier for Magnus than for herself.

"Miss Merriweather?"

Eliza glanced up, quite startled to see the butler standing before her. "Oh, Edgar. I'm sorry. What were you saying?"

"You have a visitor, miss."

Eliza waved the idea away. "Please tell whoever it is I am not—"

Magnus stepped into the library and dropped back his head against the door. He was pale, his face drawn, and his body drooped as though it took his every effort to stand.

"Magnus!" Eliza sprung from her chair and rushed to him. "Are you ill? What happened?" Taking his arm, she led him to the sofa and bade him sit.

"Edgar, some strong tea. Quickly please."

Magnus lifted his head and looked into Eliza's eyes. The despair she saw in them seized her heart.

"What happened? Tell me."

He shook his head from side to side then allowed his chin to drop to his chest. "I'm all right. Really."

Eliza sniffed the air. The scent of alcohol was plain. "You've been drinking this morn."

He nodded. "My ship. *Missing*. Wasna insured."

"What? Please, explain from the beginning."

Magnus flung his head back against the headrest, covering his face with his palms. "*The Promise*. She wasna insured," he said, letting his hands slide from his cheeks to slap atop his thighs. "I've lost everything. *Everything*."

"No insurance at all? How can that be?"

Magnus swallowed deeply and explained about Lambeth's father and the loss of the underwriters' confidence. "So there ye have it. Nearly every coin I had left sailed with *The Promise*."

Eliza sat with her hands folded primly in her lap. It pained her to restrain her feelings, when all she wanted to do was hold Magnus to her breast, kiss him and comfort him.

"When will the creditors call the loan?" she hesitantly asked, not truly sure if she wanted to know the answer.

"At the end of the season."

"Is there naught you can do to delay payment?"

"Tried that." Magnus shook his head slowly. "Nay, I will lose everything . . . in less than a month."

"What about your town house, here, in London? Surely they cannot cast you out." Her words were tinged with the alarm she felt.

"Aye, they can. When the time comes, the town house will be sold. 'Twill *all* be sold. All I'll have left is the wee cottage on Skye that me mother left me. Everything else . . . will be gone."

Eliza swallowed hard. There was a frightening finality about his words. An acceptance.

Slowly, she rose and moved toward the highly polished desk in the corner of the room. Sucking her lips into her mouth, Eliza forced a reluctant hand to slide open the small, right-hand drawer. She reached inside and tentatively withdrew the square of foolscap she'd prepared the night before.

When at last she turned and started toward him, her legs felt inordinately heavy, as though they were shackled in weighty irons. Oh, that she did not have to do this. Not now, when Magnus was broken, at his lowest.

She lifted the paper to Magnus. "Take this," she said, her words dripping from her lips in not more than a whisper.

Magnus looked up at her, utterly confused. He bent the foolscap from its folds then read the single name inscribed upon it. "Caroline Peacock?"

"Our arrangement," she answered softly. "I have investigated the season's debutantes—as you requested."

"I dinna understand."

"*She* is the one. The one you must marry. The one who can save you from ruin."

Magnus rose. "But Eliza—"

Eliza lifted her chin, willing herself the courage to stand firm. "She possesses everything you desire in a wife. She is intelligent, beautiful, charming, and poised—"

Magnus was upon her in an instant. He grasped her shoulders and forced Eliza to look at him. "But she isn't *Eliza Merriweather*."

"Miss Peacock is also quite rich. Something I am not. You must marry her before it is too late to save Somerton."

"How can ye say this after last eve? I thought—"

"What?" She raised her chin in false nonchalance.

"Why, that ye loved me."

How she wanted to cry. Here Magnus stood before her, baring his soul to her. But she could not back down now. Summoning every ounce of strength within her, Eliza shook her head, driving an icy blade of lies into his heart.

Stunned, Magnus let his hands fall away from her shoulders.

Eliza turned away. She couldn't bear to look at the shock and pain in his eyes any longer. She was breaking his heart, along with her own.

Magnus moved behind her and hugged her back against him. "I love ye, Eliza. And I know ye love me."

Her anguish peaked, and Eliza grappled for her last shred of control. For a brief moment, she closed her eyes and savored the warmth of him, knowing all the while it was wrong.

She drew in a deep breath.

"No. You are quite mistaken." She turned within his arms until she faced him. "Yes, I am attracted to you. I do not deny that that much is true. But love?" She shook her head, unable to deny her heart aloud.

Magnus released her. "I dinna believe ye."

"No? Do you need proof?" Eliza whirled and returned to

the desk. Fumbling in its drawers she withdrew her billet of passage and thrust it into his hand. "Go ahead. Look at it."

Magnus turned the document over in his hands. "Passage to *Italy*." He looked up at her, disbelief plain on his face.

"At the end of the season I am leaving London to study art. I never changed my intentions. Nothing has changed. *Nothing*." Plucking the ticket from his fingers, she crammed it back into its drawer.

"Marry Miss Peacock, Magnus, or do not," she told him as she stared blindly at the innards of the desk. "But do not allow your mistaken beliefs about my feelings pollute your decision."

Eliza heard Edgar's distinctive shuffle, could smell the tea he'd brought them. She heard the clink of cups as the butler placed the tray on the table. "No thank you, Edgar," Eliza said, at last turning her gaze to Magnus. "Lord Somerton is leaving."

Magnus stared at her. But it was more than that. He studied her, making Eliza highly aware of every move. She knew that she had to remain in control. That she mustn't let him see into her heart.

"You do not want the tea, Miss?" Edgar said, notably confused. "But you asked me to fetch some for you. Mrs. Penny was at the market, so I made it myself . . . because you asked for it. I assure you it is quite good."

She could feel dampness in her lashes and knew her grasp on composure was slipping. "That will be all, Edgar. Thank you."

"So, shall I retrieve the tray, or will you take your tea after all?"

"Oh, for heavens sake, Edgar, *leave the tea*. I shall be delighted to take a cup," Eliza said. As she watched Edgar scuffle from the room, she felt an errant tear splash on her cheek. She wiped it away with the back of her hand, then looked back at Magnus, bit the inside of her cheek and schooled her features. She said nothing more. Could not. Instead, she raised her hand and gestured to the door.

Almost mechanically, Magnus turned and slowly walked from the room. He did not look back.

The click of the closing front door drew Aunt Letitia and Aunt Viola. From either side of the doorway, they peeked into the library.

"Was that Lord Somerton, dear?" Aunt Viola asked with some trepidation.

"Yes, it was." Already Eliza's strength drained from her limbs. Her head felt as heavy as her heart.

In the next moment, she collapsed against the desk and slid down its polished side to the floor. She rested her forehead against its upper drawer.

"Oh my!" Aunt Viola gasped. "Edgar, help us, please."

Together, Edgar and the two old women lifted Eliza to her feet and drew her to the sofa. Eliza felt Aunt Viola's thin hand stroke her hair, whilst Aunt Letitia's fleshier palm patted her hand, in useless efforts to comfort her.

"What happened, dear?" Aunt Viola asked.

"Yes, we thought things were going so swimmingly between you and Lord Somerton," Aunt Letitia added.

Eliza shook her head, forcing her words through her growing sobs. "It—it is *over* between us."

Aunt Viola's gaze locked with her sister's, then returned to Eliza. "But why, dove? Mayhap we can help."

The offer jolted Eliza to her feet. "*No!*" Taking the lace-trimmed handkerchief Aunt Letitia held out, Eliza wiped her tears away. "Please. You have done enough. Lord Somerton and I are a match not meant to be." Turning, Eliza rushed from the room for the sanctuary of her bedchamber.

Letitia followed Eliza out the door and watched her ascend the stairs. She shook her head in deep disappointment, then returned to the shelves and drew down the heavy red-leather volume. She laid it open on the table before her sister.

"We certainly have our work cut out for us now, Viola."

"But Eliza refused our offer to help."

Letitia seated herself beside her sister, blowing air through her lips like a hackney mare at sundown. "Pish posh! If ever a body was screaming for help, it is our Eliza. She is simply too proud to ask for it."

Viola nodded her head in agreement, slowly at first, then with more vigor as she took to the idea. "I believe you are right, Letitia."

Letitia puffed out her chest. "Of course I am. Have I ever steered us wrong, Sister?"

"Well, I remember once—"

Letitia lifted a stern brow, daring her sister to finish her sentence.

Viola lowered her gaze. "No, dear. Never once."

"Well then, shall we begin? We've much to do if we want to reverse this dreadful situation."

Lifting her lorgnette, Viola raised the scarlet ribbon that marked the next chapter in the *Rules of Engagement* and touched the bold black words at the top of the page.

Together, Letitia and Viola read silently, then simultaneously looked up from the volume.

"Brilliant, is it not, Sister?" Letitia exclaimed.

"Simply inspired!" Viola chortled.

Clasping each other's hands with the excitement of the next strategy, the coconspirators giggled softly.

Magnus emerged from the Featherton household, yanking the brass door handle with enough force to send the knocker double-beating against the closed door. *She lied.* Eliza had lied and he damn well knew it.

His uncle's footman opened the carriage's cabin door for Magnus. Instead of boarding, however, Magnus turned and headed down the flag way, preferring the sobering effect of the cool rain to the shelter of the carriage.

Christ, he'd lost his ship, and now it seemed he'd also lost all chances to be with the one woman he loved.

The rain grew heavier, but instead of retreating to the carriage, which stealthily shadowed him in the distance, Magnus lengthened his stride. He needed to walk, to clear his mind. To block out the maddening din of his life crashing down about him.

In his heart, he knew full well why Eliza had lied about her feelings for him. She sought to be noble. To release him, so that he might do what he must to save Somerton and her people. But this knowledge did nothing to quell the aching of his heart.

As Magnus walked, the driving rain sent channels of water trickling beneath his collar, chilling his skin and irritating him all the more. But he walked on. He had to do something to right his world. He must.

He could no longer count on his ship to refill his family coffers. What choice had he now?

As logical as it seemed, to him and everyone else, he'd *not* marry the wealthy Miss Caroline Peacock. He was through making amends for his brother's mistakes and he'd be damned if he'd relegate himself to a life of misery to atone for his brother's greed and the havoc it wreaked on Somerton.

Not when he loved another. There was only woman he would marry, if she would have him. One hardheaded, over-chivalrous woman. *Eliza.*

A new determination steeled him. He'd do whatever it took to make Eliza his own.

He turned around and when he reached the carriage,

threw open its door. In the gray light Lambeth's half-bottle of brandy glistened on the seat cushion. He snatched it up and opened it, eager to ease the twinge in his heart. Holding the bottle before his eyes, he stared at it as the rain splashed down upon its torn label. *Nay. Not this way.*

He raised his other hand and pinched the inner corners of his eyes. Drink had plagued his family for two generations. It had stripped away everything he'd ever given a damn about. Destroyed his father. His brother.

He wouldn't let it destroy him too.

Opening his fingers, he let the bottle roll from his wet hand. It smashed on the road, its sweet, damning essence trickling through the glinting glass into the gutter.

Dragging a gulp of air into his lungs, Magnus stepped into the carriage and closed the door. He knew what he must do.

For eight days more the rain continued to fall, draping the whole of London in its heavy gray shroud.

With an ache in her breast, Eliza draped a swathe of snowy linen over Magnus's portrait and readied herself to leave the house. She gave not a care to the drips of paint at her sleeves or to her mussed hair. For days she'd worked from first light until dusk, before lighting candles to work by their glow late into the night. She was near complete exhaustion, but today, at long last, her half of their "arrangement" was fulfilled.

The portrait was ready and must be delivered to Magnus this very hour. She could not bear the heartache of looking at it, at *him,* any longer.

Grace watched Eliza, her brows drawn close with growing suspicion. "Where do you think you're going?" Grace, who was always light of foot, flung her body against the door, blocking Eliza's escape.

"Grace, please step aside."

"You are taking the portrait to *him,* aren't you?"

Eliza balanced the painting against her hip and tried to nudge her sister out of the way. "This is none of your concern."

Grace stood firm, "Oh, but it is, Sister. It is of concern to all of us. Hawksmoor and I are on firm footing once more, now that he's returned from Dunley Parish, and I'll not allow you to ruin things for me."

"So you've seen each other."

"Yes, he came to the house. Not that you would have noticed, what with your eyes affixed to the canvas for days at a time."

Eliza softened her gaze. "Oh, Grace, I am pleased you have rekindled your relationship with Hawksmoor. For I must admit, I have been desperate to learn who was the woman at the theater with him."

Her sister shifted her gaze to the hem of her gown. "I—I didn't want to upset him, so I . . . didn't ask."

"You didn't ask?" Eliza slid a hand along the door until her fingers caught the lock.

Grace's palm slapped down on Eliza's hand before she could turn the lock. "Oh, no you don't! How horrid you are to try to distract me."

"Grace, *move* out of my way, please."

"Aunties, come at once!" Grace shouted. "Eliza is—"

Eliza quickly cupped her hand over Grace's mouth to stifle her alert.

A stampede of tapping canes and footfalls rolled off the passageway walls. The moment her aunts arrived, Grace warned them of Eliza's intent.

Aunt Letitia lifted her quizzing glass and studied Eliza. "Is this so, gel? Are you heading off to see Lord Somerton?"

Aunt Viola began to fan herself with her handkerchief.

"Oh, dear. What a commotion this will cause within our ranks. Someone is sure to take notice and she will be ruined beyond repair."

"Really now, Viola. Calm yourself." Aunt Letitia turned her eyeglass from her sister to Eliza. "It will cause no commotion because Eliza is not going *anywhere*."

Eliza lifted her chin. "I *am* going. For over a week, I've painted all day and night to finish this portrait of Lord Somerton. And I am going to give it to him."

"She is using this as an excuse to see him again," Grace informed her aunts.

Eliza swung round to look at her. "I am simply fulfilling my promise to him."

"Is that the truth, gel? Are you sure of that?" Aunt Letitia asked.

Eliza nodded. At least, she thought that's what she was doing. Or was Grace voicing the truth of the matter?

"Well then," Aunt Letitia continued. "You will not mind if I send Edgar to deliver the portrait. A unmarried woman cannot be seen visiting a bachelor at home. It is not done."

Eliza glanced at the portrait in her hands. Of course she was using the promise of the painting to see Magnus again. In her heart she could not forgive herself for what she had said to him. For the lies she had told him. Even though it was what had to be done for the good of everyone.

The next thing she knew, Edgar snatched the painting from her hands.

"I shall take great care of it, Miss Merriweather," Edgar told her. "I will deliver it directly into Lord Somerton's hands myself."

"Very good, Edgar," Aunt Viola said. She hugged Eliza to her. "You could not have gone to his home. This is the right thing to do, child, even if it hurts."

"I know, Auntie," Eliza murmured. "I know."

* * *

Eliza paced the floor for more than an hour, stopping to search for Edgar through the window every few moments.

Grace lounged on the sofa, rolling her eyes. "Oh, do sit down, Eliza."

Turning to her sister, Eliza glared. "I have done what you have asked of me. I have broken my bond with Lord Somerton. I would think you would be somewhat appreciative."

Grace snorted and looked into the cold hearth. At that moment, the door opened and Edgar entered the parlor.

Eliza raced to him. "Did you see him? How was he?"

"Please, Edgar. Do tell us what happened," Aunt Letitia urged. "We want your every impression. Leave nothing out."

The manservant turned to Eliza. "Lord Somerton was grateful for the painting, Miss, but it seemed he was saddened by it as well."

Eliza sat down and pressed a quaking hand to her chest.

"He's fallen on hard times, I'd wager, for Mr. Christie, the younger, from the auction house was there. His man was taking inventory of Lord Somerton's household."

Eliza looked up at Edgar, confused. "Inventory?"

"Yes," Edgar replied. "It seems that Mr. Christie will be auctioning off Lord Somerton's possessions in two day's time. A *property* auction, I heard him say."

Aunt Letitia's facial muscles fell and she turned a hard eye on Eliza. "Somerton's possessions up for auction? What is this all about, Lizzy?"

"His situation must be far worse than I imagined," Eliza softly murmured to herself.

"Well, if you won't tell them, Eliza, I shall." Grace folded her arms at her chest and waited but a moment before sharing with her aunts all the details of Magnus's financial downfall. "So there you have it. Somerton cannot marry Eliza without losing everything."

At once, Aunt Viola caned her way to Eliza's side. "Oh, you poor, poor dear. No wonder you've been so out of sorts. Why did you not come to us?"

Eliza looked slowly up at her aunt. "Because there was nothing you could do to change his fate. He must marry Caroline Peacock for her dowry or forfeit his home . . . his family's history."

Aunt Viola laid a gentle hand on Eliza's shoulder. "But he loves *you*."

Aunt Letitia nodded, sending her double chin bobbing. "Of course he does, and Lizzy loves him as well, no matter what she claims. So it's just lack of funds that stands between the two of you and the altar, is it gel? That's nothing. Sister and I can assist there."

Eliza stared blankly out the window. "He's too proud. He'd never allow it."

A puzzled look twisted Aunt Viola's normally placid features. "But not so proud as he would condescend to marry for money? That hardly sounds like our Lord Somerton."

Eliza exhaled. "H-he has not accepted the idea, despite Mr. Pender's and my own urgings. But he will. He must. He hasn't much time."

Aunt Letitia remained quiet for a long moment, then turned to Edgar. "Was there anything else you noticed while you were there—something perhaps that might help us understand Somerton's current state of mind?"

Edgar shook his head as he thought about it, then his eyes brightened suddenly. "Oh, there was something. Mr. Christie showed great interest in the portrait I brought, as well as the landscape Miss Merriweather gave Lord Somerton earlier. But the earl would not let Christie near them. He told the auctioneer that everything else in the house could be sold, but not the paintings."

"He wouldn't sell my paintings," Eliza repeated to herself. A sad smile played on her lips.

"Mr. Christie was none too happy about that," Edgar added. "He told Lord Somerton that the paintings were superb and would fetch a goodly sum."

Aunt Viola clapped her hands. "Well, now. Isn't it lovely to know your paintings are held in such high esteem by an expert, Eliza?"

Eliza barely heard her. Magnus was selling off the contents of his house. Why would he do such a drastic thing if he planned to marry Caroline? A marriage to Miss Peacock would make the sale of his property unnecessary.

No, he has another plan. Mayhap there was chance for them after all. Eliza leapt to her feet. If Magnus was selling the contents of his home, no matter the reason, he was in immediate need of funds. And she was now in a position to make sure he had it—if the auctioneer was correct, of course, and her paintings would sell.

Well, there was only one way to find out. She would contact Mr. Christie on the morrow.

Rule Fifteen

Agitation breeds motivation to engage.

Since Mr. Christie had been unable to assess her paintings within the privacy of her aunts' home that morning, Eliza decided to tote her canvases to Christie's auction house herself. If Magnus was in need of money, for whatever reason, she could ill afford to wait.

Eliza was much pleased and admittedly a little surprised when, upon hearing her name, the desk agent had ushered her family directly into Mr. Christie's private office for an immediate portfolio review.

"Honestly, Miss Merriweather, I had no idea that Lord Somerton's paintings were created by a . . . woman. The use of color is so bold, the expression so daring," Mr. Christie admitted, stopping to study each of her seven paintings in turn. "Simply amazing," he uttered beneath his breath.

Eliza bristled, but held her acid retort between her teeth. This opportunity was too important. She would not dash it simply to set Mr. Christie straight about the equal abilities of women. Instead, she trained her gaze on the collection of small bronze sculptures shelved behind his highly polished cherry desk.

But then, Mr. Christie glanced up from the third canvas, and moved silently on to the fourth, a painting Eliza especially loved.

She knew Christie would see only a simple landscape. But to her, it was much more. For in that eddy of color, she'd captured a moment—a time before tragedy touched her family. A day when sunlight blinked upon the river and set fire to yellow-leafed poplars that bounded their orchard in Dunley Parish. A day when her sisters, instead of picking the heavy fruit as their mother had bade them, swung merrily from the scaffold branches of the apple trees, which stood like soldiers, straight and tall, in four perfect rows. The memory brought an ache in her chest so great that she could hardly breathe.

This was her life she was offering him. Her past as well as her future. For without the paintings, her plans for Italy were forfeit. No master would accept an apprentice, let alone a female, without a portfolio to recommend her. Eliza looked sadly at her paintings. It would take years upon years to build another of similar quality. But she would do it.

Grace took Eliza's arm and drew her aside. "You worked for years on these. These canvases mean everything to you," she whispered. "Think about what you are sacrificing. Are you sure you want to do this?"

"Yes. I want to do this . . . for Magnus." Eliza patted her sister's hand but dared not look at her. If she did, she feared the tears dammed behind her lower lids would fall unbidden.

Grace trembled, then swallowed hard. The words that came next were thin and ragged. "I . . . didn't know, Eliza. I'm so sorry. I didn't know how much you loved him."

A single tear fell from Eliza's eye. She wiped it away with the back of her hand and refocused her gaze on Mr. Christie.

Aunt Letitia grimaced at Mr. Christie's delay in coming

to a decision. She clapped her hands loudly, startling him into granting her his full consideration. "Are you interested in my niece's work, or are you not?" Her booming voice startled Christie. "There are others who have expressed interest, you know."

Eliza cringed at her aunt's bold lie.

Mr. Christie's eyes widened. "Err . . . yes. I want them all." He glanced at the collection leaning on the wall before him. "Yes," he purred with delight. "I want every last one of them." His gaze flitted over the paintings, before returning to Aunt Letitia. "Though taking them on in this way may be somewhat unorthodox, I can assure you, my lady, I shall have no difficulty selling them."

Within the next quarter hour, Eliza found herself surrounded by oversized ledgers, documents, and receipts, all of which she was instructed to sign. In the end, she had quite literally written away her life, or her hand's record of it at any rate, for, with a few strokes of ink, she had relinquished her paintings to Mr. Christie.

"Thank you, good sir," Eliza said to Mr. Christie when the formalities of consignment were concluded. "But I wonder, would you be so kind as to see that the funds from the sale of my paintings are included with those from Lord Somerton's property—secretly?"

Christie leveled his steely gaze at her, and the look in his eye told her that her request was well outside the bounds of propriety.

"I do not wish to impinge on your generosity in accepting my paintings," Eliza began again, "but my family is greatly indebted to Lord Somerton. Still, despite his unfortunate financial state, he is not inclined to allow us to repay him."

From the corner of her eye, Eliza saw Aunt Letitia's right brow raise and her ruby lips lift as she realized the ruse.

A gleam lit Grace's eyes and she stepped up to Mr. Christie. "Dearest sir, what my sister is trying to say is that this may be our only chance to repay Lord Somerton and restore our family honor." Brazenly, she reached out her gloved hand and laid it on his arm, while pushing her pink cherub lips into a little pout. "Please, Mr. Christie. This means a great deal to my family . . . and to *me*."

Mr. Christie smiled at her and patted her hand. "A matter of honor, you say?"

Grace widened her cornflower blue eyes and nodded.

Mr. Christie looked from Grace and Eliza to their two aunts who stared back at him, completely entranced by their nieces' performances.

"Very well then. The funds shall be included in Somerton's account," he replied without asking for further explanation. After taking over the auction house from his father, Mr. Christie, the younger, appeared a shrewd and prudent businessman with enough sense to know the value of propriety . . . as well as the appreciation of a pretty woman.

Aunt Viola linked Grace's arm. "Shall we be off then?"

Eliza gave her beloved paintings one last lingering look. She stared hard at them, desperately trying to record their every detail in her memory, but she knew it was useless.

Her eyes stung as she straightened her shoulders, turned and followed her aunts out the door to Pall Mall where their town carriage awaited.

Her aunts having already taken their seats inside, Eliza had just lifted her hem to board when Grace shoved in front of her and scrambled into the cab, forgoing any assistance from the footman.

"Grace!" Eliza snapped, climbing aboard and seating herself beside her sister. "What was that was all about?"

As the footman closed the door, Grace leaned forward,

yanked the carriage's dusty curtains closed, and poked her finger toward the building outside. "It's *him*."

Eliza perked up. "Lord Somerton?"

"No, it's Mr. Dabney." When everyone simply stared at Grace blankly, she added, "George Dabney. From the Hogarts' dinner party? You remember."

Understanding finally dawned on Eliza. "Oh, the *boor*."

"Yes, the singularly most tiresome man I have ever met," Grace said, crouching low in her seat.

Aunt Viola waved a finger at Grace. "He is the son of a baronet, you know, dear. You could do worse."

"*That*, I sincerely doubt," Grace croaked out of the side of her mouth. "Eliza, take a look, will you? See if he's still there."

Eliza exhaled in annoyance at her sister's overreaction to a chance encounter. She was hardly in the mood to act as her sister's spy, but being in need of a distraction from her melancholy thoughts, Eliza lifted the corner of the curtain and peered outward. "He must have gone inside the auction house. It appears you are safe." She looked at her sister. "Why do you suppose he is here?"

"I do not know, nor do I have any intention of remaining long enough to find out." Inching upward, Grace rapped her fist on the cab wall. The carriage lurched forward and started down the bumpy road, sending them swaying to and fro like laundry line birds on a windy day.

Aunt Letitia's blue eyes sparkled with excitement. "Is Mr. Dabney still pursuing your affections, Grace?"

"Not of late, but I will not risk it. I've set my cap for Lord Hawksmoor and it would not do for him to hear of another vying for my attention," Grace replied.

"I do not know if I agree with your thinking," Aunt Letitia said, mirroring Viola's growing smile. "It seems to me that a jealous bachelor could quickly become a most motivated bridegroom."

Eliza exchanged nervous glances with Grace, then dropped her head back against the headrest and exhaled the contents of her lungs. It was all too clear. Their aunts were up to their chins in something.

"What the deuce?" Pender stood dumbfounded in the passageway of Magnus's town house, looking into the barren parlor. "Have we been robbed?"

Magnus, hearing his uncle's strained voice, met him at the doorway. He'd dreaded his uncle's return from Devonshire all morn.

"No, old fellow. Sold the furniture and the frippery. Had no need for it."

Pender turned his bulging eyes up to Magnus. "Had no need for it? Are you mad? What the blazes are we to sit upon?"

"There is a chair in the corner, should ye need one."

"A *chair*? Is that all?" Suddenly his uncle's face went blank and he started for the stairway. Magnus's hand shot out and caught Pender's shoulder before he made the first tread.

"No need to fash, Uncle. Everything in yer chamber is as ye left it. I only sold what was mine."

Pender's lips fluttered, but he spoke not a word. Instead he walked through the house, gasping as he passed through each empty room.

"Come sit down in the library, Uncle. Left yer desk and chair there."

Pender dumbly allowed Magnus to lead him into the library where he sat down at the chair behind the desk. "Oh, the books. *All* the books," he mourned. "Why, Somerton?

Why did you do it? You still have weeks before the loan is called."

"Aye. I do."

"Is that not plenty of time to convince Miss Peacock to marry?"

"Aye, it would be. If that is what I planned to do." Magnus lifted his leg and sat on the corner of the desk.

"You aren't still banking on the notion that your ship will come into port in time?"

"Nay."

Pender flung out his hands. "Then why, boy, in the name of all that is holy are you selling off your possessions?"

Magnus exhaled a long sigh. "To help Somerton's crofters."

"You cannot be serious."

"I canna save the land or the hall, but I can save her people. When Somerton is sold to pay my brother's debts, I have no doubt that they'll be cast out of their homes with the Clearances to make room for bluidy sheep. Where will they go, Uncle? What will they do, when Somerton is all they've known?"

"They will go elsewhere. They'll have no choice," Pender said sternly. "Can't expect to have everything in life handed to them, you know."

"Which is why I've sold what I could. When Somerton is auctioned off, as it surely will be, they will be able to use what little money I have raised to reestablish themselves."

Pender's eyes widened. "Make a bit of blunt from the sale did you?"

Magnus nodded. "A bit. More than I'd expected at any rate. Still, not nearly enough to cover the debts."

Pender slapped his hands to his knees and stood. "You are making this much harder than it needs to be. Marry Miss Peacock and save Somerton—all of it!"

"I canna."

"Why? Do tell me that?" Pender tilted his head back and looked down his long nose at Magnus. "It's not that Merriweather gel is it?"

Magnus came to his feet and looked down on his uncle. "It is. And I'd be verra careful about the next words that come from yer lips. For if I have my way, Miss Merriweather will soon become my wife. For I'd rather live penniless with the woman I love, than as a king with Miss Peacock."

"Gorblimey." Pender withered into the chair once more. "We're in it now."

Later that balmy evening, there was a knock at the Featherton door.

Within a moment, Edgar entered the dining room where the family was just finishing their afternoon meal. Grace's eyes brightened in anticipation of a note from Lord Hawksmoor, who'd recently begun to call each evening without fail.

"Miss Merriweather, for you," he announced, extending toward Eliza a silver tray with a letter upon it.

Eliza tentatively took the letter and held it in her hands, not daring to open it right away. She was too conflicted, wanting with all her heart for the letter to be from Magnus. Hoping, too, that it wasn't.

"Who is it from?" Grace's tone was tight with the disappointment that the note had not been for her.

"I do not know." Eliza turned the letter over and saw the letter *C* impressed in the wax wafer seal. The letter was not from Magnus, and the disappointment sent a painful jolt through her. Breaking open the brittle crimson wax, Eliza unfolded the letter and began to read. She could scarce believe her eyes.

It was incredible. No, *impossible*. She tried to swallow, but a sudden dryness tickled her throat causing her to cough. Slapping a hand to her chest, she leapt from her chair.

Aunt Letitia's eyes went wide with alarm and she rushed to her. Balling her plump hand into a fist, she pounded Eliza's back with all her might.

"Ah!" Eliza managed between coughs. She tried to wave her aunt off, but nothing stopped Letitia's enthusiastic hammering.

"Heavens, Grace. Fetch Eliza a beverage," Aunt Viola pleaded, "before Letitia pounds the poor child flat."

Grace seized a decanter from the sideboard and hastily filled a crystal. Whirling around, she pressed a glass of claret into Eliza's hand, then reached out to still Aunt Letitia's eager fist.

Eliza tipped the glass to her lips and drained it completely. The elixir worked its magic, instantly soothing her throat. "My thanks," she said to Grace, testing her voice.

"Now," said Grace. "What, pray tell, is in that letter that worked you into such a fit?

"M-my paintings," she said, still gasping for air. "They've *all* been sold—to a single patron, no less."

"So soon too. That is good news!" Aunt Viola exclaimed.

Eliza steepled her fingers over her lips. "The news grows better."

A smirk formed on Grace's lips. "What? A wealthy bachelor bought them, and now he wants to wed the artist?" Grace said, feigning sincerity.

Aunt Letitia pinched the flesh of Grace's upper arm.

"Ouch!"

"Hush, gel, just let her speak!" Letitia turned back to Eliza. "Go on. I cannot endure the suspense any longer."

Eliza bounced on her toes. "They've been sold—for five thousand pounds!"

"How marvelous!" the aunts squealed together.

"Do not keep us in suspense, dear," Aunt Viola cried. "Who purchased them?"

Eliza looked at the letter, searching for any bit of information she might have missed. "It does not say."

"Well, it must be someone very grand. Someone of quality. Five thousand pounds, fancy that." Aunt Letitia shook her head in joyful disbelief. "This is a cause for celebration. Do you not agree, Viola?"

"Entirely," Aunt Viola glanced about the room for their missing manservant, Eliza suspected. "Sister, will you help me pour?"

Aunt Letitia nodded, and the two old women crossed the room to retrieve the decanter of claret.

"Well, Eliza. The money should put a nice dent in Lord Somerton's dun," Grace admitted.

"I hope it will," Eliza said.

Then her sister seized Eliza's arm and pulled her tight. "Do not be so foolish as to think this has changed anything. Stay away from Lord Somerton. For all our sakes."

"I have not forgotten." Eliza pulled her arm away. "And, you needn't worry. I know my situation has not changed. While five thousand pounds is a fortune to you and me, it cannot be nearly enough to save Somerton."

Grace's eyes softened. "Oh, Eliza, do not think me so callous as to not realize how difficult this is for you. You know it is the right thing to do for all involved."

Eliza nodded dully, wishing her sister was wrong.

The balance of the week passed without note, allowing Eliza a modicum of time to temper her armor for the Fortnam ball—an event she was certain Magnus would attend.

But as Eliza entered the assembly room with her family and Lord Hawksmoor, her heart beat as hard and loud as a kettledrum and she realized all her mental preparations were for naught.

Worse still, her aunts had acted particularly peculiar all that week—whispering in a corner and locking themselves away with the rule book. Eliza had no doubt they had something planned for her. This only bolstered her belief that tonight would be the ultimate test of her resolve.

Scores of candles set in three massive crystal chandeliers gilded the twirling dancers as surely as they'd been touched by good King Midas himself. Normally, such beauty would have captured Eliza's interest, but with the loss of her beloved paintings, and Magnus, nothing could cheer her now.

Almost instinctively, Eliza's gaze swept the room. In an instant, she spied Magnus and her breath collapsed in her throat, sending her sputtering and gasping for air.

There, on his arm, was Miss Peacock, her head erect and proud, as Magnus led her onto the dance floor.

Try as she might, Eliza found herself unable to look away from the couple as they danced the quadrille. She watched, utterly heartbroken, as Magnus swept Miss Peacock with the same gaze that had once turned her own knees to warm tallow.

"Hide me, Eliza," Grace squealed as she suddenly ducked behind Eliza. "That odious Mr. Dabney is searching for me."

Eliza looked across the floor where the hefty blond man stood. But he didn't appear to be scanning for Grace. No, Mr. Dabney's eyes were pinned to the very couple Eliza had been watching—Magnus and Caroline Peacock.

"You've nothing to fear, Grace, for Mr. Dabney seems to be particularly diverted by Miss Peacock this eve."

"Really?" Grace crept out from behind Eliza. "Miss

Peacock? W-what do you think he sees in that sow? I am much better looking, don't you agree?"

"Of course, Gracie," Eliza placated. "But you are all but affianced to Lord Hawksmoor. You arrived together, after all. Mr. Dabney would have to be blind not to see the affection that you and Reginald share."

"Yes, that must be it . . ." Grace muttered distractedly.

The two stood side by side for some moments more, silently watching Magnus and Miss Peacock dancing.

Though she had all but forced him to choose Caroline Peacock, seeing Magnus with her gnawed at Eliza until hot tears began to well in her eyes. She fumbled in her reticule for a handkerchief, but finding none, she spun around and started for the door.

In an instant, Aunt Letitia had her arm. Concern was plain in the old woman's eyes.

"Eliza, we would like you to meet someone," Aunt Letitia said, as she and Aunt Viola led Eliza several paces to a gathering of London's first circle.

Not now. All she wanted to do was leave before her emotions betrayed her pain, but instead she found herself readying for another ploy from her aunts' rule book.

True to their natures, within moments her aunts had introduced her to a marquis and two baronets.

But the way the young men looked upon her . . . why it made her long to rush to the nearest ewer and basin! What had her aunts said to them to provoke such lecherous gazes? It made her shudder even considering the possibilities.

Still, she had to credit her aunts' dedication to their matchmaking. They wasted no time applying their strategies.

But was it their intention to usurp Magnus or simply to make him jealous? Eliza didn't really know. Not that it mattered a pinch, because it was not Magnus's heart that prevented their match. Or her own, she noted, despondently.

Eliza realized she had let her attention stray too long, too far, for quite unexpectedly she found herself whisked onto the dance floor with a dashing, but oh so young, baronet.

The music swelled in her ears and Eliza tried to keep step, but with Magnus so near, she was too distracted to follow her dance partner's lead. All of a sudden, her young man wrenched her arms upward to form an arch through which all the other couples began to file.

Only paces away, Caroline Peacock laughed as she and Magnus neared the arch to dance through.

Eliza longed to slide her foot forward, just enough to trip up Miss Peacock as she pranced by. But she knew making a cake of Caroline, as satisfying as it would be to herself, would only hamper her efforts to push Magnus into the twit's awaiting arms. And so, for Magnus's sake, she did nothing as Caroline and Magnus ducked beneath the archway of arms.

When Magnus passed through, he turned and looked directly into Eliza's eyes. Like a blow to her middle, his potent gaze knocked the breath from her and once more she longed to flee.

Just as the orchestra's last note played out, Eliza dug a crimson-edged "no thank you" card from her reticule and shoved it into her confused partner's hand. Then, whirling around, she darted through the crowd for the doors.

As she passed the busy refreshment table, she stopped to cast one last furtive glance at Magnus. It was the wrong thing to do, for he turned just then and their gazes met for one, long meaningful moment.

At once she felt a pang in her belly and lower still. But it was no longer pain that she felt. No, it was something more akin to hunger and this worried her all the more.

Leave now, she told herself, knowing if she did not, she

might do something to assuage that ache, that craving, for indeed that was what it was. Her body's *need* for Magnus.

Go! In a burst of fortitude, Eliza lurched forward. At once, she hit something solid. Liquid splashed her arms and she heard a low yelp. She squeezed her eyes tight.

Opening one eye, then the other, she saw her victim. William Pender stood before her. Streams of pulpy lemonade dripped from his waistcoat and sleeves.

"*You!*" he hissed, his countenance pinched with a mingled look of disgust and surprise.

"Egads." *Not Magnus's uncle.* Eliza cupped her hands to her eyes. *Someone, please, snuff my candle now!*

Though he knew it incredibly rude, Magnus could not meet Caroline's gaze as they danced the following set. He had no wish to be with the rich miss this eve. And, judging from Caroline's own wandering eyes, he doubted she wanted to be with him either.

Still, her parents had seen to it that their daughter was affixed to his side from the moment he first entered the assembly rooms, and there she had dutifully remained, despite the blond man across the room, whose presence lured her gaze every few moments.

Instead, Magnus watched with melancholy amusement at the messy exchange between Eliza and his uncle. God, how he missed her.

But everything had to be in place before he made his next move to claim the woman he loved. *Everything.* For days on end he'd met with bankers, drafted correspondence to his regiment's commander, even dispatched funds to Somerton's crofters. But still he feared it wasn't enough. If only there was some word on *The Promise*.

As the set lumbered on, he found himself grinning as Eliza struggled against Pender's waving arms to wipe his waistcoat dry. Failing that, she cried an apology over Pender's wailing.

But then she looked up and noticed Magnus watching her. At once her whole body seemed to stiffen, then, with a look of pure mortification in her wide dark eyes, she snatched up her skirt and tore for the door.

Magnus released Caroline and turned, meaning to follow Eliza and stop her from leaving, but Lord Hawksmoor was quicker. Leaping out from the doorway, he snared Eliza's hand.

Hawksmoor bent low over Eliza's lemonade-dampened glove, causing agitation to crest within Magnus.

Did he just see Hawksmoor caress the underside of Eliza's tender wrist? Surely not. But even at the thought, Magnus bristled and his upper lip curled back.

"Do excuse me," he said to an appalled Miss Peacock as he escorted her back to her father, something he should have done forty minutes earlier.

With long strides, Magnus crossed the dance floor to where Eliza and her dance partner were taking their positions.

He caught Hawksmoor's shoulder firmly. "Excuse me, dear boy. Might I—"

Hawksmoor glared at him, cutting him off. "I say, man, the dance is mine."

Magnus fumed and stared into Eliza's large eyes. "Miss Merriweather, I *will* have this dance."

Fury glinted in those eyes. "Nay, my lord, you will not," she said more forcefully than Magnus would have guessed her capable. "This dance has already been promised to Lord Hawksmoor."

Hawksmoor bobbled his head cockily, casting Magnus a triumphant grin. "There you go, man. Be off. You heard Miss Merriweather."

Eliza raised her chin. "Why don't you return to your partner, Lord Somerton? And if I were you, I'd be quick about it," she added, nodding toward Miss Peacock. "You left her standing and the Peacocks are looking none too amused with you at this moment."

"I will speak with ye, Miss Merriweather."

"Another time, perhaps. Please excuse us, my lord. The music is beginning." Eliza placed her gloved hand into her partner's and turned into step.

Just then, Magnus felt a fan tap on his shoulder. He spun around to see Eliza's younger sister Grace standing there. "I believe this quadrille is yours, Lord Somerton." Grace smiled prettily at him.

"I . . . of course." Magnus was utterly confused. He had no more asked Miss Grace to dance than he had her Aunt Letitia. Still, he offered his arm to her, wondering what had incited Miss Grace to dance with *him*—her least favorite person in all of England.

Grace smiled agreeably and laid her hand atop his coat sleeve. She walked confidently beside him, but something in her expression made Magnus suspect all was not as it seemed. Her deep blue eyes held a worry that was not easy to miss. As they took their places for the quadrille, she leaned close and whispered to him.

"I have a matter of great importance to discuss with you, Lord Somerton."

At her strange tone, Magnus began to feel uneasy. "Is something amiss?"

"*Yes,*" she gushed. "Very amiss. Please, after this dance, go to the outer vestibule for some air. I will meet you there. You'll come, won't you? You must. It might already be too late."

Rule Sixteen

Where not expected, appear.

Save a footman scurrying by now and again, Magnus stood quite alone in the shadows of the assembly room's cavernous outer vestibule, waiting for Grace. How odd that she should have requested an interview, given their turbulent history. He wondered at her game.

A scant three minutes later, over the swell of orchestral music, the patter of dancing slippers announced Grace Merriweather's arrival.

Whatever the purpose of this meeting, it was startlingly clear that this was no sport to her. For as she came to stand before him, her cheeks were flushed a coral-hued red and her lower lip quivered.

"Oh, Lord Somerton. 'Tis all my fault. *Everything.* I bade her to do it and now I fear I've lost Hawksmoor as a result," she cried. "But I know you will help me right the cart I've overturned. You must, for I simply cannot reverse this jumble single-handedly."

"Ye must calm yerself, Miss Grace." Magnus told her. "For if ye continue to chatter at phaeton speed, I fear I'll never know what ye're on about."

"Oh. Of course." Grace sucked in a deep breath and expelled it gradually. "After your night with Eliza in the music room, I cautioned my sister against continuing any connection with you."

Hardly a revelation. "Go on."

Grace twisted her fan then looked up at him. "Before I continue you must understand how very sorry I am for interfering. I have learned my lesson well and only hope, after I finish my confession, you can find it within yourself to forgive me."

What in the blue blazes has she done? Just then, Lady Letitia's jubilant laughter drifted into the vestibule. Magnus glanced at the open doors, then hurriedly back at Grace. "Ye best tell me what fashes ye so. Quickly, too, before we draw yer aunts' attention."

"You're right." Her eyes rounded as she nervously glanced through the open doorway into the assembly room before returning her attention to Magnus. "I suggested to Eliza that she marry you and put an end to the damage your *arrangement* has levied on this family."

"But she would not agree to that."

"No. She claimed marriage was impossible due to your brother's debts."

Grace bowed her head and peered up through her lashes. "So, I bade her to adhere to the terms of your *arrangement*. Find a suitable wife for Lord Somerton, I said, then be done with him." She laid her gloved hand to his coat sleeve and peered timidly up at him. "I know you must think me most horrid."

By God, I knew it. Eliza didn't turn him away because she didn't love him. Nay, 'twasna that at all.

So he'd been right all along. Eliza sought to be noble by releasing him so that he would be free to marry Miss Peacock and save Somerton.

It all made sense to him now. Except for one thing—why was Grace asking his help now? Magnus cast a suspicious gaze at Grace.

She looked back at him, her eyes filled with worry. "I know you have no reason to trust me, after the trouble I've caused you and Eliza. But I need your help. You see, for some reason, Eliza has begun to encourage Lord Hawksmoor's attention. Why, at this very moment, they are dancing the quadrille together, *again*—to the notice of all!"

"Yer aunts will not allow it to continue. They have chosen Hawksmoor for ye, have they not?"

"That's just it! My aunts are actively encouraging Reggie and Eliza's pairing. They've even asked Lord Hawksmoor to join us as my sister's guest on our riding excursion in Hyde Park on the morrow. *Eliza's* guest—instead of mine!"

"Perhaps they are intent in marrying her off first. She is the eldest."

"Ridiculous. My aunts couldn't care a pickle which of us marries first. They told me as much, several times in fact. Heed my words, Lord Somerton, I fear Hawksmoor has redirected his affections after Eliza gifted him with her attention. But it's *you* she truly cares for, I know it, no matter what she claims to the contrary."

Beneath his coat, Magnus's shoulders tightened uncomfortably. He recalled the sight of Eliza dancing in Hawksmoor's arms only minutes ago. Remembered the fiery jealousy that coursed through his veins when she refused him on the dance floor. And that feeling plagued him still. Just the thought of her with Hawksmoor made his jaw muscles ache.

So, despite Eliza's objections, he had not imagined Hawksmoor's robust interest in her.

And now, instead of thwarting the cad's attention, Eliza was stubbornly encouraging it. She didn't love Hawksmoor,

Magnus knew that much. Eliza was favoring the straw-haired country boy simply to drive Magnus into Miss Peacock's cold arms.

Every muscle felt tied in square knots, but outwardly, he forced himself to remain cool as a sip of springwater on a summer day. "I own, Miss Grace, ye have come to me for a purpose. Now would be the time to share it."

Grace folded her arms and looked him in the eye for a moment, taking his measure. "I need you to join us in Hyde Park tomorrow as my guest."

Magnus simply stared at her.

"Can you not see the logic of my plan?" she asked. "Though you would join our party as *my* guest, it will be your mission to usurp Hawksmoor by resuming your courtship of my sister."

"Leaving Hawksmoor—"

"In my capable hands." Grace smiled brightly.

He had to chuckle at that. "So, when ye thought I would jeopardize yer marital prospects, ye did everything in yer power to rid me from Eliza's life. But now that *she* threatens yer happiness, even though nothing of my circumstances has changed, I am now worthy to resume my courtship of yer sister."

Grace gaped at him.

"Do I have this right so far?"

She gave a long sigh. "I know I must seem perfectly odious to you. Though you must own, what I am asking is in your interest too, if you truly love my sister. And I know you do, else you would not have met me here."

Magnus peered down at Grace, considering everything she proposed. Aside from her selfish motivations, there was a great deal of truth in what she said.

"So you will join us as my guest tomorrow? If so, you

must arrive at Hanover Square no later than three o'clock tomorrow. Can you be there?"

Magnus evaluated her plan. He had nothing to lose, and by Jove, everything to gain by this adventure. Actually, 'twas heaven sent, since he had yet to devise a better course of action himself.

"While I am still unsure that yer strategy has any chance of working, as ye have assessed, my feelings for yer sister have rendered me a desperate man." Magnus paused a moment, then raised his hands in surrender. "Ye may count on my assistance, Miss Grace," he said, punctuating his words with a snicker.

Grace narrowed her brilliant blue eyes at him. "Might I ask what you find so amusing? I am quite serious about this."

"Oh, I dinna doubt that, Miss Grace," Magnus replied. "'Tis just, until now, I had thought ye and yer sister were as different as morn and eve. I can see now that I was quite mistaken."

Grace screwed up her nose at that comment. "I daresay we are *nothing* alike. I know I mightn't be held in your greatest esteem at the moment, but there is no need for insults, my lord."

Magnus grinned at that. "None was intended, I assure ye. Indeed, my statement was purely complimentary." Just then, over Grace's head, Magnus noticed her two matchmaking aunts standing just inside the doorway, beckoning a clutch of gentlemen to them.

He narrowed his eyes and focused on the small crimson-edged cards in their hands. Then he blinked, quite unable to believe what he was seeing. Both Lady Letitia and Lady Viola were handing the cards to every bachelor who approached.

"I will join ye tomorrow at three." He glanced up in the

direction of her aunts once more. "But if ye will excuse me, I have another matter to attend to just now."

In response to his bow, Grace dropped a quick curtsey, then preceded him into the assembly room. Magnus cut to the left, to avoid being seen in her company, but as he did so he caught notice of Grace exchanging meaningful glances with each of her aunts as she passed them by. Perhaps Grace was not to be trusted after all. Could it be she was in league with her aunts in this scheme?

His curiosity aroused, Magnus pressed stealthily through the crush of gentlemen hovering like a dark cloud about Letitia and Viola. As he neared the nucleus of the group, he saw two pairs of lavender-gloved hands slapping the crimson-edge cards into a score of awaiting palms.

Sidling up to Lady Viola, Magnus opened his palm, and hurriedly closed it the moment a card was set into it.

Lady Viola glanced up. "Oh dear. That card was not meant for you, Lord Somerton."

"Wasn't it?" He grinned. "But it was meant for every other gentleman in attendance this evening?"

"Why yes. With the season coming to a close, we thought it prudent to step up our matchmaking efforts since you and our Eliza are no longer a pair," Lady Viola explained. "So, if you would just return the card—"

"And here I thought we'd become close," he teased.

Lady Viola softened, taking his words in all seriousness. "My lord, be assured my sister and I hold you in the highest fondness." She nudged her sister. "Isn't that right, Letitia?"

Lady Letitia looked up and her eyes alighted on Magnus and the card in his hand. Her eyes went wide. "My, my. Silly Viola, Lord Somerton does not require a card. He is well acquainted with our Eliza already." Her hand shot out and just missed the edge of the purloined card. She pulled back her empty hand with a pronounced frown.

Magnus lifted his card in the air, well out of the ladies' reach. "Ah, I believe I see my uncle. Perhaps we will find time to chat when ye both are no longer so occupied. Good eve, ladies." With a tip of his head, Magnus was willingly absorbed by the burgeoning crowd.

When he emerged from the throng and was able to draw a breath, he leaned against a heavy pedestal and read the card.

The cards previously distributed by
Miss Merriweather contained an unfortunate error.
The message should have read:
Thank you for coming to call upon
Miss Merriweather. Mayfair, 17 Hanover Square.

Magnus stared down at the card with mounting jealousy. Why, the old ladies' distribution of these cards would bring the city's salacious bachelors in droves. He wondered if Eliza had the least notion of what her mischievous aunts were doing.

The next day, Hyde Park's tree-dotted emerald lawns were generously littered with London's ton. Like the Featherton's party, whose carriage now cut ruts in the still damp earth of Rotten Row, they too had been drawn by the long-awaited fair weather and the soft breezes blowing in from the south.

Still, Eliza would not be here at all had her aunts not convinced her that Grace's hold on Hawksmoor was slipping. In truth, while Hawksmoor had danced with her twice last eve, he never extended the same invitation to Grace. And though Eliza was deeply grateful for his company, for dancing with him made her difficult vow to avoid Magnus possible, Hawksmoor's slight on her sister disturbed her.

It meant that her aunts were correct. Her assistance was needed to facilitate a quick and secure match between Grace and Hawksmoor.

Only then would she feel truly free to go to Italy, which she fully intended to do. For though she could no longer study with the masters, she could at least allow herself to be inspired by their work as she rebuilt her portfolio.

Eliza looked up at the Lord Hawksmoor, who guided his sleek new hunter into a bouncy trot alongside the carriage in which she, her two aunts, and Grace rode. "A new curricle *and* a landau? My, how grand," she declared as enthusiastically as she could.

Hawksmoor's lips parted, revealing straight white teeth. "Mother brought the landau to town. Arrived two weeks ago, you know. Asked her to come," he panted, as he tugged back on the reins to restrain his bay's boundless energy. "Told her all about your family." He looked down at Grace then, who, quite pleased with the attention, beamed back at him.

"We shall be honored to invite your mother for tea," Aunt Letitia told him. She exchanged approving glances with Aunt Viola, then excitedly reached out and squeezed Eliza's hand.

Hawksmoor *and* his mother. *Oh, jolly good. Can't wait.* Eliza closed her eyes and prayed desperately that she would survive the last days of this wretched season. This pretense of decorum was quite taxing.

Eliza leaned her head back against the buttery leather headrest. For the first time in days, the sun shone gloriously and the warm wind soothed her skin like a gentle caress. But an elbow in her side roused her. She lifted her heavy lids to see Grace twisted around beside her in the landau's forward seat.

Grace was clearly preoccupied this afternoon, so much so

that she didn't even seem to care that she was rumpling her new walking gown—an oversight quite unlike her perfectly pressed sister.

With a huff, Grace turned around in her back-facing seat, tugging and twisting at her gloves.

"Does anyone have the time?" Grace asked, impatiently.

Hawksmoor, happy to oblige, drew his watch from his fob pocket. "Half past three," he said. At that moment, his horse flung its head to the side, shaking the watch from his hand. He lunged for the gold timepiece, but his balance failed.

With a gasp, Hawksmoor lurched forward and clutched a fistful of the horse's mane. But still, he slid from the animal's back to the soft earth beneath.

The coachman pulled the reins, halting the landau. "May I assist, my lord?" he asked anxiously.

Hawksmoor's face flamed. "No, no, no. I am quite unaffected," he stammered while kicking free his ensnared foot from the stirrup before crawling to his feet. "Ill-trained beast. Did you see, he tried to throw me?"

"*Did* throw you." Eliza raised her hand to cover the grin overtaking her mouth. The horse was clearly more than the baron could handle.

Hawksmoor's ears darkened to deepest garnet. "Yes, well . . ."

"My lord, I could be wrong," Grace began, "but when you read the watch face, you leaned forward, and the horse likely misread your command."

"I am well acquainted with horseflesh, Miss Grace—" Hawksmoor began.

Eliza broke in. "As is Grace, Lord Hawksmoor. She and I were raised around horses. And, I daresay, Grace has a better seat than most men I've seen."

As the carriage slowly edged the park on its way down

Rotten Row, Grace stared back at Eliza with what could only be described as astonishment. Eliza was taken aback. Was her compliment really so unexpected?

Hawksmoor retrieved his watch from the dirt, while muttering something unintelligible, then mounted his horse once again.

Suddenly, Grace stood up in the slow-moving landau with a great smile on her lips as she pointed her index finger down the length of Rotten Row. "Look! 'Tis Lord Somerton."

Eliza shot to her feet as well, sending the carriage swaying like one of the small rowboats floating in the Serpentine ahead. *Oh, perdition.* It was Magnus, charging forward on a gleaming black mount like some fabled knight of old. Her heart thudded riotously in her chest as she watched his approach. Why wouldn't he just stay away?

Irritated, Eliza plopped back into her seat. It was then that she noticed the expression on Grace's face. Her sister appeared much too gleeful at Magnus's surprise appearance. Why, a grimace would have been a more natural expression.

Eliza levied a suspicious gaze at her aunts who sat snickering on the bench seat facing her. Then she turned aside to look at her sister. "What a lovely surprise. I wonder how Lord Somerton knew to find us here?"

Grace smiled smugly but said nothing.

Eliza reached out and gave her sister a short shake. "You might as well confess, Grace. Your guilt is scrawled all over your face."

Grace bit her lower lip, obviously considering her response. "Why, I *might* have mentioned we were coming to Hyde Park this afternoon."

Eliza raised her brows. "Why on earth would you—"

Grace batted her long lashes innocently. "Have I done something wrong?"

Eliza leaned close to her sister and whispered to her. "You are not making this any easier for me."

"Why, I'm sure I don't know what you mean, Sister." Grace feigned innocence and stole a glance at their grinning aunts.

"Ho, there!" Magnus called out, halting his massive steed aside the carriage. "What a pleasure, and a surprise, to cross paths with ye ladies this glorious afternoon." He looked down his nose at Hawksmoor. "Ye as well, good man."

Aunt Viola clapped her hands excitedly. "What brings you to Hyde Park this fine day, Lord Somerton?"

Magnus drew his horse against the carriage and reached down for Aunt Viola's hand. "The lovely scenery, of course."

Both aunts chuckled merrily as Magnus circled around to the other side of the carriage and Aunt Letitia extended her hand up to him.

"The scenery is the very reason we are here," her aunt admitted, swatting Lord Somerton's strong thigh with her furled fan with a hoot.

"Oh, Auntie," Eliza murmured to herself. Aunt Letitia seemed to have a knack for finding just the perfect way to reduce her to a fray of stripped nerves.

Magnus squeezed his well-formed thighs around his gleaming black charger, nudging it forward alongside Eliza. Catching her gaze, he favored her with a bright smile, sending a rush of heat into her cheeks.

Stop, just stop reacting to him. Oh, how she longed to cover her cheeks. She could feel them getting redder by the second.

"Miss Merriweather. You look as lovely as a rose. Damned near the same color too," he whispered as he took her hand.

So this is how it was to be? Magnus would goad her until

she broke down and admitted her ruse, that she was not interested in Hawksmoor. Well, it wasn't going to work. She raised her eyes and glared at him.

"And where is Miss Peacock this day?"

"I am sure I have no idea, Miss Merriweather," Magnus replied tightly. "She is none of my concern."

Eliza's spirits fell, but his reply seemed to amplify her aunts' excitement at his arrival.

"Of course she isn't," Aunt Letitia crooned. "And why should she be?"

Grace leaned across Eliza and offered Magnus her hand. "Lord Somerton, I had *hoped* we would see you at the house earlier," she said rather pointedly.

Hawksmoor's brow flicked up at the exchange. And indeed, Eliza caught the secret look that passed between Grace and Hawksmoor as well.

Hawksmoor pulled his right rein and turned his bay to flank Magnus's horse. "Nice bit of horseflesh, Somerton." As he surveyed the black steed, Eliza could not help but notice the hint of a sneer on his lips.

Oh dear. A battle brews.

Magnus gave but a cursory glance at Hawksmoor's bay. "Likewise."

Then Eliza saw the edge of Magnus's lip give a telltale quiver. Oh, men were so tediously predictable.

"Fast, is he?" He eyed Hawksmoor.

Oh no. Magnus had raised the gauntlet.

"Very." Hawksmoor rose up in his saddle, then settled his gaze on Eliza for a moment. He nodded, as if answering a question he himself had asked, then turned to face Magnus again. "Care to have a go? To the Serpentine?"

"Ye're no match. I was born to the saddle." Magnus's right brow flicked upward.

Eliza winced. The gauntlet was thrown down.

"No match? For you, Scotsman? Well, my lord, we shall see if that is true!" Hawksmoor spouted, accepting the challenge.

Both aunts enthusiastically applauded at the prospect of a match. And, to Eliza's surprise, Grace clapped her hands as well, encouraging the race.

"*Please* do not do this. Both are fine beasts," Eliza pleaded with both gentlemen.

Hawksmoor guided his mount to the curve in the road and waited for Lord Somerton.

Magnus raised her chin with his index finger. "No need to fash, *lass*. 'Tis only sport."

Thump, thump. Her heart thrummed double-time and she felt herself warming to him, as she swore she would not do.

Then, his fingers slipped over her collarbone. He whisked her fichu from her shoulders and tucked it inside his waistcoat. "For luck, my fair maiden." With that, he grinned and galloped his ebony mount to join Hawksmoor at the start.

"Miss Grace," Hawksmoor called out. "Would you do us the honor of calling the start?"

Grace, loving the attention, gave a thrilled giggle and came to her feet. She untied her straw bonnet and raised it in the air.

Both men bent to a crouch, their horses dancing with readiness beneath them.

The bonnet swooshed down through the air. Both men slapped their crops to their horses' flanks and charged down the road in billowing clouds of clotted earth.

"Go, go!" Aunt Letitia cried out to the coachman. "Follow them. Don't want to miss the finish!"

The landau jerked forward, tossing Eliza to the floor. *The deuce!* She climbed back into her seat and clung for her life to the door rim, as her sister and aunts were doing, as the landau flew at breakneck speed down the earthen road.

"Faster, faster," Aunt Letitia cried between whoops of laughter. "To the Serpentine!"

"S-spell!" Aunt Viola cried out just as her eyelids began to flutter and she slumped in her seat.

Aunt Letitia wrapped her arms around her sleeping sister. Eliza closed her eyes tightly and clutched the door, white knuckled, until the carriage slowed and halted. From the smell and the sound of gently lapping waves, Eliza realized they were at last at the water's edge.

"Oh, dear," she heard Aunt Letitia exclaim.

Eliza opened her eyes just as Grace leapt from the landau, forgoing any assistance from the coachman.

"Reginald, heavens! Are you injured?" Grace called out as she ran, skirts hoisted high, toward Hawksmoor, who was splashing his way out of the water.

Eliza stepped down from the carriage. Magnus had dismounted and held the reins of his black in his right hand and those of Hawksmoor's bay in his left.

By now, Hawksmoor lay on the bank, thoroughly exhausted, drenched and muddy. Grace knelt beside him and was busy fussing over him and comforting him.

Fists clenched, Eliza stomped her way to Magnus. She was fuming. And by the time she stood before him, panting from her charge, she was seething mad. Why was he making this so difficult—for everyone?

"Why?" she demanded. "Why did you do it?" In a burst of fury, she shoved both hands against his chest. "Answer me, if you will. If you can. Why?"

"It was just sport, Eliza." Magnus offered a boyish grin.

Eliza raised her brows in disbelief. "Sport? You call what happened here *sport*?" She slapped her palms to his chest and pushed at him again. The feel of his muscles beneath her hands sent a thrill through her middle.

Magnus's ire was piqued and he dropped the reins and grabbed her wrists firmly. "Aye, 'twas a fair match between gentlemen."

"Fair match?" she laughed bitterly at that. "How can you say that in good conscience? He was no match for you. Why, only moments before you arrived he'd fallen from his mount from a halt."

Magnus laughed. "Well, if the riders wurna, the horses certainly were. And, if ye recall, I did warn him of my skill."

"This had nothing to do with sport. This had to do with jealousy. *Yours.* You didn't have to make a fool of him, humiliate him. There is nothing between you and me—any longer. Do what you must, marry Miss Peacock and put me out of your mind!"

Magnus stared dangerously down at her, his chest still heaving from the race. He said nothing.

"We will *never* be together." Her voice fell to a mere whisper. "When will you believe me?"

He looked down at her hands, splayed against his chest like two stars, then turned his gaze to her eyes and spoke a single word.

"*Never.*"

He opened his fingers and released her wrists. Then, his hand slid behind her neck and he drew her mouth to his.

Eliza didn't pull away. Instead, she reveled in the pressure, the heat of his lips upon hers. And when he urged her lips apart, she opened her mouth willing, eager for the feel of his tongue thrusting inside of her.

"I'll just . . . take my horse then," Hawksmoor said meekly, but the hint of a smile touched his lips.

Eliza spun around and stared in disbelief at Hawksmoor as he slinked around them, his boots squishing water with each step, to catch up the reins. Was it possible he was in league with her aunts? *No, couldn't be.*

A short distance behind him, Aunt Viola snored away in the carriage, as Grace and Aunt Letitia moved forward toward her. But they were not shocked or angry, as Eliza might have expected. They were smiling mischievously. In fact, they actually appeared to be congratulating each other.

"Well done, Grace," Aunt Letitia was saying in a hushed tone.

"Why, thank you, Auntie," Grace mouthed, smiling proudly as she brushed a stray golden lock from her eyes.

Eliza couldn't believe what she was witnessing. Grace, who had promised to support her in her plans to avoid Somerton had instead partnered with her matchmaking aunts.

She stared at them until they quieted and looked guiltily back at her.

"Don't you see? For so many reasons, this can never be. *Never,*" she told them, her voice sounding disconcertingly watery and thin. "Please, I beg you all, *stop.*"

Catching her skirts in her hand, Eliza turned and stalked up the slope to the landau.

Rule Seventeen

*Determine your opponent's plans,
then turn them upon him.*

The next morning, Eliza sat in the courtyard before a fresh canvas, staring with frustration at its stark, empty surface.

What was she to do? She had planned to paint a landscape, the lush expanse of the moors as seen from Dunley Parish. But today her mind's eye had fallen quite blind.

She could no longer see that familiar, comforting stretch of green grasses and crisp bracken. Though she'd studied that sweep of land, sketched it even, at least a dozen times in the past year, it didn't seem to matter now.

One lone image pushed every other aside: *Magnus*. Even now, it was as if he stood before her, as he had before the Serpentine, his silver eyes filled with an unnerving blend of jealousy, anger, and confusion.

Turning away from the canvas, she laid her charcoal stub on the table and pushed her oils aside. *Damnation. Put him out of your mind.*

But how could she, when he kept coming back—his

heart bared and vulnerable, asking only for her love? How much longer could she bear it?

Time was fast running out for Magnus. He had to marry Caroline Peacock to retain Somerton. Eliza knew she could no longer afford to be gentle. She had to make Magnus believe, with all his soul, that she didn't love him.

But how could she do that? Whatever scheme she attempted had to be bold—but not so daring as to end in disaster or injury—as it nearly had with poor, soggy Hawksmoor at the Serpentine.

Just then, the door from the house flew open. Aunt Viola burst through the opening. "Oh goodness. So unexpected!" She hurried forward on the tips of her toes, maniacally waving her cane in the air. "Just wait 'til I tell you! Just you wait!"

Aunt Letitia bounded into the courtyard behind Viola. Jockeying elbow to elbow, cane to cane, to overtake her sister, she plowed through a hedgerow of spiked rose branches, sending scores of buds and petals fluttering to the pavers. "My heavens, Eliza, you cannot believe what has happened! Never, never, *never*."

Eliza was on her feet in an instant. "What is wrong?"

As Aunt Letitia barreled forward, Eliza caught hold of her aunt's shoulders, stilling her before she could slam into the table of paints.

Aunt Viola slapped her hand to her chest as she sucked air into her lungs. "Not . . . wrong," she panted. "*G-good* news."

Grace strolled into the rose-petaled courtyard then, her thoughts aloft in the clouds as she hummed merrily. By the time she reached Eliza, Grace was positively beaming.

"Do you not wish to congratulate me, Sister?" Grace asked.

Eliza released her aunt's shoulders then shook her hands

with exasperation in the air. "Congratulate you for *what,* pray tell? Will someone please explain to me what has happened?"

"Oh, let me," Aunt Letitia said to Grace. "It is such wonderful news. And, I am the matriarch after all."

Aunt Viola folded her arms over her chest. "The matriarch. My, you're feeling quite high and mighty this day, aren't you?"

"Well, I am the eldest."

"Only by three minutes!" Aunt Viola reminded her.

Grace lifted her hand regally. "The news is *mine,* so I will share it with Eliza." With a flick of her skirt, she proudly settled herself in the iron chair beside Eliza. "Lord Hawksmoor has asked our aunts if he might marry me," she said calmly. Then, quite unable to restrain herself, she boomed, "We are engaged!"

"What is this?" Eliza looked to her aunts for confirmation.

"Quite true. Lord Hawksmoor left only moments ago," Aunt Viola said. Her sister nodded her chins in agreement.

Grace raised her hand to her brow to shield her eyes from the bright sun. "He will announce our engagement to all at the Cowper ball in two days time."

Eliza felt her mouth drop open. "*Cowper?* As in Lady Cowper—one of the patronesses of Almack's?"

"The very same!" Grace was beaming. "She is bosom friends with Lady Hawksmoor. Are you not pleased for me, Sister?"

"Why . . . of course." Eliza bent and hugged Grace tightly. "This is grand news." Then, she drew back from her sister and straightened her back. "Though quite unexpected, is it not?"

"Perhaps it might seem that way, to you. But, no, I did not think his offer at all unexpected."

When Eliza said nothing, Grace looked across at her aunts. "May I have a moment alone with Eliza, aunties?" she asked.

"Most certainly, dear," Aunt Viola said. "Sister and I have so much to do anyway. *A wedding*."

Aunt Viola snared her sister's arm and the two started for the door. "Can you believe it? We are going to plan a wedding."

"We must begin at once. Of course we'll use lavender. Everything must be swathed in lavender," Aunt Letitia replied.

"I agree, lavender is lovely. Though I wonder if we should consult Grace about color," Aunt Viola quipped as the two entered the house.

"Heavens, no!" Aunt Letitia could be heard to say from passageway. "Who could possibly oppose lavender?"

When the aunts were out of earshot, Grace turned a sad smile on Eliza. "Will you take a chair, Sister. I fear there is much we must discuss . . . about what happened at Hyde Park, I mean."

"I do not wish to discuss it." Eliza pulled another chair from the table and sat down. "I explained as much to you and our aunts only yesterday."

Grace took Eliza's hand in her own. "I want you to be happy for me."

"But I am."

"Something is wrong. Are you angry because I assisted our aunts?"

Eliza widened her eyes. "Not really. But I am confused. I thought you were my ally—that you agreed that my leaving London was the right course for all of us."

"Oh, Eliza. I was wrong when I told you to set Lord

Somerton aside. I see that now. Once I put myself in your place, imagined that Reggie and I were being forced apart, why I couldn't bear it. You and Lord Somerton belong together. He loves you and you love him. Put away your notions of painting in Italy. Reach out and claim the love he offers you."

Eliza stood abruptly. "You know that is impossible."

"Nothing is impossible, if you want it badly enough. What is life without love after all?"

Eliza stepped past her sister and stooped to retrieve a broken rose bud. "Not everyone lives for love, Grace. My art is enough for me. Painting is my life. It fulfills me. It is the window through which life appears the way it ought to be."

Eliza heard the grinding scrape of the garden chair against the pavers then felt Grace's soft hands on her shoulders.

"You're wrong, Eliza. The canvas is *not* your window. Your art is your *shield*—your protection from life. Your excuse for not letting yourself experience life and love. Besides, it makes no sense to consider Italy any longer. What master would accept you as a student now? You have no portfolio to recommend you."

Eliza whirled around and shook her sister's hands away. "I can go to Italy, and I shall. I mightn't have a fine portfolio any longer, but I can still paint and someday I will study with the masters and hone my craft. I will not give up on my dream, Grace. I will not let my art be taken from me—as Mother's was!"

"As Mother's was?" Grace looked astonished. "Is this why you still cling to this dream of traveling to Italy—to save your art? Is this why you resist Lord Somerton so strongly? Oh, Eliza, you are not Mother. And Lord Somerton is not—"

"*Please,* Grace, allow me to handle this my own way. I know what I am doing. Believe me, this is the best thing for all."

Without another word, Eliza turned for the house.

George Dabney should have seen it coming. From the moment he first saw the dour expression on Mrs. Peacock's face, he should have known her mind was set.

He sat in the diminutive silk-covered chair, which, likely for interrogation purposes, had been positioned in the center of the Peacock's ornate parlor.

"If I may, Madam, Somerton doesn't deserve your daughter. Not in the least. Hasn't a quid, you know." He tried very hard not to look at Caroline, who sat on the settee across from him, wringing her hands.

Mrs. Peacock paced a tight circle around him, tapping her nail on her teeth as she walked. She waved off his last comment and stopped to stand before him. "He doesn't need blunt. We've got that. But he has something our money cannot buy—a title that guarantees entrée into high ton."

"But he's an ill-mannered Scot!" Caroline protested. "Why, just the other evening he left me standing on the ballroom floor—alone!"

Mrs. Peacock swiped a finger at her daughter. "Quiet now! A Scot he may be, but he is also a peer of the realm. The woman who marries him will become a countess. Does that mean nothing to you?"

Caroline bowed her head at the rebuke.

Peer of the realm, Dabney lamented. The son of a baronet, a peer was something Dabney was not. He ran his finger around the glossy rim of his beaver hat. Why ever had he trailed Somerton? For all his efforts, it made no difference.

He'd been kidding himself. The Peacocks would never accept his offer for Caroline.

Mrs. Peacock leveled her beaklike nose at him and studied him with her beady eyes. "Anything else to report?"

A chill raced over the whole of Dabney, making his throat constrict. "There was something else."

Mrs. Peacock snapped her bony fingers. "Get on with it."

"Saw him at Hyde Park, near the Serpentine to be exact. The Merriweather gel was there. You know, the odd one. The artist. Kissed her mouth. Right out in the open. Didn't seem to care who was watching. Neither did she for that matter."

Mrs. Peacock's eyes looked black against her ghostly, lead-whitened skin. "Kissed her? And she allowed it?" Without waiting for an answer, she turned and began to pace anew.

Dabney nodded. "Forgive me, Madam, but I fear it is too late for a match between Somerton and Miss Peacock. His heart belongs to Miss Merriweather, and by now the whole of proper London knows it." He paused for a moment then, hesitating before making his own bid for Caroline's hand. "Perhaps if I might speak to your husband. I can assure you, as heir, when my father passes—"

Mrs. Peacock shot him a glance so icy, that he felt his smalls draw up. "You will not speak to my husband about my daughter. Do you hear me? In the eyes of the high ton you are naught but a commoner. Caroline deserves better—*we* deserve better. Somerton, it will be."

"But Mama," Caroline whined. "I love—"

Mrs. Peacock slipped her nail under her daughter's chin and turned her lovely face up to her. "*Not* another word. Your father and I decide what is right for you."

Dabney came to his feet. "Somerton will not marry your daughter, of that you can be sure. He loves Miss Merriweather."

In a moment of pure condescension, Mrs. Peacock patted

Dabney's arm and lead him to the parlor door. She snapped her fingers and her daughter obediently followed them.

Mrs. Peacock looked back at her daughter's grief-stricken face. "Now, now, Caroline. Do not fret so. Miss Merriweather is of no consequence. I shall take care of Somerton's little artist. She won't be a problem for much longer, I assure you."

Dabney straightened his back. "You never intended to consider my offer."

A throaty laugh spilled from Mrs. Peacock's thin pale lips. "Believing I would ever *think* of considering you for our daughter tells me all I need to know about your worthiness."

At that, Caroline burst into tears and ran down the passageway.

Dabney, finding his spine at last, narrowed his eyes at Mrs. Peacock. "If you know what is truly right for your daughter . . ." But then he felt his courage draining away. Nothing he could say would sway her. Nothing.

Defeated, Dabney started for the front door, opened it, then turned to Mrs. Peacock one last time. "I'll not spy upon Somerton any longer," he told her. "It ain't right."

Mrs. Peacock turned down the passageway. "Oh, you stupid, naïve man. After today, if all goes my way, there will no longer be any need to watch Somerton."

Mrs. Peacock cackled, then disappeared into the shadows of the staircase.

"Bluidy hell!" Magnus leaned forward to better observe the fair-haired gentleman skipping down the front steps of the Featherton town house.

Hawksmoor. And he was grinning like an inebriated fool.

Devil take me. He'd been supplanted again.

Well, it would not be for much longer. Magnus reached

into his waistcoat pocket and withdrew a small, diamond-rimmed sapphire ring. He held it in a single ray of sunlight and turned it from side to glittering side.

The ring was precious to him, and no matter how light in the pocket he became, it was the one thing he would never sell. The ring had been his mother's and she had worn it all her wedded life. And today he would give it to Eliza.

Magnus felt oddly nervous as he contemplated what he was about to do. In a few moments, one way or another, his life would be changed forever. Would Eliza accept an offer from a soon-to-be penniless earl? A man whose last hope to save his ancestral home likely lay drowned beneath the waves?

With the money from the sale of his military commission, he had enough blunt to set up a meager household in the cottage his mother had left him in Scotland. Perhaps even enough to revive the wee saltworks there. Aye, they could get by.

But even now, he couldn't be sure of what Eliza's answer would be. But in his heart he knew the truth. He felt her answer in the kiss at the Serpentine. Nay, despite her protestations, she loved him as much as he loved her. And he had to believe Eliza would see that he could never marry another when she alone possessed his heart.

Magnus took one last anxious look at the ring.

" 'Tis time, Eliza," he said, returning the ring to the safety of his waistcoat pocket before alighting from his carriage. " 'Tis time at last."

"Magnus!" Eliza said with alarm. "I did not know you were here." She looked into the passage. "Where is Edgar? He should have announced you."

"Would ye have received me had he done so?" Magnus asked solemnly.

"Well, that is neither here nor there, is it? You have come. The question I should ask is, *why*? We received no notice you were to call. No card."

Magnus grinned then, and stepped toward her. "Perhaps not, but I received one of yers." He withdrew a crimson-edged calling card and held it up to her.

Eliza stared blankly at the card he held out to her. "One of mine? I never . . . oh, give me that." Snatching the card from his grasp, she held it before her eyes.

"H-how did you come by this?"

Magnus lifted a brow playfully. "Yer aunts were handing them out to any and all bachelors at the assembly room two nights past. I thought I should call, before your days and eves were filled with amorous lads."

Good heavens. Eliza stared back at him. Was there nothing her aunts were too ashamed to do?

Magnus chuckled. "Turnabout, I suppose. Another strategy from the *Rules of Engagement*."

"No doubt." Eliza tucked her fingers into fists. "I cannot bear it. Everyone must think me a light-skirt! This is dreadful. Just dreadful. Dash it! When will this infernal season end?"

"All too soon." All levity dissolved from Magnus's eyes.

"*Oh*. Quite right." Eliza turned and sat down upon the sofa with timorous agitation at being alone with Magnus. "Have you spoken with Miss Peacock yet? Have you come to inform me of your wedding plans?"

"Nay."

He was being so quiet all of a sudden. So serious.

"You have the portrait. I have fulfilled our *arrangement*. So why are you here?"

Magnus lowered one knee to the soft Turkish carpet and knelt down before her. His gaze glistened as he withdrew from his waistcoat pocket a sparkling sapphire.

No. Eliza's heart pounded in her ears. *Please don't do this. Please.*

Lifting her hand in his, Magnus raised it to his mouth and kissed it. "Eliza," he said, in the deepest of tones, "I have come to ask ye to marry me, lass."

Eliza was speechless, and could do naught but stare as he slipped the ring over her knuckle and drew it down to the base of her finger. "I love you, Eliza. And I know ye love me. Please, say ye'll marry me, and accept this ring as a symbol of my troth."

She looked up into his eyes, her own filling with salty tears as she twisted the ring and drew it from her finger. "Magnus, I'm sorry but I—"

"Shh," he said, laying his index finger over her lips to quiet her. "I've sold what I can. Somerton's crofters will be helped with the profits. Somerton Hall is forfeit, but I no longer care. No more can be done."

Eliza brushed away his hand then. "You are wrong! You can still marry Caroline Peacock."

"No, I canna, Eliza. For my heart belongs to ye and ever will."

The parlor door swung open, sending Magnus to his feet. Aunt Letitia rushed in.

"Oh, Lord Somerton, is this not the happiest day? Did Eliza tell you the news?"

Confusion knit his brows as he looked at Eliza. She shook her head.

"Then I have the honor. Sister and I agree, it was most unexpected, but most welcome." Aunt Letitia looked at Magnus's expression and paused. "Oh, here I am prattling on. Lord Hawksmoor has made an offer for my dear niece!"

"An offer?" Magnus swung his gaze back to Eliza, pinning her. "And it was accepted?"

"Why, of course it was!" Aunt Letitia replied. "Oh, there

is so much to do." She glanced around the room. "I was looking for my quizzing glass. Oh, there it is." In a speed most astonishing for a woman of Aunt Letitia's advanced years, she made for the door. "Forgive me, Lord Somerton. Must get back to Sister now. So much planning to do. Good day."

Magnus stared at her. "Eliza?" His voice was thin. "Tell me it isna true. *Please*."

At first, she did not understand the pain etched deep in his eyes, the ache in his voice. Then, suddenly, *she knew*.

Magnus thought Lord Hawksmoor had offered for *her*!

At once she made to correct him. "Lord Hawksmoor's offer—" Then she stopped. This was it. The one thing that might force Magnus from her, once and for all.

She looked down at her hands. "I am sorry, Lord Somerton. I cannot accept your offer." Holding back the tears in her eyes, she handed the ring back to him. "I think, now, you know why."

Eliza could see Magnus's throat work to swallow the lie she'd fed him.

"I do indeed." The tone of his deep voice was ragged. "I—I am sorry to have troubled you, Miss Merriweather." Magnus pushed the ring back into his pocket, then walked slowly for the door. "Best wishes to ye and . . . yer betrothed."

Rule Eighteen

When ardor is exhausted and stockpiles spent,
your foe will take advantage of your distress to act.

Magnus never felt so empty, so alone, as he did now, sitting in the shadows of the carriage wheeling him the short distance home.

The ring felt heavy in his pocket, and he knew he should return it to its box for safekeeping. But he couldn't bear to look upon it. Not now.

All he wanted was to be alone with his pained thoughts. He had no money, no future. No Eliza.

When the carriage stopped before his door, he climbed the steep steps and wearily opened the door. In an instant, his uncle was upon him.

"Somerton, thank God you've arrived!" Pender howled. "I am quite out of my element. Haven't a notion what to do." Shaken as he was, the old man left his cane propped against the wall and rushed, stiff-legged, to Magnus. He thrust forward a quivering handful of papers. "We're in it now, man. Look at these."

"What now?" Magnus groaned. After being sickled like a

heavy-headed wheat stalk by Eliza's surprise engagement, Magnus wasn't sure how much more he could endure.

Pender shook the papers. "Just look. Though, I daresay, I suspect you already know what these are."

"Do ye? Well, ye'd be wrong." Magnus peeled his kid gloves from his hands and took the crinkled stack from Pender. He turned toward the light from the window and lifted the first sheet to his eyes. After the day he'd had, he was certain nothing could shock him now. Except perhaps *this*.

He looked at the second paper. The third. His brother's loan sheets. "Where did these come from? I wasna expecting these for another two weeks."

"Courier brought them. Demanded payment by the twenty-sixth or we're out on the street," Pender said, his words riding a whimper. "You've got to do something, Somerton. We haven't much time."

Magnus crossed the room and rested his boot on the brass hearth fender as he struggled to think this new predicament through. He settled his hands on the cold marble mantel and curled his fingers into fists, crumpling the duns.

No matter how he turned it over in his mind, it still made no sense. How could this be?

Magnus was quite aware that when his brother found himself outdone at Watier's, he'd gone to a moneylender in the club's basement. There, he had taken out several loans to consolidate the enormous debts he'd accumulated in London.

But those duns were not due for nearly three weeks. Why, then, this immediate demand for payment? As he considered the implications of this new time lock, Magnus grew increasingly uneasy. "Did the courier say anything else?"

"Wasn't the sort to stand around and chat. Burly chap, he was. Brief and to the point." Pender came to stand beside him. "Said he'd be back in forty-eight hours. His employer expects payment then."

"Two days? Bluidy hell. 'Tis barely enough time to pack a valise."

Panic rendered Pender's trembling fingers near useless as he struggled to open his watch case and check the hour. "Is there anything we can do in such a short time? You know I have no blunt. Lived off my sister's generosity for years . . . and yours of course. But if there is anything in my possession that might help—"

"Dinna fret, Uncle. I'll think of something," Magnus replied, praying that he would.

For some reason, James's duns had been purchased. But why? He looked down at the pages again, scrutinizing every line.

The amounts due had not changed. There was no visible profit to be gained. Then, why the blazes would someone buy up James's vowels and accelerate their call date?

Magnus slid his boot from the hearth fender. "You mentioned an employer. I dinna suppose the courier gave *his* name?"

Pender nervously threaded his bony fingers and began to pace the room. "Never thought to ask. But at this point, what does a name matter anyway? In *days* we'll be cast to the cobbles. That is . . . unless you—" As the words were released into the air, Pender looked desperately at Magnus from across the barren parlor.

"Unless . . ." Magnus began, hoping by speaking the words it would be easier to accept what must be done. "Unless I marry Miss Peacock."

The tension in Pender's shoulders seemed to dissolve. "Yes," the old man said hesitantly. "The time for ships to miraculously appear at the docks is over, lad. The duns have been called and now you must do your duty to the family."

Pender scuffled across the room and settled a comforting hand on Magnus's coat sleeve. "I do regret that you cannot marry your woman of choice, but in the end, it matters not. Miss Peacock brings to the marriage what you need most. What your estates need—money."

Magnus lowered himself into the room's lone chair, sending its ancient wooden braces groaning beneath his weight. He rested his elbows on his knees and dropped his face into his hands.

"Aye, Uncle, 'twill be the perfect marriage of convenience." Slowly, Magnus looked up at Pender and shook his head in defeat. "But whose convenience, I wonder?"

The next evening, after a day spent being bathed, needlessly coiffed and perfumed by Jenny, their eager lady's maid, Eliza and her family finally arrived at the Cowpers' ball where Grace and Lord Hawksmoor's betrothal was to be announced.

Eliza, still reeling from Magnus's surprise proposal, numbly followed her aunts around the perimeter of the ballroom. Even as she dutifully conversed with several matronly friends of her aunts, Eliza found herself breathlessly in awe of the rout's significant attendance.

Though Lady Hawksmoor, Reginald's mother, spent her days housed near the quaint moors of Dunley Parrish, it was clear that she wielded uncommon influence within London society. How else could she have convinced Lady Cowper, one of the venerated patronesses of Almack's, to host this ball for her only son?

No one of breeding would dare refuse Lady Cowper's invitation, late as it was, even though the true purpose of the gathering had not been communicated to anyone.

But all would be revealed at the stroke of midnight, when trumpeters would beckon Lord Hawksmoor to the orchestra perch and he would announce to all of elevated London his engagement to Grace.

When a tray-bearing footman passed, Eliza accepted a sparkling glass of wine and tipped it back in a single draught. Granted, the move was most unladylike, but it was also the quickest way she knew to settle her frayed nerves.

As she surveyed the expansive room, she saw that every curtain was drawn wide, and hundreds of beeswax candles filled lofty chandeliers, drenching the guests in a lambent glow.

Outside, the street was filled with sleek black carriages waiting to decant their passengers, while liveried footmen hurried to see the guests into the already overcrowded manse.

Lady Hawksmoor, who met Grace the moment she entered the saloon, now strolled arm-in-arm with her, taking great pride in introducing her son's intended to her circle of city friends.

Eliza smiled proudly as Grace, dressed in a shimmering sheath of gold and silk, moved with all confidence from a duke of royal birth to a member of parliament and his bashful wife. Her sister was glowing. She had utterly charmed them all, assuming the admiring smiles following her wake were a reliable gauge.

Yes, tonight Grace's dreams were coming true. For one brief but glittering moment her sister was the toast of London. Eliza doubted she could ever be happier for anyone.

If only, Eliza wished, she could be as happy for herself. And why shouldn't she be? Grace's security was assured, making it possible at last for Eliza to leave London behind. And to top off her own good fortune, in just days, having remained unattached for a full season, her inheritance would be hers.

Soon enough she'd be prowling the windy deck of a ship

headed for Italy. She mightn't study with the masters as she'd planned, but her dream of dabbing pigment to canvas beside the glittering Mediterranean, the dream she'd held closest to her heart, was still about to come to fruition. At least in part.

Except . . . such a life was no longer her dream.

Everything was different now. Her desires, her hopes— had all changed. Evolved.

Living in Italy wouldn't bring her happiness. Not the way it once would have done.

Not without Magnus.

At the thought, Eliza glanced around the burgeoning crowd, but fortunately saw no sign of her lusty lord. Nor would she, she hoped. She had asked Grace, as well as her aunts, to ensure that Lord Somerton did *not* receive an invitation to this eve's affair. And, for once, it would seem, Grace had done as she'd asked—instead of exactly the opposite.

Of course, the true danger lay within the possibility that Magnus would still come, even without an invitation. What a trough she would be in if he entered the ballroom, just as Lord Hawksmoor announced his engagement to Grace.

The music began, sending dancers scurrying to the floor. Her aunts locked gazes, their eyes bright with excitement.

"Come, Eliza. The dancing has begun," Aunt Viola chirped.

Eliza looked at the laughing couples lining up for a country dance. "Tonight is Grace's night, Auntie. I wish only to watch my sister."

"Well then, if that's what you desire, but we should improve our view of the floor. Don't you think?" Aunt Letitia didn't wait for a reply. Instead, she linked her sister's arm, and led her through the crowd toward the open floor.

Eliza watched them go and tried to stop scanning the

crowd for any glimpse of Magnus. *He is not coming,* she tried desperately to convince herself. For a full hour, her hawkish gaze still hunted the sea of dark coats filling the ballroom.

She had just finished her second glass of wine when a gloved hand grasped her arm and spun her around.

"La, Eliza! Your brooding is spoiling my evening," Grace admonished, looking more miffed than concerned for her well-being.

"I am not brooding," Eliza replied flatly.

"You are," Grace countered in a half whisper. "And there is no reason for it. Tonight you should feel entirely at ease. For once, you can rest assured our aunts have no secret suitor stowed behind their skirts ready to leap out and make an offer."

A nervous laugh grazed Eliza's teeth. "You're right, of course," she admitted as they watched the two old women flit around the ballroom, prattling merrily with anyone who would tolerate them. "At the moment, they're quite focused on celebrating your success."

Mayhap a little too focused, Eliza thought. How unlike her aunts to give up so easily on Magnus, especially while he was still unattached. Their distraction with Grace's success must truly be complete, she decided, for tonight the all-important fact of his bachelorhood seemed to have slipped their notice entirely.

"Come then. Let's join the merriment," Grace said. "Here, have some wine. 'Tis exactly what you need to re-light your candle."

"Wine, oh no . . . pray I've only just—" But her sister was already tipping the crystal, sending waves of liquid over her tongue and down her throat.

"That's right. No, no, do not fight me. Just a bit more. There. How do you feel now? Better?" Grace grinned.

Eliza brought her fist to her breastbone. "Warmer. And a little dizzy."

"That's the wine. It's French. From the Cowpers' own cellar," Grace boasted. "Lady Cowper spared no expense for my celebration . . . I mean mine and *Reginald's,* of course." She rose up on her toes. "There, I see Lady Hawksmoor. Come now, I'll introduce you."

Eliza closed her eyes and at the count of three shoved all diverting thoughts of Magnus out her ears. She opened her eyes and hoisted a smile. "Ready."

She would celebrate Grace's evening properly now. Or, so Eliza thought, until across the room, she was startled to see Mrs. Peacock glaring at Eliza's with a sharp eye so poisonous that the tiny hairs on her arms stood uncomfortably on end.

Grace followed Eliza's gaze. "What is Mrs. Peacock's disagreement with you now? She should be down on her knees, crooning her appreciation, for goodness sake. You all but trussed and served up Lord Somerton on a silver platter."

Eliza looked around desperately for the footman with the wine. "Indeed. By now, I would have thought it blatantly clear that I am no threat to her Caroline."

"I agree." Grace narrowed her eyes at Mrs. Peacock. "I wonder who invited her? Not I, certainly."

Eliza turned Grace in the opposite direction as she grappled for a distraction of sorts. "Let us put Mrs. Peacock out of our heads tonight. We have better things to occupy our attention. For instance, you promised to introduce me to Reggie's mother."

"That I did." Grace's eyes rounded. "She is so very youthful looking. Oh! I've been meaning to tell you. Do you recall the woman we saw Hawksmoor with at the theater the other night—that was *her.* Oh, what a jealous goose I was. But it was all for naught. Just wait until you meet her!"

"Then, pray, keep me waiting no longer," Eliza replied, flashing a convincing smile. "Lead the way." She gave a worried glance back at Mrs. Peacock one last time, then turned and followed her sister through the crowd.

When the clock in the great hall struck eleven that evening, Eliza was standing with her aunts in a thickly fo-liaged corner of the main room where they might survey the partygoers from a slight distance.

This suited Eliza quite well, for she had absolutely no de-sire to cross paths with Mrs. Peacock—or her daughter, whom she'd seen pecking scraps from the refreshment table like a starving vulture.

Grace hurried back across the room to them, bouncing with such exuberance that Eliza was sure her sister's generously-powdered bosom would pop from her daring French-cut gown at any moment.

"I've done it," Grace announced, her eyes were shining like cabochon sapphires. "I made it my mission, for your sakes, to meet every *one* of the patronesses. For you realize they are *all* here. And, well, I have done it! I've charmed them all. Can you believe our fortune? Almack's doors will be thrown wide to us."

"Splendid, sweeting," Aunt Letitia replied. "How kind of you to look out for those of us not quite as fashionable as yourself."

"You are very welcome, Auntie," Grace replied, before wrinkling her nose. "Why are you all hiding in the potted greenery?" She gasped and brought her fingertips to her pink mouth. "Oh, dear. You are not planning something, are you? Do tell me you are not." With great drama, she clapped her hand to her forehead. "*Horrors,* I already feel faint. You know I cannot abide any nonsense this eve."

"Calm yourself, Sister," Eliza said gently. "You will surely erupt in strawberries if you do not." Then, a wicked urge overcame her and she raised a finger to hover over Grace's cheekbone. "Oh my. I believe I see the beginnings of one right . . . *there.*"

Grace slapped her hands to her cheeks. "Oh no! Where?"

Aunt Letitia shot Eliza a warning glare.

"Oh, my mistake," Eliza corrected. "Nothing there . . . at least not *yet.*"

"My darling Grace, let me assure you, we are not hiding, as you put it. We are simply surveying the party from this vantage point," Aunt Viola explained. "And, I must say, dear, I rather take offense at your assumption that we are up to something nonsensical. I ask you, when have we *ever* done such a thing?"

Eliza choked back an incredulous snort.

Suddenly Aunt Letitia spun round and gasped. "Heaven forbid. Do not move, Eliza. Do not even blink."

Eliza froze, immobile as a glass-eyed shop doll. Seconds stretched miserably into a full minute, forcing Eliza to risk a tiny whisper. "Auntie, why must I stand here like a stone statue?"

Her aunt gestured behind them with a backward tilt of her nose. "'Tis Lord Somerton—with the Peacocks!"

Eliza felt a trembling in her lower limbs. Her heart beat in double-time. "W-why is Lord Somerton here?"

"'Twas your Grace's doing, you may depend on that," Aunt Viola told her.

"Auntie!" Grace protested indignantly.

"Well, gel, you know it's true," Aunt Letitia whispered back. "Your sister was not convinced of your course when it came to Lord Somerton, Eliza. And I must say, I am half inclined to agree with her."

"Grace, how could you invite him?" Eliza hissed.

"I tried not to, really I did." Her sister shrugged her shoulders. "But just before we left the house I changed my mind and sent over a footman with a personal invitation to attend. I made no mistake. Talk to him, Eliza, before my engagement is announced." Grace's golden brows fluttered like the wings of a finch. "That would be one hour from now, Sister. Hurry and tell him the truth—that I am engaged, not you. You'll look quite the goose if he learns of *my* offer along with everyone else."

A finger of dread skewered Eliza.

Heavens above, what was she to do now? Of course she'd known Magnus would learn the truth eventually. She only hoped for a little more time.

Against her better judgment, Eliza ventured a quick peek at Magnus, but by unfortunate chance, caught Mr. Peacock's notice instead. He smiled in acknowledgment and started her way.

Oh, drat! Stay calm. Think of gentle waves. Summer breezes, singing birds . . . peacocks.

Odious, awful peacocks.

"Careful, dear. Your thoughts are leaking from your head again," Aunt Letitia whispered to Eliza.

Lud! To escape further mortification, Eliza clamped her lips shut. Within an instant, Magnus, along with another regal looking man and the three-member Peacock flock had joined them.

Mr. Peacock drew so near, that Eliza, locked in place by the shackles of propriety, could discern his every dinner course from his odorous exhalations.

"Oh, it was providence that we found you this eve." Mr. Peacock bowed before her. "Somerton, here, was only just telling Lord Stanhope, that you, Miss Merriweather, are a portraiturist of unsurpassed talent. Quite the thing."

The gentleman tipped his head in greeting. "I daresay, Miss Merriweather, might I convince you to accept a commission for a portrait of my mother? She'd feel so much more at ease sitting for a woman." His eyes and mouth remained wide as he awaited her answer.

"How good you are, Lord Somerton, to recommend me." Eliza offered him an agreeable smile, then turned to address Stanhope. "I do so appreciate your kind interest, but I fear I am unable to accept any commissions."

It was true, she desperately needed the money. Indeed, would have leapt like a starving cat on such a meaty opportunity a mere month ago. But now, there was no time to complete a portrait, for her ship to Italy would set sail in a matter of days.

Eliza allowed her gaze to drift past the preening Miss Peacock to Magnus, who was studying her through narrowed eyes, hard and brilliant. Was it anger she saw there? In truth, she deserved his anger . . . and yet, at the same time, she did not. For her only desire was to do what was right by him, not to cause him pain.

Mr. Peacock frowned. "Are you quite certain you've no time to spare?"

"Oh, no. Not one bit," Grace cut in. "For Eliza must replenish her own portfolio—now that all of her other paintings are gone."

Eliza gasped with shock at Grace's unexpected revelation, then cringed when she saw Magnus's eyes widen in surprise.

"Oh, dear. I fear you've said too much, Grace." Aunt Viola clapped her hands over her own mouth.

In a single stride, Magnus was suddenly before Eliza. His shadow cloaked her and suddenly she felt very insignificant.

Powerless. Suddenly, the music, the candlelight, the people around her all seemed to fade away leaving only the two of them.

"What happened to yer paintings, Miss Merriweather?" he demanded. From the ferocity of his tone, Eliza half expected him to snatch her up off the floor and shake an answer from her.

His eyes were wide, but puzzled, too, as if his mind was struggling to resolve some vexing riddle. His breath came faster, harder. She could feel the heat of it upon her cheeks.

"Well?" he prodded.

"I . . . I sold them," she finally managed to squeak, avoiding his gaze.

His expression grew thunderous. "What did ye say?"

"You might as well admit everything, Sister," Grace said, jolting Eliza into reality once more. "It does not take a great scholar to figure out why you sold the gems of your talent."

Eliza sealed her lips and shook her head.

"No?" Grace said. "Well, Sister, I am not so timid."

As Grace walked to Magnus, Eliza reached out and grabbed her sister's hand. "*Please,* do not do this. Not *here.* Not now."

"Why not? I should think Lord Somerton deserves to know what you've sacrificed for him." Grace defiantly looked Magnus straight in the eye. "Eliza sold her paintings at auction for *you.* Every last one of them—well, except the two she'd already given you. She directed Mr. Christie to secretly add her proceeds to the sum from your own property auction. My lord, do you realize what this means?"

Magnus was stunned, his mouth fully agape.

"Well, I shall tell you," Grace said. She lifted her gloved hand and poked a single finger hard into the center of Magnus's broad chest. "It means, my lord, that my sister sold what she held most precious to help you save your beloved

Somerton. She has sacrificed her greatest dream *for you*. What say you now?"

In the throes of her impassioned monologue, the volume of Grace's voice had swelled, and Eliza heard several gasps behind her. "Grace, *please!*" Eliza tried to turn away, but Magnus snatched her wrist and spun her back, forcing her to acknowledge him.

His eyes glistened. "Why, Eliza? Why did ye do this for me?"

Aunt Letitia gave a great snort and swatted him with her fan. "Why I should think the answer quite obvious, Somerton, you great ninny. Because she—"

"No! Do not say it," Eliza pleaded. "For it makes no difference now."

"Indeed, it does not," Mrs. Peacock's triumphant voice broke in as she wrenched her daughter forward and thrust her beside Magnus. "For you see, only today, Lord Somerton has requested Caroline's hand in marriage." A slow, slick smile eased over her thin lips as she plunged her poison-tipped words into Eliza's heart. "Lord Somerton and our daughter will be married by special license in less than two days."

A dreadful chill iced Eliza's skin and her eyes began to sting horribly. If she did not leave at once, unbidden tears would disgrace her before the entire assemblage.

"Please excuse me—" she muttered, already headed for the door and the street beyond.

"Eliza, wait!" she heard Magnus call out from behind her. She glanced over her shoulder and was horrified to see he was coming for her.

At least a dozen people separated them, and for a moment, it was impossible to see Magnus at all. This was her chance to elude him, she decided. Her only chance.

Instead of fleeing through the open door, she turned and

raced up the curved stairway for the sanctuary of the ladies' withdrawing room. Near to the top of the stairs, she stopped and peered through the balusters just in time to see Magnus dash through the front door and into the night.

At five minutes until midnight, Eliza emerged from the ladies' withdrawing room. Having adequately culled her wits, she needed to find her aunts and take leave of the celebration. Eliza glanced about the room, hoping to catch a glimpse of their matching purple frocks.

She must make haste. Grace and Lord Hawksmoor's engagement would be announced at the stroke of midnight. And, if Magnus had realized his mistake and returned, he would see her supposed betrothal for the stellar lie it was.

Well, she did not want to be around if that happened. She would leave *now*. Before it was too late.

Her eyes scanned the room until at last she saw Aunt Viola's mountainous snowcapped coiffure. Her aunt stood before one of the front windows with a small group of ladies, but even from a distance, Eliza could see that something was wrong. Dreadfully wrong.

Her aunt's usual serene countenance was pinched and twisted with worry. Beside her stood Aunt Letitia, whose cheeks had gone scarlet with fury.

Eliza hurried across the room. As she drew near, she saw that the ladies flanking her aunts were none other than Lady Cowper, Lady Hawksmoor, and Grace. But her sister's eyes were startlingly wide and her lips were trembling.

Devil take her! *What was going on?*

Suddenly, Eliza noticed that not only was every eye in the ballroom focused upon her, but conversations quieted as she passed by. She raised her fingertips to her cheeks. No, no errant tears. She checked her dress. Nothing was amiss. Still, people stared at her in silence. Scores of them!

How peculiar. For some unfathomable reason, she'd become the center of attention. This could not be a good thing, she decided, as foreboding crept icily up her spine.

Still, she continued toward her family, returning timid, reticent smiles to those who ogled her shamelessly. How she longed to tiptoe out the nearest door or leap head first through the front window—anything to escape this scrutiny.

Grace's hands were set indecorously on her hips, and as Eliza drew up behind her, the volume of her snapping voice swelled. "She has done nothing wrong." "I stand by my sister—no matter the consequence!"

Lady Hawksmoor caught notice of Eliza's appearance and lifted her nose. "Thank heavens the announcement hasn't been made. No one will know that our family was nearly contaminated by this scandal."

With a chill look at Eliza, Lady Hawksmoor whirled around, giving her back to her. Then, with a swoosh of her skirts, Lady Cowper lifted her chin and turned away as well.

They'd given her the cut direct!

Grace gasped, but when the shock of the insult waned, she also raised her chin high, as if she were Queen Charlotte herself. "Come along, Eliza, Aunties. I will not stay here a moment longer."

Eliza followed willingly, too confused to do anything else.

The four women stepped out into the night and the Featherton footman rushed forward. Aunt Letitia slapped her miser's bag into his palm, whispered something, and sent him on his way.

Without wasting a moment, the footman dashed down the street, emptying the money bag into his palm. He shouted directions to the drivers and tossed guineas into their waiting hands. Amid the groan of shifting cabs, the whinny and clop of matched pairs, the coachmen somehow managed to crowd the fashionable carriages to one side of the road, allowing the Featherton town carriage just enough room to squeeze through.

At the door and windows of the Cowper residence, London's sophisticated ton shoved, pushed, and argued with one another, like a hoard of fishwives on market day—all to get a glimpse of them.

This was maddening. Eliza raised her palms before her. "Will someone please tell me what is happening? What have I done?"

"In a moment, dear. In you go." Aunt Letitia shoved Eliza into the carriage, then shimmied in herself, allowing Grace and Aunt Viola to scramble in behind her.

Eliza stared blankly out the window as the carriage jolted forward. Then, to her astonishment, she saw Lord Hawksmoor emerge through the swarm of partygoers crowding the doorway.

"Grace!" he shouted. "Grace, come back . . ."

Eliza looked into her sister's startled, wet eyes as the sound of Hawksmoor's plea faded into the rumbling grind of the carriage wheels upon the cobbles.

Eliza put her arm around Grace and held her against her. "There now, it will be all right."

"No, it won't. I am ruined," Grace managed through her tears.

Eliza looked up at Letitia. Something was terribly wrong and she was at the center of it all. "Please, Auntie, what happened inside?"

Hesitantly, Aunt Letitia explained. "It seems that a rumor was spread this evening—that you sold what was *most precious* for Lord Somerton."

"My paintings, you mean?"

"Of course, gel. We know as much. But this is how the rumor began. The most regrettable part is that by time it reached Lady Hawksmoor, what was *most precious* to you had somehow evolved into your *favors*."

Eliza gulped. Was she actually being accused of selling her body? "Surely, Lady Hawksmoor does not believe such drivel," Eliza said in utter disbelief.

Aunt Viola looked at her sadly. "My dear, the ton loves nothing more than juicy gossip. They will believe even the most outrageous of accusations, if it amuses them."

"This is incredible." Eliza sat motionless, holding her sobbing sister and staring blankly out the carriage window. She felt numb.

Grace lifted her head. "Lady Hawksmoor demanded that her son withdraw his offer of marriage."

Eliza snapped her head around. This could not be happening!

Aunt Viola reached across the cab and patted Grace's arm. "Hawksmoor's a good man. What happened tonight will be of no consequence to him. He'll make you a fine husband yet. You'll see."

Grace sniffed loudly, then smiled a little. "I hope so."

Eliza squeezed her eyes, praying that she'd soon wake to find this night had all been a very bad dream.

Rule Nineteen

To truly surround him,
you must leave a way of escape.

Magnus slashed his crop through the still air and decapitated the nettle's head from its reedy stalk. He watched it fall, with a surprisingly heavy plop, into the green lapping water of the Serpentine. Then, his irritation still high, he set about hacking at its jutting stem, which had the bad taste not to fall with its mistress.

The air was abnormally moist this day and already, after such little exertion, Magnus felt the coolness of sweat breaking across his back. *Where the hell is she?* he wondered, as he lopped off another nettle top in frustration. Miss Peacock should have arrived thirty minutes earlier.

It was imperative that he speak with her, alone, before their wedding on the morrow. He had made arrangements with Caroline, herself, to meet secretly at the water's edge, sure that her parents would not otherwise grant him an interview with their daughter so close to the wedding.

Nay, they had worked hard to see Caroline betrothed to a peer. Had gone so far, Magnus believed, as to have purchased his brother's duns in a devious attempt to force him into their betrothal vice. And it had worked. They'd squeezed from him an offer for their daughter, Caroline.

Now that everything sailed precisely in the Peacock's current they would hardly risk allowing Magnus a moment alone with Caroline—a moment through which he might wriggle free from his betrothal bonds.

But that is precisely what Magnus hoped to do this very afternoon. Before it was too late. He had to convince Caroline to cry off, to break their connection herself, to avoid ruin.

For how could he marry another after Eliza sold her paintings, her dreams, her heart and soul, for him? She'd cast her dreams to the breeze all to help him save Somerton's loyal crofters. Did she know just how much that meant to him? How it touched him?

Though she vehemently denied her feelings, Eliza's heartfelt offering showed Magnus a depth of love and sacrifice he had never known in his lifetime. A love so powerful that it made him ache inside. How could she marry another? How could he?

From the moment Eliza fled the rout upon hearing the news of his engagement, Magnus felt the hollowness of his decision to marry Caroline. It was wrong, no matter how logical it seemed. Wrong for both of them.

But today, he'd correct his mistake and break his engagement to Miss Peacock. If it was possible. If Caroline was as ambivalent about their upcoming nuptials as he suspected.

For, though he and Miss Peacock had been affianced only a very short time, Magnus had not missed the lass's ever wandering gaze at Society events. Quite likely, her heart lay elsewhere and she had only agreed to Magnus's halfhearted offer under strict orders from her parents, who plainly desired a title for their daughter far more than her happiness.

Only a furlong away, a shiny black coach drew to a halt on Rotten Row and from it alighted Caroline Peacock and her diminutive lady's maid.

Caroline slipped her fingers through her saffron ribbon ties and removed her modish bonnet as she walked toward him across the verdant lawn. Pausing for a moment, she handed her hat to her maid and bade the woman, Magnus gathered, to allow her the privacy of a few yards.

She came to him then, smiling brightly in the golden sunlight. But somehow her supposed joy at seeing him never quite reached Miss Peacock's eyes, and Magnus became more convinced of his suspicions.

"Lord Somerton, how wonderful to see you."

He bowed to her then, but before he could speak a word, Miss Peacock started again.

"Pray, why have you asked me to meet with you in secret? As you well know, should my parents learn of this, they would be most displeased. The wedding is tomorrow, after all."

"Aye," Magnus agreed. "Which is why I must speak with ye today." He offered her his arm, which she politely took, and they began their stroll around the Serpentine.

As they walked along the footway, Caroline nervously glanced back at her carriage, as though she longed to be inside it headed for home. Magnus wished she were there, too, and that what he was about to do was but a distant memory.

"Miss Peacock—"

"You may call me Caroline, my lord." She feigned a pleasant smile for him. "After all, we are soon to be husband and wife."

"Aye." Magnus squirmed uncomfortably beneath his overwarm coat. "About our marriage—"

"Mother is so excited. Despite the rush of it all, she has seen to every detail herself, no matter how inconsequential."

Bluidy hell. Enough prattle. He couldn't endure this mindless prelude any longer. He whirled before her. "Look here, Caroline. I am about to ask ye something, and ye must answer me truthfully."

Miss Peacock pushed a coiled lock of her copper hair behind her ear and squinted at her maid in the distance. "Of course, my lord." She couldn't even look him in the eye.

"I know that ye dinna love me."

"I think everyone knows *most* arranged marriages don't begin with love." She looked up at him with false confidence gleaming in her eyes. "But I—" she began, but Magnus quieted her with a finger laid vertically across her lips.

"All right, ye dinna love me *now*. But do ye think ye could? That ye might learn to . . . someday? I must know."

He held his finger before her lips for some seconds more, allowing her time to think her reply through. To come to an answer not drilled into her mind by her mother, but an answer straight from her own heart.

She lowered her head and toyed with the frothy lace upon her sleeve. "You've seen through me, Lord Somerton." Finally she looked him square in the eye. "I do not love you. Just as *you* do not love me. Best not fool ourselves that it will ever be otherwise."

Magnus nodded his head. At least she was being honest.

"This is naught but a match of convenience for us both," she added. "Surely you know that. Payment of your brother's vowels and money to restore Somerton is why you are wedding me. My family will benefit from my becoming a countess, the wife of a peer. Doors that were once closed will be warmly opened. My parents will overcome the stain of low birth."

She looked off across the rippling water. "It's so simple really. This marriage is everything Mother wants for me."

Magnus knew he had to be gentle now. Careful in his words. "I know our union will benefit yer family, lass. But if it were yer choice alone . . . what is it that ye want?"

Caroline forced a small laugh and shook her head. "I tell you, it is of no consequence. Even if you did not exist I would never be allowed my heart's desire. *Never*." Caroline eyed the carriage again.

"Does that mean there is someone?" he asked, hopefully. "Someone ye love?"

Caroline tempered her emotions before speaking again. "My lord, we should not be discussing such things. We are to be married on the morrow."

Magnus took her hand in his. "Caroline, 'tis exactly why we must discuss this now. Before 'tis too late. It appears our hearts, both yers and mine, reside with others. How can we forge a marriage from such unhappiness?"

When she looked up at him, Magnus could see tears welling in her eyes. "Because I do not have the strength to do otherwise." Then, she looked away, embarrassed by her admission.

Slipping his fingers beneath her chin, he turned her head up to face him. "I think ye do, lass. If there is love enough in yer heart."

His words seemed to startle her, and she flinched, freeing a lone tear from her lashes to stream freely down her cheek.

"I cannot defy my parents, my lord," she said, sniffing back any more tears. "I—I simply cannot." Caroline pulled back from him. Catching up her skirts, she ran toward her maid and together they hastened to the carriage.

Magnus's spirit plummeted as he watched her go.

The footman reached for the door, but surprisingly, it swung open for them from the inside.

There, in the dimness, sat the very man Magnus thought he'd seen weeks before at the docks. The man he suspected of trailing him through the predawn streets of London.

A moment later, Magnus's eyes met those of the gentleman and he tipped his hat, sure now that this man was Caroline's forbidden heart's desire.

He knew now. This man, whose love for Caroline was about to be sorely tested, was his only hope for surviving the morrow a free man.

Standing before the open valise on her bed, Eliza checked the date on her billet of passage to Italy for the fourth time this morn, almost unable to believe the ship would set sail this very eve.

There was no use remaining in London. Here, she had become a liability. Already her presence had damaged her sister's chances to wed respectably. If she remained much longer, she might also ruin Magnus's chances to marry and to save Somerton as well. No, tonight, quietly, so her family would not stop her, she would leave for Italy.

Crash.

Eliza jammed the ticket into the valise she'd been secretly packing for her voyage. She whirled around, blinking with surprise at the swinging door and her aunts who now stood just inside her bedchamber.

Panting and wheezing, the two old women struggled to speak. Finally Aunt Letitia sucked air deep into her lungs and found her voice. "Grace—Grace is *missing*!"

Aunt Viola began to whimper and pace before the bed. "She isn't in her bedchamber. We've searched the house, the grounds, the square. She isn't to be found."

Sliding her paisley mantle from her shoulders, Eliza tossed it in a backhanded motion atop her bulging case, hoping to conceal it from her aunts' notice.

After what had happened at Lady Cowper's ball two nights past, Eliza had a deep suspicion where her sister might be found. "Perhaps not. Follow me." Eliza passed by her aunts on her way down the hallway. "I suspect her abigail will confirm Grace's whereabouts."

Aunt Letitia and Aunt Viola anxiously followed Eliza below stairs.

Sure enough, Mrs. Penny's daughter, Jenny, had participated in Grace's rushed departure. As the lady's maid sat in a chair before the kitchen fire, surrounded by the mistresses of the house and Eliza, she was more than willing to confess all she knew.

"Miss Grace rang for me at first light. Needed some help, she did, getting ready for a journey of some sort."

Eliza touched the maid's shoulder. "A journey? Did she mention where she would be going?"

"No, miss, but Lord Hawksmoor was waiting for her in the parlor while she readied herself. If you ask me—"

"Well, we are!" both aunts blurted, startling the poor abigail near witless.

Eliza patted the lady's maid's shoulder. "Go on, Jenny."

"Well, I think they were running off to be married," she said, her eyes wide and fixed on her employers.

"Goodness!" Aunt Letitia shrieked. "What was she thinking, running off like this?"

"Indeed!" Aunt Viola pounded her heart. "Why, we could have gone along with her to arrange her nuptials. Organization is our strong suit."

Eliza shot a smug glance at her aunts, before questioning Jenny further. "Did she say when she would return?"

"She didn't say one word about that. Wait . . . she did mention something about showing them *all* at the masquerade." Jenny looked up at Eliza. "Who do you suppose she meant by that, Miss Merriweather?"

"That she would show the ton, I would guess."

Aunt Viola looked toward her sister. "The masquerade ball is in two weeks. You do not suppose she intends to remain in Scotland until then?"

"All alone on her wedding day, without her family to support her," Aunt Letitia sniffed. "*One* of us must be there." Then, her wayward eye found Eliza.

"Oh no, Auntie." Eliza was astounded. "Surely you are not asking me to trail after her?"

"Young lovers always take the Great North Road," Aunt Viola said. "Quickest way to Gretna Green and a swift wedding. No doubt you can catch her up if you take the town carriage *now*."

"I seriously doubt that. If Jenny is to be believed, my sister left at least an hour ago."

Aunt Letitia caught Eliza's head and hugged it to her pillowy bosom, nearly smothering her. "But you will *try,* for us, won't you, dear?"

Eliza struggled free and took a deep breath.

"If you will not go after her, Eliza, then Sister and I shall." Aunt Letitia stared at Eliza, challenging her silence.

"*No!* Goodness no. If anyone is getting into the carriage, I suppose it will have to be me," Eliza told them as she started back to her bedchamber. But she would not be taking the Great North Road.

What good would it do her to chase down Grace? She would never catch her before they wed, for they would certainly exchange vows the moment they reached Gretna Green. All she would end up doing is interrupting the happy couple in their marriage bed. *Heaven forbid.* Well, she was not about to do that.

No, she would be heading east, for the docks—and on the evening tide, she would set sail for Italy.

She had planned on leaving anyway, and this Gretna Green folly provided as good a chance as any to do just that.

"Brilliant, dear," Aunt Letitia said as she followed her. "Here, take my purse. You'll need money for lodging and the sort. While you are gone, Sister and I shall prepare your costume for your return."

"Costume?" Eliza's eyes rounded. "Really, Auntie, I have no need for a costume."

"Oh, nonsense!" Aunt Letitia cooed. "If Grace is planning to attend the masquerade, then we all shall stand with her. We are united in purpose. Rule One, remember?"

"You do not suppose Grace would truly go to the ball after her humiliation at Lady Cowper's rout," Aunt Viola chimed after Letitia.

Lifting a brow, Aunt Letitia nodded. "I do indeed. I'd say our Grace is made of stronger bones than we know." She looked at Eliza, then at her sister. "Good for her, I say. We should all take a cue from young Grace."

"We do already have our vouchers," Aunt Viola remembered aloud.

"Yes, we do, Sister. Therefore we shall all attend the masquerade at Almack's, *en force,* and prove to the ton that their wicked gossip has not conquered us."

"Hear, hear!" Aunt Viola hooted. "Besides, the queen is rumored to be in attendance." Then, no doubt in response to some secret signal from her sister, Aunt Viola instantly sealed her lips and said not another word on the subject.

This struck Eliza as queer, and she detected the beginnings of another strategy. But, since she did not truly plan to attend the masquerade, for she would be sunning herself in Italy in two week's time, she let the comment pass unchallenged.

"How will you . . . I mean *we* even pass through the door?" Eliza asked. "One of the patronesses, Lady Cowper to be more precise, is sure to bar our entry to the establishment. It is a private affair."

Lifting her brow, Aunt Letitia circled her eyes with her index finger. "The ball is a *masquerade,* my dear."

Eliza chuckled at Letitia's demonstration and found herself already missing her peculiar little aunts.

Magnus paced the length of the cramped sacristy as his uncle checked his watch for the fifth time in as many minutes.

"Just a bit late, 'tis all," Pender assured him, his fidgeting conveying his own nervousness. "You know the ladies. Want to look their best on their wedding day."

"Aye, I know," Magnus replied, but the comment did nothing to assuage his nervousness—not that she would not come—but that she *would* after all.

"Calm yourself, Somerton." Pender reached out and caught Magnus's shoulder, stopping him midstride. "She'll be here soon enough and your financial woes will be a worry of the past."

Magnus looked up at Pender before turning away and opening the door a finger's width.

The congregation, likely having grown weary of waiting on the church steps for the bride and groom, had come inside the chapel and taken their pews. The hiss of whispers rushed toward the altar as the Peacock's friends and family joined the congregation for the ceremony.

The morn was warm and the church was rapidly heating with the day. Silver filigree vinaigrettes made their appearance under the noses of the old, reviving senses, yet ripening the scent of the crowd twofold.

Just then, the vicar opened the outer doors, and leaving them both ajar, charged down the center aisle and ducked into the sacristy.

"My lord. I do apologize that you must learn of this from me . . ." The vicar twisted his thinly skinned fingers nervously around his ruddy knuckles.

"What is it?" Pender stepped forward. "Something wrong?"

"Please, do continue," Magnus urged. Could it be Caroline was not coming this morn? *Lord above, let it be so.*

"Oh, there is no gentle way to make this known to you." The vicar swallowed deeply, then looked into Magnus's eyes. "Miss Peacock, I fear, cannot marry you this day, kind sir."

"What?" Pender yelped. "Why in hell not?"

Magnus's heart began to pound with joyous anticipation as the vicar, visibly shocked at Pender's words, continued.

"It seems she is already married to a Mr. George Dabney, a baronette's son. Ran off last night and did the deed at first light by special license. Dreadful that she left you standing this way. Just *dreadful*. Only learned the news moments ago."

Magnus clasped the vicar's hand and pumped it wildly. Then, overcome with relief, he lifted the astonished little man off the floor in a heartfelt embrace and danced him around in a wide circle, like a well-loved rag doll.

"Thank you! Thank you for telling me, kind sir." He dropped the vicar to his feet and raced from the sacristy with an elated hoot and holler, grinning like a madman as he dashed down the aisle, past the astonished congregation and out the doors.

He had to find Eliza. He would ask her to marry him this very day, Hawksmoor be damned. And this time, he wasna taking nay for an answer.

Rule Twenty

Engagement is often predicated by deception.

Though winded and disheveled from his harried ride through Mayfair, Magnus had finally arrived at Hanover Square. He leapt from his mount and looped his leather reins through the hitching post, then bounded up the steep stairs to the Featherton's front door.

He was *free*. Free of the Peacocks. Free, now, to claim Eliza as his own—if only he could convince her to cry off from Hawksmoor and to wear *his* ring instead.

And by God he would. He was far too close to let anything bar his way now.

Pausing to collect himself, Magnus groped inside his pocket until he felt the reassuring presence of the special license which he'd secured at Doctor's Commons only an hour ago.

Everything had been arranged. He and Eliza were legally licensed to marry. All she need do was consent and he would whisk her before the agreeable old vicar who awaited his word.

Deep within his chest, Magnus's heart pumped madly as he twice slammed the brass knocker to its rest. But a full minute passed and Edgar still had not responded to his knock.

Lucifer's stones! Could it be that the family was not at home? Magnus leaned his ear closer to the door and listened.

From the ruckus inside, this clearly was not the case. On the other side of the door, cabinets slammed. Heels clicked on the entry hall's marble floor, nearing then receding, and the shrill calls of the Featherton sisters ricocheted from one end of the house to the other.

Then, quite suddenly, the door swung open and tall, stoic Edgar stood before him.

Magnus struggled to retain his composure, but there was no concealing what he felt, for he was near bursting with excitement. Lurching forward, Magnus slapped his hands to Edgar's cheeks and smacked a kiss on the unsuspecting old man's shining pate.

"Edgar, my man. Is this not the most joyous day?" he expounded.

Edgar stared back at him, utterly aghast.

"I've come to call upon Miss Merriweather, if ye please." Magnus knew he was grinning like a fool, but he couldn't help himself. At the sounds of light footfall, he glanced down the passageway and glimpsed Lady Viola as she shot through the hall and ducked into the music room.

Edgar cleared his throat and as if by command, Lady Letitia, walking stick held before her like a sword, hurried through the parlor doorway. Her eyes were wide and her left hand waved frantically in the air as she cut across the passage and disappeared into the library.

"Good lord, Edgar. Is something amiss?" Magnus asked, "Or are the ladies simply playing hide and seek?"

Edgar hesitated, then released his grip on the door and nervously shoved his fingers through the wild white wings of hair at the sides of his head. "Well, my lord, I don't quite know how to answer, for you see . . ."

At that moment, Lady Letitia darted out of the book room and caught sight of Magnus. She halted midstride. "Oh, Lord Somerton, how very good to see you. But heavens, you will not believe what has happened! Just wait until you hear this."

Lady Letitia pumped her thick arms, sending both·her chins jiggling, as she charged toward him. "*The gel's done it.* Gone off and eloped with Hawksmoor. Not a word to us, mind you. Just ran off a short while ago, lickety split. All the way to Scotland no less."

Magnus's heart seized in his chest. "Eliza?"

"Headed up the Great North Road to Gretna Green," Lady Letitia murmured as she looked into his eyes. "What a scandal this will cause!"

"Forgive me, my lady, but on this point I must be *completely* clear—*Eliza* is headed to Gretna Green?" Magnus asked.

"Yes, yes. Eliza is off to Gretna Green," Lady Letitia repeated. "Am I not making myself heard?"

"Perfectly."

Just then, Aunt Viola scuttled up the passage, her walking stick twitching up at Magnus like a divining rod. "Oh, good day, Lord Somerton."

Though his head felt light from the blow of the elopement news, Magnus bowed in greeting.

None of this could be happening. Everything had been going so well. He even had the damned license.

Lady Viola brushed the invisible dust from her palm onto her skirt then lifted her hand to Magnus as she gifted him with a hostess's smile. She glanced at Lady Letitia and spoke through her still smiling teeth, as if she believed if her lips did not move Magnus wouldn't hear her. "Have you told him about the elopement?"

"Aye," Magnus interrupted. "Yer sister just informed me of it." Mayhap there was still time yet. Time to stop this nonsense. There must be.

"Whatever shall we do?" Lady Viola asked him, her countenance pulsing with anxiety.

"Perhaps *I* might be of some assistance in persuading her to return home," Magnus offered. "However, to do so, I shall require more information."

"Oh, my lord, we would be most grateful for your guiding hand. Mayhap you can persuade the pair to reconsider elopement. For I own, no matter the circumstance, a wedding must be conducted properly . . . else tongues will wag. Can't have that now," she replied.

"I agree wholeheartedly," Magnus looked from one Featherton sister to the other. "Time, however, is of the essence, ladies, so will ye tell me how long ago Eliza left?"

Lady Viola looked quizzically at her sister. Then, after receiving an affirmative nod, she returned her gaze to Magnus.

"*Eliza* left only an hour ago . . . wait, maybe two."

"I shall ride after her directly." Both aunts smiled broadly at him as he turned and rushed out the door.

"You best hurry for she has quite a lead," Letitia called after him.

Moments later, Magnus was atop his steed, laying crop to muscled flank, as he set off for the Great North Road. He would stop Eliza from making this grave mistake.

If Eliza Merriweather married anyone this day, it would be he. And no one else.

As Lord Somerton turned the corner, heading in the direction of Oxford Street, Letitia signaled for Edgar to close the door. She clapped her hands excitedly and turned to her sister with a grin. "How fortunate you saw him through the window."

Viola laid her hand to her chest. "My heart is still pounding. What do you think, Letitia? Have we succeeded?"

Letitia chuckled softly. "I do indeed, Sister. In truth, after our impromptu performance, I would not be the least surprised if we hear of *two* Merriweather weddings in Gretna Green."

"Though, in case we are mistaken in our assumptions," Viola hesitantly added, "we really ought to locate the rule book. Now, where do you suppose Eliza has hidden it?"

Letitia chewed her lips thoughtfully. "Well, she seems to favor the high shelves in the library. Clever gel. Knows neither of us can abide heights."

Then, Letitia's gaze shifted to Edgar with clear intent, making the poor man reticent to meet her eye.

"But you, dear sir, have no fear of the climbing ladder," she said, with a leading edge. "Perhaps *you* will climb up and have a look for the rule book?"

Edgar cringed noticeably, but he did not falter. "Jolly good idea, ma'am," he croaked.

The moist air heated and dried, and morning faded into noon as Magnus galloped relentlessly up the Great North Road. He passed a handkerchief over his eyes, rubbing away the gritty dust lodged in their corners and squinted ahead at the golden spirals of earth billowing up in the distance. Could it be? *Aye, a carriage.*

He cut his crop down along his steed's sweaty flank to begin his pursuit and was quickly able to overtake the carriage.

Though the coachman followed Magnus's fierce command and had drawn the carriage to a full halt, the cab still rocked violently and lusty groans emanated from within.

Images of Hawksmoor clumsily groping at Eliza's pale skin flashed angrily in Magnus's mind as he tore open the carriage door. But when he poked his head inside the cab, intent on throttling the man, Magnus was startled to find himself looking into the barrel end of a pistol trained on his nose.

Bluidy hell. It wasn't Hawksmoor.

"What the blazes are you on about, man, breaking in on us?" the gunman asked, his hand trembling under the weight of the moment.

"Percy, are we to be robbed?" Lying skewered beneath him, quivering thighs spread, was a buxom brunette, struggling to draw down her skirts. "Do something, *please.* Save us!"

Not Eliza. Thank God.

"I . . . uh . . . beg yer pardon," Magnus stammered, trying to avert his eyes from the evidence of passion he'd interrupted. "Thought ye were someone else. Sorry to be a bother. Carry on then." He flung the door closed again, wincing at his ill-chosen words. Then, with a wave of his hand, Magnus beckoned the startled driver on his way.

At last the carriage rolled over the gentle rise in the road and disappeared from sight, Magnus shook off the tenseness of near disaster. *Damn it all.*

This carriage was the second he'd forced from the road within the past hour. But for all his exertions, he'd only mistakenly stopped no less than three eloping couples, one of which he'd caught coitus interruptus.

But Magnus would stop at nothing until he found Eliza. And that had to be soon. He usually traveled at nearly twice the speed of a carriage, even on the best of roads, which the road he now traveled certainly was not. He must be close.

Shoving his dusty boot into the stirrup, he raised up and swung his leg over the saddle, then urged his horse down the pitted and pocked highway.

His mouth was parched and gritty from the road, so when a quarter of an hour later he neared St. Albans and came upon the White Hart Inn, he decided to avail himself of a quick refreshment. He was about to dismount when an enclosed landau wheeled around from the side corner of the brick establishment, sending a stinging spray of gravel into his face.

When he opened his eyes a moment later, he seized upon the crest emblazoned on the landau's black door. *Hawksmoor*.

Got ye now. Magnus nudged his horse into a gallop and struggled to draw alongside the carriage until finally he was able to reach out and pound the door. "Stop! Stop, I say!"

From inside, Hawksmoor's voice called out to the coachman and within moments the carriage stopped in the center of the road.

Billowing clouds of dry saffron dirt rose into the air around the landau forcing Magnus to squint his eyes. He wasted no time and leapt from his horse, pressed the brass handle on the carriage door, and thrust his hand inside the dim cabin.

The moment he felt a soft arm, he wrapped his fingers around it and pulled its owner from the carriage.

"Well, you had better have a riotous good explanation for yanking a woman from her fiancé's arms," its owner hissed.

Magnus stared in disbelief. 'Twas not Eliza at all. But her sister Grace! And she was snarling mad at him now.

Dumbfounded, he ignored Grace's sputtering rebukes and lowered his head to peer inside the carriage for Eliza. He saw nothing, except for Hawksmoor's livid eyes glaring back at him. At once, he felt the tapered end of a walking stick poke the hollow of his throat.

"Explain yourself, Somerton, before I run you through!" Hawksmoor demanded.

"With a walking stick?" Magnus lifted his brow. "That, sir, I highly doubt."

"What? Oh," Hawksmoor muttered, as he unsheathed a thin blade from the hollow of the cane.

"There ye go man, much more menacing."

Magnus eased himself backward into the daylight, guided by the point of Hawksmoor's tiny saber. The moment they both cleared the coach steps, Magnus slapped the blade from Hawksmoor's hand and shoved him to the dusty road. "I would not try that again if I were ye."

Turning around to Grace, Magnus found himself in the path of a whirling reticule. The heavy bag came down with a whoosh, slammed into his middle and knocked the breath from his lungs.

"Leave him be!" Grace cried. "You are not going to ruin this for me, Somerton. We *will* be married. No one can stop us!"

"God on earth, Miss Grace," Magnus gasped, as he clasped his hands over his stomach. "What the blazes have ye got in that bag, paving stones?"

She tilted her nose upward. "Twenty guineas." With an exasperated huff, Grace helped Hawksmoor to his feet, then turned back to Magnus. "Now, if you please, I demand to know why you've delayed us." She narrowed her eyes and raised her reticule threateningly.

Hawksmoor moved closer to her side, as if for protection—*his*. "Yes, who sent you to stop us? My mother?"

"Why, no one," Magnus said, looking to Grace as he raised a hand against any possible swing of her lethal bag. "I thought Eliza had run off to marry Hawksmoor here. I was trying to stop *her*, so I could convince her to marry *me*."

"You did not marry Miss Peacock then?" Grace asked, though she did not wait for an answer. "How wonderful!" The tightness around her eyes relaxed and she let out a small laugh. "But why would you believe my sister was off to marry my Reggie?"

"Why? Because Eliza . . . yer meddling aunts—" Magnus stopped then, and blinked stupidly back at her. Why had he thought it? Had anyone ever told him outright that Eliza was to marry Hawksmoor? He tumbled the question through his mind for several seconds.

The answer was . . . *nay*. But their engagement had been deceitfully implied, by Eliza and both of her aunts.

Why, those cunning little ladies. They'd tricked him into heading for Gretna Green. He'd been entrapped by another strategy from that misused book of rules!

No doubt the two old ladies had hoped to orchestrate a double wedding in Gretna Green.

Still, as frustrating as their games were, he could not be angry with the two conspirators. What they wanted so badly to achieve, a match between he and their niece, was no less than what he wanted with all his heart.

Magnus looked back at Grace, growing ever more frustrated with the situation. "Yer aunts told me Eliza was headed to Gretna Green."

"Did they? How odd." Grace shook her head then. "No, Eliza might have led our aunts to *believe* she was coming to Gretna Green, perhaps to stand witness for me or some such nonsense, but actually coming, no, that is highly unlikely."

With an exasperated huff, Grace tilted her blue eyes up at the cloudless sky, then pulled at the satin ribbon bowed at her throat and removed her bonnet. "Even if she wanted to, Eliza wouldn't have reached us in time. You, yourself would not have caught us so quickly had we not stopped to break our fast at the inn."

"Why are ye so sure she wouldna come north?" Magnus prodded.

From the corner of her eye, Grace glanced tentatively up

at Magnus, making him confident that she knew more about Eliza's flight than she was letting on. Grace shifted her weight from one foot to the other.

"Today is the thirtieth, no?" she seemed to wince a little. "A few weeks ago I gave her a billet of passage to Italy. The ship was to set sail on the evening tide—*tonight*. I believe our Eliza may be headed for *Italy*!"

Eliza stood on the gently swaying deck of the tethered ship that would soon spirit her down the Thames and away from all she knew. All she loved.

It was an odd sensation, her world shifting beneath her feet. But Eliza knew, in time, she would become accustomed to it.

A forlorn sigh slipped from her lips as she gazed out at the bustling London docks, at her aunts' town carriage still waiting below—"in case you change your mind," the coachman had said. But she would not.

For now it was too late to reverse her destiny.

Early this morn, instead of heading north for Gretna Green, she'd directed the coachman to take her to the small chapel where Magnus was to wed Miss Caroline Peacock. It would be torture to wait outside as Magnus pledged himself to another, but she could no more ignore the draw to the place than a moth could disregard the beckoning flame.

Eliza sat alone in the carriage for nearly an hour, until she saw the vicar open the doors to the congregation and invite them inside.

It took great strength of will for Eliza to remain several minutes more. But she waited, though hopelessly teary-eyed and wet-nosed, until she was confident that Magnus and Caroline had exchanged their solemn vows. Until she knew Somerton was saved.

Only then did she signal the coachman to drive onward to the docks, to her future, however bleak it now seemed.

Ship hands, burdened with trunks and bags, filed up the gangplank and disappeared into the dark hull one by one like an army of great ants. The sun-bleached deck planks creaked and groaned under their loads, and the ship tugged against the hemp ropes that bound it to the pier, as though protesting the delay in leaving.

Eliza wanted to cut the ropes herself, wanted to unfurl the sails, so painful was the thought of remaining in London a moment longer knowing Magnus was married to another.

She turned her back to the dock and walked to the stern, preferring to stare out at the lapping gray water and imagine her new life in Italy instead of lamenting what could have been.

Suddenly, strong hands seized her shoulders.

"Come with me, lass."

Magnus. She spun around and looked up into his sterling eyes as his hands slid down her ribs to cinch her waist. A whirl of emotions, thoughts, and words sped through her mind as he held her so tight she couldn't move. "What are you doing here?"

Magnus smiled at her, but his eyes were deadly serious. "Why, I should think that obvious, lass. I've come to take ye home."

"You will do no such thing! *I* am going to Italy. My new home. And *you,* my lord, should return to your *wife.* It is your wedding day after all."

"Aye, 'tis my wedding day, but how can I enjoy the afternoon when my bride is hell-bent on sailing away?"

"Your bride?" Eliza blinked. "What are you saying? You did not marry Miss Peacock?" An errant pang of elation shot through her middle.

"Nay, I didna."

"But you must! You can still save Somerton." After all her sacrifice, her heartache, here he was with her—throwing it all away. "It is not too late."

"Aye, 'tis. Ye see, I spoke with Miss Peacock yesterday and found she wanted to wed me as little as I wished to wed her. Something I said must have found a home in her heart, for she eloped with another last eve." He smiled then. "Christ, I thought no news could make me happier—'til I discovered ye were not betrothed to Hawksmoor after all."

Eliza turned away and refocused her gaze on the leaden water. "I am sorry for my deception. But I had to do it. I could not allow you to lose Somerton because of me."

Magnus spun her around to face him. "Because of *ye*? What are ye saying, lass? Somerton is lost because of my brother, not ye."

"But if you married Caroline Peacock—"

"Then I would have forfeited my future, my happiness, all for a pile of stone. Eliza, my life is with ye. Without ye, I have nothing. And if ye've yet to understand that, ye soon will."

Magnus cupped her cheeks in his hands. "Eliza, I *love* ye. Och, 'tis true, I have no riches or a fine house to offer. But I have a few quid and a wee cottage in Scotland. And if I work hard, and swear to ye I will, I can bring back my mother's family saltworks on Skye. It willna be much at first, but enough, if ye love me as I love ye."

He reached inside his pocket then and drew out a folded paper. "'Tis a special license to marry. I spent a fair bit of what I had left to make clear our way. The vicar is waiting, lass. Ye need only say ye'll marry me."

Eliza began to shake. Every part of her screamed *yes, yes*. But giving into that voice inside would be wrong, and both of them would live to regret it. She could not live with his resentment for losing Somerton.

Once the ship set sail and she was far away, Magnus would be free to offer for a more worthy, wealthy woman. And in time, he would understand how wrong it would have been to let his heart rule his head.

In the moment her decision was made, Eliza felt a rip inside her chest. "I am sorry, my lord, but I cannot," she whispered.

Magnus shook his head. "Now see, I knew ye'd need a little convincin', so I asked yer footman and driver to wait for us." He caught Eliza's arm and began to drag her across the deck toward the gangplank.

Eliza was so stunned that she barely registered what was happening. She never dreamed Magnus would use such extreme measures to detain her.

Other passengers, and indeed the captain himself, turned to stare.

"Help me! Please, help me!" Eliza screamed as she struggled fiercely against him.

Magnus turned around in time to see a group of angry-looking ship hands closing in on them. Then, Eliza saw a flicker of mischief spark in his eyes.

"Now, lass, what will the children do without their dear mother? I canna raise them all alone," he said, in a most convincing tone. "Think of the bairn, only three months old. She'll never know her ma."

Eliza's mouth fell open. She couldn't believe what he was saying, much less that these strangers seemed to take him at his word. The encroaching crew turned away and returned to their own business.

"No, 'tisn't true. I have *no* children!" she cried out, but it was futile. No one was listening anymore.

She heard Magnus chuckle softly and then felt herself being lifted and thrown over his shoulder like a sack of flour.

"Let me go, you great oaf!" she howled.

"Now, is that any way to refer to yer husband and the father of yer six children?"

"*Six?*" she repeated, earning her another chuckle. "My, you must think very highly of yourself."

As he headed down the wobbly plank running from the deck to the pier, Eliza clung to Magnus. From this upside-down view of the world, her sky became a slurry of murky water and muck.

"You may be able to kidnap me, force me to miss the sail, but you cannot make me marry you."

"I canna?" he asked, seeming quite pleased with himself.

"I should like to see you try," Eliza shrieked, feebly pounding her fists against his broad back.

"Verra well then, lass. Ye shall have yer wish."

Wide strides carried them fast across the pier to where her footman waited.

"Rufus, help me," Eliza called out to him, but to her astonishment, he only grinned back at her. This was a conspiracy! What had she done to deserve this?

"Are we ready go then, guv'nor?" the coachman called down to Magnus, fully discounting Eliza's pleas for help.

"We are indeed," he told the driver. The footman opened the door and Magnus tossed Eliza onto the seat cushion. "Ye know the way."

"That I do, guv'nor," the driver replied. "Have ye there in no time at all."

As the coach jerked forward, Eliza scrambled for the door handle, but Magnus pulled her back to the cushion and rolled atop of her.

"Ye're going to marry me, lass. Within the hour. So ye might as well get used to the idea."

Rule Twenty-one

When you are equally matched, engage.

Fury flared within Eliza as she stared up into Magnus's rather amused eyes. "Marry you?"

"Aye. And ye have no say in the matter. The time for foolish, noble delays is over. Besides, ye know ye love me and dinna try even once to deny it." He cocked a brow at her and grinned a bit, goading her all the more. "Think of this as yer reward for yer martyrdom and sacrifice."

"You're mad." Eliza lurched against him and, finding herself quite unable to move her arms, bit at his throat to show her frustration.

Magnus reared back, his eyes wide with surprise. Then his gaze darkened, growing ever intense as his interest in her new game increased.

Before she could take another breath, his lips came down hard upon her own, just long enough for her to taste the salt on them. Then he pulled back, as if he thought she might lay her teeth to his skin again.

Or perhaps, he was inviting her to do just that.

Strangely, the possibility thrilled her. Already she felt her resistance giving way beneath his searing kisses. Seizing the last tatters of her resolve, Eliza slammed her hands to his shoulders and shoved with all her strength to knock Magnus from atop of her.

For a moment, his weight shifted, and she reveled in the thrill of approaching success. But before she could taste her victory, his hands swung upward and cuffed her wrists.

"Let go of me, you great Scottish beast!" she cried, though the outburst only netted her a chuckle. Enraged, she bucked against him, but the action seemed only to embolden him.

Magnus held her fast and stared deep into her eyes. "Fight me all ye will, lass, but yer struggles will get ye nowhere. I canna be swayed. Ye are mine, Eliza, and I will not rest until God and England agree."

When her mouth fell wide open with the shock of his words, he kissed her, exploring her mouth with his tongue, sending rivulets of sensation deep within her. She moaned at the pleasure of it.

A slow smile eased across Magnus's mouth. "If this has become a battle of wills, lass, ye've lost already."

Magnus's chest pressed Eliza deeper into the seat cushion with every inhalation and she gasped a broken breath, all she could do beneath his weight. She could feel him harden against her, a sensation that sent heat pooling between her own legs.

Lightly, she ran her tongue across her bottom lip and as she softened beneath him, Magnus sighed. Their battle was finished. And to the victor went the spoils.

This time, when his mouth hovered above her own, she closed her eyes and parted her lips, inviting his tongue inside, wanting to feel its warmth and slickness against her tender flesh.

As his lips touched hers, he opened his fingers and released her wrists. She brought her arms down to his shoulders and threaded her fingers through his thick hair until her hands met and clasped behind his head.

But then a burst of fresh air raced between their bodies. She opened her eyes and saw he had leaned back. There was a tug at her neckline. In the next moment, his fingers lifted her breasts from her rigid stays and his teeth bit down ever so gently on the tip of her aching nipple. She groaned at the wanton pleasure of it.

Somehow he knew just where to touch to heighten the tautness building inside of her. Under her skirt, Magnus fumbled against her underpinnings while twisting for position between her knees.

He looked down at her with a disablingly sexual gaze, drew her skirts high, and slipped his palms silkily against her bare thighs, pushing them apart. Her eyes locked tight with his as he guided her knee over his shoulder, until he disappeared beneath the crumpled drift of skirts and she felt his mouth between her legs.

Heat suffused her cheeks. This was wicked. So wrong. But then his tongue slid over the throbbing nub at her center and she arched against him, too astray in the tingling sensations to feel embarrassed. He licked at her, lapping at her need.

Eliza let her head loll back against the seat cushion. She was too lost in physical bliss to do anything but feel. She bit her lower lip and squeezed her eyes tight as he slipped his tongue deep between her folds and into her, driving her to utter madness.

Her body pulsated with satisfaction as the rhythm of his touch teased her until her grasp on sanity barely existed. Even her heart began to drum in her ears and between her quivering legs too.

"Magnus," she cried out. She opened her eyes and

pushed him back from her. She lifted her leg from his shoulder and bent forward.

She could see the defined bulge of him straining against his tight breeches as she slowly, tentatively, released his buttons. Looking up at Magnus for assurance, she slid her hand beneath the fabric until she held him, hot and pulsing, in her hands. Hesitantly, she ran her fingers up and down his shaft, gently, slowly at first. Then, as he grew impossibly large and rigid in her fingers, and she learned the power of her touch upon his skin, she quickened her stroke with authority.

They were moving to one unavoidable end. She knew there was no way to stop now. For either of them.

Without releasing his startling darkened eyes from her gaze, she eased back slowly onto the cool seat cushion, guiding him with her hand to the moistness between her legs. When her back flattened against the seat cushion, Magnus brushed her hands away and he positioned himself above her. Touching her *there*. Just barely.

She fought the urge to push against him, to take him inside of her. Instead, she raked her bottom lip with her teeth as he slid his hands under her and squeezed her buttocks.

Sucking in a breath against the burning sensation to come, Eliza grasped the bulk of his muscular arms for leverage and arched up as Magnus thrust into her. He filled her completely. Stretched her.

But it was easy this time. No sting. No pain. Only pressure. Only need.

And then it returned. The warm tightening, deep inside of her. The climbing pleasure, growing, intensifying, with each powerful thrust. She lifted her knees and locked her legs around his waist, wanting only to draw him deeper into her.

Magnus groaned and squeezed his eyes tight as she matched the rhythm of his thrusts. Eliza closed her lids, too, sinking her nails into his arms as every push brought her closer to her breaking point.

Nothing mattered now. All too willingly, she surrendered to the maddening sensation as Magnus thrust relentlessly inside of her, driving her into some deep, mindless abyss.

And then, when the tension could wind no tighter, something inside of her released, and she cried out. Fingers of warmth raced through every nerve of her body.

Magnus's body shuddered within her. His thrusting stopped, and for a moment neither of them moved.

Eliza opened her eyes to see Magnus smiling down at her. He lowered himself atop of her and kissed her slowly, gently.

She sighed and smiled as she wrapped her arms around the man she loved. Never did anything feel so right.

As the coach raced through the summer-baked streets of London, Eliza never felt closer to Magnus or more alive in her own body. She no longer cared about what was right or where they were headed. Or why.

So long as they didn't stop.

For a while afterward, they lay together, clothing askew, bodies damp.

Lud, if someone had told her that before her midday meal she'd be laying inside her aunts' carriage with Magnus between her legs, she'd have thought them quite mad. But here she was. And, as much as she was loathe to break their intimate moment, the time to settle things between them had arrived.

"This changes nothing, Magnus," Eliza finally managed. "You can still save Somerton, if only—"

Magnus cupped his hand over her mouth, hushing her. "Listen to me for once. Eliza, I love ye," he began softly, "and that will never change."

The sincerity in his voice touched her, and her eyes began to sting.

He bent and kissed her forehead. "I can live without fortune. Without land. Without my home. But I canna live without yer love."

Tears of happiness breached Eliza's lashes and came coursing down her cheeks in hot streaks. She sniffled, unable to form words. Not a single one.

Balancing on his elbows, Magnus took her face in his hands. "Ye are my life. Ye can sail to Italy or to the far reaches of China for that matter. But I will find ye. I'll never stop, until ye are mine . . . forever."

All at once, her noble vow to do what she *thought* was right seemed ridiculous to her. She sacrificed so much, but she had been so wrong. The only truth was their love and the rightness of their being together. Why hadn't she realized this before?

"But what about your home?" Eliza asked, her voice was thin from the growing lump in her throat.

"Somerton is as good as gone, I know, though it never truly mattered to me anyway."

"Not mattered to you? But I thought—"

"Nay. 'Twas always her people, lass. For their loyalty over the years to my family, I owe them much. But I'll find a way to help them, I swear it. I'll call in favors, talk with other landowners. I'll do what I must. But I canna do it without ye."

Magnus rose from her, taking a moment to straighten his clothing. As he did, Eliza hurried to do the same. Though looking her best was an impossibility, she at least wanted to look presentable, for she knew that in the next minute they would together carve a memory.

Magnus knelt before her. Rocking with the sway of the

carriage, he raised both her hands and kissed them, then looked into her eyes.

"I know I have nothing to offer ye but perhaps my meager earnings from what I reap from the land and sea. But if ye will do me the great honor of becoming my wife, Miss Merriweather, I will certainly be the richest man alive."

Eliza drew a ragged breath, sure her heart would burst with happiness.

"Say ye'll marry me, Eliza. Say it now."

There was no impediment between them anymore. No reason not to be with the man she loved . . . *forever*.

"Yes, I will," she said, laughter mingling joyfully with her tears. Eliza leapt up and threw her arms around his neck.

As he gathered her to him and held her body close, it all became astonishingly clear. She never really needed Italy at all. Never needed to run away to protect her passion. Her artistic soul would thrive, wherever she was, in the warmth of their love.

She parted her lips and raised herself to meet his kiss, sighing with pleasure as his firm mouth claimed hers. She couldn't remember ever feeling so blissfully happy.

Suddenly the carriage halted and they both pitched abruptly forward. They hit the forward seat, then crashed to the floor. Wherever they were going, they had, rather unceremoniously, arrived.

Eliza sat up and rubbed her aching head. "Where are we?"

But before Magnus had a chance to answer, the carriage door opened. Pender stood outside, peering inward at them, his mouth rounded in shock as he noted their disheveled condition.

Magnus charged forward, blocking his uncle's view, and stepped down from the carriage. He slapped Pender on the back, with such force, that the older man stumbled forward.

"Congratulate me, Uncle," Magnus said, grinning like a cat with several feathers jutting from its mouth. "Miss Merriweather and I are engaged."

Pender turned his head to look back through the open carriage door at Eliza, all hooks and buttons finally fastened, blinking out at him.

"Oh," he muttered. His lips hinted of a smile. "So that's what you young folk call it these days."

The next hours held such a whirlwind of activity that Eliza later wondered if it had all really happened. But the ancient Somerton sapphire on her finger, the ring that had belonged to Magnus's own mother, was proof that it had indeed.

With Pender and her well-rouged aunts standing as witnesses, and fragrant orange blossoms in her hair, Eliza and Magnus had exchanged their vows before the vicar in the Featherton's own rose-rimmed courtyard that very afternoon.

Her life had been utterly transformed with a single promise. But outwardly, nothing had really changed—not yet.

In the two weeks after the wedding, Pender oversaw the preparations of the Somerton townhome for debtor's auction, while Eliza and Magnus made their marriage bed in her own chamber at Seventeen Hanover Square. But soon they would be heading north to the Highlands of Scotland to begin life anew as husband and wife.

And while their plans thrilled her, Eliza had never spent more than a few hours away from Grace. Though many times over the years she had fantasized of a day when her nagging sister was no longer part of her daily life, her heart ached just thinking about how much she would miss her.

In a gesture of thoughtfulness, Grace had sent word to her family of her nuptials, along with details of her plan to spend her first days of married life at Hawksmoor. She did not include, however, any indication of when she might return to London.

Aunt Letitia had remained stalwart in her belief that the married couple would return for the masquerade. And Eliza, unable to bear the thought of leaving without bidding farewell to her sister, had attached her hopes to the notion as well.

And so, as the masquerade commenced, Eliza stood, her face hidden behind a bejeweled domino, scanning Almack's famed dance floor hoping to catch a glimpse of Grace's golden curls.

After all, this night's masquerade had been heralded in every newspaper as the crowning Society event of the year. Of course, Grace and Hawksmoor would attend. Everyone of consequence would be present—including, or so it was rumored, Prinny, the Prince Regent, and Queen Charlotte.

As a precaution, Almack's doors and windows had all been closed, owing to the Prince's fear of taking ill from a draft. The heat inside was rapidly becoming unbearable, due to the warmth emitted from those mad enough to dance in the swelter.

Candles sparkled brightly overhead. Vibrant flowers splashed the eye and assailed the nose with heady fragrance, scenting the all-too-still air.

Though their masks had allowed them to slip through the assembly room doors unnoticed, as Aunt Letitia had predicted, Eliza doubted the rest of the evening would pass as smoothly.

It would take a strong heart to stare down Society after the lies that were spread about her only two weeks past, but Eliza vowed to do it. For Grace's happiness. But for herself, she no longer cared. Her own contentment was already firmly secured. Eliza smiled to herself at the latent realization.

"Eliza, yer aunts," Magnus said, taking her elbow and turning her to see the Featherton sisters and with them, Grace and Lord Hawksmoor.

"Now we are all here together!" her aunts cheered, clapping their gloved hands together.

"Ladies," Magnus said, bowing before each aunt in turn. "You both look lovely this eve."

Wrapped in yards of snowy gossamer sheeting, edged with frothy silver lace, Aunt Viola reached into her golden quiver and withdrew an arrow from her shining bow. She playfully aimed it at him and giggled happily as he flinched for her.

"Let me guess. You are Cupid."

Aunt Viola laughed. "Of course. And my sister is Aphrodite, the goddess of love."

Eliza gazed upon Letitia and her filmy lavender Grecian gown with a plunging neckline, cut far too low for a lady of such advanced years. She forced an uneasy smile. "Such . . . hmm . . . appropriate costumes. Do you not agree?"

"I do, indeed," replied Grace, who, like Eliza, donned only a domino as her disguise.

"Grace!" The moment Eliza's gaze lit upon her sister, tears rushed into her eyes, making her wonder at her all-too-sensitive emotions of late.

Grace rushed forward and kissed her ridiculously wet cheeks. "Oh, I heard all about your wedding. I am so happy for you, Eliza. Or, shall I say Lady Somerton?"

Eliza hugged her sister to her, laughter mingling happily with her tears. "I can scarce believe it myself. Everything occurred so quickly."

"Funny how that happens, is it not?" Grace said, grinning.

"Wait a moment—" Eliza took Grace by her shoulders and held her at arm's length while she looked at her sister's left hand. "Show me!"

Grace bounced on her toes, waving her finger bearing a golden ring in the air.

Stepping forward, Lord Hawksmoor took his new wife's hand into his. "May I present, Lady Hawksmoor," he said proudly as Grace swept back her leg and offered an exaggerated curtsey.

"Oh, my." Aunt Viola reached a feeble hand to the back of an armless chair and collapsed into it.

"It's one of her spells," Grace cried out. "*Here,* of all places."

The others rushed to encircle Viola as Aunt Letitia patted her shoulder. "No, it's not a spell, is it, Sister?"

From her wilted position in the chair, Aunt Viola shook her head. "No, no, no," she said with a sniff.

"Then, what is it?" Eliza asked softly.

Aunt Viola raised her head and lifted away her hands to reveal two pink-smudged gloved palms. Wet streaks cut pale tracks through the heavy poppy-hued rouge on her cheeks. "This is the happiest day of my life."

"Oh, Auntie. For us as well," Eliza replied, as she and Grace hugged Viola and Letitia to them.

Suddenly a great crash of applause shook the air. Startled, Eliza jerked upright. Magnus, already a head above the crowd, rose up to see what had caused the commotion.

"By Jove, 'tis the Prince Regent and Queen Charlotte. They are moving this way, toward the orchestra."

"They're here. Did you hear, Viola?" Aunt Letitia asked.

"Of course I heard!" Aunt Viola scrambled to her feet and snared Eliza by the wrist. "Out of our way, please!" she muttered as both she and Aunt Letitia pushed their way through the crowd, dragging Eliza with them, for a better look.

"You two go ahead. I do not care to—oh, Auntie, *please,*" Eliza protested, helplessly glancing back at an amused Magnus as she was hauled along with them.

As the roar of the crowd quieted, the queen began to acknowledge those lucky enough to line her path on either side.

Despite the looks of protest they garnered, Aunt Letitia and Aunt Viola squeezed their way into two of these prime spots and even managed to shoehorn Eliza between them.

Then, as her aunts' mission suddenly occurred to her, Eliza felt a plummeting sensation in her stomach. *No. Oh, please no.* "Auntie, you cannot mean for the queen to acknowledge *me*?"

Aunt Viola smiled up at her. "Aren't you the clever one."

"You are making a mistake. She won't do it, I tell you that. Not only did I sneeze in her face, but surely she has heard the horrible rumor about me selling my favors."

"Hush now, gel. She must, don't you see, Eliza? Our family must regain her pleasure."

"Why should her opinion matter?" Eliza asked in a hushed whisper. "Grace and I are already married into good families."

"True, but young Meredith is not," Aunt Letitia reminded her quietly. "Can't have the stain of foul rumors reducing her prospects, now can we?"

"Meredith? Good heavens, she is but a child."

"Do you not realize she will be of age for presentation in less than two years?" Aunt Letitia whispered in Eliza's ear. "Though I daresay, it might do to delay her a year or so. Let all the chatter about her antics at school die away, you know."

"Quiet now. She is nearly here," Aunt Viola scolded. And she was. Queen Charlotte was about to reach them, when suddenly, Mrs. Peacock, standing in the line opposite them, lurched forward.

The Queen turned her head and looked at her, denying the attention Eliza's aunts so desired. Aunt Letitia glowered at Mrs. Peacock, who now stood directly before the queen.

Aunt Viola nudged Letitia's side, then raised the back of her wrist to her forehead. "SPELL . . ." she cried out, and promptly collapsed to the floor.

With a startled gasp, Queen Charlotte whirled around and stared down at the old woman, as Eliza knelt at her side.

"There, there, Sister," Aunt Letitia crooned, while Eliza lifted Viola's head to her lap.

The Prince Regent rushed forth, his bloated face flushed with concern. "Find my doctor!" he ordered a footman, which Eliza thought uncharacteristically kind of him—that is, until he added, "What felled her might be catching."

" 'Tis just one of her sleeping spells," Eliza replied without a thought to whether a direct reply was appropriate. But as she gazed down at her motionless aunt and saw a faint smile stretched across her brightly painted lips, Eliza's heart skipped a beat. Then another. God above. It was now blatantly clear that she'd lied to the Prince Regent!

"Miss Merriweather?"

A chill shot up Eliza's backbone. Jupiter! Did the queen just say her name?

"Miss Eliza Merriweather?" the queen repeated.

Aunt Letitia instantly dropped to the floor in a great billow of skirts and took Eliza's place as Viola's pillow, allowing her to stand and face Queen Charlotte.

"You are Miss Merriweather, are you not?"

Whisking her domino from her eyes, Eliza bowed her head and dropped a deep curtsey. "Yes, your majesty . . . I mean *no*," Eliza stammered. "Oh bother!"

The Prince Regent, quite possibly the widest human

being Eliza had ever seen, stepped forward. "Which is it, woman?"

Magnus strode into the breach and spoke, to the gasped horror of the crowd. "Miss Merriweather is now Countess of Somerton, Yer Highness." He leaned down to Eliza's ear and whispered. "Ye might want to curtsey again, lass."

And so Eliza did. Though she wasn't at all sure her trembling knees hadn't temporarily given out just then. For without thought, her dip precisely coincided with Magnus's bow.

The queen drew nearer to Eliza and inspected her. Taking Eliza's hand, she drew her upright. "I had not expected that one so talented would also be so very young."

A murmur rolled through the ballroom at the comment. The queen seemed almost to smile at her audience's reaction.

Talented? Eliza smiled timidly. Her heart pounded in her ribs and her stomach tied itself into great aching knots.

"Through Mr. Christie, I was fortunate enough to be *favored*," the queen turned her head and lifted a disappointed brow at Lady Cowper and several other of the *ton*'s gossips, "with seven of your paintings."

Like an ebb tide, the crowd flowed away, and Eliza was surprised to see a number of high-ranking women bowing their heads in shame.

Eliza raised her gaze to the queen slightly, glancing at her only long enough to discern if she was jesting. But it appeared she was not. "I—I am honored."

"The honor is mine, Lady Somerton, to have discovered such a talented artist."

Eliza swallowed the stone in her throat.

"Mr. Christie mentioned there are two other paintings."

"Yes, your majesty." Eliza glanced sidelong at Magnus. "They belong to my husband, Lord Somerton."

"Somerton." The queen gestured to Magnus. "I want them."

Magnus bowed most regally. "I must apologize to the Crown, but the paintings are tokens of my wife's love. As much as I wish to please Yer Majesty, how can I oblige?"

The queen said nothing for several moments, then, turned a knowing smile upon Magnus. "Very well. I understand the bonds of love, all too well, Lord Somerton. Therefore, I shall forgive you. I would not think of taking the landscape, or your portrait." She leaned close to Eliza. "Oh yes, Lady Somerton. You needn't seem so surprised that I know of them. Mr. Christie is very thorough."

"Did you say *portrait*?" Prinny, the bulbous Prince Regent, cut toward Eliza. "Lady Somerton, *I* would sit for a portrait."

"Of course. I am your servant," she said, hardly able to believe this was happening.

"Splendid. I shall have my man of affairs contact you."

With that, Queen Charlotte and the Prince Regent turned for the doors and made their way through the throng, cueing Aunt Viola to cease her charade and get up from the floor.

But Eliza could only stare wide-eyed at Magnus, astonished at his fortitude. "Y-you defied the queen!" she said, still finding it difficult to catch her breath. "I could have replaced the paintings."

"But ye could not have replaced the memories that went along with them. Besides, what would Queen Charlotte do with a portrait of me?"

"Well, you are quite handsome." Eliza giggled as she and her husband linked their arms and passed through the crowd, nodding tentatively in response to adoring smiles, as they strolled back to Grace and Lord Hawksmoor.

When they neared, Eliza was stunned to see the Dowager Lady Hawksmoor standing before Grace, the first time the two had been in the same room since Lady Hawksmoor had tried to break Grace and Hawksmoor's engagement. *Good heavens*. Eliza hurried toward the pair, girding herself to diffuse a particularly nasty confrontation.

But as Eliza descended upon the pair, she was shocked to hear the dowager speaking kindly.

"How lovely for your sister to be honored by the queen and the Prince Regent."

"It is a great honor for our family to have the Crown publicly recognize my sister for what we have known all along—Eliza is a great artist."

The Dowager Lady Hawksmoor lowered her head. When she looked up at Grace, her lower lip was shaking. She placed her hand on Grace's. "After losing my husband, I wanted what was best for my son. I was only thinking of him." She turned a bit and glanced at Eliza, as if to be sure she heard.

Grace graciously patted her hand. "I understand, Lady Hawksmoor. And Reginald will have the two of us looking out for his welfare now." Grace matched the dowager's civil tone.

"Please, call me Mother, now that you have become my daughter." She leaned forward and kissed Grace's cheek.

"Thank you, Mother."

The dowager turned to Eliza offering a hopeful smile.

Eliza reached out and squeezed the older woman's hand. "Welcome to our family, my lady."

Looking over the older woman's shoulder, Eliza met Grace's gaze. *Thank you,* her sister mouthed.

"I say, where have yer aunts gone?" Magnus asked. "Ye dinna suppose they have it their heads to invite Prinny to tea?"

Eliza and Grace laughed at the utterly ridiculous thought. But not *too* hard.

*   *   *

Three days later

Eliza settled her paint case and palette into the portmanteau Jenny had packed for her and glanced nervously out the window for Magnus. He should have been back more than two hours ago.

She turned to her aunts. "Well, I believe that is the last of my things. I still cannot believe Magnus and I are truly married, and that in just over a week's time, we will be living in his cottage on Skye." She walked across the room and hugged Letitia and Viola and kissed their cheeks. "But Scotland is so very far away. I shall miss you both terribly."

Aunt Letitia ran her hand along Eliza's arm. "We shall miss you as well, dear. Sister and I have grown so accustomed to having young people in the house."

Aunt Viola agreed. "Now, with both you and Grace married, I do not know how we will get along."

Eliza glanced at Edgar, who kept his eye on Viola from the passageway. She grinned. "I've a suspicion you will survive quite well."

Grace returned to the parlor and handed Eliza two hats. "Do not fret, Eliza. Before our aunts know it, they will have our dear sister Meredith to guide through the season." Grace grinned then winked at her aunts. "And, believe me, *she* will be even more of a handful than Eliza. Just you wait and see!"

Eliza laughed. "What a thing to say, Grace. You will surely frighten them away."

"Our aunts will be fine, Eliza. You've no reason to worry," Grace reassured before heading back up the stairs to collect a few more items for her own trunk.

Aunt Viola moved to a nearby table and lifted the *Rules of Engagement* into her hands. "Never you mind about us.

We are prepared for Meredith. We have the rule book, after all."

"You do indeed." Eliza grinned broadly. She glanced into the passageway to be sure Grace was out of earshot. "But there is something I think you should know about *Rules of Engagement*."

"What do you mean, gel?" Aunt Letitia looked up at her, blinking innocently.

Eliza didn't know why she was having such a hard time forming the words she'd wanted to shout for well over two months. "The rule book is—"

"A war manual?" Aunt Viola asked.

"W-why, *yes*." Eliza was astounded.

"Oh, we knew that, Eliza." Aunt Letitia laughed and waved Eliza's concerns about hurt feelings away. "But strategy is strategy, Papa always said."

"He did indeed, Sister," added Aunt Viola.

Eliza brought her hand to her mouth. She couldn't believe it. Her aunts had known the book's true purpose all along! These two loveable old ladies never ceased to amaze her.

Outside, the slowing clop of horse hooves on the cobbles called Eliza to the window. "At last, Magnus has come for me." She turned and gave each of her aunts a quick departing peck on the cheek, as Grace raced down the stairs toward the open door.

Magnus crossed the parlor threshold and Eliza smiled brightly at her husband. Since the moment they were married, she and Magnus had been afforded very little time alone, and Eliza was quaking with eagerness to board the carriage for Scotland and start their life together. She called out to Edgar. "Please ask the footman to fetch my trunks."

Magnus caught the old man's arm. "No need, Edgar. We're not going anywhere."

Eliza sank onto the window seat. "What do you mean? 'Tis all arranged."

Magnus dashed across the room and kissed her. Then he leapt up and kissed Grace, before whirling around to kiss both aunts. He rushed up to Edgar, who covered his mouth with his hand.

Magnus laughed. "I was only going to shake your hand, man."

Eliza rose and moved to the center of the Turkish carpet. "My, you're in a jolly mood."

Magnus took Eliza into his arms and twirled her around the room as he laughed and laughed. "*The Promise,* she's made port!"

Eliza stood there, utterly stunned. "How can this be?"

"Somehow, she survived the storm."

Eliza shrieked with delight and hugged her husband tightly. "So Somerton—"

"Is saved—intact." Magnus gave her an elated squeeze, then drew back and looked at her with all seriousness. "I need some time to handle the shipment and to settle my debts. Ye dinna mind postponing our departure for another month or two?"

A month or two? Eliza let a smile turn her lips. "Of course not. The delay will give me time to complete Prinny's portrait . . . and to buy a bit more paint. For I fear I do not have enough to realistically capture his rather . . . generous form."

Both her aunts hooted merrily.

"Be sure to buy as much ye need. Brushes, canvas. Oils. Enough for a year." Magnus was nearly bursting with excitement.

Eliza was puzzled. "A year?"

Magnus withdrew several papers from his pocket and handed them to Eliza. She opened the folds and gazed down at the print. Lord above. She couldn't believe her eyes. "Italy? We are going to Italy?" Her heart began to ache.

"What better place to spend our first year as husband and wife?"

Eliza looked up at him slyly, then put her lips to his ear. "I can think of one place," she whispered.

Magnus grinned and swept her up in his arms. "Ye are an original, Lady Somerton."

"Why thank you, Lord Somerton," she said, as he plucked her right out of her slippers and kissed her with such passion that she felt her toes blush.

Rule Twenty-two

Learn from each engagement, and apply successful strategies to future engagements.

London, April 1818

Meredith Merriweather's vivid blue eyes rounded with great reverence as her aunt Letitia laid the great leather volume before her. She could smell fresh oil on its spine as she ran her fingers over the gilt lettering pressed into the crimson leather. She read the title. "*Rules of Engagement?*"

She looked up at her aunts. They were smiling at her. "I do not understand."

Aunt Letitia cleared her throat. "Our father acquired this rule book many years ago for our season. This same rule book provided us with the stratagem to direct your sisters into very successful marriages."

It did? How astounding. Meredith wondered why her sisters had never bothered to mention this to her.

Aunt Viola lifted her lorgnette to her eyes. "Now, we will use its wisdom to successfully see you through your first season. Are you ready to begin?"

Meredith nodded warily. What else could she do? Refuse and disappoint her aunts who had always been so kind to her? No, she knew she must listen carefully the same way her sisters must have done.

Aunt Viola cleared her throat quietly, then opened the cover and read the heading of the first chapter.

"Rule One."

About the Author

Kathryn Caskie has long been a devotee of history and things of old. So it came as no surprise to her family when she took a career detour off the online super highway and began writing historical romances full time.

With a background in marketing, advertising, and journalism, she has written professionally for television, radio, magazines, and newspapers.

She lives in a two-hundred-year-old Quaker home nestled in the foothills of the Blue Ridge Mountains with her greatest sources of inspiration, her husband and two young daughters.

Rules of Engagement, winner of Romance Writers of America's prestigious Golden Heart award, is Kathryn's debut novel.

Readers may contact Kathryn at her Web site
www.kathryncaskie.com.

More
Kathryn Caskie!

❧

Please turn the page
for a preview of
LADY IN WAITING
Available in bookstores
everywhere.

Entry 1

Scientific Diary of Miss Genevieve Penny
December 20, 1817

I have made an important scientific discovery—one that will change my life forever.

By crossing two particularly vigorous varieties of Mitcham peppermint, I have produced an essential oil of unmatched potency. Alas, which two varieties, I have no memory, having no mind for storing such dreary details. Hence, the introduction of my exquisite new scientific journal with fashionable marbled facings, satin page marker, and soft leather spine. I purchased it today, along with a gorgeous cairngorm brooch I saw in the window of Bartleby's, which has fast become my favorite shop on all of Milsom Street, if not all of Bath. But I digress.

Through a most fortuitous accident, I found that this particular oil has the curious effect of causing the skin to flush with youthful vigor immediately upon contact. Thus far, there have been no ill side effects; therefore I shall

*commence blending a half dozen gallipots of the peppermint
cream for the Featherton ladies. No doubt they will be
pleased, as will the shopkeeper at Bartleby's, for the guinea
the Feathertons will likely gift me must be applied directly
to my overdue shop bill before I am barred from the establishment forever.*

*Bath, England
January 2, 1818*

Genevieve Penny spun around and stared, quite unable to
believe what she was hearing. "What, pray, do you mean she
used the cream down *there*? My God, Annie, it's a *facial*
balm. Did you not explain its intended use to her ladyship?"

" 'Course I did, Jenny. I'm not daft." Her friend, an abigail like herself, punctuated her words with a roll of her eyes
and settled her plump behind on the stool before the herb-
strewn table. "But how could I have known Lady Avery and
the viscount had a more *amorous* plan for the cream?"

"And now she wants a pot of her own?" Jenny nervously
tucked a loose dark curl behind her ear. "I gave the Feathertons' cream pot to *you*. My gift was meant to be our secret.
I never intended for the cream find its way above stairs."

Above stairs? What an awful thought. Jenny's stomach
muscles cinched like an overtight corset and she gasped for
a breath.

What if the Featherton ladies learned of her little entre-
preneurial endeavor born of supplies *they* paid for—
blended in *their* own stillroom? Heaven forbid. She might
find herself out on the cobbles without a reference! Where
would she be then, hawking oranges on the street corner for
her daily bread?

She seized Annie's shoulders. "You did not tell your mistress that *I* gave you the cream."

"Nay, of course not. Said a friend gave it to me." But as she spoke, Annie's keen eyes drifted across the table to the sealed clay gallipots on its edge. With a twist of her ample form, she broke Jenny's grip and made her way across the stillroom.

"Have some made up, do you?" Prying open the lid, Annie lifted a pot to her nose and breathed deeply, letting out a pleased sigh. "Well, my lady wants two pots of the tingle cream to start—"

Jenny's cheeks heated. "Lud, stop calling it that! It's *not* tingle cream. It's a peppermint *facial* cream."

"You can call it what you like, but I tried a dab myself. You know . . . *there*." Annie flushed crimson and looked away. "And I own, Jenny, the way it made me tingle . . . positively *sinful*. I do not doubt it revived my lady's desire."

Jenny heard Annie return the clay gallipot to the table, but then she heard something else. Her ears pricked up at a faint but unmistakable jingle of coins.

As Annie turned around, she withdrew a weighty silken bag from her basket and pressed it into Jenny's palm. "My lady bade me to give the maker this, *if* that maker could be persuaded to oblige her with two pots today."

Jenny loosened the heavy bag's satin tie and emptied ten gold guineas onto the table. It was a fortune for a lady's maid like herself. A blessed fortune! Her blood plummeted from her head into her feet and she sank onto a stool, unable to stop staring at the gleaming mound of riches.

"You do have two spare pots, don't you, Jenny? Her ladyship would be most displeased if I returned to the house without her cream."

Jenny nodded absently and pushed two of the three gallipots forward. This was certainly not the use she intended when she blended the cream. But what else could she do but oblige? This was more blunt than she'd ever seen in her lifetime.

"Jolly good. Knew you'd come around." With great care, Annie wedged the pots into her basket and covered them discreetly with a square of linen. "Must run now. Haven't much time, you know. I'll be needing to dress Lady Avery for the Fire and Ice Ball this eve."

"Of course." Jenny glanced at the rough-hewn table and the lone gallipot sitting amid the crushed herbs. "Only one left," she muttered to herself.

Annie set her fist on her fleshy hip. "One? You mean that's all you have—at all? Well, dove, if I was you, I'd set about making more of that tingle cream right away."

"Why should I need more?" Jenny raised her brow with growing suspicion.

Beneath the snowy mobcap, Annie's earlobes glowed crimson. "Well . . . I *might* have overheard Lady Avery telling Lady Oliver about her thrilling discovery of an amazing cream. Of course, I knew she was talking about the tingle cream. And Jenny, Lady Oliver was *most* interested."

A jolt raced down Jenny's spine. "Do you not mean others in Society know of this? Lud, this is a bloomin' disaster."

"Oh, Jen, you're getting all foamy for nothing. What's so wrong with an abigail making a few quid on the side? Who knows, a Society connection could be the very thing to catapult your sales and help you remove yourself from debt for good."

Jenny forced a snort of laughter, but as the idea settled upon her, she became very still.

Criminy. The idea was intriguing, even if a little mad. But the more she thought about it, the more enticing the suggestion became to her.

No, no, this was ridiculous. She couldn't possibly produce enough pots to clear her accounts—not without getting the sack from her employers.

Could she?

Rising, Jenny walked to her supply cupboard, twisted the wooden door wedge and peered inside. She was keenly disappointed at what she saw—or rather at what she didn't see. The cupboard was nearly bare. She'd need more emulsifying agent. Plenty more. Gallipots, too. Of course she'd have to distill some more Mitcham peppermint.

This was going to be *real* work.

But she would do it. In fact, if she very worked hard, she might even come to terms with her accounts before the last spring leaf unfurled. If not before. She had a Society connection, after all.

"Jenny, are you listening?"

She looked up blankly.

"I need to stop by Bartleby's and retrieve some ribbon for my lady. Care to join me?" Annie scooped up a guinea from the table and flipped it spinning through the air. She grinned as Jenny opened her palm and caught the coin before it hit the table.

"Why not." Tossing the glittering coin atop the pile, Jenny cupped her hand and neatly corralled the ten guineas in the silk bag. She looked up and flashed a jubilant smile.

Annie laughed. "Won't the shop keep be gobsmacked when you actually *pay* ten guineas on your account?"

Jenny winced a little. "Well, maybe not the *full* ten. I think I might stop by the apothecary and fetch a few more supplies."

Annie's eyes widened with excitement. "Does this mean you're going to do it—start a business?"

"A business? Oh, I don't know." Moving to the wall hooks, Jenny crowned herself with her new velvet bonnet, then swept her perfectly coordinated pelisse over her shoulder. "But it can't hurt to have few more pots of . . . *tingle* cream on hand, now can it?"

Muffling their giggles so they wouldn't be overhead by the Featherton ladies above stairs, Jenny and Annie headed out the door in the direction of Milsom Street.

"The man is entirely unreasonable!" Jenny jerked the handle hard, slamming Bartleby's shop door behind her. "Eight guineas I paid him, and still he wouldn't let me put the pearl earbobs on my account." With envious eyes, Jenny glanced down at Annie's neatly tied packet of ribbon.

Annie stuffed the parcel into her basket and drew the linen doily over top as if purposely hiding it from Jenny's view. "You must owe him an awful lot."

Jenny shrugged. "I suppose. But I am a loyal customer. He should have more faith."

"Can I ask . . . how much you owe?"

"I don't know really. Dropped all his notices in the dustbin. After all, he needn't remind *me* that I owe him payment. It is not as if I've forgotten."

"There's Smith and Company, too, don't forget. What was it you put on account there?"

"A black bear muff. You should buy one. Most fashionable this season." Jenny wrinkled her brow as they walked. "I should have brought it today. Would have kept my hands warm as embers."

Annie sighed. "And then there's the jeweler on the Lower Walk—a quartet of garnet buttons, wasn't it?"

"Now you must admit *those* were a bargain. All I need to do is replace the shell buttons with the garnets and my pewter gown will be transformed. Why, I've actually saved the cost of a new gown simply by buying the buttons. Really very economical."

Annie stepped before Jenny and caught her shoulders.

"Just look at you, Jenny. We're headed for the markets and you're wearing a pelisse of apple green Kerseymere, vandyked with satin! Why do you do it? What need have you for fine gowns, and trinkets? You are wasting what little money you earn on this nonsense. You are a lady's *maid*, Jenny. Not a real lady."

"I *am*." Jenny caught Annie's wrists and yanked them from her. "Or I would have been . . . had my father married Mama. He was a highborn gentleman, you know."

"Yes, I do know. But, ducks, he *didn't* marry your mother, and you are not a lady, no matter how you dress and adorn yourself."

Jenny was about to snap a retort, when the sun reflected off a large shiny object blinding her for an instant. Oh, *bugger*!

When her eyes refocused she found herself looking at the most exquisite, certainly the most modish, carriage she'd ever seen in Bath—or even London.

"Gorblimey! Will you look at that, Annie? Have you ever seen anything so grand?" Jenny started slowly toward the conveyance, feeling quite incapable of stopping herself. "Come on, Annie, I have to see inside the cab."

"Jenny, *no*." Annie ticked her head toward the first pairing of ebony horses. "The footman. He's bound to stop you."

"Oh, botheration. You can keep him busy for me. Come on, Annie, be my friend and chat him up, whilst I just go and have a tiny peek inside, all right?"

"Jenny, you *can't*."

But Jenny's boots were already upon the cobbles and she was making her way to the far cab door.

Once Jenny heard the sultry tones of Annie's voice mingling with those of the footman, she crouched low and skulked around the gleaming carriage. Rising up, she peered wide-eyed through the door's lower windowpanes.

To her delight, the cab was empty. Now, if only the door was . . . she pressed the latch down, and the door opened. Jenny smiled and gave a wink to the heavens, for someone up there was certainly looking out for her this day.

The scent of new leather slipped through the crack and she greedily breathed in its essence. Oh, this was better than she'd hoped.

And what with the door being open, this was practically an invitation to slip inside, was it not? Besides, it would hurt no one for her to indulge herself just for a moment.

Jenny glanced warily in both directions, then, confident she'd not be seen, put her foot on the step and eased herself inside the cab.

Oh, it was all simply glorious. She was almost giddy with pleasure as she ran her hand over the interior walls, resplendent with a gold-pressed crimson silk that perfectly set off the dark burgundy leather benches.

Eagerly, she fluttered her fingertips over the leather-wrapped seat, which was quite easily as soft as fresh churned butter. She eased herself back, allowing her bonnet to settle against the headrest. "Oh, *yes*," she purred. It was like resting on a cloud.

Jenny had just closed her eyes, imagining herself being whisked to the Upper Assembly Rooms for the Fire and Ice Ball this eve, when she heard a man's stern voice.

"Madam, might I be of some assistance?"

Startled, Jenny snapped her eyes open and jerked her head upright. She blinked into the cool afternoon light streaming through the open door. Outside, on the opposite side of the carriage, stood a huge, kilted gentleman. He was stooping down and peering back at her.

Oh my God. Don't panic.

Just stay calm.

But already, as she stared back into the man's dark brown eyes topped with scowling brows, she could feel her heart slamming madly against her ribs.

Lud, what must he think? She knew what she would think if she found a strange woman relaxing in *her* town carriage. Well, if she had one. She'd think the woman was quite mad. Or . . . maybe a thief.

A thief? Gorblimey. What if he called a constable?

"I believe ye have mistakenly boarded my carriage," the Scotsman said with a controlled level of gentility that surprised her. "Might I help ye find yer own, my lady?" He leaned back then and glanced down Milsom Street, grimacing slightly when he obviously saw no other fine conveyance parked upon the cobbles.

"Oh, I—" But no other words were coming. Lord help her. *Think, Jenny, think.*

Then, inexplicably, the perfect explanation planted itself in her mind. "Kind, sir," she managed, lifting her hand weakly to her brow. "Pray, forgive me. My head began to swirl and I needed to sit down. The sensation came upon me so quickly, I was forced to seek my ease inside your carriage."

"Och, I see." The Scotsman seemed to take to her words immediately, and his eyes softened with concern. "Has it passed—the spell, I mean?"

She nodded her head and offered a thin smile. "Indeed it has. Just this moment, in fact." Furtively, Jenny laid her hand on the door latch and pressed down. The door sprung open. "I am sorry to have troubled you. I will go now."

A look of surprise lit the Scotsman's eyes, and quite suddenly, he disappeared from the far door.

Jenny shoved the carriage door beside her wide and leapt

down, hoping to escape, but the Scotsman had already circled around and caught her elbow before she could flee.

"Please allow me to assist ye by offering a ride to yer home."

A few yards away, Jenny could see Annie, her eyes wide and mouth gaping, standing with the footman near the lead pair of horses.

Jenny turned back to the Scotsman. "No need, sir." She wrenched her elbow from his grasp. "My abigail can escort me. I own I have fully regained my strength and my residence is not so far away. Again, I am sorry, sir. Do excuse me."

With that Jenny shot up the flagway, hooking Annie's arm as she passed and dragging her along with her.

"Very well, then. Good day," the gentleman called out in a confused tone as the two women scurried around the corner on their way to Queen Street.

"Lord above! You're mad, Jenny. I told you not to do it," Annie lamented. "But no, you climbed inside the bloody town carriage anyway."

Jenny slowed her step and stilled. "I know, Annie, but the carriage was *so* lovely. You can't imagine how extraordinary it was. I only wanted to board and see what it felt like to travel like a lady of the ton. Just for a moment."

"When are you going to give up your impossible dream of becoming a lady? Do you not see the trouble it causes you? You are indebted to half the shopkeepers on Milsom."

Jenny looked away and shrugged, then urged Annie forward up the walk. "I am well aware of my financial circumstances. But I'll find a way to pay my debts."

"Well you had better, before Bath's markets send the constables after you for stiffing them."

Jenny focused on the swish of her skirts and the rhythm

of her boots as she walked, anything to keep from looking her friend in the eye. Annie was right, of course.

But this time, she might actually be able to do something about her debt. The cream could solve all her worries.

Reaching inside her reticule, Jenny retrieved the two guineas she had left. "Come on, Annie. I need to stop at the dispensing apothecary on Trim Street. I have some supplies to purchase."

Later that afternoon, above stairs, Jenny fastened the last button of Miss Meredith Merriweather's ball gown, then tossed the back of her mistress's skirts into the air, so she could see the luminous effect the sheer, rose-festooned over-dress created.

"Oh, you look like an angel, Miss Meredith." Jenny smiled, proud of her own handiwork. "You'll be the envy of every lady in attendance."

Meredith chewed her lip, and twisted a thick coil of copper hair around her finger. "I'm just not sure, Jenny. I think I might like the saffron gown better. This is my very first ball—and even though I've not come out yet, I want to look my best. What do you think?"

"Both gowns are lovely, miss. And you know as well as I that 'tis the woman inside that makes the gown beautiful."

"I suppose . . ."

Jenny folded her arms across her chest. Meredith was damned lucky to be allowed to attend any Society event—even in staid old Bath. True, young ladies often were permitted to hone their social skills in the spa city before later coming out in London, but Meredith was a real hoyden.

Meredith peered at her reflection in the cheval mirror, then whirled around to face Jenny who stood behind her. "I wish I could see them both at the same time." She arched her brows expectantly.

"What do you mean?"

"You and I measure for size more closely than the Brunswick twins. Will you not slip into the saffron gown, then we can both go downstairs to the parlor and let my aunts choose which is best suited for me."

"Oh, no, I couldn't possibly." Jenny knew she ought to protest, owing to her position in the household, but goodness, she could barely restrain herself from dashing to the bed and throwing the gown over her head that very moment!

Meredith took Jenny's hands into her own and pushed her bottom lip outward in a pretty pout. "Please, Jenny. For *me*?"

Jenny glanced down at the floor, as if considering the proposition. She counted to ten, for anything less would not be convincing, before returning her gaze to her mistress. "Oh, very well. But only if you explain to your aunts that this was *your* idea, not mine. Wouldn't want to cause trouble with the ladies, you know."

Meredith giggled at that. "What a thing to say, Jenny! You've been part of this household since you were a child. Why, they think of you more as a daughter than a lady's maid. Now, raise your arms for me."

Jenny laughed as Meredith assisted her into the saffron gown. "This exercise will likely all be for naught anyway for I doubt the gown will fit my form." But of course, she knew it would.

Perfectly in fact.

For more than four days after Mrs. Russell, the modiste, had completed the gown for Meredith, Jenny had secretly sequestered the finery in her own small chamber. Each night she'd withdrawn it carefully from her trunk, eased into it, adding the requisite citrine earbobs and pendant she'd acquired from Smith and Company, then slipped up the stairs to peer by candlelight at her reflection in the cheval mirror.

Meredith fastened the last button then stood side by side with Jenny. They both blinked into the mirror with astonishment.

Jenny could not help but stare at her reflection in the cheval glass. In the daylight, the gown emphasized the golden highlights in her ordinary brown hair, and the vibrant green in her hazel eyes. For the first time in her life, she felt pretty.

She felt . . . like a lady.

"Oh, Jenny," Meredith gasped. "You're . . . *beautiful.* I mean it. I always thought you were pretty, but . . . just look at you. You look like a princess."

It took Jenny a moment to find her voice. "Well, I don't look like the old Jenny Penny anymore, that's for certain." She gave a small laugh as she turned and dropped a pronounced curtsey to Meredith. "So pleased to meet you, Miss Meredith. I am Lady Genevieve, Countess of Below Stairs."

Meredith laughed, then turned Jenny to face the mirror once more. "You are truly beautiful."

Jenny bowed her head, hoping the ridiculous tears swimming along her lashes would remain in place.

Suddenly, Meredith's hand was in hers and Jenny was being whisked down the stair treads to the parlor.

Giggling, Meredith threw open the parlor door. "Aunties, may I present my dear friend, Lady Genevieve."

With that, she propelled Jenny through the doorway and into the center of the parlor.

In an instant, Jenny regretted setting foot outside Meredith's chamber. Regretted leaving her bed that morning. For her employers, the grand ladies, Letitia and Viola Featherton, who might have enjoyed Meredith's game under more intimate circumstances, were not alone.

There, standing before Jenny was a towering, dark-eyed, kilted gentleman. The very same Scot, in fact, whose carriage she had had the audacity to invade only two hours earlier.

Both of the elderly Featherton ladies, who had come to their feet the moment Jenny entered the room, were wearing like expressions of pale shock.

The Scotsman lifted a sardonic brow as he slowly surveyed Jenny from boot to crown.

"My lady," he said, in the deep, dulcet tones of the Highlands. "I am so verra pleased to make yer acquaintance"—amusement played briefly on his lips—"*again*."

THE EDITOR'S DIARY

Dear Reader,

Love comes in many disguises. But sometimes love comes while you are in disguise. Just ask Eliza Merriweather and Molly Shaw in RULES OF ENGAGEMENT and MAN TROUBLE, our two Forever titles this May.

Julia Quinn calls **Kathryn Caskie**'s Regency-set first novel, **RULES OF ENGAGEMENT**, "a delightful debut" and Eloisa James raves "clever, frothy and funny—an enthralling read." So hold onto your muslin skirts, this one's going to blow your stockings off! Eliza Merriweather has no desire to get married. But her two scheming aunts Letitia and Viola have other plans. They've enlisted the help of an old military guidebook called "Rules of Engagement' to secure her offers of marriage. After all, engagement is engagement no matter the context. But Eliza, a worthy adversary, has hatched a scheme of her own. She's persuaded Magnus MacKinnon, a Scottish earl, to pose as a suitor to discourage other callers. Before long, Magnus's brogue sends shivers down her spine and his kisses make her heart race. Could what began as a lark blossom into real love?

Journeying from the wiles and the guiles of the ton to the warm sun and the gentle surf of the Caribbean, we present **Melanie Craft**'s MAN TROUBLE. *Romantic Times* called her "a fresh new voice" and the praise couldn't be more well-deserved. Dr. Molly Shaw is leading a double life. By day, she's a history professor on the tenure track and by night, Molly is bestselling romance author Sandra St. Claire. These parallel lives never intersect . . . until a journalist friend asks her to pull off the story of the century: transform herself into billionaire playboy Jake Berenger's perfect woman to get the inside scoop. But Jake is anything but an innocent victim. In fact, his reputation as a ladies' man is so overexposed that his business is suffering. His only solution is a radical makeover into a family man. And for that he needs the perfect wife. Could she be right under his nose, hidden beneath Sandra St. Claire's sexpot act and her spandex? It looks like there's trouble brewing in paradise!

To find out more about Forever, these May titles, and the authors, visit us at www.hachettebookgroup.com.

With warmest wishes,

Karen Kosztolnyik, Senior Editor

P.S. The temperatures are beginning to rise so treat yourself to some ice cream and these two reasons to relax: **Sandra Hill** pens a spicy contemporary about a woman who's on the lam from a loan shark and discovers that she's still married to a man she thought she divorced years ago, in **CAJUN COWBOY**; and **Edie Claire** delivers the poignant tale of a woman who inherits half a mountain inn and a tangled web of untruths she must unravel before she can claim a love that was **MEANT TO BE**.